THE HELIX

The Helix

Yasmeen Cohen

ISBN 978-1-3999-3738-2

For the mother who has always loved you.
For the generation yet to be born.
For my grandmother who inspired a better world.

For Tio Danny.

Contents

≈

Chapter 1

'Why are you fighting me on this?'

'I don't know,' I admitted, aligning the final corners needed to solve my Rubik's cube. The early birthday present from Neer revealed a photo of us on one of its faces – he'd picked the one we'd taken straight after finishing our GCSE exams last year. Standing outside the school gate, Neer smiled a broad carefree smile with his arm around me while I stood awkwardly next to him. One glance at the memory had me wondering why I hadn't returned his hug, said *yes* when he'd asked me to join the class celebration and just conformed – for once.

Placing the cube aside, I positioned my mobile back to my ear. 'I don't know why I'm like this,' I sighed in forfeit.

'No need to get all melodramatic on me. You love a science project! Just imagine it, you can be the research hero while I dazzle them with my animated presentation skills,' Neer tried to reassure me but I wasn't convinced. 'Listen, you know I love you and think you're amazing,' he said, repeating the phrase he'd told me many times in his soft, warm voice. 'We've all got stuff to work through. It takes courage to admit it.' His words only made me grumble, it was hard to remain stubborn when he was being so sweet and caring.

'You know I only want what's best for you,' my best friend pressed, automatically making me roll my eyes in response.

I turned on my back, letting my mobile fall beside my face. I stretched my arm, which was still aching from holding my mobile for so long, before taking a deep, steadying breath, momentarily focusing my attention on the darkening skyline. Three shooting stars whizzed past my bedroom window, the shock sending a thrill through me. We hardly saw stars anymore, not since the new building development, and yet they shone unnaturally bright now, their tails disappearing as quickly as they'd appeared.

Three stars, the same number of times I'd felt the pull within the pit of my stomach filling me with a brief but burning urge to revolt. First, I'd noticed it at the supermarket, then during Krav Maga training and again on my way to school. Something in me was brewing, leaving me feeling rowdy for a fight.

'Will you do it, then?' Neer asked, interrupting my wandering thoughts.

'You know you can sound like a real dad sometimes?' I shot at him. Although it was merely a guess, I could hear Neer snicker on the other end of the phone.

'I'll even give your second present *early,'* he cooed. 'They say the sequence in this one is practically impossible to crack,' he bragged, knowing I was a sucker for trying to solve the unsolvable and would have long exhausted the Rubik's cube by then.

'Fine, I'll do the group project,' I conceded, not knowing why I had resisted so much to begin with. I could socialise with our new classmates, even if I knew it would only be a matter of time before they started distancing themselves from me. But I could try to show Neer how helpless I was at making friends. Maybe he would finally stop worrying and accept that I only needed one friend. Just because I was alone didn't mean I was lonely. One exceptional friend – like him – was enough.

I took another calming breath. 'But the moment it gets awkward—'

'I'll come to the rescue,' Neer interjected, finishing my sentence. 'It's not my first rodeo,' he said pointedly. I could hear his smile through the phone, making me chuckle, easing some of the tension in my shoulders.

'Plus, it's good practice for all that environmental lobbying you're going to do,' Neer pressed, still trying to convince me. It was just like him to find the bright side to the most impossible of situations.

'Don't you have to deal with your nightmarish sister or something,' I joked and right on cue, I could hear yelling in the background. Neer muttered a quick goodbye and then there was nothing. I was alone again with my thoughts.

I tried not to think about the group project, about having to introduce myself and how every time my stomach would inevitably turn while my brain scrambled, only to find a black pit of empty thought. How do you introduce yourself when you remember nothing of your childhood but your name? The usual dizziness that accompanied these thoughts suddenly washed over me. It was as though my body was actively trying to stop me from recalling my forgotten memories. I sighed, looking up at the dark sky once more before shutting my eyes. Taking three slow exhales, I let the world around me disappear.

There I was. But at the same time, I wasn't. I felt like I was floating. I looked at myself from the outside, divided into two distinct beings. My mortal body was sleeping in my childhood bed, turning, and tossing like a caged bird, restlessly waiting to be released while the other watched from above. My gaze followed the golden thread holding us together. Cast from the core of my belly, I found an orange flame had ignited inside my physical body. I knew I should feel scared, but how could I when its warmth beckoned me like an evening bath? I tried to hold back. Part of me wanted to stay away, safe, but I could no longer resist and plunged in its direction.

My heart beat loudly in my ears. My breath caught as I faced the burning orb trapped under a translucent veil. Nothing this beautiful should ever be hidden. Mesmerised by the rhythm of its flames, the golden thread pulled me close towards the hand-sized sun. I wanted to help. Set it free. But the coward in me held it at a distance. I dared reach towards it, only to pull back when its rays pulsated brighter in response. It wanted me to unleash its power. Without hesitation this time, I leaned back in, ready to find out what was on the other side.

'Ella!' called Mum, breaking through the all-encompassing trance, jolting me awake. My hands automatically flew to catch my A-Level textbooks just before they slid off my bed. Propping myself up against the bedframe, I rested my head against the familiar wood, taking a deep, steadying breath. I knew this meant there was no turning back. If I wanted to sleep again, I would have to start confronting my past despite promising myself long ago never to unlock that painful door. Pulling my legs up tighter against my body, I let the weight of my head fall between my knees and let out a low sigh.

It all started a few days ago. At the same time, I began to dread my upcoming birthday. Following my not-so-subtle teary outburst while watching *Anastasia*, a '90s animated film about an orphan girl looking to discover her past, Mum had volunteered to offer me an ancestry DNA test. Surprisingly, I hadn't automatically pushed the suggestion far, far away.

Mum, or Dr Barnardo as she prefers to be called when providing her medical opinion, reckoned my brain was repressing my memories, protecting me from past trauma. She was probably right since my body flooded with crippling nausea every time I contemplated the first seven years of my life. It's why I had avoided talking or even thinking about it, despite Mum's unconditional support. I simply didn't feel brave enough to peek down memory lane – well, until recently.

Even then, I knew I would undoubtedly chicken out a few times. The thought of having that first uncomfortable conversation with Mum, asking what she'd learned about my past, made me shudder. I let out a loud exhale – it would take a *long time* to uncover what had happened to me.

But, at last, interrupting my thoughts, I could hear the irritation in Mum's voice from three stories below as she shouted once again from the kitchen.

'Honey, please can you hurry? Dinner is getting cold!'

Unwilling to move, I sighed, knowing I had to get going if I didn't want her to drag me out of my room. Taking two steps at a time down the pine staircase, I slid down the remaining handrail, gliding over the final steps before landing steadily on my feet.

As expected, I found Mum standing by the kitchen counter, perched over her laptop, drinking a glass of wine.

'Which do you think?' asked Mum as she rotated the screen towards me. She was still working on her funding campaign for the hospital.

'Mum…' I frowned at her, my tone disapproving, noting tonight was her girl's night, which meant...

'I know, I know, 24 hours without work,' said Mum, reading my mind. 'But I have an ungodly early shift tomorrow, and I won't have time to review it again before the presentation.'

I eased my frown and skimmed through her speech as she served me a plate of her famous Thai curry. 'Definitely the second one – they won't have a choice but to act if you link it to their publicly announced targets and long-term strategic objectives.'

Giving me a nod of recognition, Mum saved the copy I had suggested before closing her laptop. Waiting for me to start eating, she took a large sip of wine before placing it back down.

'Talking about objectives,' she started in her 'casual voice'.

'I've been thinking, and while I know you don't like to celebrate your birthday, how about we throw a little party tomorrow for you and your friends?' she asked innocently. 'It could help you branch out,' she suggested.

Well, this explained why she'd topped up her glass of wine. I hated celebrating my birthday: almost seven years ago, Mum had thrown me a surprise tenth birthday party, scarring me for life. All I remembered was the actor's all-black outfit from *The Matrix* scaring me to death, making me wet my trousers and cry in a corner while my whole class looked on and laughed. It was safe to say that I hadn't been particularly eager to recreate the moment.

'It's really not necessary, Mum,' I urged, squirming uncomfortably. I never understood why we couldn't just go to my favourite Ethiopian restaurant down the corner, just the two of us. I suppose it was the classic conflict between an introverted child and an extroverted parent – neither one of us would ever be satisfied. Still, it wouldn't stop us from constantly trying to push each other from our comfort zones. In a way because we were different, we were better together. It's what kept life interesting.

She lowered her eyes and pressed her lips together. I could tell she was upset. She was always encouraging me to spend more time with my classmates, but other than my best friend Neer, I didn't feel comfortable around them. We sat silently, knowing that one of us would eventually give in. I just hoped it wouldn't be me. In a feeble attempt to distract myself, I scrapped my plate clean, trying to ignore the guilt building inside me. Avoiding eye contact, I kept my eyes cast down. I knew if I looked into her kind, familiar eyes, I wouldn't be able to stand the thought of disappointing her.

But all that did was make me look down at the bracelet on my wrist: the one she'd given me the night we first met.

I threw up my hands in surrender. 'Okay, fine, you win. Let's throw a birthday party,' I mumbled as enthusiastically as possible.

Mum couldn't hide the smirk that had begun spreading across her face at my words.

'It'll be great, trust me,' she said evenly, still grinning as she threw back the rest of her wine. She kissed me on the cheek before heading out.

My mind was racing, already contemplating every possible worst-case scenario. But I tried to remind myself my birthday was tomorrow, and there was no way she'd be able to organise anything drastic under such a tight deadline. Right? I placed my bowl in the sink, waiting to hear her cab pull away before grabbing my jacket and heading out.

≈

Zipping my collar as high as it could go, I tried to shield my face from the bitter cold. Holding out the torch from my mobile, I lit the way as I jogged through the brittle leafy path, making my way into the surrounding forest. Relishing the silence, I let out a long exhale as soon as I was finally deep enough to be away from the constant sound of the road. Taking six long breaths, I continued pacing as I listened for the eerie, raspy call of the barn owl sweeping the air above, stopping only for the last breath.

Closing my eyes, I let the air from my lungs flow out heavily – as though banishing the last of the weight that had set upon me. Blinking my eyes open, I spotted a fallen oak leaf. Kneeling, I placed it between the tip of my fingers, recalling the beckoning I had felt in my dream just an hour ago. I brought my torch closer to it, illuminating its pattern. Zeroing in on its design and veiny details, I committed my focus, letting its repeatability soothe me.

A voice was calling me somewhere in the distance, but the pattern had already captivated my thoughts. Unwilling to break away from the warm feeling, I closed my eyes, searching for comfort from the orange sun. I directed my focus to my stomach, hoping to find it there. I saw nothing but could feel its flames pulsing against its cage. I breathed deeply, urging its flames to break free. Pushing. Harder.

The voice was closer now, a distant thrum vibrating in my head. A hand grabbed my shoulder, but I could hardly feel it. A seal had broken. Bursting. Its long, magnificent flames extended freely. Its golden silk wrapped around the whole of me. I let out a final gasp. The hypnotic pattern – pulling me deep, down into the dark and far away from the forest path.

Something had changed.

Panting loudly, I could no longer taste the damp moisture in the air or hear the harsh screams of the owl. I burst my eyes open as I tried to comprehend the dimmed sight that met me.

Tall, volcanic mountains loomed above me. The air around me was arid, and I could already feel my throat getting drier. Unable to process where I was, I stood very still, my face warming from the adrenaline coursing through me. The land around me was utterly barren – empty and broken. I turned, frantically searching for the person who had grabbed me, but there was no one. Looking around the arid wasteland, I saw nothing – nothing seemed capable of surviving on this treacherous black rock extending across the deserted land.

Crouched on the floor, I steadied my footing wearily on the sharp rock. Slowly standing up, I could feel my throat tighten as my panic grew. I wanted to scream for help, but my gut told me to remain silent and hidden. Looking around for any apparent dangers, I saw no one. The only thing of note was an old iron gate at the edge of a steep vertical mountain. Just beyond the gate was a small stone structure.

Uncertain about what I was doing, I moved closer to the entrance of the single-levelled square stone building to examine the wooden entrance door. There was nothing different or unusual about the door itself. It was six feet high and plain, with no discernible patterns – and yet, I felt consumed. My heart was palpitating widely in response.

I stood there for a moment, frozen. While my brain was telling me to run, my instincts urged me to enter. Something was driving me towards the other side of the door. Looking around, I knew that even if I wanted to run, there would be no escaping the death that surrounded me. I had no choice but to find out what lay behind the door. I only hoped my way back home would be on the other side.

I bobbed up and down, psyching myself up as though preparing for one of my fights. Trying not to overthink it, I gathered all my courage, extended a trembling hand to the handle, and pushed it down. Opening the door slowly, I could hear noises on the other side. Holding the handle down to keep it from making any noise, I pressed my ear gently against the door and listened intently.

'Well, it looks like we're almost ready,' came a raspy voice from inside the stone building.

I didn't know what I was expecting to hear, but somehow a demonic cry of horror would have seemed more appropriate. The voice sounded like it belonged to a middle-aged Yorkshire woman. Without thinking further, I let my instinct lead me and walked through the door.

My gaze swivelled around the small rectangular room. It was dark except for a few rays of light coming from a small, barred window and an old lamp hanging in the middle of the room, despite there being no signs of electricity. The walls were bare. In the corner was a wooden chair next to a light frayed with wear and tear. The room was sparse and functional, and at the centre of it all was a nurse fussing over a straw bed. As my eyes adjusted to the light and I looked closer, I realised a woman was lying deathly still on the bed.

My heart tightened at the sight of the pale woman as I watched the nurse inject a black vial of sludge into her arm before tucking it under the blanket. Although I had never seen this woman before, I felt an undeniable pull toward her. Laying immobile with her eyes shut, I watched as the nurse brushed her short dark hair away from her face. Her cheeks were hollow, and I wondered how long she had been here – and how much longer she had to live.

Feeling compelled to touch the sickly woman, I moved forwards before stopping in the middle of the room, wondering if the nurse would notice me. I stepped closer, but the nurse continued her tasks, almost as though she was purposefully ignoring me. Unnerved by her silence and somewhat frustrated by the complete lack of response, I strode across the room, walking around the bed to stand next to the nurse. Finally acknowledging my presence, she stopped, slowly turning her body to face mine. Then everything seemed to happen at once.

Striking me like lightning, her hand leapt out like a snake and wrapped around my throat in a vice-like grip. I felt her gaze pierce through me as she squeezed tight, my neck burning like fire. Spasms burst through my body, the sparks of pain cutting my breath short as I clawed at her grip, trying to free myself. The pain pulsated from her hand, growing in intensity as she unleashed invisible flames across my every limb, spreading like wildfire through my body. I desperately tried kicking her, scratching her face, but she had me pinned at a distance and by the time I tried breaking the tension in her arm, my movements were weak and sluggish. I was paralysed with pain.

My heart thumped erratically as I desperately gasped for air. Looking into the nurse's eyes, I searched for any indication of empathy, but they were empty of all emotion. Unable to look away, compelled by her gaze, the flames grew the more I struggled. The void in her eyes intensified, darkening the inky black veins in her paper-thin skin until they framed her gaze like a mask. Her lips peeled back into a smile. Strengthening her grip, her eyes gleamed purple as she stole every ounce of life from my body. She was going to drain me until I was dead.

Gasping, I desperately tried to regain control of my limbs but couldn't focus on anything beyond the burning sensation consuming me. My heart was growing weaker by the second. My vision started to blur, and black spots danced morbidly before me. Drifting, I managed to catch a last glimpse of my murderer. The creature was watching me slowly die, gazing intently at me – so intently that it failed to notice the shadow behind it that was growing larger and larger. I watched weakly as the shadow grabbed the creature and it shrieked, jerking back in surprise, breaking its gaze. As soon as its eyes were off me, I felt its hand loosen around my throat, and the pangs of pain began to subside. Free from its deathly grip, my body dropped like a hammer, and my head slammed into the floor. I took a few sharp inhales, still spluttering, my head spinning.

The creature growled a thick, angry buzz, the piercing sound interrupting my hazy vision and unleashing a fresh wave of adrenaline through my body. I forced myself to stay conscious. Dazed, I used my arms and legs to slug myself along the floor. Its scream was growing louder, reaching a painful pitch as it started spasming. Covering my ears, I tried to shelter myself from the piercing sound. I turned just as the creature slumped to the ground with a sickening thud, black sludge oozing out of its body. Two golden blades gleamed as they were pulled out of its back. They were dripping with blood. The last thing I saw was the light emanating from the pair of brightly glowing black stones set in the hilt of each blade – then darkness fell over me.

≈

Tingly heat spread across my face and neck, gently waking me. I wanted to open my eyes, but I struggled to see past the haze. I blinked in and out of consciousness, noting the soreness of my neck easing as the unusual warmth spread to where the creature's grip had held me. My head felt clearer every moment as the pain dissolved until it stopped altogether. The heat source disappeared, leaving my neck once again exposed to the cold, bitter wind.

'Are you okay?' a low, breathless voice asked.

I pried my eyes open, squinting against the bright torch light shining towards me. I quickly realised that I was back on the forest path near home, my body slumped across the floor. I was still holding onto the oak leaf. I was silent for a long moment, absorbing my surroundings before I heard the smooth, warm voice again

'Do you feel any pain?' There was a twang to his voice, a hint of a Scottish accent.

' I... I don't think so,' I stammered, rubbing my hand along my still tingly neck. It was sore, but it didn't hurt nearly as much as it should, and I suspected it had something to do with the boy.

'I'm fine,' I confirmed in a strained voice. Releasing his hand from my jacket, the boy moved away, giving me space as I tried to sit up.

'Be careful,' he warned as I struggled to lift myself from the ground.

I raised my hand protectively to my head, suddenly aware of a throbbing ache above my left ear. He noticed as I suddenly winced.

'Ow,' I said, surprised.

'That's what I thought.'

'What the hell...' I trailed off, trying to clear my head from the lingering haze. Lifting my torso off the ground, I turned to look at the boy for the first time. He was tall, fair-skinned, with hair that gleamed like bronze against the artificial light. But what captivated me the most was the glorious intensity of his glowing emerald eyes, boring into mine. My breath caught in my throat. I must have hit my head really hard. I took a deep breath as I tried to reorient myself. And then I noticed the two glowing, golden blades in his hands. I watched as a drop of inky-coloured blood dripped down the sharp edge of the blades, slowly falling off their tip before falling onto the footpath.

I gathered myself, trying to control my breathing as I planned my next move. I steadied my hands on the ground behind my back, readying myself. As quickly as I could, I mustered all my strength and propelled my body forwards, directing a powerful kick at the boy. Throwing him backwards, I sprung up, determined to make my escape. My muscles burned with physical exertion and relied on the adrenaline thrumming through my body to keep me going. Without hesitating, I charged past him and broke into a run.

Sweat poured down my face, but I kept running, gasping for air as I tried to brush away my footprints leading back home. I was a fast runner yet I felt slow, like I was running through wet sand – I couldn't seem to get enough traction from the dirt beneath my feet. I almost tripped several times as I looked backwards, checking for any signs of pursuit. I couldn't tell if he was following me, and the thought of not knowing only made me sprint faster.

The trees swayed as a gust of wind blew through the forest, surrendering their leaves without a fight. Then came the first drops of rain.

'Just a little bit further now,' I encouraged myself, pushing to accelerate as the rain started to fall.

The rain was cold on my skin, but the downpour was getting more aggressive, and it was becoming harder to see. My breath felt like daggers in my throat as every limb in my body burned, but I kept on running. White hot lightning split the dark sky on the far hill, and then it was gone. The thunder followed only seconds after, loud in my ears as blood pumped around my body.

The driveway was only a few yards away, but, unable to run anymore, I jogged the rest of the way. Wheezing heavily, I finally saw the familiar, reassuring metal gate entrance to home.

Chapter 2

I snoozed my alarm for the third time, knowing I probably couldn't postpone getting up any longer without risking being *very* late for school. I had ended staying up most of the night, listening for any signs of danger, only to collapse in the early morning.

Disgruntled but ultimately safe, I dragged myself out of bed. I rushed to the bathroom, checking my neck in the mirror, looking for traces of the Defacer's grip. Anything to prove that last night had been real. I checked again, but there was nothing there. The bruises had miraculously healed.

Pushing the worrying questions aside, I threw on my usual outfit: black jeans, a sky-blue t-shirt, a navy jacket and black combat boots. I'd always prioritised practicality over fashion, not to mention that I spent so much time training at the Krav Maga studio that there was no point in wearing anything that might get ruined. Hurrying out of my bedroom, I ran downstairs.

Rushing by the kitchen counter, I swiped an apple and peeked through the window before stepping out the front door. Clinging tightly to my yellow umbrella, I took a large bite of my ruby-red apple. I chewed to stop my teeth from chattering while my eyes did a final sweep of the forest ahead. I'd walk along the main road today.

My feet tapped against the pavement. Protected only by a small stream separating me from the forest towering above the road, I pressed myself against the forest wall every time a car squeezed by. Just as it had the night before, my mind bounced relentlessly. The supernatural attack I had barely survived. The pulling sensation that had led me to the dying woman. The green-eyed boy's bloodied blades. To thoughts of my past, Mum, biological parents (whoever they were) and the dreaded feeling of having to stand in front of a room full of staring classmates for the group project, I had begrudgingly agreed to join. Everything that caused my skin to crawl had bundled into one massive, clustered knot throbbing relentlessly in the pit of my stomach.

'It's okay,' I tried to soothe myself. 'It's okay,' I repeated, the words enough to recall unbidden memories to the surface of my racing mind, calling me into the past.

It was a deafeningly dark night. I didn't know how I had arrived here or where I came from, only that I was cold and hungry. I had been roaming the street for what felt like ages looking for help, but I seemed to be invisible to all.

Wearing nothing but a dress, I ate leftovers from bins and sheltered in the corner of a dead-end alley, hiding as best as I could from the dangers of the night. I don't know how much time had passed since I'd first arrived, but I felt weak and cold. Shivering, I curled in on myself in the relative comfort of my corner, too drained to move.

I was convinced it would have been the last night of my existence if it hadn't been for the angel that had flown to my rescue. Wearing a long white coat, she was wandering the streets with a flashlight when she spotted me trembling in the corner. As she approached, she slowed down her pace, eventually stopping a few yards away. Crouching down, she held up her empty hands in the air.

'I'm here to help you,' she said in a soft, melodic voice as she pointed the torch towards her face so that I could see her better. Her eyes were calm pools and the edges of her eyes creased as she smiled encouragingly. Although eased by her kind expression, I continued to stare, fixated on her golden hair. Gleaming against the light, her face shone as though framed by a halo. I watched as a single loose strand of hair dangled in front of her face, blowing in the wind, while her eyes took in the remains of my raggedy dress.

Determining whether I understood her, she continued talking deliberately, ensuring I heard every word. 'My name is Doctor Barnardo. Can you tell me if you are hurt?'

Uncertain of the answer, I shook my head sideways. I approached her carefully, not knowing what she wanted from me. When she put her hand in her pocket, I tried to push myself further into the wall, closing my eyes and hoping to become invisible.

'Don't worry, I'm only getting you some food,' she explained, pulling out a granola bar. Unwrapping the packaging, she extended her arm to offer it to me.

Painfully aware of the pit in my stomach, my belly rumbled audibly at the sight of food. Warily, I examined the cereal bar before unwrapping it to take my first bite.

'I'm going to take you in my arms now and take care of you, alright?'

Nodding my head, I stayed still as she lifted me into her arms. Feeling the warmth of her chest and the reassuring scent of vanilla, I let my eyes drift with exhaustion.

'You're safe now,' she whispered.

I closed my eyes, wanting to give into the warm sensation that came with the memory when a branch snapped behind me – its sound tearing me back into the present. My head shot up, turning towards the direction of the running deer in the surrounding forest. Catching a glimpse of inhumanly bright green eyes, I did a double take, watching attentively where I thought I had seen the dark silhouette. I waited, hearing only the blue tit's song. My phone started buzzing in my pocket. Knowing it was Neer telling me to hurry up, I started jogging towards school, emerald eyes lingering in my thoughts.

≈

Standing in our usual spot outside the school gate, I saw Neer holding his red umbrella high, looking around anxiously when he noticed me running in the distance.

'C'mon, hurry, you're late!' he called out, agitated as the bell rang for our first class. He waved his arm in encouragement and I rushed the final yards.

'What's taken you so long? You look like a wreck,' said Neer offhandedly as he pulled me under his umbrella despite having brought my own. I hadn't noticed the drizzle.

Judging by the exhausted look I gave him, he seemed to reassess his question.

'What happened?' he asked, and this time his voice was soft as he stopped to look at me properly.

'I'll tell you later,' I replied breathlessly. We rushed through the gates and sprinted the length of the corridor into the Physics lab. Neer sat next to me during class, watching me intently as I tried to maintain my composure. His leg was bouncing below the table. I squeezed his hand under the table like I always did when he worried.

Starting secondary school at the same time, Neer and I had found ourselves naturally gravitating toward each other, forever grateful for the seating plan that forced us together. I remember being struck by how much older he sounded when we first met, despite only being one year my senior. Introducing himself with natural ease, I knew he would blend right into his new home. Sure enough, within a few months, he had integrated himself much better than I ever had. There was something about his joyous outlook and his persistence that made him the ultimate people-pleaser. With that came a flock of new friends, yet he always seemed to want to hang out with me. I kept waiting for him to tire of me and move on, but he kept sticking around – he always joked that no one else would put up with him for as long as I had.

Against all odds, we suited each other – he loved asking questions and I loved thinking up fantastical answers. Not to mention, I loved hearing about Neer's rich background. Born in Kenya to Indian-Kenyan parents, he had spent his whole life living there. That is, until his parents moved to the UK a few years ago. Leaving everything they knew behind, they'd moved in the hope that a British education would give their children a chance at a better life. As much as Neer had settled in his British home, his eyes lit up whenever he told me stories of growing up in Kenya. Watching him talk about his childhood with such unfiltered joy made me feel less empty about the loss of my own.

But we only became best friends the day I noticed he'd gone missing. Looking for him, I'd caught him having a panic attack in the bathroom. Not knowing what to do, I kept asking him how I could help when he grabbed my hand as he worked on calming himself. Neer told me everything that day, about how behind his sunny smile, he'd been struggling to adjust to all the changes in his life. Since then, I had been fortunate enough to hold his hand whenever he looked like he needed reassurance.

Squeezing his hand once more, I tried to reassure him that I was okay, but it didn't seem to help ease his preoccupation, and he continued to tap his foot nervously throughout the class.

Unable to concentrate on the lesson, I let my mind wander as I thought of the strange green eyes. The gentle pull of the leaf's pattern came to mind. It had felt welcoming, like the orange sun of my dreams. I knew I should learn to dread the sensation. It had lured me with whispers of innocence only to lead me straight to the claws of a deadly creature. I rubbed my hand against my stiffened neck, remembering the effects of her burning grip.

Suddenly, Neer's elbow was nudging me in the ribs drawing my attention. Ms Lancy was standing in front of me, peering down at me expectantly.

'Umm…' I muttered as I frantically sat up straighter. I could feel my brain scattering helplessly for some sort of clue. 'Would you please mind rephrasing the question?'

'Certainly – please could you summarise for the class the many-worlds interpretation?' Ms Lancy returned an equally innocent smile, knowing very well I had no idea what the answer might be. I shrugged my shoulders apologetically, slumping down in my seat as Ms Lancy turned away.

'The many-worlds interpretation is the theory that multiple worlds exist parallel to Earth, in the same space and time as our own. In other words, Ella, unless you're planning on joining another world, we'd quite like to keep your focus in this one please,' Ms Lancy said sweetly, the edge to her voice only slightly apparent.

'Yes, Ms Lancy,' I responded obediently.

Satisfied with having caught my attention, Ms Lancy returned to the front of the classroom. I didn't dare daydream for any of the remaining hours.

'Ella,' she called from the front of the room as everyone exited to their next class. I walked over, expecting to be told off, only for her to pull out a wrapped gift from her desk drawer. 'Please could you give this to your Krav Maga coach?' she asked coyly, extending it towards me.

Waiting for my response, she explained, 'He won't pick up my calls anymore. I don't know what else to do.' I could hear the desperation in her voice.

I sighed in resignation, putting the book she was gifting him carefully into my bag. 'I'll do what I can, but no promises – Darren's stubborn beyond reason.'

'Thank you,' she added, but I could see the bright sparkle in her eyes that would soon extinguish.

≈

I spent the rest of the morning rushing between classes, trying to update Neer on what had happened in the forest last night, but I was at a loss for words. How could I explain my near-death experience without sounding like a total nutcase? Although, if anyone were to believe me, it would be him. Since seeing his first panic attack at school, we'd done everything together. When we were younger, he'd even helped me set up cameras in my room when I'd had night terrors. Even then, he'd helped without question, which was rare for Neer. I looked over at him fondly.

Standing outside the entrance to the canteen, Neer held two sandwiches in hand. It looked like we'd be heading to the library for a more private conversation.

'You look calmer. How are you feeling?' Neer asked as we started walking. I simply gave him a look.

'Why don't you finally tell me what happened?' he asked. I could hear the anticipation in his voice, but I didn't know where to start.

Sensing my hesitation, Neer continued, 'If it helps, I've brought you your new puzzle.'

My eyebrow raised along with the small smile that now curved my lips.

'"Forever unsolvable" is how I believe the website described it,' Neer challenged, extending my grin.

Somehow not knowing anything about my early childhood had made me obsessed with trying to solve every puzzle I came across – to the point where it had now become a part of our daily lives. Neer would bring me a new puzzle and I'd spend my time trying to crack it while he told me about his latest assignment at the school paper. This time he smirked as he handed me a mini-cylinder that looked like something out of the Da Vinci Code.

'You've got to crack the code to find out what's inside,' enticed Neer, already seeing the cogs in my brain go round, easing the knot in my stomach.

‘It has the highest difficulty rating from its range,’ Neer boasted, only accelerating the speed at which I worked through it. ‘The awesome thing is that you can create your own sequences – by locking the positioning of certain rings and assigning the number of variables you want in each sequence. If solving for two sequences isn’t enough, you can choose whether to make them interdependent or not.’

I looked up, stopping just long enough to glance towards Neer before focusing them back down. He smiled widely, recognising the intrigued expression on my face. I was going to have a lot of fun. Having given me a few seconds of breathing space, I could sense Neer’s bubbling impatience. He watched me intently. I knew I’d have to reveal something. I debated what before deciding there was no story to tell – not until I could explain what had happened to me. I wouldn’t even be able to tell him if the stranger with the deep green eyes was a hero or a villain.

‘Mum is throwing me a birthday party,’ I divulged, knowing that would be explanation enough.

To my surprise, Neer laughed. ‘That’s it! You looked like you’d seen death. I assumed it was something serious. You’re so dramatic! It’ll be fine. For sure, it’ll be a small event,’ he reassured me.

‘You don’t know that.’

He gave me a look that let me know we were at risk of falling back into his ongoing lecture about how I needed to expand my friend group. We’d had this conversation way too often, and it always ended the same, with Neer telling me I had to give others a chance. I was convinced he'd teamed up with Mum on the issue – the winning arguments had seemed way too aligned for it to be a coincidence. I knew they meant well, but I was happy being alone.

'I'm looking forward to the group project,' I tried to convince him, reminding him I had renewed my efforts. He nodded in agreement. It looked like he would let me have this one.

Looking out the library window towards the darkening sky, I tried my best to discuss a new topic before he changed his mind.

'Have you finally watched *A Life on our Planet*?' I asked, knowing Neer would love it as much as I did.

'I can't believe it's taken me this long to watch it. It was eye-opening!' he added, bewildered, reflecting the reaction I had had.

'Can you believe only 35% of Earth's wilderness remains?' I said, feeling my heart sink as I remembered the cost if we didn't change our way of living now.

'Can you imagine…'

I didn't need Neer to finish his sentence. I knew what he was thinking – a sixth mass extinction caused by us and for what? I thought back to the beautiful footage of colourful coral reefs, leaping cheetahs and the grandeur of the forests. I thought of the hypnotic pattern of the oak leaf I'd picked up last night, and something in my chest pulsed at the memory.

'No, I can't. I won't. As Christina Figueres said, we need to be "stubborn optimists". The world has already given us part of the solution – we just need to make it happen.'

'Yeah, right, all we need to do is cut our current greenhouse gas emissions in half over the next decade; re-wild the planet; increase the use of renewable energy; regulate the fishing industry and all through population growth,' added Neer sarcastically, but I wouldn't give in – we could do this, we had to.

'Exactly,' I said, pouting in defiance. 'And we can start by doing our bit.'

'Oh no, here we go again. Who have you targeted now?'

'I may have sent a strongly worded email to the school on how we can reduce our carbon, food waste and water usage. Not to mention rewild the playing fields.'

Neer raised his eyebrow. 'And what did they respond?'

'I haven't heard back yet,' I admitted, 'But it's okay. I've already decided you'll help me start a petition if the school doesn't get back with a satisfactory response.'

He laughed, shaking his head, knowing there was no changing my resolve – we were going to save humanity, one climate activist at a time.

As though in reminder, the school bell rang a nasal, buzzing sound. There was no time to lose, yet our planning would have to wait until the end of class.

By 4 p.m. classes had finished. Relieved that the day was ending, my knuckles ached for the punching bag. I'd started the martial art of Krav Maga shortly after moving in with Mum. She thought it would help me feel more confident in myself. I'd hardly missed a day of training since I'd signed up and had just received my black belt.

Neer was driving me to training like he'd done most days since his 18th birthday. I would meet him at the school car park, and he'd usually read his book during my session, saving me the unsafe cycle along the motorway. He was considerate like that.

Walking out of the school building, I saw a few people holding the same leaflet and smiling at me. Okay, kind of weird, but I didn't think much of it as I continued walking towards the silver e-Golf where Neer was sitting, bobbing his head to the beat of the music in his car. But that's when I noticed someone was walking alongside me.

'Are you going to wet your trousers again this time?' taunted Arthur.

Just the thought of having to engage with this idiot had my rolling my eyes. Despite being perfectly sweet when he was younger, Arthur had become a jerk since his growth spurt and made a point of tormenting every girl in the class.

'Is that the best you can come up with?' I shot back. He just laughed, thrilled to have prompted a response, instantly making me regret acknowledging his stupid games.

'Should I bring you nappies, just in case? Call it a birthday gift,' he poked.

I could feel my nails digging into my palms.

'Is your mother worried you'll end up old and alone, just like her?'

Throwing my fists to my side, I let my backpack slide down my shoulder onto the floor. I stormed towards Arthur, sweeping his feet from under him in one tactical move. His ass slammed into the floor. Grabbing a fistful of his collar, I jerked his head towards me.

'Say that again!' I yelled, unconcerned by those around me. I didn't care what he said to me, but no one would insult my family – least of all Mum. I could see the tremble in my hands, shaking with adrenaline.

Suddenly Neer was next to me, hand on my shoulder. 'C'mon, Ella.'

I let go, remembering where I was. Grabbing my bag from the pavement, I threw it once more over my shoulder. I slid into Neer's car, eager to escape the crowd that had gathered around us.

'I know he's a jerk. But, that was a bit much,' Neer pointed out, his voice concerned. He was of course right. I'm not sure what had taken over me.

'Please can we go?' I hid my face with my sleeve.

As though noticing the growing crowd, Neer nodded and turned on the car. It wasn't until we were exiting the school grounds that Neer spoke again. 'I know this isn't going to help, but you should probably see this,' he said, thrusting a piece of paper at me. It looked like the same one I had seen across the school.

YOU'RE INVITED!
Please join us for Ella's birthday party!
12–6 p.m., Saturday 17th November
SEE YOU THEN!

Looking out the car window to confirm my suspicion, I could see that everybody at school had a copy or at least it felt like it.

'No, no, no! This party can't be happening,' I groaned. 'How could she? I only agreed this morning.'

I grounded my teeth together, strongly this time, feeling the red-hot mix of anger and embarrassment boiling up inside of me.

'I can't believe it. I knew something was off; everything was too casual, too last minute, especially for Mum.' I mean, she ran a whole medical practice where she knew what every one of her employees was doing daily for the next six months. Of course, she had come up with a plan to celebrate my birthday. Even if it meant organising it behind my back and without my consent.

Neer kept quiet during my monologue, knowing better than to comment as I seethed next to him.

‘Everything was planned, down to the day when she would ask for my agreement to have a party. Of course, she would only ask me the day before: one, because it meant I would never suspect a big party, and two, even if I did refuse, it would have been too late to cancel. She’s been playing me like a fiddle.’

I sat back, still fuming but feeling slightly better after my rant. I couldn’t deny that I was also quite impressed, knowing my sweet and compassionate mother was capable of such cold, calculated manipulation. I sighed as I stared out the window. This day was becoming too much. It just had to end.

‘I guess it’s a good thing you’ve got training today,’ chimed Neer.

I hummed in agreement.

When we arrived at the studio, my long-time coach, Darren Rose, was waiting on the mat.

‘Your mother asked me to train you extra hard today – she warned me that you might have some extra energy to blow off.’ His laughter made his deep grey eyes light up. ‘I’m guessing it might have something to do with the birthday invitation I received a few weeks ago, although she did ask me to keep quiet about it.’

‘A few weeks ago!’ I shouted louder than intended, unable to help myself.

'Okay, it's a sensitive subject… I won't say any more,' he said, putting his hands up in surrender as he struggled to maintain a straight face.

'Just tell me this, when did you find out?' he asked as a broad smile spread across his disfigured face.

I shot him my darkest look, making him lock his grinning lips with an invisible key.

I dropped my bag to the side, pulling out the wraps for my hand – Ms Lancy's gift staring me in the face. The small note card taped to the front of the wrapper open for my eyes to read – 'I'd love nothing more than to have my debating companion back.' I cursed under my breath, quickly wrapping my hands before joining Darren on the mat – gift in hand.

I shoved it in his direction. 'From Ms Lancy.'

His lips pressed into a hard line before tossing her gift aside – discarded without a second thought.

I bit down on my lip, the pain sharp in my mouth.

I should have never brought it up.

He held the boxing pads by the sides of his face, indicating for me to begin. I started punching softly, my eyes lingering on the book, now laying on the floor behind him. He pushed the pads against my hand, forcing my focus until I directed each punch with maximum precision. As I fell into the rhythm of the repetitive workout, I felt my body relaxing a little further with every hit.

'Yesterday evening...' I finally said, breaking the silence. Darren looked at me quizzically.

'That's when Mum asked me about having a party,' I admitted sourly.

My confession seemed to win him over as he roared with laughter, making me smile.

'You've got to give it to June, she's got game,' he chuckled, wiping the sweat from his eyes.

'Mum's making university abroad sound like a dream,' I objected, punching harder into the pads.

'Come on. It's not that bad. You'll have some food, drink a little, see a few people and at most you'll have to give a short speech,' he reassured me.

I stopped punching and looked up at him in desperation. 'I hadn't even thought about giving a speech!'

'It'll be okay, kiddo. You'll have Neer by your side,' he said, waving to Neer, who sat on the bench reading another political science book.

'Enough chit-chat, let's fight,' I said.

By the time we were done, I was beyond shattered. Neer had had to leave early after receiving a call from his parents, pleading for him to come home and help with his nightmare sister. It seemed no one else in the house had enough patience left to deal with her. Usually, I relished my quiet cycle home, but after last night's attack, I asked Darren to drive me back home. He'd been surprised but hadn't questioned me.

Luckily, all the lights were off when we arrived at the house. If anything were to happen, I'd prefer it happen to me alone. Locking the door thoroughly behind me, I looked out the window, making sure no one was in sight before drawing the curtains and finding a note on the counter from Mum on top of the birthday invitation I had seen spread across school:

'With great power comes great responsibility.'

Unfortunately, being your mother's only child has some downfalls but also its benefits – you'll find I made your favourite, hopefully earning your forgiveness.

P.S. Still at the presentation, don't wait up for me.

Love you,

Mum

Too exhausted to think any further, I took my food upstairs and locked the door to my bedroom. Barricading the entrance with a chair, I watched it intently as I gulped down Mum's Mexican fajitas. I listened for a while, my haunted thoughts now combined with anticipating the horror that would be tomorrow. Finally deciding it was as safe as it was going to get, I plugged in my headphones. Blasting mindless music until it drowned my every thought, I fell asleep once my mind was nothing but a void.

Chapter 3

The room was dark and deadly silent. Looking ahead, I could only make out the back of an old wooden chain next to a rusty lamp, the lightbulb flickering incessantly. Recognising the room, I approached slowly. I could hear the sound of shallow breathing only a few yards away. I stood still as I tried to look closer, the shadows revealing the angular edges of her disappearing face. It was the sickly woman from my recent escape. She was saying something. I focused on her wheezing breath, only to hear the despair in her echoing voice.

'Eloisa... Run, Eloisa...'

A jolt coursed through my body and jerked me awake. Taking a few short, sharp breaths, I tried to steady my racing heart. The cool air entered my lungs, slowing down with every elongated breath. Brushing my tangled hair away from my face, I wrapped my hands around me, holding myself tightly, feeling exhaustion sink into my body. The unexpected trip to the desolate volcanic land, the nurses' deadly grip around my neck and the boy's glowing golden blades. Nothing I did helped me find the rest I sought. The images circled relentlessly throughout the night, and now they were haunted by the sickly woman's voice.

I shuddered, wrapping myself tighter in my blanket. I couldn't quite shake the haunting familiarity I'd felt when I heard the woman's voice. Why did she want me to run, and from what? And how did she know my birth name? Few people knew my real name was Eloisa. Turning my face into the pillow, I glanced at the clock by my bedside, burying my face deeper into the pillow when I saw it was already 11 a.m. Unwilling to get up, I simply stared out of the skylights in my ceiling, hoping to feel reassured by the swirling greyness of the sky above as I mentally steeled myself. I had to get ready – guests would arrive in the next hour.

I rushed into the shower, shaved my legs, washed my hair and then spent a good half-hour drying my thick, black hair until it fell in waves down my back. I looked closely at my face in the mirror. Maybe it was the light, but I looked different. My grey eyes seemed darker than usual, contrasting with my skin which had become increasingly pale with the sunless autumn.

I felt wired, on edge. I didn't know what it was or why, but I could see it on my face too. It must be the nerves. The nurse's pit-black eyes flashed before me, making me wince as I placed my hand over my heart, feeling the memory of her invisible flames tearing me apart. I shook my head, it must be a delayed shock reaction. I brushed off the feeling.

I wouldn't let myself linger on her anymore. I needed to focus on the party for Mum's sake. Even if I didn't like being the centre of attention, especially around people I didn't really know, she'd clearly put a lot of effort into the party.

Despite Mum and Neer's best efforts I'd never managed to integrate myself properly at school. I had tried! But no matter how much effort I put in, I just seemed to struggle to relate to people. I thought, well, actually, I *knew* I could come across as being quite intense. I couldn't help it. I was someone who always looked to create a deeper connection with people, and I couldn't be satisfied with less. That was the way it was. Even Mum, to whom I'd consider myself closer than anyone else on Earth, sometimes struggled to cope with my awkwardness.

Sometimes, I wondered if I was experiencing the world the same way as everyone else. It was like I was missing something, something vital to my being. But then again, maybe relationships simply weren't meant to move you to your core. If that was the case, I was chasing after relationships and connections that simply didn't exist.

But it was my birthday and the turn of my thoughts seemed to have kick-started a wave of negativity within me. Unwilling to let myself be depressed like this, I cranked up some music in an attempt to lift my mood. I chose to wear my favourite cherry-coloured sheath dress. It was vaguely warrior-like, which I loved – perfect for the battle ahead.

I peeked at the driveway through my bathroom window as the clock struck twelve. Multiple minivans, filled with my classmates, had already started to arrive. Feeling an instant pang of nausea mixed with dread, I ignored the growing pain that had started burning in my chest. Gathering my courage, I headed towards my impending doom. Catching a first glance at the garden, I couldn't help but admire Mum's work. She'd put up multiple connecting marquees in the garden, each perfectly sealed and equipped with hydrogen heaters to shelter guests from the cold outdoors. Looking through the open entrance, I could see stunning white blossoms hanging in garlands, dripping with long lines of red gossamer ribbons.

I searched the small crowd of early comers, blushing as I took in the crowd of faces focusing on me until I found Neer's reassuring presence. He looked relaxed as he happily chatted to a group of people making their way into the marquee. Dressed in skinny black jeans and a poorly ironed white shirt, his bright-pink socks stuck out, and I smiled despite myself.

A few years ago, Neer had insisted he needed a signature style, something to complement his South Asian features. Something 'exotic,' he had quoted, which had me rolling my eyes so deeply that we laughed about needing to get them pulled back out. But soon after, my best friend started exclusively wearing brightly coloured socks, usually matching his mood.

When Neer finally saw me, his eyes shone with excitement, taking in my unusually polished appearance. Staring too long with a look of confusion, he quickly composed himself and waved me over to join him.

'Wow, Ella! You look great!' he said enthusiastically, giving me a bear hug.

'Thanks. You scrub up nicely, too,' I complimented, although I couldn't keep the nerves from my voice, despite my best attempts.

Pained by the intense burning spreading rapidly through my body, I said a quick, awkward hello to the rest of the group as they meandered into the marquee. Letting them walk ahead, I took a moment to compose myself. I let my hand fall over my chest, wishing the burning would disappear and give me a chance to be normal at my own birthday party.

'Are you sure you're okay?' asked Neer in a hushed tone. Shooting him a dark look, I bit down my tongue, holding back the suddenly fierce retort bubbling up. Turning my face away, I fought to get a grip over myself, but the more I fought, the hotter the flames burned inside me.

'I'm sorry,' I pleaded, ashamed of my behaviour.

Neer's frown deepened as he continued to watch me. 'You seem off,' he finally said.

'I'm fine,' I snapped, desperate for him to leave.

'Jeez. Just try to relax,' Neer said, taking a slight step backwards. I clamped my jaw down in response – he was right. I was losing control. My heart hammered in my chest. Yet I was increasingly intoxicated by a fit of raw anger I had never felt before. Barely clinging to my rational side, I willed myself to behave as we walked to rejoin the group.

'Nice party, Ella. Who knew you could throw such a badass event?' offered one classmate, interrupting the darkening spiral of my thoughts.

I looked up at her – Fei, my brain supplied – composing my response, indulging for a moment in what it would be like to tell her what I really thought.

'Thank you,' I eventually managed. 'Although I can't take any credit for it. Mum put all of this together.' My voice sounded strained even to my own ears. I knew she hoped I would elaborate or choose another subject of conversation, but I couldn't find anything to add, causing an awkward silence as she tried again.

'I overheard Mr Wise in the corridor saying he was very impressed by your pitch for the Climate Innovation Competition,' offered my classmate, ignoring my intensity. I had proposed a water filtering system catching microplastics seeping through our drinking water. There were so many things I could elaborate on; plastic's devastating impact on marine life; our exponential production of it despite knowing its harm; how we needed to curb our unsustainable consumption. Yet I could only manage a nod, not trusting what I might say.

Fortunately, Neer jumped in, sensing my distress. 'I'm sure he also loved your idea, Fei! Upcycling unwanted laptops and iPads to donate to students who don't have access to their own to complete homework is a fantastic initiative!'

The group around me nodded in agreement and started discussing the various competition entries, speculating who might win. Nodding along, I let my posture hunch under the burning sensation raging through me. Hunched over, I could no longer stop scrunching up in pain.

Letting the group carry the conversation, I desperately looked to the crowd, appearing behind Neer, hoping to find something to calm me, only to see Arthur gorging himself on the canapés. My jaw tightened as my anger grew. What nerve he had showing up to my party, especially after he had insulted Mum. I turned back to the group, trying to control my laboured breathing. I could feel my eyes glazing over slightly as I struggled to listen to the conversation. Distracted by rage, I couldn't help but continue to spiral in the bitter yet satisfying hatred for everyone and everything in my surroundings.

I turned my head from side to side, taking in the room, allowing my gaze to wander from person to person. I was breathing faster now, but no one seemed to notice. Until I spotted him, there he was. Staring back with his bright green eyes, he'd stopped speaking to Darren, letting his natural smile disappear into a firm line.

Never letting go of my gaze, he leaned in to whisper something to Darren, making Darren turn to look in my direction. Raising both hands in front of his body, indicating for me to wait for him, they started pushing through the crowd towards me. I felt another jolt of fire course through my veins.

'He must be kidding himself if he thinks I'm going to wait around for him,' I muttered as I turned to leave the group. I thought I heard Neer ask if I was okay, but I wasn't sure, and I didn't care, anyway. The burning inside me was growing hotter, and it was hard to think of anything else. Gently grabbing my arm, noticing how my chest had collapsed forwards, Neer asked again, but before I knew what I was doing, I jerked my arm away and out of his grip. He stumbled and his drink sloshed unceremoniously to the ground as I shoved past him.

I could hear him calling after me, following me through the crowd as I dove deeper. My irrepressible rage eventually got the better of me. I turned on him. Stopping him in his tracks, I grabbed him by the arm. He froze. His eyes were wide, and his face set in an expression I'd never seen. Before I knew what I was doing, my hand tightened against his skin.

And then the rush began.

I could feel my muscles strengthen, the texture of my skin brightening, the excitement building with every heartbeat that pumped the additional energy flowing through me. I pulled him closer, responding to the insatiable thirst that screamed for more.

Catching a glimpse of myself in Neer's glasses. My face was rigid, jaw clamped shut, teeth grinding. My eyes were pitch black. The inky disease that lived in them had leaked into the skin around them. The fire burning inside me was now raging. Every extra ounce of energy I sucked out of him acted like a gasoline bomb, sending the fire further into havoc – along with my thirst.

I looked behind the glass that covered his eyes. Rolled back, he stood limp in my grip.

Spinning. Spinning. My head started to sway. I forced my lips to open. Swallow. Let go. Run.

Out of the marquee, the images around me faded into barely a blur as I ran towards the surrounding forest. I sprinted to the edge of the garden faster than ever before, quickly disappearing into the dense comfort of the trees.

Collapsing to my knees, crushed by the flames coursing through me, I let the tears pour uncontrollably down my face, sobbing with pain before letting out an agonised scream. And then I could hear them. And the creatures could see me.

Bursting through the surrounding canopy. The two creatures flew through the branches before landing effortlessly around me.

Instinctively, I wrapped my hands protectively around my head. One of the creatures turned to me, and her lips curled back over her teeth. Her jaw unlocked as she screeched in response to my call.

Their bodies were like those of humans, but their eyes were black like mine. No, darker, and seemed to have similarly leaked into the surrounding skin forming a darkened mask around their eyes – a mask of death.

'Strat, get behind her' barked Darren to the boy. The two creatures crouched protectively around me, swords in hand.

Pulling out his two golden semi-circular blades from behind his back, the boy's emerald eyes momentarily gleamed charcoal. The black stone lodged in his blades, shining brightly in response.

Within a blink of an eye, the two creatures combusted into dust – sliced in half, straight through their core.

'Quickly,' urged Darren, already positioned. They had circled me as though they were trying to trap a wild animal.

'There must still be traces of the Defacer within her!' shouted Darren to Strat as I let out another wild scream.

Crouched on the ground, I drew further into the trees, still sobbing. The fire inside turned into an icy cold flame, and my body started shutting down as it grew numb.

'What do we do?' yelled Strat, panicked, looking towards Darren for guidance.

'Give me a minute!' replied Darren, more urgently this time as he scrambled to figure out a solution.

'Hold her down!'

I launched myself forwards to the boy, but I was too late. They had pounced first.

Taking out a large syringe filled with golden liquid from his pocket, Strat tactfully dodged me as Darren pinned me to the ground. Secured under the weight of Darren's body, I fought to escape, but it was useless. Rushing to my side, Strat injected a needle into my thigh. Shrieking, I tried to unsuccessfully rid myself of Darren until I felt the flames start to dampen. Feeling my vision blur, I stopped fighting Darren altogether, my body slumping in his hold.

Still holding me gently, Darren whispered, 'It'll be okay.' Feeling the last of the burning flames go out, I let go.

And then, darkness.

≈

I woke up with cold sweats, my arms glistening. Looking outside the living room window, it was already night. I must have blacked out the whole afternoon. I was lying on the sofa, covered by a blanket with a cool towel on my forehead. The room was dark except for the reading lamps on either side of the couch. Barely conscious, I could hear two voices bickering in the corner of the living room.

'How could you not tell her she's an Elan? Train her to use her Energy?' I heard the boy, Strat, shout in hushed outrage. That was his name, Strat. Not quite what I expected for a Scot, yet it seemed to suit his rugged look. He wore black jeans with a stone-coloured long sleeve shirt. His dark grey suede-like jacket was tossed across the chair, yet he still seemed too hot as he pushed his sleeves further up, exposing muscular forearms as he ran his hand through his unruly chestnut hair.

He leaned against the high armchair, tilting his body unevenly as he looked back towards Darren, his piercing green eyes matching those I had first seen in the forest. I should have probably said something then and there, letting them know I was awake, but I was too curious to interrupt and wanted to uncover more about these Elans. their Energy and how it all related to my attack.

I allowed myself a glance, seeing Strat press the tip of his fingers to his creased forehead. We were about the same age, yet he seemed so familiar with the gesture, with the worry.

'I could feel the Defacer tearing away her Energy, claiming it for itself…' Strat elaborated, his voice quivering as he tried to explain what we had gone through just a couple of days ago. 'And then for her to go through that again this afternoon…' He took a sharp breath in, his eyes haunted.

Darren placed his hand on Strat's shoulder. 'You couldn't have known. We don't train you to endure a trip to Pamatan, let alone kill a Defacer in the process,' reassured Darren, patting his shoulder before letting his hand drop.

Strat leaned deeper against the armchair for support before straightening himself. Shoulders squared. 'I'm sorry for my part in this, I should have checked she was clear of traces from the Defacer, but we need to prepare her better.'

Darren slowly turned toward him, the full weight of his authoritative gaze bearing down on Strat.

My body went numb. I could feel the warm fire creeping into my cheeks. The burning of nausea crept up my throat. I forced myself to blink.

'Unless I say otherwise, Ella will continue to lead her life as humanly as possible,' Darren ordered, his tone ice cold.

I took a silent breath, trying to keep my insides in the interior of my stomach. What did Darren mean by 'as humanly possible'?

Again, I should have intervened and demanded answers. But I couldn't. My coach wasn't someone you crossed lightly, and the child in me crawled into a tight ball. I waited, expecting Strat to do the same, but he just held his gaze, matching its intensity.

'This is insane,' he enunciated, shaking his head in defiance. 'She deserves to make her own choice. Two Defacers materialised out of nowhere, protecting her too. This isn't something we can just move past,' argued Strat, looking incredulous.

My body went cold as I realised that whatever had happened to me was bad and a big enough deal that it had broader implications. My senses heightened at the prospect of danger. My instincts urged me to listen more closely.

'No, no, we can't,' agreed Darren, his voice level. I could feel him glancing my way, checking I was still asleep before continuing. He continued, his voice lower than before. 'But we can resolve this ourselves, and you're going to find out how she got summoned to Pamatan without descending through the Gates. And if there's a gap in our defences, we'll find a way to let the others know, but I want both Ella and the Committee knowing as little as possible while we do.'

'Even if we don't report this to the Committee, we'd be doing ourselves a massive disservice,' challenged Strat, holding firm to his opinion. 'You say I'm your most talented student, but I'm nothing compared to what she should be.' I could feel his finger pointing in my direction. I tightened my eyes shut, sensing their eyes on me.

'That's enough,' directed Darren, but it did nothing to stop the speed at which Strat's words were now flowing.

'I was in Pamatan for just a few minutes, just enough time to find her, and it felt like my Energy was being sucked straight out of me. And that's with over a decade of training.' He took another sharp breath. 'Yet she's travelled to the home of our archenemies, completely untrained, somehow survived and had the strength to kick me in the gut afterwards. We can't just ignore that sort of talent, pretend like she wouldn't make all the difference to our fight against the Defacers.' I could hear the plea in his voice.

'This isn't a negotiation,' cut in Darren.

'And what happens if they try to summon her again?' retorted Strat, unwilling to give up. 'Let me at least train her how to control her Energy. Even if it's just the basics, it could make all the difference between life and death.' I swore my mouth dropped open at the audacity of this boy.

'That's enough!' Darren hissed.

My face drained of blood at his answer. Black spots once again formed into my vision. I had to close my eyes to stop the spinning. I couldn't prevent my hand from sliding to the top of my heart as though it could protect it from the pain.

A moment of silence passed between them.

'She's going to have questions,' obliged Strat, his tone more cooperative despite crossing his arms across his chest.

'That, she will,' agreed Darren, his tone calmer than it had been a minute ago. He was familiar with my somewhat relentless questioning, I'd inherited from Neer. Nothing would stop me if I wanted to get to the bottom of something.

Darren exhaled loudly. 'I need to check up on Neer. Handle this,' he added, looking in my direction.

'Tell her nothing,' he warned, grabbing his jacket.

Chapter 4

'Oh no, no, no!' My chest started to heave. I threw my legs to the floor as soon as I heard Darren shut the front door, only to have Strat's hands hover over me the moment my toe touched the cold wooden floor, urging me to stay put.

'Where is he?' I almost yelled. I couldn't help but turn my head frantically, needing to see him myself. My breath caught when I couldn't find my best friend.

'Who?'

'*Neer!*' I shot back, finally breaking through the last of my brain fog. The memory of my white knuckles burying into his lifeless skin hit me with all its might.

'He's fine,' rushed Strat in a soothing voice. 'Just a little frazzled, but fine. Your mum insisted he go home and rest.' I stared into his emerald eyes, grabbing my hair as I looked to verify the truth of his statement.

'Just breathe,' said Strat, never letting go of my gaze as he sat back down. 'Neer is fine. Luckily he can't seem to remember what happened and has no injuries other than the tiny bruise on his arm.'

I couldn't help the tears of relief that trickled down my cheek. I looked away, wiping the moisture from my eyes. I grabbed my chest, trying to contain the guilt that followed. I had done this to him.

'Ella,' cooed Strat softly. A thrill shot through me just hearing my name uttered by his lips. 'I know what you're thinking – but it wasn't you,' he tried to reassure me. He handed me a glass of water and waited for me to take a sip. 'You were infected by the Defacer that attacked you the night we met in the forest.'

I flinched at the bluntness of his response, recognising the darkness that had coursed through me. He spoke slowly but with intent, his eyes searching mine. 'Your body's removed the final traces of the Defacer's poison, but you still need to rest up.'

I quickly scanned through my sore body before catching a glimpse of myself in the antique hand mirror resting on the coffee table. I pulled it towards my face. My eyes were once again clear. I couldn't help but touch the skin around them, remembering the inky taint that had inhabited me. How did I know that darkness wasn't hiding somewhere inside me?

'You're safe now. The poison's all gone,' added Strat, noticing my apprehension. Even then, I couldn't help feeling like I shouldn't trust myself. I had sought the rush of Energy and liked it.

I cringed at the sound of metallic pots crashing down. We both turned our heads towards the kitchen, listening to Mum unleash a string of angry words.

'Let me tell her you've woken up,' Strat announced. Before I could stop him, he walked across the living room and into the kitchen, pausing briefly before leaving the living room to say, 'Just run with the story I've told her, okay? It's for the best,' he pleaded, his previously confident voice coloured with new worry.

Before I had a chance to wonder about our cover story, Mum was rushing toward me.

'Oh, darling! I was so worried! You poor thing, you've had all the nasties that come with a concussion,' she said, hugging me awkwardly. 'Let me examine you quickly,' she demanded as she pushed my legs to the side so that she could sit on the sofa. I hadn't even had time to put my water down before I had her flashlight in my eyes and her hand on my wrist as she started counting my pulse.

'Your temperature is gone. That's good. You're not feeling dizzy or sick?'

'No,' I confirmed, letting her fuss over me.

'Strat tells me you met at the Krav Maga studio? He's also one of Darren's students?' she asked, to which I nodded in confirmation.

'And you'd been feeling nervous about giving a speech, which is why you went into the forest?' Mum enquired, unconvinced.

‘Yeah…’ I said slowly, glancing at Strat, who gave a slight nod. ‘Yep, yep,’ I added with more conviction. ‘I’m sorry I left the party. I needed a moment to clear my head,’ I lied with as much confidence I could muster.

‘And Strat followed you because…?’ she persisted.

Before I could think of an excuse, Strat intervened. ‘I, too, sometimes suffer from stage fright and thought I might be able to give Ella a few pointers to help her out. When I finally caught up with her, I found that she had tripped over a root and had knocked herself out. Which explains the bump on her head.’ I marvelled at the ease with which he lied, his voice melting like honey.

Mum ran her hand gently through my hair, stopping when she found the bump on my head from my fall on the forest path leading home.

‘Yes ... I guess so.’

I could tell she was deliberating whether we were telling the truth, especially since it was hard to believe Strat ever being shy. ‘You’re not usually clumsy, darling. Well, I’m just glad you’ve woken up. You need to stay hydrated.’

‘It must have been the nerves. I wasn’t quite myself,’ I explained, thinking of the lengthy apology I needed to make to Neer. We’d need to find a better explanation for him because I doubted he would have believed our lie.

‘I wonder why,’ Mum added with her not-so-subtle sarcasm, her eyes lightening up with amusement as she glanced towards Strat and back to me. ‘Your pulse is a little quick, but apart from that, you seem fine.' She smiled widely, her eyes bright.

Trying to ignore the embarrassing blush blazed across my face, I gave Mum my fiercest look, begging her to stop. Her smile stretched a little further before she started to recompose herself.

'You should try and stay awake for a little while before you go back to sleep, just in case,' she advised, her tone finally normal again. 'Best to message Neer, too. He was worried about you. He wanted to stay until you'd woken up, but I insisted he went home.'

Just the mention of his name had my eyes burning. I breathed in, counting my breath as I let out a slow exhale. *Neer is safe. I'm safe,* I repeated over and over in my head, trying to keep it together. It seemed to work as Mum didn't seem to notice.

'You should go home, too, Strat. It's late, and I'm sure your parents will be worried,' insisted Mum. She must have been trying to get him out of the house for a while now.

But I could feel Strat glance towards me, taking in my impending meltdown before deciding he would stay.

'Ms Barnardo, you've had a long day. Please let me keep Ella company so that you can rest,' Strat said, flashing her his dazzling smile.

Looking at me for guidance, I nodded encouragingly at Mum. 'I'll be fine, I promise,' I tried in my steadiest voice.

Even if Strat had agreed to go along with Darren's plans, it didn't change the fact he had stood up for me, for a stranger, because he thought it was the right thing to do, and that spoke mountains about the kind of person he was. Something in his demeanour told me he wouldn't be afraid to make his own decisions, even if it involved defying Darren. It gave me hope. If anyone was going to tell me the truth, Strat would be my best shot.

Mum held my gaze, waiting to see if I would change my mind, but it was set. I needed some answers, and I knew I wouldn't get any with her lounging around.

'I'm fine,' I tried, my pitch squeakier than usual.

'Okay, but I want you resting,' she ordered. 'And you let me know the moment you start feeling unwell,' she added sternly, leaning over to kiss me on the forehead. 'Strat, you're welcome to sleep in the guest room if you get tired. It's just above the dining room on the second floor. I'm off to bed. Goodnight.'

≈

Grabbing an issue of *Country Life*, Strat leaned back in the adjacent armchair flicking through the pages. We waited patiently, listening to Mum's footsteps as she walked up the stairs and into her bedroom.

I couldn't help but twitch every time I thought back to Darren's order. *'Tell her nothing'* were the exact orders he'd given Strat. After everything I'd gone through, did he really think he could just keep me in check? Was I just a submissive student to him? And yet I had laid there – mute – while they discussed *my* future.

Mum would have been ashamed. She was always outspoken, strong-minded, and I had kept silent. I hadn't even had the guts to intervene, defend myself, or ask for answers. I squared my shoulders, turning to face Strat, resolved to seize the opportunity in front of me. I promised myself I wouldn't let him leave without telling me everything.

But he seemed to have a different idea of how we would spend our time.

I couldn't help but watch him skim pages. He looked sad, almost pained, and I felt an urge to reach over and comfort him. Blushing, I let myself examine him further. Framing his deep-set eyes were softly rounded eyebrows pulled into a deep frown. I hadn't noticed it before, but the tip of his nose was slightly crooked, another imperfection, yet perfectly fitted.

There was something about him, though, that made me feel anxious and, more than anything, engrossed by his presence. He noticed me looking, glancing up at me through long dark lashes. My eyes went wide as I realised I'd been caught staring. My cheeks heated up to my utter dismay.

Luckily the thump upstairs saved me as we both looked towards the ceiling, listening to Mum close the door to her bedroom. Once we were sure she was out of earshot, I drew my full attention back to Strat, fully prepared to start my interrogation. Before I could say anything, he jumped in.

'I'm Strat, by the way,' he said with criminal ease, pulling his hand towards me. 'It's only right you know my name after assaulting me twice,' he teased, his lips curving up at the corners.

I looked at him sceptically – his sudden charm-offensive unnerving me. I wondered if this was how he planned to distract me from asking critical questions.

He seemed to interpret my apprehension as doubt when I didn't extend my hand in response.

'I promise we're on the same side,' he said, the side of his mouth pulling up into a cocksure grin. 'Plus, don't you think if I had wanted to hurt you, I would've done it by now?' he joked with ease. 'I certainly wouldn't have waited until your party! I've got better things to do, you know.'

He let out an enchanting laugh, revealing a perfect set of white teeth, and I felt a little dazed. I glared at him, doing my best not to ogle and probably looking ridiculous with the hot blush on my face. But I was determined not to let my judgement be compromised, yet looking into his deep green eyes, I felt something within me ease.

'I have questions,' I pre-warned Strat, ignoring everything he'd just said.

'I've been warned that might be the case.' He smiled that cocksure smile.

‘Who are the Defacers? Why did they attack me? How did I suddenly end up in … that place?’ I could hear the desperation in my voice, but I’d had enough of being completely clueless.

Still tucked under the blanket, I pulled my knees towards my chest. He was so close that I could pick up on the citrusy smell to his skin.

He sighed heavily. ‘It hasn’t been the easiest of days. Are you sure you don’t want to rest, and we can talk about this tomorrow?’ His tone suggested he already knew there was no chance of that happening.

‘No!’ I exclaimed, making his eyes light up. The corner of his lip twitched. My impatience clearly amused him.

‘Alright, alright,’ he said, raising his hands defensively. ‘But for the record, it’s only because you’ve given me no choice.’ He was surely banking that excuse for the explanation he’d undoubtedly have to give Darren later.

‘Just so I know what I’m working with, tell me, did you have any inkling of the existence of your Energy?’

I shook my head, making his frown deepen. ‘And I still don’t,’ I prompted, thinking back to the leaf’s golden light and its pattern pulling me into the depths of its embrace.

‘Your Energy is probably still too depleted from Thursday’s attack for you to feel its presence,’ he explained. ‘Although it’s unheard of for it to have Awakened so late. I wonder what triggered it …’ he mused to himself as he looked at me, as though assessing my age.

'What were you doing that day in the forest just before you got summoned?' he enquired.

Sneaky, he was trying to get the answers he needed from me before he'd have to answer any of mine. 'I'm not falling for that. If you want to get what you need from me, you're going to have to give me some information in return.'

He lifted his eyebrow. 'I can't do that,' he admitted, another truth, but it didn't discourage me.

'Well, you're going to have to tell Darren you've been unsuccessful in your mission.'

Strat chuckled in response as he rubbed his chin. 'Or … you can tell me what I need to know and you can discuss your questions directly with Darren?' he hustled.

He wasn't going to play ball; I had to try another angle. 'It's not that simple,' I replied honestly – our relationship was complicated. Although I trusted Darren, he wasn't the most forthcoming with the truth, especially when it came to the past. 'I know he won't tell me anything. You're my only hope.' I gave him my most innocent look, screaming 'damsel in distress' – boys loved to feel like the hero and I knew if I played it right, he'd give in. 'Please,' I added as sweetly as my pride would allow.

Strat held my gaze before softening his expression. 'I can't say I hadn't been warned,' he said, shaking his head, relaxing his stance. 'But you'll eventually need to speak to Darren,' he warned.

I wiped the tears that had boiled over my eyes and smiled in victory. Obviously, I didn't want to speak to Darren about this, but it was worth the trade-off if it got me some answers. Plus, Strat had never specified 'when'.

'Deal?' Strat insisted.

'Deal.' I smiled satisfactorily, shaking his hand. I jerked my hand away at the feel of his touch, stinging me as if an electric current had passed through. Making sure not to touch me anymore, he stood up and paced away. He seemed to gather his thoughts before settling on the sofa's armrest.

'Firstly, I want you to know that Defacer attacks like yours should never have happened in the first place and, most importantly, you are not alone.' He paused, reconsidering his words. 'Or, should I say, you are no longer alone.' He was trying to sound reassuring, but I could hear the bitterness in those final words. Before I could continue my interrogation, he lifted his index finger, indicating he wasn't done.

Moving swiftly back down to the seat next to me, he repositioned himself to face me directly, sending flutters to my stomach.

'I'm also really sorry for what happened to you today. It was my fault. I should have checked for Defacer traces after the attack.' I could hear the shame in his voice. Looking briefly down, he glanced back up through his dark lashes, revealing an expression so sad that it made me want to reassure him.

‘It’s not your fault,’ I disagreed, using the words he had just used on me. ‘Plus, I’m fine,’ I said, stretching out my sore arms to prove my point.

‘I still should have checked,’ he finally accepted, although I got the impression he didn’t feel like he deserved Darren’s mercy.

‘Either way, it’s not the introduction you deserve.’ He spoke softly, the hurt obvious in his eyes, and much to my surprise, I found myself gravitating towards him. We had just met, yet he made me feel like he cared, like I mattered.

But then again, I had never been good at reading others, so perhaps this was how he was with everyone. No matter the explanation, it didn’t erase the depth to which his words had touched me. It was like my whole world had stopped and pivoted as I considered, for the first time in my life, that maybe I wasn’t so alone.

Without a second thought, I leaned across the sofa to hug him. Still exhausted from the events of my birthday party, I misjudged the distance. Almost falling on top of him, I grabbed his shoulders for balance, sending that unusual electric shock between us. I pulled myself straight. This wasn’t something I was used to feeling – that connection.

Managing to hold my balance, we briefly embraced. ‘Thank you,’ I whispered in his ear, feeling deeply grateful for everything he’d done for me, least of all saving my life. ‘That’s twice now.’

We hadn't clarified anything, yet it was amazing how much safer I felt. Releasing him before the connection between us grew too palpable, I sat back down on the sofa.

I was the first to break the silence. 'Let's start from the beginning?' I suggested. We had so much to discuss, and I couldn't wait any longer.

≈

Holding my knees tightly against my chest, I could feel the intensity with which my heart bashed against my ribs. My palms were sweating despite the cool air. Taking short, shallow breaths, I pushed the knot down my throat as I took the first step towards unlocking the door to my past.

'What were *you* doing in the forest yesterday evening?' I asked. I tried to keep my voice steady, but even I could hear the wobble as I watched him carefully for any tells that he might be lying.

'Checking up on you, of course. I promise you I'm not some freak lurking in the shadows,' Strat assured me, flashing a devilishly innocent smile.

'Okay, fine,' I yielded, feeling my traitorous lips twitch upwards into a smile before I rolled my eyes – I wasn't sure if it was at him or myself.

'I did call out at first to check everything was okay and to let you know I didn't intend to sneak up on you, but when you didn't respond, I came closer. It's then I started to feel glimpses of your Energy and saw you staring at the leaf, realising you were in a trance, but it was lasting too long to be normal – usually, we're only in that deep meditative state for a few seconds before being pulled through to the Helix.'

I had to interrupt him. '*The Helix?'* I asked, needing further clarification.

'It's a six-levelled multiverse that connects us to the Defacers in Pamatan and them to Earth.'

'Explain,' I squeaked, blinking my eyes in a double take.

'The Helix is where our Energy allows us to teleport ourselves.'

'And you've… travelled to this *parallel universe*, *the Helix,* before?' I asked him, searching for the right words.

My question seemed to amuse him because his eyes lit up as he struggled to contain the laugh bubbling behind his sealed lips.

'Don't laugh!' I whined, kicking him softly in the thigh. But it only seemed to make his laughter grow.

'I know! I shouldn't – how can I describe it to you? It's as though a goose had asked another goose if it could fly. You and I being the geese in this example,' he chuckled in disbelief at the situation. 'I've had all my best fights crossing through that multiverse,' he continued enthusiastically. 'You're going to love it, even if you sometimes get a bit of a kicking.'

I shook my head in disagreement. This guy was obviously a lunatic.

'Although I'll admit, I've never travelled like that before, or to Pamatan, so that was … new …'

'Pamatan?'

'The home of the Defacers,' he stated, taking in the blank expression on my face as I remembered the bleakness of the land. My stomach fluttered anxiously. Even those creatures deserved better, I couldn't image how they survived.

'My turn now,' interrupted Strat, pulling my mind back to the room. 'Any idea how the Defacer could summon you into Pamatan and why it was trying to steal your Energy?'

I shrugged but did my best to recount the event, from the engulfing silkiness of the leaf's pattern to entering the concert structure. 'There was a woman. She was really sick, on the straw bed in the room – you must have seen her?'

His expression turned quizzical, his frown deepening.

'Don't we need to go back and help her?' My voice rose in panic as I remembered the fragility of her state.

'I didn't see anyone, Ella,' he answered with sympathy. I couldn't help but love the way my name sounded off the roll of his tongue. 'It all happened so quickly. It was probably a trick, the Defacers that cross into Earth do it all the time to lure innocents.'

I gazed out the window wondering how I could have imagined it, but again, I was new to all of this. I turned back to Strat who was still deep in thought.

'Why bother tricking me if the creature just wanted to kill me?' I posed.

'To get you close enough that she could easily absorb your energy – feed herself,' guessed Strat. 'But that wouldn't explain why they bothered leaving traces within your system – unless they were expecting you'd get away.'

'Or because they always planned to turn me into one of them.' My statement rang in the air. The possibility sent a shiver down my spine. I didn't need Strat telling me it would have been worse than death – I had felt their evil first-hand.

'It would explain why the serum worked.'

'How did you know it wouldn't combust me like it did with the other two?' I asked, my tone accusatory. My eyes were wide with outrage.

Strat's eyes twinkled with guilt as he got up and paced along the coffee table once again. 'Call it a hunch…' he replied sheepishly, as though he was used to cheating death.

I was gobsmacked for a moment, and then I could feel my face turning bright red with outrage at his recklessness.

'What?!' I hissed sharply – I would have yelled if I wasn't painfully aware of Mum eavesdropping upstairs. 'You injected me with a serum of god knows what, based on a hunch!' I exclaimed.

'What choice did I have? You were getting all 'Defacery'.' Strat shrugged, but I could hear the defensiveness in his voice. I continued to pout incredulously, but he only smiled back in response. 'You can't argue with the results.'

That was true, but I'd never tell him that.

'As long as I can prevent it, nothing bad will happen to you,' he promised, his voice melting my anger away like honey, leaving me with a warm fuzzy feeling.

Looking down, I couldn't hold back the tiny smile curving on the side of my mouth.

'Plus, in the future, you'll be better prepared,' Strat added as an afterthought.

My eyes popped open again. 'Wait, say that again?' I said, putting my hand up in protest. 'What do you mean 'in the future'? I was hoping this was a once-in-a-lifetime thing!' I could hear the hysteria building in my voice again.

Smiling ruefully, he sat next to me. 'I won't let anything bad happen to you. Don't need to worry so much.'

The sincerity of his words touched something deep inside me. 'Says the guy who injected me with a serum containing god knows what,' I teased back.

'Okay, I'll admit it maybe wasn't the most fool-proof plan, but you're an Elan! Admittedly, you're quite late to the party, but you're naturally talented. Training you will be a breeze. You'll quickly become so good that you won't even need me anymore,' he joked. This did reassure me. I didn't like depending on Strat, no matter how much the thought of spending more time with him made my heart flutter.

'What did you mean earlier when you said I could be the difference in the fight against the Defacers?' I finally asked, remembering his comment to Darren.

He raised his eyebrow. 'Did you sleep at all this afternoon?' he asked rhetorically. We heard another thump upstairs. Quickly straightening myself, I realised we had been leaning towards each other, our bodies almost touching. Coughing self-consciously, Strat stood up and walked a few yards away.

'Sorry,' I apologised self-consciously, not wanting to scare him off.

'Don't be. I like your questions,' Strat quickly reassured me again. 'But maybe we stop here?'.

I, of course, had a million more questions pop into my mind. But even I knew I had to let him go. 'You'll tell me later?' I tried.

Strat let out a lyrical chuckle while letting out an exasperated sigh. 'I promise,' he vowed. 'But speak to Darren *soon*. I'll be in enough trouble as it is,' he added with a wicked grin.

'I better go. It's getting late,' he said, louder than necessary. He must have known Mum was listening, too. He stood still for a moment, waiting to see if there'd be any more noises coming from upstairs. Silence.

Walking past me to grab his jacket, he leaned in to whisper in my ear, sending my heart into double time. 'I'll be back by midday tomorrow. Don't get into too much trouble until then,' he said, giving me a wink.

The promise of tomorrow with him combined with his low, rusty voice sent a hot blaze around my face. He turned to leave but looked back one last time, his eyes still smouldering. He mouthed, ‘Good night, El,’ before closing the front door firmly behind him, leaving me and my pounding heart wondering how I’d ever get back to sleep.

Chapter 5

I woke up to the warm smell of freshly baked bread. Rising from the sofa, I lazily followed the aroma of breakfast to the kitchen, where I found Mum. There she stood over a plate of fried eggs and a buttered slice of crusty bread. Kissing Mum on the cheek, I sat at the kitchen bar.

'How are you feeling this morning, darling?' she asked, concerned for what she believed was a concussion. I could only imagine her reaction if she knew that my body had actually been fighting off lingering traces of Defacers still present in my bloodstream from my almost murder.

Stretching my arms over my head, I gasped, realising all my sores from the previous night had vanished. 'Really good, actually! This delicious breakfast definitely helps,' I sucked up with a big, childish grin as I tucked in.

'I don't suppose Strat would have anything to do with that, now?' Mum teased, raising her eyebrows, almost making me choke.

'Mum!' I groaned, blushing furiously as I remembered the sweetness of Strat's breath on my skin, promising answers to my endless questioning. There was no point trying to hide it. I knew Mum would recognise the blatant signs of my attraction to Strat.

'I don't blame you. He's *gorgeous*!' she said, exaggerating, 'Like a young Gerard Butler.' She grinned as though she had just tasted something delicious, only making me laugh as I shook my head in disapproval.

'And you *really* need to go on a date,' I teased her, wiping my plate clean with a final bite of bread before throwing it in my mouth. 'And before you say no, just tell me you'll think about it.' It had been years since I'd last heard Mum get excited about anyone. After the fiasco with her last boyfriend, the chef, she didn't seem to want to get back out there.

'Okay, I got it. Perving on teenage boys is the line, no need to get all "Mother" geisha on me. I'll pay my debts.' She stuck her tongue out. 'But don't let him go to waste,' she warned. I could only roll my eyes in response. There was no stopping her. Catching a glimpse at the kitchen clock, I jumped as I realised Strat would pick me up in half an hour.

'I'm running late! I promise to do the dishes when I return,' I called out, already running up the stairs.

'Where are you going now? It's Sunday!' she shouted behind me, but I was already gone.

I had to be super quick. I needed to ensure I intercepted Strat before he rang the front door. I couldn't have Mum find out I was running around like an idiot to meet Strat. At this rate, she'd think we were dating. The thought made me feel even more jittery than I already was. For all I knew, he was a total playboy and used those twinkling eyes on every girl he met! Pushing aside the start of my character analysis, I tried to focus on the information provided yesterday and organise my thoughts while getting ready. I tried speaking out loud to keep my mind from drifting to Strat's dreamy words, 'I won't let anything bad happen to you.'

Walking into my ensuite bathroom, I stared at my reflection. 'I'm an Elan,' I stated, pushing a lump down my throat. 'Giving me access to some sort of Energy,' I continued, forcing myself to take what I was saying seriously before rushing through the last part. 'Allowing me to travel to a parallel universe called the Helix, in which I'm meant to stop the evil Defacers from …?' I trailed off, no longer holding a straight face. I sounded ridiculous. It was difficult to believe the truth behind those words when I didn't feel or look any different, yet even my imagination couldn't have made up the last few days. 'Maybe there's a way to activate this *Energy*?' I wondered aloud, adding it to my long list of questions for Strat.

There was a final discovery, but it hurt too much to say it out loud. It was the fact that Darren knew what I was and hadn't told me. He knew how insecure I'd always felt about my forgotten childhood. Everyone knew where they came from, and I didn't have the faintest memory of anything since my adoption – my mind was utterly blank, thoroughly erased. He should have told me, even if it meant finding out I wasn't quite human. I knew Darren was a private person, but since this secret was about me, he should have at least hinted I was different. It would have helped me understand why I always felt at odds with my classmates, and I would always feel that way.

The saddest part is that I wasn't surprised to hear he'd been keeping secrets. The one time I had asked Darren about his past, he'd given me such a murderous look that I'd never dared ask again. Since then, there had been this unspoken rule between us never to ask about his past, and he would never bring it up.

In many ways, I considered Darren to be a father figure. I'd seen him daily for Krav-Maga training since I was seven. I trusted him, I believed he'd always had my best interest at heart, but even Strat had seemed surprised by the extent of his concealment.

'I just need to find out why Darren kept this secret,' I said, fortifying my resolve.

Having refocused, I already felt calmer, knowing I had a plan, although it didn't last long. By the time I looked back in the mirror, the expression on my face seemed to reflect my state of mind, but my body didn't seem to follow suit. My excitement was all over my face – eyes too bright, hectic spots of red across my cheekbones. After brushing my teeth, I worked on taming my hair's tangled chaos. I splashed my face with cold water and tried to breathe normally, with no notable success.

I half-ran back to my room to decide what to wear before giving up and putting on my usual clothes. I'd look less suspicious if I left the house dressed this way, plus I doubted there was a designated outfit to kill Defacers. Checking the clock incessantly, I kept peering into the driveway from my bathroom window only to see Strat pulling up outside the main gate on a motorbike. Sending urgent palpitations to my heart, I rushed down the staircase as stealthily as I could manage. The hardest part would be closing our creaking front door unnoticed. Successfully creeping outside the house undetected, I couldn't stop myself from shushing at the door.

Finally, I was out! I turned around, enthusiastically launching myself forwards, only to bump straight into Strat. I sucked in a sharp breath as my face hit his solid torso. Lurching, I desperately tried to stabilise myself, making the mistake of grabbing onto Strat's flexed bicep. My heart spluttered hyperactively as one blush blended into the next. Mortified, I fumbled as I rushed to push myself off him, landing awkwardly. Desperate to escape the situation, I practically ran out of the main gate, expressly avoiding all eye contact. I could hear Strat's low, hearty laugh follow me as he jogged lightly behind me.

Securely out of sight from the house, I shouted out behind me, 'Sorry! I must still be drowsy from the serum last night!' forcing out an exaggerated laugh, which only made things more uncomfortable.

Slowing down my pace, I realised I had no idea where we were planning on going. Looking around me, Strat wasn't walking next to me and, turning to look back, I spotted him leaning against a black glossy dirt bike, the type you would have only seen in an action movie – he was trouble. Restraining my mouth from dropping open, I did my best to portray indifference at his gorgeousness.

'Are you ready? We've got plans, you know,' Strat teased, grinning. I could see him studying me as I strolled over, his eyes wandering slowly over my outfit before stopping on my face. Keeping my gaze focused on the path to him, I did my best to play it cool. Stopping beside him, I remained quiet. Still smirking, he said nothing as he handed me a black helmet and protective jacket.

'Thanks,' I replied as casually as I could manage, looking at him properly for the first time today. His chestnut hair was dishevelled, and his eyes were narrow and red from what looked like a lack of sleep.

'Long night?'

'I needed to find answers,' he replied, smiling tiredly.

Deciding not to probe him further on this now, I changed my questioning. 'Where are we going?'

'To get help,' he replied mysteriously as he put on his helmet. Straddling the bike, he put his hands on the handles, waiting for me to mount. Hopping on, I delicately placed the tip of my fingers on his shoulders, trying my best to limit unnecessary physical contact going forwards, especially considering I'd exhausted all acceptable levels of body contact within the first minute of our encounter.

Sighing loudly, Strat grabbed my hands and wrapped them firmly around his waist

'You've already escaped death twice under my watch, let's not make it a recurring theme.'

I gripped the material of his jacket tightly, thankful he couldn't see my face. Roaring the engine to life, he kick-started the bike and propelled us forwards. I held onto him for dear life as we raced down the street, spraying dirt behind us. He drove quickly but steadily. Leaning over the handlebars, head low, face forwards, he never hesitated as we weaved through the cars. I looked at the people passing by as we raced through the town, enjoying the continuous motion of the curves and the autumn air whipping through my clothes.

Unguarded, I closed my eyes for a moment, only to be haunted by the sound of an unwelcome voice.

'*Eloisa*,' the voice pleaded faintly.

Adrenaline flooded my system. Bursting my eyes open, I was greeted by the sight of the Krav Maga studio. We stopped before the entrance, and Strat waited for me to move my frozen arms. When I didn't move, he frowned and unclasped my trembling hands, scrambling to get off the bike. I tried to say something, but I knew Strat could see the confusion and fear that widened my eyes.

'Don't worry. We'll take them down,' promised Strat as he lowered my hands, knowing the Defacers were trying to reach me again. I tried to hide the tremor in my hands by placing them between my legs, but I knew he had noticed them. Pursing his lips, he removed my helmet before grabbing me from under my arms and lifting me off the bike.

'Let's put an end to this,' he exclaimed, his voice full of determination. Sliding his hand easily into mine, he pulled me into the studio, his warm hand easing the tension that had claimed my body. Holding my hand firmly, we walked through the empty gym. My body still trembled despite the comforting warmth of the solid concrete walls and the smell of sweat. My heart tightened as we marched towards Darren's office. I could see him through the glass door, with a crossword puzzle in his hands. Leaning backwards in his office chair, he was relaxing with his feet on his messy desk.

My mind raced as I prayed this wouldn't be the moment I'd finally have to confront Darren on his secrecy. My legs continued to drag along, suddenly gripping the floor. My hand tightened around Strat's, urging him to stop. The sirens wailed in my mind. I wasn't ready.

'What's wrong?' Strat asked, concerned. His emerald eyes bore into mine, looking for signs of another Defacer summoning.

'I can't do this,' the coward in me begged. 'I know we had a deal, but I just can't. Not with Darren,' I whined, tearing my eyes to the ground. The tension in his hand loosened, my heart ached, but he didn't let go, not yet. He just continued to watch me, probably debating what to say.

'I thought you wanted answers,' he finally said softly, puzzled by my reluctance. He didn't understand what was at stake. I couldn't lose Darren.

'I can't confront him,' I tried to explain. 'He won't forgive me,' I said, thinking back to all the friends Darren had readily discarded when they started asking too many questions, Ms Lancy amongst them.

Strat frowned. His eyes flashed to the floor before baring them back into mine. Full of fire, his eyes gleamed like emeralds in the sun as an enigmatic smile curved his lips, offering nothing but trouble.

'Then let's not give him a choice,' Strat challenged as he pulled me once again, but my feet wouldn't move. He stopped again, pausing for an explanation.

'I'm scared,' I admitted.

'I'll be right here with you,' he promised.

≈

Strat let go of my hand as he walked into Darren's office.

'What took you so long? I would have thought that flashy bike of yours would at least get you here on time!' Darren joked loudly before quickly dying down as soon as he saw me standing behind Strat, his expression turning firm.

'Tell him what just happened!' Strat commanded. My eyes widened at the unexpected change in emotion.

'Well, I... I...'

Seeing that I was unable to get the words out of my mouth quickly enough, Strat jumped in. 'The Defacer just tried summoning her again on our ride over here! They're getting more frequent, Darren!' replied Strat, exasperated. 'I checked, and there's no record of an Elan ever being summoned and pulled through the Helix by a Defacer. We need to get her under the protection of the Academy.'

'I told you before, it's not an option,' cut in Darren, eyeing me.

I retreated nervously where I stood, uncomfortably feeling the tension between both men, understanding Strat's plan. He wanted to corner Darren into involving me. It was brilliant but high risk. It would be over if Darren thought we were playing him at any moment. I waited for Strat to drop it. But, to my surprise, he didn't back down.

Strat calmly appealed, 'I know what you said, and that might have been the case yesterday when you could barely sense her Energy, but it's now fully Awakened. She might as well have a beacon signalling where she is.'

The news caught my breath. Strat could feel my Energy, which meant it was there. I couldn't feel it yet, or I hadn't given myself enough time to look.

'If they could summon her when her Energy was barely ignited, they'll be able to summon her again in no time now.

She has to go to the Academy. The shield will keep her safe,' argued Strat with the same intensity, holding Darren's gaze.

I held my breath, fully expecting Darren to shut him down, but he said nothing, just holding Strat's gaze. Swinging his feet off the table, Darren stood up, his expression easing. 'Maybe you're right,' he finally admitted.

My stomach fluttered in sheer admiration. If Strat had been able to sway Darren, the least I could do was say my part – after all, they were making decisions about my life.

I swallowed hard, pushing the nausea back down my throat. 'If it'll stop me from getting summoned again…' I trailed, urging my voice barely above a whisper. I pinched the insides of my hand, forcing myself to stay calm.

'If my Energy is in the open, we may have no choice?' I asked, carefully avoiding any words that might trigger Darren to shut down. The air hung still as he deliberated, my heart racing in response, feeling both dread and excitement. I hated how some part of me hoped for an alternative where I didn't have to be different from everyone else.

Still sensing hesitation on Darren's part, Strat swooped in to close the deal. 'There's no going back once your Energy has come into full fruition. Once it's Awakened, it's there forever. There's no other choice. We need to get you trained and in a location where the Defacers wouldn't be able to summon you into the Helix.'

Darren sighed loudly. 'That's enough, Strat,' he ordered, his tone annoyed – after all, Strat had explicitly gone against his orders and had told me way too much. I glanced towards Strat, but his expression gave nothing away. This would be the moment we'd found out if our act had worked.

Darren frowned, pinching the bridge of his nose as he walked around his desk to place his hand on my shoulder as he looked at me properly for the first time.

'I wish I could tell you otherwise, Ella, but for some reason something has caused your Energy to unseal, and we won't be able to protect you until the Defacer summoning you has been eliminated,' replied Darren regretfully. 'The decision is yours, we can either stay here and do our best to protect you, or we can go to the Academy, face things straight on and get this over with. Which will it be?'

The choice was mine and for the first time since this madness had started, the gravity of the situation hit me. Unlike my original plan, this wasn't going to be something I could just mull over for a few years until I felt ready to deal with my feelings. This was either fight, flight or cooperate and Darren knew it.

That's why he was giving me a choice – maybe he hoped I might still back down. I usually would have, and it would be easier for him to continue hiding things from me if I stayed put. It was tempting, and the coward in me wanted to stay home and ignore the reality. But Strat had inspired me. I had a right to know about this other world, to know who I was, and this was my chance to unlock the door to my past.

In return, I would have to accept this new reality in which I would never be like Neer, Mum or any of the other kids in my class I had struggled so desperately to connect with. I was something else, and ready or not, I was going to find out what Darren was hiding me from even if it meant fighting off Defacers.

Looking towards Strat, I could see the corners of his lips curve as he subtly tipped his head, encouraging me to take the leap.

'I'll go,' I said, determined, my insides clenching. I had finally jumped in, with both feet.

≈

'Okay,' agreed Darren after I'd accepted to go to the Academy and help defeat the Defacer summoning me. He seemed to take a moment to let the decision sink in before adopting a stern face with Strat. 'Have you told anyone about Ella?' he checked.

'No,' replied Strat, his face matching the seriousness of the mood.

'Good. We can't have the damn Committee finding out,' replied Darren, providing no further explanation. I could sense my eyebrows raise at Darren's curse. He never swore and made a point not to, said our manners were the only things that made us civilised. My eyes flickered to Strat, his features tensing, pursing his lips, but he said nothing.

Letting out a long, exhausted sigh, Darren continued, 'Strat, please can you organise the logistics around training at the Academy for the three of us and make sure no questions are asked. We go today.'

Strat nodded, giving me a subtle wink before disappearing out the door, leaving the two of us alone.

'Let's talk about this over some sparring?' Darren suggested. Both quiet, tension hung in the air, we walked out of his office, each thinking of the days that were and those to come. Handing me my hand wraps, we made our way onto the mats. Starting with a light warm-up, we moved on to controlled kicks.

'You've become very good,' commented Darren, breaking the silence. I noted that the previous annoyance in his voice was almost gone. 'I'm proud of how dedicated to your training you've been,' he complimented me, making me smile despite recent events. He was being kind and I knew he meant it. Darren never said things he didn't mean and he knew his good opinion meant everything to me.

Not expecting a response, he moved the pad to his other hand. Repositioning myself, he waited for me to start kicking with my left leg before continuing. 'It's more important than ever that you continue to develop the depth of your concentration. Being able to quiet your mind and focus internally will be vital when coming to grips with your Energy.' I continued kicking out, mind focused on the pad but taking in his words. 'When channelled correctly, our Energy allows us to travel to a series of interconnected parallel universes, collectively called the Helix. Using your body as a portal, your Energy will bring you to the first Level in the Helix, after which it will be up to you to rationalise your Energy and find the next gate, crossing into the following Level. That is, of course, assuming you have enough Energy and want to descend into the Helix in the first place.'

'So, there's a limit to my Energy?' I clarified, taking a moment to wipe the sweat from my brow.

'Exactly, but the more control you have over your Energy, the longer you'll be able to make it last. Think of travelling through the Helix like scuba diving and your Energy as your oxygen tank. The moment you start engaging your Energy, you start consuming the oxygen in your tank, giving you only a finite amount of time to stay underwater. If you stay close to the surface or Levels One to Three in our case, your body won't be under too much strain, allowing you to consume your oxygen steadily. But the deeper you dive, the more hostile the environment and the more oxygen you need to consume simply to survive. Similar to divers, the more experience you have, the better you will become at rationing your oxygen and prolonging the life of your tank.'

I thought about what he said. 'Does this mean you also need to ration Energy for the return?'

'Yes, although there are two ways we can return to Earth. Using the diving analogy – you can either acclimatise and use the Gates interconnecting the Levels to return using some Energy, or you can shoot straight back up to the surface.

'We have something called a Lifeline – an unbreakable link to Earth that allows us to teleport ourselves directly from any Level back to the place you first travelled from.' Darren could see the relief sweeping through me as my shoulders relaxed. I realised then that my Lifeline had brought me back to the forest path after the Defacer's attack.

'But you need to be careful,' he warned. 'Although your Lifeline gets you out of the Helix faster, it also takes up more Energy than if you were to return through the Gates. The deeper you are in the Helix, the more Energy it will require to get you home and the more strain you will put on yourself.

'The same way divers can die from the bends, we can die from exhaustion. If we deplete too much of our Energy without leaving enough reserves to travel back home, there's a risk our bodies won't be able to recover. You must constantly check in with yourself and make sure you have enough Energy to fight any unexpected Defacer attacks and can travel back home without burning out.'

A million thoughts were racing through my head. According to Darren, I should have been 'starved for oxygen' when I was summoned into the deepest Level of the Helix, and yet I don't remember feeling particularly strained. I guessed that it was probably to do with the fact my Energy hadn't been wholly Awakened. Mistaking the line between my brows for worry, Darren interjected.

'Of course, it shouldn't come to that,' Darren said. 'Especially since they've found a way to summon you directly to their homeland, the final sixth Level, Pamatan. It'll allow us to save most of our Energy to kill the Defacer summoning you, rather than having to use it to travel through the Levels.'

'Do you think it's just the one?' I clarified, thinking back to Strat's comment about the sickly women never existing.

Darren shook his head. 'I hoped this would end with the Defacer Strat killed, but it looks like the Defacer after you has decided to pair up, which is most unusual. Unfortunately, it means we have to eliminate another powerful Defacer.'

I now worried as I thought back to the pale woman lying in the straw bed – it couldn't be her. She wouldn't have the strength to defend herself, let alone escape. Did it mean Strat was right? Was the whole thing a set-up to get me close enough for the Defacer-nurse to steal my Energy? *No*, I thought, pushing that conclusion aside. I knew nothing could have faked the connection I felt to the woman. There had to be another explanation.

'Why do you think they're going after me?' I asked.

'I don't know,' he huffed in frustration as he ran a hand along his scar. 'Unexpected things have been happening, things that shouldn't be possible.' He paused before lowering his pads. 'You, for instance, were never meant to be part of this world,' he said, his words sorrowful as he looked far away. Lowering my arms in kind, I placed my leg back steadily on the training mattress.

I wanted to ask him why and what had happened, but I didn't have the courage. It hadn't taken long for us to trust each other and yet I knew he wouldn't be afraid to pull away if I asked too many questions like he'd done with Ms Lancy. If you were lucky enough to win his affections, he would go above and beyond for you, but it didn't mean he didn't reserve the right to change his mind. I, for one, was determined never to jeopardise our relationship, even if it meant playing by his rules.

So instead of asking, I waited for him to shake off the memory. His expression quickly turned to fiery determination. 'We've encountered a slight hiccup, but we'll put things right again. Most Elans choose to lead human lives, and there's no reason you shouldn't continue to do the same.'

Placing the pads back to the sides of his face, he anchored himself, preparing himself for my punches. Uncertain, I raised my arms once more. He smiled, and his voice regained its natural enthusiasm. 'Before the end of the week, this will all be forgotten. But until then, we need you to be able to defend yourself!'

My face broke out in sweat. I aimed each punch towards the pad, despite knowing how useless I would be against a Defacer. The nurse had been so strong, so powerful. How could I compete? As though sensing my discouragement,

Darren intervened my thoughts. 'You can do better,' he encouraged, but his tone had an edge of mischief.

'Over the next few days, I will mainly focus on teaching you how to sense and harness your Energy. Sharing the same principles as in yoga and meditation, I'll teach you how to engage with your Energy, make it flow through and beyond your body, giving you a greater understanding of your strength. Unbounded by the skin, you will be able to open your Energy to engage with other objects, people and universes – like the Helix,' he said encouragingly, despite the impossibility of what he was saying.

'You'll see,' he said unwaveringly, seeing the scepticism of my expression.

'I want you to start looking internally, try to find and engage with your Energy. Focus deep within, and you should find a warmth within you. You might even see a light in the form of a colour. When you find it, harness that burning light in your belly, visualise a flow of Energy to your fist, and direct it towards the pad,' coached Darren.

In a front stance, I nodded with trepidation as I placed my fists on either side of my hips and breathed deeply. I closed my eyes as I searched deep within, quickly finding the Energy within me. Attentive to my body, I scanned the top of my head, down to my eyes, chin, along my arms and chest, stopping at my stomach. Sensing something new and robust, I searched deeper within my chest, feeling more invigorated with every millimetre I reached closer until I finally saw it. Within me lay a bright orange light, shining like the sun. I let out a loud breath, mesmerised by its beauty.

I tried hard to focus on Darren's voice. 'Hold your focus. Remember, it's a bright hot energy ball ready at your command. Picture it, feel its warmth, draw it out through your body and concentrate its force into your punch.'

I pictured the Energy at my core and slowly, slowly, it became vivid again. Amazed by its warmth, I felt radiating heat and concentrated on rolling it through my body, moving it wherever I wanted. It was a burning white ball with orange flames expanding outwards, focused in my fists. It felt fantastic, with every part of my body engaged and alive. I illuminated it more fully in my mind and imagined it as a weapon I could use against the Defacers. I pictured the orange flames shooting Energy from my fingertips.

'Good, now listen to the direction of my voice and guide your Energy through, channel it through your punch.'

Following his voice, I pulled my arm back and placed my thumb outside my knuckles, calling upon my Energy. Using all my strength to channel the power within the orange sun, I concentrated all my focus. The Energy vibrated throughout my body until it grew so powerful that I felt its force flow into my fist before swinging my eyes open. Half expecting actual flames to burst out of my hands, I anchored my gaze on the boxing pad, using my entire body to propel my punch at my target. My fist made contact and I directed the whole of my Energy into the pad.

Stunned, I stood there, my arm fully extended, panting. Darren lay on the floor before me, my Energy having thrown him off balance and onto the floor. Recovering my breath, I rushed over. Stunned at first, he dusted himself off and roared with laughter, laying himself flat on the floor.

'Are you alright?!' I asked, as I crouched next to him to have a better look at him.

'I'm fine, I'm fine.' He waved me away as he sat up on the mat, still laughing.

'It's been a while since I received such a powerful punch! Well done! At this rate, we might be able to wrap things up before the end of the week! You've just done something that takes most Elans years of training!' Stretching his hand towards me, he grunted as I pulled him up. 'You're strong, Ella. I'm guessing you're pretty tired from that?'

I nodded, encouraged by his optimism.

As we walked back to his office, his voice grew serious. 'I know that was fun but listen to me carefully for a moment. You've got a good life here, with people that care for you. We can't jeopardise that, now can we?' he asked, although it was more of a statement.

'No,' I agreed despite feeling like I'd been cornered into my answer.

'We can't forget about your mother and Neer, who have built a life around you and will need you to return swiftly by their side,' he persisted, staring at me intently. Although I didn't like the whole secrecy around the situation, he was right; I had to think about my family, so I nodded in agreement, letting him know I'd abide by his plan.

'I'm glad we're on the same page. Unfortunately, I doubt I can get to Pamatan without the Defacer summoning you again, so we'll have to train you to use your Energy and do this together. Okay?'

'Yes, sir,' I complied, excited by the prospect of learning how to use my Energy, even if it was a short-lived affair.

'But we've agreed, no using your Energy without me and we're not dragging this out one minute longer than it needs to be. One week, that's all I'm giving us to train you and kill the Defacer summoning you. I want you back home worrying about homework by Sunday, agreed?'

'Sounds perfect,' answered the scaredy-cat inside me. Although I was curious, this was all moving too fast for my liking. I was terrified by this new world and to my ashamed relief, Darren's restrictive boundaries limited the amount of digging I would be able to do.

'This isn't a joke, Ella. The Helix is dangerous and can be deadly.' His voice grew grave. 'Countless Elans have died going to Levels insufficiently prepared. Even if you were lucky enough to escape an attack by a Defacer, you could have been left battling for your life upon your return.' He showed the same pained expression I had seen earlier on his face before opening the door to his office. 'No matter the universe, death is always final.'

He handed me a cold glass of water, and we sat opposite each other, sipping our drinks pensively as we recovered from the workout. Darren's fingers clinked rhythmically against the glass in his hand, setting the rhythm for the knot growing in my stomach. Gathering my nerves, I thought back again to what Strat had said about having a right to know about this world, my world. This was my opportunity to ask the questions I'd usually never dare speak. I could feel the nausea crawl up my throat as I hoped Darren wouldn't shut me out because of my impertinence. I thought twice before daring myself – his decisions affected me. I had to ask, but I was still afraid.

Breaking the silence, I let out a strange whisper. 'Is that why didn't you tell me I was an Elan?' I tried to ask as calmly as possible, but my voice's tremor was unmistakable. Looking up at me curiously, Darren stopped tapping the glass. I had never dared confront him before.

Remaining composed, he moved his glass to the corner of his desk, choosing his words carefully. 'Yes, partially,' he replied honestly, much to my surprise, but didn't elaborate. I wanted to ask more, but something in his demeanour was letting me know that further questions would be unwelcome, and I didn't have the nerve to speak up again. One question was enough, I told myself. It was already progress. Once certain I wouldn't ask any more questions, Darren stood up.

'If the summonings are becoming more frequent, we will have to move quickly.'

Pacing the room, Darren put his arms behind his back as he walked up and down the office. After a few moments, he stopped, having devised a plan. 'I don't particularly like the next bit, but I don't think we have much of an option: we're going to have to lie to your mother...'

Convincing Mum wouldn't be too difficult, she wasn't an unusually strict parent, but she wouldn't want me missing class unless ...

'We could tell her that someone's dropped out, and I was selected to participate in a Krav-Maga championship for the week,' I suggested.

'Great idea,' approved Darren. 'Let me drive you home, and we'll tell her together. It's best if we leave this evening.'

Chapter 6

It was already getting dark when we arrived home, and it would be pitch black by the time the three of us would arrive at the Elans' Training Academy. That is, assuming Mum buys into our elaborate lie to cover for the week of Defacer-killing training ahead.

'Mum! Darren and I have some exciting news!' I called, walking through the front door.

I continued to walk towards the sitting room, where I found her on the sofa, serving a cup of tea to Neer. Catching me off guard, I felt mortified for not calling him sooner, especially after attacking him at my birthday party. The guilt only got worse when I caught a glimpse of the purple bruise covering his forearm. It still didn't stop me from running toward him. Giving him a long hug, I pressed him tightly against me, feeling beyond relief that he looked so well.

'I'm sorry,' I whispered, sensing his apprehension, which only made me squeeze him tighter.

He sighed in resignation. 'I'm still mad at you,' he warned but wrapped his arms around me.

'I thought you couldn't remember the party,' I apprehended, stiffening in his embrace. Neer seemed to pick up on the fear thickening my voice as he paused to look at me, before pulling down his sleeve.

'I can't, of course not,' he stumbled. My chest heaved in relief, knowing my secret was safe.

'Can I get one of those?' interrupted Mum, a smirk spread across her face. I couldn't help but smile. Wiping the tears that made their way to my eyes, I hugged Mum before sitting in the armchair.

Never letting go of Neer's hand, we launched straight into our cover story, shortly convincing Mum to let me go to my week-long 'Krav-Maga Championship'. 'After all, it is the opportunity we have been training for.' Nodding enthusiastically along to our story, I could feel Neer's withering gaze on me. His timely squeeze of my hand let me know he wasn't buying our story. Doing my best to ignore him, I smiled encouragingly at Mum.

'And you feel well enough to do this?' asked Mum, referring to my 'concussion', which was only a tiny bump in the head from my fall.

I nodded. 'I can't miss this opportunity.' If only she knew the depth of that statement.

'You've convinced me, but Ella, I want you to ensure that you keep on top of your course content. Neer, please will you help me make sure of it?' asked Mum kindly.

'Of course, June,' he replied. 'Assuming Ella bothers to answer my messages,' he added in a snide tone.

Sensing the mood, Mum thanked Neer and stood up, asking Darren if he'd like to help her make some more tea in the kitchen despite the full teapot.

'Gladly,' Darren agreed, but he was sure to stare at me with urgency. 'Ella, let's leave in fifteen?'

'Sure,' I replied, understanding the time pressure of the situation; after all, we didn't know how long we had until the Defacer would next try to summon me and *finish the job*. We had a plan, and there was no time to lose.

As they exited the room, Mum leaned towards Darren, whispering, 'She's going to struggle to get out of that one.'

Embarrassed, I looked down at my hands as I placed them between my thighs, collecting my thoughts, only to have Neer immediately burst into giving me a lecture.

'You need to start checking your phone. Did it ever occur to you that I might be worried?'

'I'm *so* sorry. But are you really alright?' I asked, looking over him for any other injuries.

'Am *I* alright?'

Neer laughed, a sharp, unhappy sound. 'Ella, do you have any idea what I've been through these last 24 hours? I was so worried after I'd heard you'd knocked yourself out. Then I didn't hear back from you and I didn't know what to think.'

'I'm fine,' I insisted. Neer looked at me from under his lashes unconvinced. 'I tripped, that's all,' I lied. 'If anything, I'm the one who should be fussing over my best friend.'

'You should be,' he pouted, letting go of the matter.

'I was going to call you,' I consoled him.

'So, where are you really going?' Neer said, his eyes dark with suspicion.

He could see the hesitation on my face as I debated what I should do. I didn't want to lie.

'You didn't think you'd fooled me, did you?' he said, almost offended. 'You've always been a terrible liar. I'm surprised your Mum bought it.' He was right – I couldn't even lie about the prank I had set up for him last Halloween.

Of course, I was itching to tell him the whole story, but I also knew I wouldn't be allowed to share the truth. Darren had been adamant that I get as little involved as possible with this other world so that I could swiftly return to my everyday life. I already knew if I told Neer anything more than he already knew, his curiosity would get the better of him. He would insist that we find out everything we possibly could about Elans, the Helix and Defacers, which would involve digging deep into my past. I couldn't risk it. If I was going to attempt to uncover my origins, I'd do it on my terms.

'Surely, you wouldn't dare give me the same BS excuse you gave your mother?' he said, staring at me intently.

My heart beat faster at the prospect of confrontation. 'No,' I replied. I glanced to check Darren and Mum were still chatting in the kitchen. 'Help me pack?' I asked, giving Neer a look that let him know we needed privacy if I was going to say anything.

'Happily,' he replied, smiling in satisfaction as he followed me up the stairs towards the attic.

Glancing toward the clock, I picked up my pace, knowing we'd soon have to leave.

As expected, the questioning started the second we crossed the threshold of my room. 'So, where are you really going?' pressed Neer, folding his arms across his chest.

'Look, I can't tell you much.' I breathed, giving in. 'But what we told Mum isn't a complete lie. I am going to some sort of centre and will hopefully go there to "beat" some things.' I hoped this would be enough to ease his curiosity.

'"Beat something"? That's what you're going with?' he replied, his eyebrows raising. 'Because of your dying need for drugs and alcohol,' he added, sarcastically.

'What? No! What's wrong with you? Mum's a doctor. It's a training centre, and I said, "beat some *things*". Plus, I'd be much more afraid of being murdered by her if that was even remotely the case.'

'Who's looking to murder you?' Neer enquired, his frown deepening.

I bit my tongue in response, tightening my jaw, afraid I'd said too much.

'Are you in trouble?' Neer probed, his arms dropping to his side as he stepped towards me.

'No, not really,' I tried to reassure him, but that was a lie. So I added, 'Maybe, but we're going to deal with it.'

'What, with Darren and the hot guy?' I could see the confusion deepening.

If I wasn't careful, I would never get out of here. 'Yes, but I can't say anymore. Okay? Please, can you just help me pack?' I asked, although it sounded more like a plea. Neer held my gaze as he most likely debated in his head. 'Please.'

'Fine, but you know if you ever need anything, I'm here for you, alright?' he urged, only making me smile.

'I know.' I smiled, squeezing his hand.

'Ella, are you ready?' enquired Darren urgently from the ground floor.

'Almost!' I called back as I stared wide-eyed at Neer, mouthing a curse. Grabbing my empty suitcase from under my bed, I flung it open as Neer started throwing me clothes from my closet. I filtered them as they arrived, shoving anything I thought might be useful into my bag.

'What do you need?' asked Neer, equally panicked, looking for direction while continuing to toss me a seasonal spectrum of clothes.

'I have no idea! Although probably not the bikini!' I laughed throwing it back out. If only it were that type of trip.

'I don't know!' defended Neer, laughing as we nervously hurried, both knowing how impatient Darren could get.

'Are you sure you can't tell me anything else?' Neer asked again, unable to keep his questions at bay. 'I might be able to help,' he pleaded, flashing an innocent smile as though that would sway me.

Zipping my suitcase shut, I took a moment to calmly walk towards my best friend before placing my hand on his firm shoulder.

'Oh no … You're pulling "a Darren". This must be serious,' he teased. He was, of course, referring to Darren's classic 'hand-on-shoulder' move he unconsciously did whenever he had something important to say, much to our continuous amusement.

Looking into his eyes, trying not to laugh, I took a moment, knowing I needed to convey the sincerity of my words. 'I know you're concerned, but I can't involve you in this.' As he released the tension in his shoulders in acceptance, I hugged him. 'It'll be over soon,' I tried to reassure him. He wrapped his arms tightly around my waist, and we stayed like this for a while.

Interrupting our embrace, I heard a familiar voice. 'Sorry, Ella, but we need to go,' said Strat in his usual smooth alluring voice, sending butterflies straight to my stomach. I quickly extracted myself from Neer's arms. Neer looked at me weirdly, but I refused to meet his eyes. Strat was standing at the entrance of my room with my suitcase in hand. Crimson spread across my face as I realised Strat had walked around our embrace to pick up the bag from my bed. Taking another step away from Neer, I could feel my panicky awkwardness taking over.

'Okay! Bye!' I shouted too loudly at Neer as I proceeded to pat him on the shoulder. Mortified by my absurd reaction, I couldn't stop patting his shoulder, which only made the tension sweep faster back into his posture.

As Neer looked at me confused by my bizarre behaviour, I eventually managed to take control of my arm and stop.

'Ready?' asked Strat, to which I nodded before heading down the staircase. Offering Neer a small comforting look, I followed Strat down the stairs, where we met Darren and Mum. Anxious to limit the amount of lying I had to do, I rushed over to hug Mum goodbye, only for her to try and hold me back for a joint group conversation.

'Ella, did you know Strat was also going to participate in this competition?' she asked rhetorically. 'How great is that!' she exclaimed, taking great enjoyment in my discomfort.

'Umm, super exciting,' I replied blandly. I was determined not to give in to Mum's tormenting shenanigans.

'Anyways … We probably need to get going, so we'll see you next week,' I cut Mum off before she could say any more, ushering Darren and Strat quickly out the front door. Glancing back, I took in Mum's and Neer's dumbstruck faces for a final time before I closed the front door.

Guided by the small lamps that lit up the driveway, I let a small smile of relief spread across my face as I rushed ahead towards the car.

I could hear Strat chuckling as he leaned over toward Darren. 'Ballsy.'

His comment made me smile further. I, too, was surprised by my audacity. Luckily, I knew Mum would think it was funny rather than rude.

Beeping the car open, I heard Darren shout, 'Please let Strat sit in the front with me. We need to sort out the logistics of getting you inside the Academy under the radar.'

More than happy to abide by his request, I hopped into the back of the car after thanking Strat for his chivalry and plugged in my noise-cancelling headphones. Rejoicing in the familiar lyrics accompanied by an acoustic guitar, I pushed away thoughts of what was ahead and let my mind drift aimlessly. Listening to my music peacefully, I enjoyed watching as we zipped past lit-up homes only to fall asleep a few moments later.

≈

When I woke up, my stomach was rumbling; several hours must have passed, and it was time for dinner. Pushing myself to sit up straight, I looked out the car window. We had stopped at an electric charging service station. Strat was perusing the shop, and Darren was outside plugging in the car. Stretching my limbs, I stepped out for a moment. It was dark, and, as far as I could tell, we were surrounded extensively by farmland except for a few houses lit up in the distance.

I yawned, reaching my arms over my head before turning to Darren. 'How much further is the Academy?' I asked, rubbing my eyes.

'We're here,' Darren replied, his voice bland and monotone. My gaze swept across the empty fields and the run-down service shop. Usually, Darren would have laughed at my imitation of a meerkat, but it seemed he was in the mood to joke around,

'It's under the shop,' he replied, his voice equally as tight as before.

'Very 007,' I said, impressed.

'Yeah, well, unfortunately, it's so secluded that it makes it impossible to find a decent curry anywhere around here,' he moaned, making me chuckle in response – pleased to have eased some of his tension.

'A hefty price to pay,' I added, mocking Darren's obsession with curry houses. I was surprised he hadn't asked Mum to make him a batch to take with him.

But Darren's dark eyes were quick to whip the grin on my face. 'Be on your guard,' he warned. 'The Defacers aren't the only monsters we need to worry about.'

I rubbed my hand against my now chilled arm, released by Darren's gaze only when something behind me had caught his attention. Turning to see what he was looking at in the service shop, my eyes locked with Strat's. Waving me over, a heart-dropping smile spread across his face. I could feel Darren's burning eyes pierce the back of my head as we grinned at each other across the street.

'I'll meet you out back,' he said. I waited for a beat to see if he would mention his apparent displeasure with our friendship, but he kept quiet even if his eyes said otherwise. As soon as he closed the car door behind him, I jogged towards Strat. My eyes were glued to his until I walked into the shop.

'Strat,' I called out, feeling a thrill go through me as I said his name.

He was in the snacks' alley deciding what nuts to buy. Funny enough, everything was packaged in clear, standardized containers – no logos or bespoke shaping, just a series of container options. Even the glass bottled water he handed me wasn't your standard shape.

'So, this is it!' Strat exclaimed. 'Well, almost. How are you feeling?' His voice was soft and concerned, yet I could feel his excitement as he bobbed up and down like a hyperactive child.

I could feel myself responding to his infectious optimism. 'Good –' I lied, smiling nervously. 'I mean, I have no idea what to expect, but I feel good about being here,' I admitted more truthfully. There was no denying the hole in my chest, the hollowness I felt as I relentlessly sought to find a sense of belonging, which is when I felt it—the orange fire within me.

Although I couldn't see it, I knew it was the same flame I had seen in my dreams, beckoning me to it. I recognised its warmth, spreading through my body, leaving behind comforting ease. And just like that, in a matter of moments, my sense of self had wrapped around it, calming my increasingly unsteady nerves.

Having walked to the cold drinks section to grab another bottle, Strat turned around, watching me inquisitively, looking deep into my eyes. I could sense he was looking for something like he was trying to read me. I quickly looked away. It somehow felt too personal, too vulnerable. Respecting my limits, he broke his gaze, giving me a slight smile while grabbing a drink from the shelf.

'At least you'll be safe here,' Strat tried to reassure me, referring to the Energy shield around the Academy that would protect me from any unexpected summoning.

'Darren doesn't seem to think so,' I let out.

'Don't worry about him. He's got a chip on his shoulder. Just stay out of the way of the Committee, and you'll be completely fine.'

'The Committee?' I asked.

'Our irreproachable leaders,' he answered sarcastically. 'A bunch of pompous cowards if you ask me.' I raised my eyebrows in question, but Stat didn't seem to want to elaborate on this one beyond his quick-fix response. 'If you see someone in a golden surcoat, just walk the other way,' he said. 'It's those in the turquoise surcoat you really need to watch out for. They're the real trouble,' he warned with a glint in his eyes, but even his humour did nothing to ease my heart's racing.

I wrapped my hands around my arms, the reality of the situation settling in. I let the orange flame inside me glow, hoping it would help fade the needles exploding in my stomach. I cast my eyes on the floor, trying to draw the line of the tiles with my gaze – hoping to settle the apocalyptic ping-ponging of thoughts in my mind. Strat turned towards me. I could feel his eyes absorb the mess that was untangling before him.

'Hey…' he said softly, caressing his hand along my arm before pulling me into his embrace. 'I'm sorry, I didn't mean to scare you.'

I couldn't help but breathe him in, he smelled of sweet citrus, brought out by a light musk at the base of the fragrance – both relaxing and intoxicating.

'I want you to enjoy this moment,' he said as he pulled away. 'I remember my first day at the Academy. I just couldn't wait to do my bit – there was nothing nobler than the thought of protecting Earth against the ever-invading Defacers! And there still isn't, not in my opinion.'

Almost spitting out the content of my drink, I was left coughing, trying to process what Strat had just said. 'Ever-invading?' I exclaimed.

'They need to feed themselves, and since they're driven by their thirst and never satisfied with their source in

Pamatan, they're always trying to cross into Earth. Just think about it, every living thing around us has its source of Energy – it's the equivalent of an endless honey pot. Instead of bears, it's Defacers; rather than honey, it's Energy.'

I frowned at his poor analogy but got the point.

'So, it's our job to keep them on their side of the Helix?' I guessed, to which Strat nodded. 'What happens if there is a gap in our defences? Aren't more of them going to get through? Kill more innocents?'

The haunted look in his eyes, confirmed the answer.

'Let's enjoy this moment,' he said, seeing the blood drain from my face. 'Coming to the Academy was one of the best days of my life.' His enthusiasm was evident, easing some of the dread of having to fit in someplace new. Who would I be here without Neer coming to rescue me from my inevitable faux pas?

Returning our empty snack containers to the cashier, I stared as he wiped them down and ran them over with a neon blue light before refilling them with their original content. I could feel my heart stop as my brain processed. There was zero waste. They were buying in bulk and using standardised packaging containers to store their products, which they could then wipe down and disinfect before the next customer reused the same containers.

I couldn't help but smile widely. I could feel my eyes shine as I turned to look at Strat. 'This is amazing! So simple,' I whispered, not wanting to draw the attention of the cashier, who I assumed was also an Elan.

Strat raised his eyebrows at my enthusiasm, clearly picking up my passion for sustainability.

'There's a lot more of where that came from,' he assured, finally coaxing a smile out of me. 'Just wait and see,' he promised before we slipped out the back into the night.

Letting our eyes adjust to the darkness, we spotted Darren with my suitcase leaning against the service station's wall next to an iron door. Staring at the oval symbol carved into its centre, I noticed the bulging round scanner lodged in the middle of the design.

Gathered around the metal door, Darren grabbed my hands tightly in his. 'The most important thing is that you don't draw any additional attention to yourself, Ella – promise me.'

I could see the slight sag of relief in his shoulders when I promised I would.

'We're just here to use the Academy's shield against the Defacers while we get you sufficiently trained. The moment we kill the one after you, we're out of here, not a moment later. Got it?' Watching us intently, he paused, waiting for us to confirm we had understood him.

Letting go of my now damp hands, Darren turned to Strat. 'It's best we stay apart. I'll go first and draw attention to myself, so you can sneak in. Meet me at 7 a.m. tomorrow for our first session in the Grounding Room.'

Standing behind the service station, we looked at the silver door. Lifting his chest, Darren raised his hand and wrapped it around the biometric scanner before closing his eyes. Taking a deep breath out, his hand started to glow – the intensity of its light slipping between his fingers. The lock clicked open. He pushed the door, turning one last time to look at us.

'I bloody hate this place,' were his last words before he stepped through, letting the door slam firmly behind him.

Chapter 7

Hearing only the chirp of the crickets, we waited patiently outside the backdoor to the service station shop, giving Darren enough time to divert the attention to himself as we sneaked after him into the Academy that lay underneath.

With every passing minute, I could feel my heartbeat intensify in anticipation. As though hearing it too, Strat squeezed my hand reassuringly.

'It'll be fine, trust me,' he comforted with the warm tones of his voice. Not wanting to let go of the security of his hand, I intertwined my fingers in his, not caring if it might be too forward. After all, I needed him. Luckily, he didn't seem to mind as he gave me a small, reassuring smile before rechecking his watch.

After what felt like an eternity to me but was likely the span of a few minutes, Strat spoke up. 'That should be long enough,' he confirmed.

Placing his hand around the biometric sensor bulging out of the door, Strat let his Energy glow through his hands, the unique frequency of his Energy unlocking the door. Picking up my suitcase effortlessly, he pulled us inside the service station underground.

The corridor was dark, long and narrow. It was so tight that we had to walk behind one another. Unable to see where we were going, I let Strat's trusted hand guide us through.

'Careful, we're going to start descending,' he said kindly. He was clearly at ease down here while I could barely regulate my breathing. Placing my hand on his shoulder to help me balance better, we carefully walked down each step, taking one at a time. Trying to focus all my attention on not falling, I couldn't help but feel Strat's muscles rippling under his jacket every time I leaned my weight onto him to walk down another step. Tightening my grip, I gently spread my fingers across the top of his shoulder and along the nape of his neck, touching the smoothness of his bare skin, sending my nerves ablaze.

Exhilarated by the thrill of darkness, here I was, alone with a beautiful man only inches away from me. His shoulder was soft, yet the thickness of his skin was robust, resilient and comfortingly warm. I could feel Strat's heartbeat through his skin, each pulse sending vibrations along his body and mine. His heart was racing, only intensifying the butterflies that seemed to have exploded in my stomach.

Unable to bear the intensity any longer, relief flooded me when I saw a small light flowing under the exit door.

Rushing down the last few steps, Strat threw himself against the large metal door, swinging it wide open, allowing me to let go of his shoulder, to our relief. Sighing out a deep and loud alleviating breath, Strat took off his leather jacket in one smooth motion and folded it across the front of his body.

Adjusting to the newly found brightness, I was surprised by the openness and the vastness of the space. My jaw dropped in complete amazement.

'The training centre of the Academy spans two floors. The accommodations are by the manor above ground,' offered Strat, swiftly moving past our earlier moment.

Formed of glass walls, the space allowed you to see the full extent of the floor. Slick, modern and open, this was a fantastic training facility, at least four times the size of the station above.

Equipped with railing, they seemed to be able to move around the walls and adjust the floor plan according to their needs. From the sweep of my gaze, it seemed like the current rooms provided various functions. Everything from practice weapons for archery, swordsmanship and every other killing form was stored on display. Tables were filled with screens cantered around beautiful intricate drawings of unknown landscapes. A meditation room was in use with students sitting in a symmetrical circle, and centre stage were 30 students, wearing identical navy outfits, undergoing combat training and moving in perfect synchronisation.

Oblivious to our presence, they attentively watched the teacher at the front, following her instructions. I didn't recognise the martial art, but I was mesmerised by the harmony of the rhythmic movement as the whole class moved seamlessly between the role of attacker and defender. Never breaking the flow, they effortlessly transitioned between each deliberate action, adopting new, carefully prescribed stances. My eyes moved to their feet, studying the seemingly prickly surface they trained on.

As though reading my thoughts, Strat answered my unspoken question, 'They've got rounded tips, so they don't hurt. Think of it as an extended acupressure mat.' He reassured me. 'It's to teach them how to surrender to the feeling of pain.'

'Pain?' I asked, unable to mask my worry.

'Stabilising your Base Energy's burn rate while travelling in the Helix can be… challenging, both physically and mentally. It's why we need to practice managing our Energy levels.'

I don't know what expression laid on my face, but it was enough for his tone to soften radically.

'It's not like that,' he explained. 'Once they surrender to the pain, it doesn't hurt them anymore – well, less. Unlike what our mind wants us to believe, pain isn't ever-increasing. It eventually hits a ceiling. When it does, it will linger there for a while, and your mind will tell you it will keep on getting worse forever, but if you commit to it, the pain will at some point transform – and in their case, release a flood of endorphins when their muscles release built-up tension. It's incredibly effective at helping open your Energy flow. Just look at the boy over there.' He pointed to a young boy with ruffled blond hair guided by a blue-haired girl, slowly running through the motions.

Looking closely, I noticed tears flowing down his face. Not of joy, not of sorrow, just of aliveness. Of beingness. Of release. His body remaining soft with calmness and ease.

'Pain is our greatest teacher. Surrender to the pain, give up control, and it will let you feel closer to the essence of your being. Not to mention, it's an incredibly helpful guide when having to augment the use of your Base Energy levels in the Helix or during a flight with the Defacers.'

I had so many questions, but alas, we had stopped by the entrance of the changing rooms.

'We should change into our uniforms to avoid drawing any further attention,' advised Strat, keeping my questions at bay. Moving towards one of the used lockers just outside the entrance of the changing rooms, Strat looked briefly around for any unwanted passers-by. Placing his ear against the cabinet, he swiftly pulled the locker open. Quickly taking out a navy outfit, he put it in my hands before ushering me toward the women's changing rooms.

'I'll meet you out here in five. The class will soon be over, and it's best if we blend in with the group going to dinner,' urged Strat. Despite the time pressure, I felt momentarily relieved by the mention of dinner. I didn't function when I was hungry.

Matching the rest of the décor, the changing room was clean-cut and minimalist. The lockers and benches were painted white. There were individual showers and private changing rooms for those who preferred privacy. I saw plenty of mirrors, hairdryers and even a steam room. Jumping into one of the private changing rooms, I threw on the blue outfit. It was a type of kimono. I wrapped the top around my waist, adjusting the collar, and slid easily into the trousers, which seemed to hug my curved body perfectly. It wasn't my usual outfit, but I admitted it was quite flattering.

Throwing the rest of my clothes into my suitcase, I could hear people entering the changing room, happily chatting about the intensity of the training. Smiling timidly, I couldn't help but glance over them, trying to find something that would have hinted to me they weren't human.

Their expressions and mannerisms were the same. They were physically indistinguishable from humans despite being able to augment their strength. It's probably why most of them could get away with leading human lives, yet they fit in here with such ease that it made me envy them. Showing the familiarity of a well-aquatinted team, they chatted away as they helped each other strap their weapons onto their backs and hips.

Fitted in protective sheaths, each weapon bore a coloured stone on the hilt. Flashing my eyes from sword to knife to bow, I could count only four colours – black, amber, green and white. One sword caught my eye with its vividly glowing crystal. Catching me by surprise, I couldn't help the small gasp escaping my lips. Meeting my eye, the girl holding the sword flashed me a reassuring smile before returning her weapon securely into the sheath strapped to her back. The stone immediately lost its glow when she released it. It was drawing its power from her touch.

Conscious not to draw any more attention, I tore my gaze away, keeping my head down as I exited the changing room, only to find Strat standing outside.

Wearing the same uniform as everyone else, we looked the same except for his sleeveless surcoat. Laying straight on his shoulders, its silky texture flowed effortlessly across his front, hanging open to his waist. Lined with a golden rim, the turquoise of the vest looked magnificent against the navy kimono. The shimmer of the material only further accentuated the intensity of his emerald eyes, making my breath hitch in my throat. As he stared straight at me, I couldn't help but admire the intricacy of the design on the high open collar, perfectly framing the squareness of his jaw. My eyes widened as I hoped to take in every detail, every sensation, and engrave it in my memory. His eyebrows raised in response as a smirk spread across his smooth face, causing a flush to spread across my face as I tore my eyes away.

'The navy looks lovely against your dark hair,' he complimented as he walked toward me. Surprised, I looked down, flushing, of course. Pausing, he watched me as he caught a stray lock of hair that was escaping the twist of my hair, brushing the tips of his fingers against my neck as he rewound it in place. My heart spluttered hyperactively, and I didn't know where to look.

Just as I was trying to come up with something to say, we were interrupted by someone standing next to us. 'Are you both coming to dinner?' asked the middle-aged man, still dabbing the sweat from his face. Not wanting the moment to end, I regretfully stepped back from Strat as he affirmed we would be joining.

'That reminds me,' Strat said, handing me a sunburst pin.

Holding it delicately in my hands, I turned my new item around. Centred around a purple crystal, two bold sunrays shot out from either side while the rest of its core was surrounded by several thinner rays.

Meeting the curiosity in my eyes, Strat explained as I pinned it to my chest. 'If anyone asks who you are, you're a confused teenager, who has finally managed to travel to Level Two,' he said, pointing to the two bold sunrays on my badge. 'In light of your recent breakthrough, you've come to the Academy for a few days with the hope of finally discovering your position.'

'Confused teenager?' I said, faking bewilderment.

'I wanted to keep it as close as possible to the truth,' he teased, smiling.

I couldn't stop myself from lightly punching him on the arm. 'And what's your part in this whole story?' I pouted, furious at his audacity.

'Ah! I'm your dedicated mentor during this trip, helping you achieve that clarity.'

I couldn't help but scoff loudly, rolling my eyes at his smugness. 'Is that why you get a different rock?' I asked, glancing towards the black stone lodged in the centre of his badge, matching the one I'd seen in his weapons. I had better assess his skill before I let my arrogance get the better of me – after all, I had no idea how talented Strat might be.

'That's because I'm a Striker. My crystal helps amplify my mental and physical endurance as well as stamina. Archers get an amber Oliupite to calm their nervous system, helping them stay calmly focused on their target. The Scientists have an electric green Calmond, amplifying their intuition and creative aptitude, and the Healers get a Quartz allowing them to channel their Energy better. The crystals help us augment our Energy, levelling the playing field when we fight the Defacers – especially those whose brute strength double with the help of their Marcax crystal.'

This explained the different stones, but Strat could see the scepticism on my face, my mind saying, *Crystals, really*?

'They may differ slightly from the crystals you find in your regular online shopping basket.'

Now he had my interest. 'How, so?' I asked.

'By transferring a bit of our Energy into the crystal, we change its molecular composition, causing it to produce a unique vibration and frequency. We enhance them with additional properties so that the more Energy you flow through your crystal, the more those benefits are reinforced. Since you always want to receive those abilities, the brightness of your crystal also becomes a good indicator of how much Energy you're burning through.'

'How do you know what crystal to choose?'

'It's the synchronisation of your vibrations which draws you to choose what will become your crystal. The assertiveness and the courage I felt from the Demnite was what bonded me to it and finalised my position as a Striker. It was the best fit for me then and will forever be.'

'So, the crystal determines your position?' I confirmed my understanding.

'You could argue that, since the four crystals only get enhanced by the Elans with the corresponding position, they tend to draw those with the same abilities. I prefer to believe it simply accelerates the process. The Demnite, for example, only reinforced traits already in my character. Those characteristics just happen to be those that make the best Strikers.'

Strat could see the frown on my face, as I thought this sounded a bit arbitrary.

'You're free to choose, of course, which is why we encourage all the newbies to explore the different positions before the Weapon Ceremony. But everyone has always ended up in the position to which their crystal best aligned.'

'And I don't get a designated position because as a 'confused teen', I still haven't yet decided who I want to be,' I said, making sense of the whole system.

'You said it, not me.' Strat laughed.

'Rest assured. We don't leave you empty-handed. All newbies get a Tetresia crystal to help activate their spiritual awareness, open their intuition and enhance their Energy.'

'But I don't get it engrained in my weapon?' I said, referring to the brightly glowing crystals forged in Strat's golden blades.

'Observant as always,' complemented Strat. 'That's because your crystal is temporary. You will only get an engrained weapon during the Weapon Ceremony when you finalise your position. That's also when we get a new badge engrained with the same crystal forged into the weapon of your choice.'

'I'm guessing I don't get a position or a weapon then?' I complained, feeling shorthanded. 'Can I at least get the cool samurai vest? Or do I need to get into trouble first?' I cooed, biting my lower lip. He seemed to stare blankly at my mouth, immediately making me regret my failed attempt at flirting.

'Because "*they're the real trouble,*"' I explained, reminding him of his earlier comment. Strat swallowed, clearing his throat before blinking his eyes and returning my gaze.

'So, cool, vest? Aye,' he commented, swiftly moving past my awkwardness. His eyes once again crinkled with their familiar shine as he put his hands around the collar of his surcoat, showing it off.

'You do look like a true warrior,' I admitted, unable to rein myself in.

'Well, I'd hope so! This is an original Jin Baori made for actual Samurais. I wouldn't let Hiryuu find out you ever doubted its authenticity,' Strat said proudly before lifting his hand, anticipating my flood of follow-up questions.

'I already know what you're going to ask.' Strat smiled. 'Although we've been spread across the world, we've been fortunate enough to have had the ability to exchange knowledge continuously. With the Helix being the ultimate Silk Road, we've developed a global culture, giving us the advantage of being able to pick and choose the best – food, clothes, battle techniques, weapons, and training methods. When you think about it, it's amazing the advancements we've been able to make because of it.'

'That's incredible.' That was the only thing I could think to say before remembering my previous question. 'So where did we land on getting me a vest?' I asked cheekily.

His shoulders shook with laughter as he waved his head from side to side. 'Unfortunately, we don't quite hand these out,' he said apologetically. I couldn't help but feel a sting of disappointed.

'How about this,' Strat proposed. 'If you agree to slow down with the questioning, I'll do my best to get the Committee to reconsider letting you pick your position. And, if you decide to stick around, maybe I can even help you get a vest of your own. Get you into some real trouble,' he teased, although there was apprehension in his voice.

Despite my best efforts, I couldn't contain the smile spread widely across my face. Even then, I pretended to ponder my answer. Of course, I didn't need a second longer to decide that any offer involving a future with Strat was worth taking, even if the odds of Darren allowing it would be slim. Weighing up the benefits, I made up my mind.

'I do have a billion more questions, but then the vest does look pretty cool… And I would like to work on the whole "confused teenager" thing…' I said, pretending we both didn't know the true motive for accepting his offer.

'If we limit the questions to half a million a day, you've got yourself a deal,' he negotiated.

'Deal,' I agreed, shaking his hand.

Strat released an exaggerated sigh of relief, followed by one of his enchanting chuckles. 'Now, let's catch up with the others,' he said, and we rushed to the back of the flock.

Keeping my head low, we followed the crowd silently as we walked back towards the metal front door, taking a right past the studio and going into a long corridor. I felt a thrill course through me as I followed the Elans, feeling for the first time in a long time like I might belong.

Chapter 8

Following the other trainees, we walked deeper into the Elans' training centre. Funnelled into a long corridor, we suddenly emptied into a large, expansive space below. I moved closer to the glass wall, finding an Olympic swimming pool spread along the bottom floor. Exchanging a surprised look with Strat, he smiled warmly. I could forever stare into his emerald eyes. Still, my attention was drawn to the wall-length thermometer showing the Academy's healthy battery levels. As we passed, everyone gave one big jump, further powering the battery through the kinetic floors laid everywhere across the training centre.

'We continue to hold the top spot, despite being one of the smaller training centres,' bragged Strat before giving the floor a mighty stomp. He was right. They were top of the leader board and were ahead of the 30 other centres featured.

It was incredible the amount of power that was being generated simply through everyone's training. I couldn't help but wonder if this was something we could expand, 'self-powered gyms'. Now that was a million-dollar idea.

'You really should try to stop looking so surprised. Give us a chance to blend in,' scolded Strat. 'No matter how cute you look,' he added sweetly, giving me a wink. I couldn't help but bite my lip. His distractions kept my immediate questions at bay, even though I still couldn't believe our numbers. There must be hundreds of Elans spread across the globe, training in various Academies.

'I thought I was a newly trained Elan?' I objected, believing I was blending into my cover story.

'Yes, but no one would expect this to be your first time in a training centre.'

'Oh,' is all I said, realising the abnormality of my delayed Energy 'Awakening', making me feel like an awkward teenager that hit puberty late.

'Especially since we don't want anyone mentioning you to the Committee,' Strat elaborated, suddenly tense.

'Is that very bad?'

He seemed to deliberate. 'It's not good. I didn't object because I know Darren doesn't trust the Committee, which is understandable after how they treated him, but we need to be careful. They wouldn't like us going behind their backs and won't be afraid to punish us for it. Especially since the repercussions of your summoning go beyond us. I don't like what we are doing, but if Darren says we need to keep this on the down-low, he must have a good reason.'

I nodded in agreement, glancing one last time at the pool, hoping that no one would get hurt because of our secret.

Moving further away from the service station above, I suspected we were walking under the surrounding farmland. Gathering closer to the group, I kept silent as we walked down the tunnelled corridor before stopping by a small electric shuttle. A few pupils rushed by as soon as the white, glossy doors opened, grabbing a seat along the benches.

'Did you guys see Darren Rose? I thought he was dead! It's been about ten years since we last saw him!' a blonde girl exclaimed dramatically. Unable to hide my intrigue, I leaned forwards on my elbows, watching the small squeamish boy next to her jumping in on the gossip.

'He's the only living Elan to have figured out the sequence to the Gates and survived traveling through all the Levels into Pamatan and back,' added the boy eagerly.

'He used to be my teacher,' shot the blonde smugly. 'That's before he disappeared. I'm pretty sure he'd given up on being part of the Committee after the Defacers murdered his sister.'

I pretended to tie my shoes to hide my surprise. My stomach tightened in response. Darren had had this whole other life– brother, leader, celebrity. One I knew nothing about. I couldn't help but feel the ache in my heart before tightening the lock to my box of unspoken things.

I forced myself to focus on the blonde sitting opposite. Having captured her audience, the girl continued, 'He must have finally realised his mistake. He's probably coming back to convince them to take him back. I bet they won't, though. My mother's not the forgiving type ...' Her voice trailed off as though remembering an experience of her own.

I wished to hear more, but her interest seemed to lead her elsewhere. Following her gaze, I realised her eyes had settled on Strat. I tried to ignore the sudden tug of irritation but couldn't help but glance at the twenty-year-old. She was attractive and judging by the tightness of her perfectly fitted kimono, she knew it. Clocking my judgmental gaze, she scanned me from top to bottom before deciding I was no threat. Angling her body towards Strat, she batted her long lashes in his direction, waiting for him to notice her as she shyly flicked her beautifully coiffed braids. Of course, her hair was miraculously unaffected by her intense workout.

Discretely using my peripheral vision, I waited to see if Strat would react. To my gratification, he seemed to ignore her advances even if it didn't discourage her. When he turned his head toward the small group, she pounced confidently at her opening.

'It's always nice to see another Striker,' was her opening line. My eyes shot to her badge, seeing she was sporting a black crystal with three bold rays. 'I see you've travelled to Level Five! That's very impressive. I've just made it to Level Three myself,' she said proudly, thrusting her bosom forwards while pointing to the last ray. It shone brighter than the others. I had to stifle myself from rolling my eyes in response, forcing myself instead to gaze at the other passengers. It was only then that I noticed that no one in the shuttle seemed to have travelled beyond Level Three. I looked over at Strat – he must be particularly advanced, even more so now that he had travelled to Pamatan, although he never mentioned so himself.

'Is that so?' he mused, looking solely at the blonde. She edged closer while he kept his arms folded across his chest. He didn't even need to lift a finger and had girls throwing themselves at him. The thought tightened my chest.

'And you're part of the Squad? So young?' she observed. 'Also, very impressive,' she purred.

I had to stop my eyes from rolling to the back of my skull. Honestly, if I hadn't been so intimidated by how obviously beautiful she was, I would have told her to tone it down.

I glanced at Strat only to find her flattery had worked. He was smirking and giving her a look that would make anyone want to pounce him, including me. The blonde leaned even closer. To my horror, he reciprocated by leaning forward ever so slightly. His eyes locked with hers as though sharing a secret and whispered, 'It always helps being First Spear.'

I didn't know what this meant, but this news seemed to conflict with her previous enthusiasm as she unconsciously leaned back in her seat. I swore I saw the corners of Strat's lips curve in response. As though perfectly timed, the shuttle doors whistled open. We had arrived at our destination.

Lifting himself to his feet in one swoop motion, Strat turned to offer his hand to me.

'Hungry?' he asked, appearing unfazed.

'Always,' I replied, my voice higher than usual as I grabbed his hand, allowing him to lift me up. Unable to restrain myself, I sneaked a final peak at this girl's face only to see her disappointment clearly displayed. Doing my best to hold in a devious chuckle, I pushed my head further down, unable to suppress the smile that had spread across my face. *That's right, get in line*, I thought.

≈

'What was all of that about?' I asked Strat, leaning closer.

'About Darren?' he clarified.

I also wanted to know about Darren's unexpected fame, but I had promised to halve my questioning. 'No, the "First Spear" thing?'

He winced. He'd obviously hoped I'd ask about Darren before brushing it off. 'Just reminding her, the packaging doesn't always reflect what's inside.'

I stopped in my tracks. Misinterpreting my reaction as apprehension, Strat's expression softened once again. 'Don't worry, I'm right beside you,' he encouraged holding his hand towards me. Grabbing it, I let him pull me closer to him as we followed the crowd. Walking up a set of stairs, we exited the underground garage disguised as stables.

Enjoying the freshness of the cool outside air, we arrived over ground into what looked like a wooden stable.

Astounded by the stunning décor, I shared a look of confused excitement with Strat, but he kept his lips sealed. His eyes were playful, and his grin mischievous as he led me to the outdoors.

Bewildered wouldn't even begin to describe my amazement. I let out a small cry of surprised pleasure. Surrounded by the vast and beautiful grounds, I looked around in total awe. A perfectly lit gravel drive descended to the entrance of a large two-storey red brick house best described as a manor. A three-yard wooden gate bridged the gap between the driveway and the manor, granting passage across the water circling the house.

Turning to stare at Strat, I got caught up in all the excitement as he grinned at my wonder. I tried to absorb every detail of his glimmering eyes and seal it in my memory. Pointing toward the scene before us, Strat brought my attention back to the manor.

'The manor was originally built in 1474 and turned into a school after World War One,' offered Strat. 'We have about seven hectares of land, featuring a stableyard, kitchen garden and ponds, a meadow and a grove,' he said with pride. 'We've turned the stable into a transportation station from the manor to the training centre, which we've just exited. And we transformed the stables into additional rooms.' Looking in the direction he was pointing, I distinguished lights from a building a couple of hundred yards away.

I immediately spotted the solar panels installed on every roof, the rainwater tank that fed into the house and the kitchen gardens. While the grass around us was mowed, the rest of the land was left wild and, judging by the number of bugs flying past the lights, this was a biodiversity hot spot.

'Do you grow sufficient food for everyone?' I asked, trying to size up the kitchen gardens vs mouths to feed.

Strat seemed to pause and think about this. 'We'd have to ask Gabe to be certain, but I'd assume so since we're carbon negative.'

'That's... incredible!' I stammered. Here were all the solutions the world had been speaking about, tested, trialled and working! This place was a sign of hope. 'Who's responsible for all of this?' I asked, my mind already racing at the possibilities of what we could do together, the world needed to know.

'Everyone contributes, but there's a group that leads the effort. When all of this is over, I could introduce you to some of them if you like?' Strat offered, making my eyes light up in response, to which he chuckled, a low enchanting sound.

'I'll warn you though, some of them can be pretty full-on. I heard this one guy mistakenly electrocuted himself from exhaustion. He's fine, but they had to start giving him a curfew he was spending so much time re-engineering the place.' I couldn't help but frown at Strat's incredulous tone.

‘I mean, I get it. What’s the point of defending the world against the Defacers if there’s nothing left worth protecting,’ I argued, feeling the need to shield the unsung hero.

‘I agree. I just prefer being the one travelling through the Helix, slaying Defacers trying to cross into Earth,’ smiled Strat. ‘You’ll soon see what I mean. Protecting innocent humans from getting their Energy sucked out of them is *really* fun,’ he said, his eyebrows popping up.

We reached the bottom of the drive, lined by young apple trees, and stood at the bridge’s entrance. I briefly stopped to admire the manor, which stood majestically on its island, contrasting with the dark trees planted in the rough pasture of the parkland behind. Presenting an imposing Georgian façade, a plain tiled roof hung to the first floor with tall brick chimney stacks and small dormer windows at attic level. It looked like a newly built tower on the east end of the façade. Overlooking the gardens, it had protruding solar glass windows on the ground and first floor levels and a high-pitched roof with eight inclined faces meeting at a single point high above the roofline of the existing building.

Looking at the direction of my eyesight, Strat stated, ‘That’s where Ms Roberts lives. She’s the owner of the estate.’ I gave him a quizzical look, and he filled in the gaps. ‘She’s the heir to a wealthy aristocratic Dutch family and married a similarly rich Italian Duke. Together they bought this place and turned it into an Academy for Elans.’

He offered no further explanation, but I suspected there was more to that story. 'It's very generous of them,' I replied as we walked into the house, making a mental note to ask him for more details later.

As we walked across the bridge, I noticed the same oval symbol on the station door carved into one of the stone bricks. I knew it must be significant, but I couldn't make it out. At the bottom of the oval border lay a semi-circle covering a third of the shape with thick straight lines shooting out from it before meeting the shape's border.

'It's a sunset,' offered Strat, as I finally recognised the image of the sun setting, its rays of light shooting out from its core. 'It's become a symbol for us,' he added as we walked into the manor. I wanted to ask why, but I noticed a small crowd gathering next to us. I'd have to add it to my list of questions.

Mirroring the grandeur of its exteriors, the entrance arcade had the date 1861 carved in it. The house had been remodelled to reflect the Victorian Gothic style of the time. There were loads of gabled, dormer windows crowned with mini-pediments, some of which were covered with luxurious, thick curtains most likely kept for decoration. As soon as we walked through the entrance, everyone started removing their coats, comforted by the warmth of the house.

We walked right past a large staircase leading to the second floor, through a wooden arch and straight into a large, open dining hall. Beautiful dangling chandeliers filled the room with sparkling light. Below were six large dining tables, each seating about 20 people, most of which seemed to be filled with ordinary people eating and chatting. Everyone was dressed in a navy kimono except for one other, who also wore the same surcoat as Strat.

Following the others, I stood in line for the food buffet. Piling up on vegetables, proteins and carbs, I layered my plate with delicious food before sitting opposite Strat. Eyeing my full plate, I could see Strat's lips curve in the corners. Ignoring him, I continued to spin my plate as I tried to figure out the best place to start digging in.

'I don't think you'll find an inch of that plate that isn't covered by food,' he said, his green eyes sparkling playfully.

Pushing some of my food aside to create an opening, I looked back at him with an expression of smug defiance as I took my first bite. Almost burning my tongue, I tried to mask the pain with little success, much to Strat's amusement, as he shook his head with quiet laughter.

After appeasing some of my hunger, I finally asked, 'So, what does the sunset represent?'

'Well, do you remember how we need to keep the Defacers on their side of the Helix to stop them from invading Earth and consuming life's Energy?' he asked casually, as though the risk of a Defacer invasion was part of everyone's everyday life.

'Sure,' I replied, incredulous we were having this conversation.

'Well, part of the reason we manage to keep the Defacers contained to their end of the Helix is that we keep on beating them to the Gates interconnecting each Level. By the time they start figuring out the Gates' sequence and discover their location, we've set up two layers of defences between Pamatan and the Level One gate crossing into Earth.'

'What do you mean by "figure out the Gates sequence"? Aren't the Gates always in the same location?' I asked.

He pulled his chair closer. I could see the excitement in his eyes, sending goose bumps through my body. Our faces were only inches away, his mouth curved up in his classic mischievous grin as he spoke in a low voice. 'Here's the twist. Between every ten to fourteen days, the sun starts to set across all the Levels in the Helix, signalling its imminent collapse. When the sun rises again, the landscape in the Levels will have changed as well as the sequence determining the location of the Gates.'

Speechless, another cold wave rushed across my entire body, sending shivers down my spine. I was starting to understand the impossibility of what Darren had achieved. Satisfied with my reaction, Strat let out a low enchanting chuckle as he picked up his fork again.

'You must think this whole thing is crazy.'

'If I hadn't been summoned and felt the strength of my Energy, I wouldn't have believed you.'

'You wouldn't have believed me?' he repeated incredulously, his eyes playful.

I shook my head slowly and formed a smile. 'I thought you were a little crazy, actually.'

'Is that right? So, the truth finally comes out.' He feigned offence. 'Here I was thinking I had you under my charm, and I find out you already think I'm nuts.'

'Well, aren't you? Maybe just a little? I mean, you did stab me with Defacer-killing venom without knowing if I would survive,' I joked, letting a huge smile spread across my face. 'And what do you mean by "already"? Are you trying to hide something from me?' I probed, fixing him with a suspicious gaze.

This seemed to upset him as his face quickly grew serious. 'Maybe, a little,' he admitted.

'Are you finally going to explain the "First Spear" thing? I pursued, remembering the girl's wary reaction in the shuttle between the training centre and the manor.

The way Strat's body stiffened confirmed I had hit the nail on the head. He cast his eyes down towards his hands as his shoulders pulled forwards. I had a hard time believing anything could impact my feelings for Strat, but something about his expression let me know he was wary of sharing.

'Well, then?' I asked courageously, uncharacteristically addressing the topic straight on. 'I'm sure it's not that bad,' I added more softly this time. I wanted him to feel comfortable sharing things with me. 'How often do you get the benefit of an unbiased opinion? Plus, you already know by now that I won't drop the subject until you eventually tell me,' I teased, giving him a look that showed my determination, making his shoulders drop back down.

'Okay, I see your point. Although, I wished we had had more time,' said Strat as though this might be goodbye. 'Promise you'll listen to everything I have to say first?'

'Deal,' I replied eagerly, using what I suspected was his favourite word.

'As I mentioned, each Elan is assigned a position to help us better organise ourselves in battle, giving us a critical advantage over the Defacers who go in just with brute force. It starts as soon as the sun rises again in the Helix. The Archers immediately set off as soon as it's safe. They scout for the Gates, interconnecting each Level using their exceptional spatial awareness and drawing skills. Bringing back vital information, the Scientists can get a head start on cracking the sequence to the Gates, while the Strikers use their understanding of the landscape to devise war tactics. All the while, the Healers prepare themselves to act as Energy-transferring-vessels to cure the wounded for the fight ahead.

'Everyone behaves like one team, under the leadership of the Committee. Acting as the ultimate decision-makers, their instructions are executed by the Squad – we're their second in command. Demarked by our "cool" surcoats, as you call them, we're a group of highly trained individuals dedicated to protecting the Helix. We both mobilise and defend the Troop of lower-skilled Elans, who are either training to join the Squad or choose to predominantly lead human lives.'

'Okay…' I said, waiting for the bad part to come.

'We do that by acting as the first wave of attack.'

I frowned. I wasn't thrilled about Strat being in the frontline fighting off Defacers. Of course, Mum wouldn't approve of Strat's killings, and I can't say I was too keen either, even if they were Energy-thirsty, murderous Defacers. But this was by no means a deal-breaker. There was something else.

'And where does being First Spear fit in?' I finally asked, barely above a whisper, dreading the seconds ahead.

Staring deep into my eyes for a long beat, he eventually said, 'I'm the one who casts the first blow.'

'I don't understand,' I frowned.

He watched me carefully as he spoke, 'I'm the first to throw myself into enemy territory, to cross "no man's land", to lure the Defacers out and break the battle open.'

I could feel the blood drain from my face as the reality of what Strat had just told me sunk in. I had seen enough World War Two documentaries to know this massively reduced his life expectancy. I couldn't comprehend why he would choose to play this role. Past soldiers prayed they wouldn't be sent to the front and he was purposely making it his full-time occupation.

'Are you alright?' He sounded worried.

'How long have you been doing this?

'Couple of years, it's what got me into the Squad.'

'How old are you?' I breathed.

'Eighteen.'

I kept my face composed, aware of his scrutiny as my blood boiled – so young. It was easier if I didn't try to believe it. How could the Squad permit it? I could feel my orange core ignite in fiery response, fuelled by my urge to protect him.

I wasn't paying attention to my expression, but something in it made him grow sombre. His hands dropped to his side, and he stood very still, his eyes intent on my face. The silence lengthened.

'What is it?' I whispered, leaning into him.

His face softened as he edged himself closer, and he sighed. 'I keep waiting for it to happen.'

'For what to happen?'

'I know something I tell you or something you'll see will be too much at some point. And then you'll run away. At least promise me you won't turn your back on this, on who you are. Even if there are a few nutters amongst us.' He smiled half a smile, but his eyes were serious.

'I'm not running anywhere,' I promised. 'Maybe I'm just a little concerned about why you feel the need to put yourself in imminent danger?'

'Perhaps it was reckless to start with, but then I got great at it, and it became part of who I am.'

So, there was more. 'Are there any more revelations you'd like to unload today?' I probed sheepishly, knowing my chances were slim to none.

'Not today, thank you,' Strat replied sarcastically, admittedly to my relief. I didn't think I could fuel my anger any more without giving myself away.

'Are you sure?' I probed anyways, knowing I was on the verge of becoming irritating.

'Absolutely! At this rate of questioning, I'll go crazy by the end of the week, and I'll have you to blame!' he faux-accused. 'Any man would go mad under such intense interrogation!' I couldn't help myself from playfully snapping his hand in outrage.

'It's what happens when an incredibly hot guy comes to your house and tells you you've just travelled to a parallel universe. Only to kidnap you for a week to his secret "Academy". It's not exactly your everyday interaction.'

'Fair point. Incredibly hot, eh?'

'Yes,' I confessed, 'as if you didn't already know.'

'I like hearing you say it anyways.' His emerald eyes locked with mine, and I suddenly had difficulty remembering what we were discussing. So, we didn't talk and enjoyed each other's presence. Falling into a comfortable silence, I suddenly felt exhausted from the emotional roller coasters over the last few days.

Not feeling the need to fill in the silence, I observed my surroundings. I counted a total of about a hundred people, all from different ethnicities and backgrounds. What looked like a sixty-year-old lawyer with a tidy side parting and expensive glasses was happily chat to a fully tattooed punk girl and the teenage boy sitting opposite him.

I also noticed that, apart from a handful of pupils with a Level Four badge, everyone else seemed to have only been able to travel to the earlier Levels. How was it possible that my Energy was able to survive a trip to Pamatan with no training? My Energy should have immediately burnt out.

Pushing the concern to the back of my mind, I eavesdropped, trying to gather more information on Darren's past life; after all, it seemed to be the only thing anyone was discussing.

Spotting the young boy with the ruffled blond hair from the training centre, I watched him sneak under a nearby table. It was curious enough to direct my attention to the busy conversation happening between the heads above.

'I heard his sister used to be a superstar around here. I bet he got jealous and killed her, which is why he had to run away,' speculated one guy, sitting in a small group, only to be interrupted by an older woman wearing a golden surcoat.

'You were barely born when it happened, Raj!' the woman joked, pushing her long blonde, wavy hair aside. 'Why don't you ask someone who was around rather than spreading nonsensical rumours?' she lectured him, much to his embarrassment.

'But I'll give you this, you weren't completely wrong,' she said in a kinder voice, putting the boy back at ease. 'Darren's sister, Amelia, was in many ways a "superstar" as you say. She was exceptional,' the woman marvelled, remembering her young adulthood. 'Amelia was fierce, strong, intelligent and brave like no other. It was her curiosity and influence that got us first exploring the deeper Levels of the Helix and ultimately confirmed there was a sequence to the Gates. It's how she managed to find her way down to Level Six in the first place. Although tragic and deeply mourned, her death will always be remembered as an important moment in our history. She was the first Elan to ever go to Pamatan, and Darren was the first to return alive.'

'But how did she die?' probed Raj impatiently, oblivious to the sadness that had entered the woman's voice as she retold Amelia's story.

'That we don't know, he never told anyone,' she said patiently. 'The most probable scenario is that a large group of Defacers attacked them, and only Darren was able to get away. He tried to convince the Committee that Amelia might be alive and they should send their best Elans to rescue her before the Gate sequence changed again, but his request was denied. They told him it was too risky and they wouldn't help him. Everyone knew this was a big betrayal for the Roses, but no one dared go against the Committee. I feel ashamed every time I think back to how we treated him.

'After the incident, Darren made it clear that he would no longer be a part of our community, but he stuck around, for a while anyways. Eventually, they searched for Amelia's replacement and to Darren's dismay, they choose his sister's rival and Diamor was given her place on the Committee.'

I couldn't stop the bewildered expression crossing my face. No wonder Darren hated this place. The Academy was where he experienced the biggest betrayal of his life.

'Diamor sucks though,' slagged off Raj. He didn't seem to have a filter, and judging by the elbow slammed into his side, he had said something potentially offensive. I bit down on my lip when his leg jerked under the table, missing the boy hidden by a hair.

Raj's friends looked apologetically at the woman with the golden surcoat, but, rather than scowl, she seemed amused. This seemed enough for the spying boy, who slowly untangled himself from the maze of legs undetected. My gaze followed him as he smoothly collected himself before rushing towards the girl with the fiery-blue hair at the end of the hall and whispering in her ear.

She seemed to nod as she listened. The boy looked back in the direction of my table. I quickly cast my eyes down, hoping I wasn't caught staring. I breathed, pretending to pick at my plate and continued to listen to the nearby table.

'She's no Amelia Rose, that's for sure,' continued the woman with the golden surcoat, agreeing with Raj, forgiving his impertinence. 'But her conservative approach has worked well throughout these years. We can only hope that it continues to be enough.'

With the conversation naturally ending, the Elans got up and left with a lingering suspense of what was to come. Excited by the gossip, you could feel the vibrations in the air, everyone bonded by the same cosmic Energy.

Chapter 9

I followed Strat up a third flight of stairs. He was taking us to one of the manor's attics. Flinging open the trap door, we clambered into a large studio bedroom. Setting our bags aside, Strat threw various items of scattered clothing into empty cupboards as he turned on the lampshades dotted around the room.

I glanced from the back to front, making a note of the unused kitchenette on the back wall, small lounge area centred around a sealed fireplace, and massive king-size bed placed centre stage. I tried to ignore the clenching that came over me when I looked at the crimpled bedsheets and focused instead on the bareness of every surface. While functional, the whole place missed personalisation, the little things that turned a lodging into a home.

'So, this is where you live?' I asked Strat, somewhat uneasy with his set-up.

'You sound surprised,' he noted, glancing towards me.

I shrugged, not trusting myself to speak without judgement in my voice.

'I can find you somewhere else if you'd prefer?' he asked, his voice quieter than usual, turning his back to me as he peered under the kitchen cupboards.

'No,' I replied too quickly. 'It's just unexpected, that's all. I like it – it's very minimal,' I tried to compliment. Strat glanced back in my direction. I seemed to have convinced him as his shoulders visibly relaxed before returning his attention to wiping the dusty kitchen surface.

'It's easier this way,' he said, his tone trailed as he tried to recover the situation. 'Until they rotate me to another Academy,' he backtracked, but I already knew what he had meant – in case things ever went wrong. He was First Spear, after all, death was part of his every day and living like you had owed nothing seemed to be part of it. *Less to clean up,* I thought cynically. 'Although Ms Roberts would probably have me stay forever if it was up to her,' he chuckled, trying to recover the mood.

I forced a grin despite the unsettling news that included his eventual move.

'Do others board here too?' I enquired, keen to change the subject.

'Nope, just me,' he replied with practised ease as he finished up, wiping his damp hands on his trousers. Scrutinising his reaction, a moment of wordless communication passed between us. He realised that I knew he was keeping something from me. In turn, I realised that he wouldn't give anything away. Not now.

'It's getting late,' he stated.

'Aren't you staying?' I asked wistfully, stepping towards him, painfully aware of the slight desperation in my voice.

He shook his head. 'As long as you're staying here, I want this to be your safe haven, which usually means no teenage boys crashing on the sofa.' His eyes were soft, the green in his eyes deep. Only a step away, he tentatively reached out his finger to my face. He hesitated. I grabbed his hand and pushed it towards my face. He traced the back of his knuckles against my cheek. I warmed under his touch, my heart leaping in my chest, savouring every second.

'I'll come to get you first thing in the morning,' he promised. Picking up his bag, Strat opened the trap to the attic and started walking down the ladder.

'Strat!' I called after him, not wanting the moment to end. I rolled my neck to try and rid myself of the goose bumps on my nape as I said his name. He turned around, his emerald gaze burning into mine, my mind scrambling for words. He lifted his eyebrows as he waited for my response and I finally managed to find words.

'Good night,' I whispered, heart still pounding.

'Sweet dreams to you too, El.'

I let myself collapse onto the bed. Gosh, it smelled like him: an intoxicating, comforting smell that washed my anxieties away. Grabbing my phone to set my alarm, I saw a text message from Neer. I'd reply later. I didn't want to lie to him, and I couldn't muster the willpower needed to answer his inevitable interrogation. I set the alarm for 5:30 a.m. and sent a quick text to Mum, letting her know we'd arrived safely and would be training non-stop over the next few days.

Kicking my boots off, I let myself relax for a moment, but my mind couldn't seem to steady itself as it jumped to and from every piece of information I'd recently learnt. I still felt uneasy knowing Darren was keeping secrets, but why? And how long had the lie gone on for? I found it hard to believe that it was a coincidence that one of the closest people in my life also happened to be an Elan and hadn't thought to mention I was too. It hurt to know he didn't trust me. I'd always believed we had an unspoken connection, but then again, it might just have been in my head or because we're both Elans.

Letting out a long sigh, I accepted that I wouldn't be solving the mystery tonight. Focusing on calming myself, I inhaled and exhaled, slowly tuning out the chatter in my mind. Scanning through my body, it was incredible how much more liberated I'd felt since my Energy had Awakened. It was as though I had finally been set free. Lying still, I tuned into myself, trying to find the orange fire I had felt earlier. I started by scanning the top of my skull, taking my time before moving down along my body. Soon, I could see the orange flames emanating from my Energy, centred in my body.

Marvelling at its intensity, I explored its uplifting sensation when I noticed the tight ball in my gut. Taking in a long exhale, I released some of my Energy through my body and dove deeper to examine the knot. Using my breath, I directed my light towards my gut as I tried to soothe the tightness. I visualised my Energy untangling and melting away the tension.

I told myself things would be okay, and I had to let go of my fears. It was the only way of overcoming my trauma and potentially recovering my memories. I reminded myself that I was safe and could let myself open up. I no longer needed to be afraid. Feeling courage enter my heart, I turned the palms of my hands up to face the sky, letting the vibrations of the room flow through me. I let go and allowed my natural flow of Energy once again to circulate through me, feeling something in me release as I drifted off to unconsciousness.

I was singing and running in an empty fenced courtyard. I started to swirl around, letting the airflow through my hands, sending me into fits of giggles as the air passing through my fingers tickled my palms. Swirling faster, I saw a man standing nearby, just past the fence behind a large black rock. Trying to stop, I had to steady myself but needed to close my eyes as I swayed from side to side. When I opened them again, the man had disappeared.

Chills ran along my body, waking me long enough to pull the bed cover across my fully dressed body. Rolling myself into the sheets, I drifted back to sleep.

My head hit the side of his hard chest, feeling the dampness from the sweat that had transpired through his shirt. I could still smell its mustiness when my head rolled backwards, hanging unsupported across his hairy arm. My eyes felt like cement blocks, but I urged them to stay open, fighting the insistent pull of the heavy, unnatural fogginess seeping through my body and into my brain. I couldn't make out his face, but something about his heavy rasping breathing let me know he was hurt. I had wanted to look for longer, but I couldn't fight the fog anymore. I had to let my eyes fall shut in oblivion.

≈

BEEP! BEEP! BEEP! BEEP!

Grunting, I threw my hand out, searching for my wretched phone. Completely disoriented, it took me a moment to remember where I was and that I needed to get up. My head was pounding as I tried to make sense of my dream. I shivered despite the flush in my cheeks, thinking back to the fenced courtyard in my dreams and how it reminded me of the stone structure I'd been recently summoned to.

Turning on the bedside lamp, I looked through the window, pushing the dream aside. It was still too early. It was still pitch black and freezing cold. Bracing myself, I got up, grabbing my suitcase with one hand while holding the covers around me. I turned on the bathroom lights, wincing and shutting my eyes instantly from the sudden piercing light. I turned on the shower tap and didn't have to wait for the hot water to come gushing out. Equipped with a purifier that cleaned and recycled the water, I hopped into its warm embrace, and for the first time since I could remember, I permitted myself the luxury of a guilt-free shower, letting the rolling water gently wake me up. Unwilling to get out, I indulged myself, safe in the knowledge I was using significantly less water, only for my thoughts to be interrupted by the slamming of the attic trap door.

Sending my heart in double time, I found myself rushing out of the shower and throwing on my new kimono, still partially wet. Running a brush through my thick hair, I looked at myself in the mirror, only to see the excitement that had stung me awake like a child on Christmas day.

Carrying out the covers with me, I made my way out of the bathroom, feeling nervous and thrilled all at once when I saw him. Standing in the kitchenette, my smile broadened as I watched him prepare a cup of breakfast tea.

Turning in my direction, a single strand of hair fell from his perfectly slicked hair. He raised his eyebrows in response. Gosh, he was handsome. 'Good morning to you,' he greeted cheerily. He was obviously a morning person while I struggled to keep my eyes open. 'Have any Defacers managed to break through our impenetrable protection while I was away? Or did you just choose to sleep in the bathroom?' he asked inquisitively with a wicked grin spreading across his face as he handed me my cuppa.

I forced myself to blink. Darted my eyes away from his irresistible lips. Think, words. 'I'm not good in the mornings,' I explained.

He hummed in response and took a step forward. I gripped my mug tighter, trying to focus on the cloudy brown colour. 'I was struggling to get out of bed this morning, and then I thought, *Why suffer when I can just take the covers along with me*?' I blabbed.

'Is that so,' he purred. He was so close, I felt the heat from his body. I finally allowed myself to glance at him. He pulled out a single white feather lodged in my hair, bringing it out in front of us. One tiny feather stood between his lips and mine, and oh boy, how my body tingled in response.

He reached out to grab the duvet I'd abandoned on the nearby chair and stepped around me towards the bed. A million thoughts were rushing through my mind, and none were innocent. He draped the covers over the mattress before directing his darkened eyes towards me, only to catch me staring again. I forced myself to take my first sip of tea.

'Where did you sleep?' I asked, trying to clear my thoughts from the morning fog.

'I found an empty room for the night. Luckily, there aren't many Elans staying over these days,' he answered, his voice rougher than usual. I couldn't help the smile that tugged my lip. Was it possible he was equally affected by me as I was by him?

'Thank you for letting me stay in your room. It's very thoughtful of you,' I murmured, unable to contain the blush spreading across my face.

Smiling timidly, we finished our cups of tea in companionable silence and headed for the Grounding Room. The halls were empty, and the air was still; everyone was still asleep, as they should be at this ridiculous hour. Making our way through the manor, I noticed we walked past the dining hall without grabbing any food. Slightly irked by the lack of breakfast, I mimicked Strat's silence as we exited into the morning dew.

It was still dark, but the lights along the path guided us to the stable, into the shuttle and back to the training centre. Apart from a few cleaners preparing the studios, it was equally empty here. Walking past the entrance gates, we grabbed the stairs to the level below before arriving at the Grounding Room.

After taking off our shoes and socks, we walked into the studio, the soothing sound of ocean waves welcoming us. Surprised by the obscurity of the room, I noticed the cool air in the room tickling my skin. It was dark except for one focal light directed to the centre where Darren sat. Wearing the exact navy kimono and turquoise overcoat worn by members of the Squad, Darren had the amber Oliupite of the Archer on his badge with all six rays extended. A shiver of realisation coursed along my spine at the sight of his badge.

Sitting sideways, I could see Darren's face: his eyes were closed, but his expression was serious, focused and unmoving. As Strat and I moved closer, he finally looked up at us.

'Thank you for bringing her, Strat,' said Darren. We both waited for more instructions, but Darren stayed silent. 'You may go now,' he clarified, glancing at Strat.

Distressed by Darren's sudden dismissal of Strat, I looked nervously at Strat. I hadn't expected the nausea that followed learning we'd be apart. Glancing down from the corner of his eyes, Strat remained tranquil. He smiled reassuringly, making me ease slightly, even if I could feel my heart beat louder with every step he took away.

Wishing he could stay, I felt powerless as I watched his protective presence walk out the door when I suddenly saw his head peer out from behind the door. Flashing me with a wicked smile, he winked at me before disappearing behind the closing door. Just like that, my fears lessened, and my lips curled up involuntarily.

Raising his arm, Darren invited me to sit. Copying his stance, I sat opposite him, directly under the spotlight, cross-legged with a straight back. Lifting my hands, Darren gently took hold of my wrists and faced my palms down towards the ground, letting them float slightly above my knees as he placed his upwards-facing palms directly under mine. Not touching, he hovered his hands above mine when I suddenly felt a slight vibration intensifying as the air between our hands grew warmer. Amazed by the heat emitted from the palm of his hands into mine, I could feel Darren channelling the vibrations around us.

'Take deep breaths. Direct it to the base of your stomach, up along your lungs, throat and out through the mouth,' instructed Darren.

Doing as instructed, we sat in silence with closed eyes listening to the rhythmic oceanic sound playing as Darren led the pace of our breathing.

'Now breathe in for ten, hold for five and exhale for ten through a loud exhale.' Breathing a long, deep sigh, I followed his instructions before releasing a coarse exhale from the back of our throats.

After a few repetitions, Darren interrupted the silence. 'Do you feel the Energy flowing through?'

'Yes,' I replied, feeling the orange sun within me shining. I saw it in my mind's eye, the orange flames of my Energy glowing in the centre of my body, and felt its heat radiating outward through my limbs.

As if reading my mind, Darren continued. 'Can you feel how strong it is? Its unwavering intensity?' Feeling the growing presence of my Energy, I nodded in confirmation.

'When you're ready, extend its warmth through your body and try to release some of it through your fingertips by imagining its light shimmering out.' I shifted in my seat. 'You don't have to worry about depleting your Energy while on Earth – its source is infinite while we're here and will refuel as soon as you release it into the world,' explained Darren, pre-empting my worry.

As directed, I concentrated on my Energy, feeling it vibrate through my body and out of my hands. Its warmth made me wonder how I had ever lived without it.

'Now, can you also feel a pulling sensation within the centre of your Base Energy keeping you anchored here?' he guided me. I explored the incredible sensation of the Energy within me, immediately finding the feeling he described, grounding me to the surface below me.

'I found it,' I choked out in proud satisfaction, exploring the unbreakable thread between my Energy and this world, constantly keeping me bounded.

'Good. That's your Lifeline – whenever you're in the Helix, you can use it to teleport yourself back to where you originally travelled from on Earth. The deeper you are in the Helix, the more Energy you'll need to get you back, unlike the Gates, which don't require any additional Energy to cross through.'

'When we decide you are ready, we will try and prompt the Defacer to summon you from this room. Holding onto you as Strat did, in theory, we will be teleported together even though our lack of Lifeline grounding in Pamatan means we will land in slightly different locations. Strat reckons he was only a few yards from where you landed in Pamatan, which is reassuring. Just in case there are multiple Defacers, you will need to be able to defend yourself until I catch up. As soon as you see me and I know which Defacer is summoning you, you'll immediately use your Lifeline to return to safety,' explained Darren.

'Okay,' I obliged, knowing the plan wasn't up for debate.

'Good. Today, I want you to focus on associating the grounding feeling of your Lifeline within this room, this surface, this Level.'

I nodded, now understanding the coldness of the room: it was to keep us alert. Using the continuous and constant sound of crashing waves, playing on repeat, I used to dictate the rhythm of my breath. I refocused on the sound of the crashing waves every time my mind started to waver.

'That's it,' encouraged Darren. 'I want you to remember every sensation you feel: every sound, every inhalation and exhalation, and the feeling that brings you.'

Trying to stay focused, it was incredible how busy my mind was. I tried my best to banish my thoughts as they appeared, using the rhythm of my breath to guide me back to the present moment. Darren slowly pulled his hands out from under mine. I let myself breathe out in sweet release, the connection broken.

'That's enough,' Darren declared. Taking the cue, I threw my eyes open.

Standing up, he pulled me up, and we exited the Grounding Room. I soon realised I had no idea how long we'd been meditating, but the pit in my stomach told me it had been a couple of hours.

‘You did well,’ encouraged Darren. ‘It’ll become easier with practice,’ he said, seeing the effort on my face as we put our shoes back on. ‘This grounding exercise will allow you to use your Lifeline more easily when in the Helix,’ he explained as we walked the first few steps of the staircase.

‘Darren!’ a woman called out from behind us in a kind but assertive tone. Freezing on the spot, Darren snapped his head back, looking at the woman and then at me, standing behind him.

‘Go grab breakfast in the manor. I’ll find you later,’ Darren commanded, his voice full of urgency.

‘Darren!’ called the woman, closer this time. Ignoring her, he held my gaze so I wouldn’t look in her direction.

‘Go now,’ he urged as he ushered me past him and up the stairs. Taking each step at a time, I could feel his eyes watching my back, ensuring I was on my way out.

Prolonging my exit, I heard him walking back down the stairs toward the woman. Reaching the final few steps, I took the opportunity to steal a glance before leaving. Directing my gaze downwards, I looked past Darren to find her eyes fixated on me. Dropping her jaw, I could see the colour in her face begin to drain as horror crossed her face. Noticing her reaction, Darren started to turn in my direction, only for me to sprint out of sight up the second flight of stairs.

Reaching the top of the stairs, I stood by the lockers, trying not to draw any attention to myself as a few Elans hurried out of the changing rooms, probably running late to the classes starting all around me. Pausing, I listened carefully, trying to eavesdrop on Darren's conversation, but heard nothing. They must have gone into one of the rooms.

Giving up, I started making my way back to the manor. Keeping my eyes cast, I made my way to the shuttle and crossed the garden between the stable and manor until I was inside. My mind was still buzzing as I asked myself how she knew me.

Chapter 10

Starved from my first training session with Darren, I followed the smell of breakfast, leading me back to the dining hall where we had eaten the previous night. Most tables were empty by now – I was lucky I had made it to last call. To my relief, I found Strat sitting by himself. He was munching away, and I couldn't help the automatic smile spreading across my face as I saw him. I rushed to fill my tray with food before sitting opposite him. Looking up at me as I took a seat, he flashed me one of his dazzling smiles.

'Hi,' I greeted him timidly.

'Hey, yourself,' he replied warmly. He studied me for a moment. 'How was this morning?' He lifted his eyebrows to match the curiosity in his voice.

'Hard,' I replied honestly, dropping the weight of my head into my hand. 'But something weird did happen as we were leaving,' I whispered conspiratorially, edging closer. 'This woman started calling for Darren, and he immediately panicked. You should have seen how he rushed to get away.

He borderline pushed me up the stairs. And that wasn't the weirdest part. When I finally managed to get a glimpse at her, she looked equally as freaked out. Honestly, it was like she'd seen a ghost.'

'Hum? What did she look like?' he asked, intrigued.

'Tall, slim, probably in her late forties. She had light brown skin and a messy black bob,' I answered, realising we were, once again, leaning towards each other.

Amused by my childish stance, Strat had imitated my pose with his opposite elbow so that our faces would only be inches apart. Comfortable with his proximity, I could feel the softness of his breath and the intoxicating muskiness of his scent. Staring into my eyes, I could see a teasing smile making its way to his lips.

'Why do I get the impression that weirdness follows you?' he mused, and the shine in his eyes made me smile back. I let myself lean in ever-so-slightly, losing myself in the emerald green of his eyes.

'You have such beautiful grey eyes,' he complimented as though reading my mind. Lifting his free arm towards my face, he paused hesitantly before delicately caressing the small area above my ear, tucking my hair behind my ear. Completely immersed in our own little world, I could have stayed like that forever if it wasn't for the relentless pinging of incoming text messages vibrating in my pocket.

'You should get that. It sounds like someone is desperate to get hold of you,' suggested Strat as he leaned back.

Reluctant to move, I pulled out my phone. Flicking through my messages, I saw three new texts from Neer, on top of the two from last night. Instantly feeling guilty for forgetting to message him back, I decided only to read the ones from today:

'Hey, how is the "competition centre"?'

'I just wanted to check something hasn't killed you yet?'

'Hellooooo? Should I call the police yet?'

I cursed myself under my breath for not answering his messages earlier. He had likely worried about me, and I had utterly neglected him. I sent him a quick reply:

'Sorry! All's good. Darren's been training me all morning, pre-breakfast! I'm expecting the rest of the day to be the same. Speak to you later. Thanks for checking up on me.'

I pressed send. More than ready to pick up where I'd left off with Strat, I started putting my phone away when it pinged again.

'You're popular,' teased Strat.

'It's probably Neer again,' I replied to his unasked question, trying not to make it a big deal. This news didn't seem to please him as his teasing smile quickly disappeared behind an accentuated frown. Unconsciously crossing his arms across his chest, he seemed to deliberate his next move.

Leaning back across the table, he propped his elbow back onto the table. Balancing his chin on his knuckles, he moved his face closer to mine, closer than before – his sudden proximity sent my heart beating. Targeting my free hand lying on the table, he started running the tip of his fingers in a circular motion along the top of my hand, sending tingles along my whole body. 'I hope I'm not stealing you away from him?' he purred.

I blinked, my mind going blank as I stared at him dumbstruck. Trying to clear my mind, I struggled to get my brain working again. Were his lips always so desirable? Cupping the bottom of my chin, he pulled me in closer, so our noses brushed against each other. I could feel the warmth of his sweet breath against my face. My heart was pumping mercilessly, ready to burst out of my chest.

Holding me still, he repeated his question. 'Am I interrupting a blooming romance?' Waiting attentively for my response, he held my gaze as I scrambled my brain, only to choke out one syllable.

'No,' I breathed, although the thought of Neer and I as a couple would have usually sent me into hysterical laughter. Neer wasn't even sure he'd ever be interested in anyone that way, but I wouldn't tell Strat that just yet – I was enjoying this too much.

A victorious smile began to spread across his lips, but he didn't move away. 'Is there anyone else I should be concerned about?' he asked with faux innocence, his warm breath brushing against my lips.

'Nope, I'm single … available …' I muttered clumsily, unable to stop myself from leaning closer.

Revealing a perfect set of teeth, he released me as he leaned back into his chair. 'Good, because I may never give you back,' he threatened with a wicked shine in his eyes, melting my heart like butter.

He picked up my tray and stood up to leave the table. Looking around, I saw we were the last ones in the dining hall. I was about to follow him when my phone started to vibrate again. It was Darren calling.

I picked up. 'Hello?'

'Where are you?' Darren asked, anxiety bleeding through his tone.

'In the dining hall. Why?'

'I sent you a text message to meet me in the Grounding Room ten minutes ago.' Darren sighed loudly before muttering, 'I should know better by now than to text you.'

'I'm on my way,' I exclaimed, getting to my feet and sprinting past Strat, hoping I could get there before Darren became too irritated.

'Where are you going?' called Strat behind me, his voice suddenly pitched.

Flashing him a rosy smile of my own, I cheekily replied, 'To console my other lovers!' and exited the dining hall.

≈

The rest of the day was much like the morning, spent in utter concentration, leaving me for dead in the evening.

'It gets easier with time,' Darren reassured once he'd decided that was enough training for the day. 'We must build a strong foundation. We can't rush it, even if I'm determined to leave this place as soon as possible.' I felt a surprising pang of sadness at the mention of leaving when we had just arrived. I still had so much to learn, and Darren wanted to take me away so soon. I wondered if it was perhaps why he had been keeping Strat at a distance. Maybe he didn't want me building any ties.

We walked silently, enjoying the night sky as we approached the manor. I headed directly towards the dining hall and wondered if Strat would be waiting for me again. I couldn't keep at bay the little sprouts of hope budding inside me, building with every step. Growing more impatient, I began to walk faster, leaving Darren to struggle behind

'Hold up a second!' Darren exclaimed, stopping me at the arch that marked the entrance to the dining hall. 'What's the big hurry?' he asked as he scanned the empty room Empty except for one. Sending a tsunami of dopamine my way, there was Strat. He was engrossed in the massive volume in his hand. Sitting in all his glory, he patiently waited for me. He must have asked the cooks if we could stay past closing time since they had removed all the chairs except two: the one he was sitting on and another directly opposite him, which I hoped was for me. If physically possible, my heart would be jumping out of my chest. Impatient to join him, I turned to face Darren, only to find his face crumpled up with displeasure. He definitely didn't want me building ties.

'I guess it's later than I expected,' he admitted as he checked his watch. He eyed Strat before turning back to me, deliberating. My stomach knotted up. With my whole being, I wished Darren wouldn't say anything to jeopardise my relationship with Strat. My heart stopped when he finally said, 'Quick dinner and off to sleep. I will see you at the same time tomorrow in the Grounding Room.'

'Yes, sir,' I replied dutifully, smiling wider than I knew possible, before dashing off towards the beautiful boy waiting for me. Gleaming, I couldn't hide the joy I felt. When I thought I couldn't be happier, I noticed the enormous plate of food carefully placed under a glass cloche, keeping it warm. I sneaked up on Strat, spooking him enough to make him drop his book on the table.

'Wow! You're happy!' he beamed.

'I'm always happy to see you!' I replied, making his smile widen.

'You're happy to see me?' he enquired, surprised.

The look in his eyes made me laugh. 'Of course, who doesn't want additional protection against evil Defacers,' I added, pretending to be serious.

'No, no, no, you said happy to see *me*, not some generic hunk. I won't allow any take-backs.' He gleamed like a young boy. His eyes lit up as I laughed, almost making me forget about the smell of food. Quickly releasing him, I pulled the lid off as I sat down, inhaling the dreamy aroma of roasted vegetables. Savagely making my way through my food like an animal after a long chase, I inhaled my meal.

'I thought for a moment all the excitement was for me, but it seems I've been able to unlock a greater source of joy,' Strat teased. 'I've been ploughing through the Academy's archives and found something that might interest you.'

He paused dramatically to see if his sweeping statement would draw a reaction from me. I remained unmoved, making Strat sigh disappointedly.

'It's about the lady gaping at you earlier,' he enticed.

'I'm listening,' I said, lifting my head.

'Her name is Dr Lily Vera. She used to run a chemistry lab about twelve years ago before it got shut down by the Committee. There is hardly any record of her work. Still, I found a document suggesting she used to experiment with plant extracts, sending patients into an induced coma while keeping their consciousness awake so they could travel deeper into the Helix. Something must have gone wrong because the whole thing was suddenly closed down. I assume the Committee thought whatever they found was too dangerous to be recorded, which would explain why there are hardly any records.'

'Why would they do that?' I asked, mortified by the Committee's actions. 'Surely they would benefit more from being transparent about the failure than hiding it?'

'I agree, but the current members of the Committee don't respond well to change, or innovation for that matter. They probably hid it out of fear it lands in our enemy's hands or because they were afraid.' Strat shrugged.

I opened my mouth to speak, only to be interrupted.

'Before you bombard me with your questions, hear out the rest,' he teased, anticipating my reaction. 'I did a little snooping with the manor's staff – most of whom have been here forever. It turns out that Darren and Dr Vera used to be quite the item.'

'No way!' I blurted out, unable to contain myself.

'Apparently, Darren's sudden disappearance from the Academy happened just after they broke up,' he finished, clearly feeling rather pleased with himself.

'Who knew I was in the presence of the next Sherlock Holmes,' I applauded, while also flattered and flustered by his close attention to my life.

'I came prepared for the drill sergeant,' he joked, causing a warm wave of gratitude.

'Although it doesn't explain why she was so appalled by my presence,' I noted.

'No, it doesn't,' said Strat contemplatively. 'I also haven't been able to find anything helping us understand how you got summoned to Pamatan or why your Energy hadn't Awakened until now…' He trailed off thoughtfully.

'But?' I enquired. There was more.

'There's no keeping anything from you, is there?' Strat sighed, making me smile.

'Nope. So, spit it out.'

'Don't get too excited. It's just a theory, but what if someone purposefully sealed your Energy?'

'Is that even possible?' I asked, bewildered by the possibility of my stifled Energy being manufactured.

'I don't know… All Elans are born with Energy, but it's only when it's Awakened that you are strong enough to transport yourself into the Helix. For most of us, it happens in our early teens, and even then, it usually takes us a few years to muster enough Energy to go beyond the first Level. You're way past the expected age; and if your Energy had just matured, it shouldn't have been possible for you to survive a trip to Pamatan.'

'Unless my Energy has been Awakened for years and had had the time to strengthen, even if it was sealed. It would explain things.'

'It's possible the serum or the Defacers' attack unsealed it,' suggested Strat.

'It's possible,' I nodded, thinking back to the veil that used to be around my orange sun and how it was set free the night I was summoned to Pamatan. 'We just need to figure out *why*?'

Running his hand through his hair in frustration, Strat exhaled a long breath. I could relate to his unsatisfied curiosity. I hardly understood how my Energy worked, let alone how my untrained Energy had strengthened in one moment, what took experienced Elans years to develop.

‘I hate not knowing!’ Strat’s voice was strained, a feeling I could easily relate to daily.

‘Now imagine what it feels like not remembering the first seven years of your life or having the faintest idea of how you ended up becoming an orphan,’ I said, trying to keep the bitterness from my voice.

His eyebrow raised before his expression softened. ‘I didn’t know. I’m sorry. It must have been difficult always wondering what had happened to you and your biological parents,’ he said kindly.

I shrugged. ‘It’s why I agreed to this quest.’

‘You’ve come looking for answers …’ he said softly.

I nodded in confirmation. It felt good to tell someone – especially Strat. I felt he understood who I was, even if I was still figuring that out.

His face lit up when he seemed to remember something. Reaching under the table, Strat searched for something.

‘In that case, you might like what I brought you,’ he said, handing me the 500-page brick he was reading earlier. ‘I’ve noticed you’ve had a few questions on your mind about the Defacers, why they want to invade Earth, etcetera.’

‘Is this the moment you finally decide to end the ridiculous cap on my questioning?’ I asked, hopeful.

‘Not a chance. I’d be a fool to put myself through that line of questioning again,’ Strat shot back teasingly. I couldn’t help but bite my lip in response. I knew he was joking, but I couldn't help but feel like I had been punched in the stomach. He seemed to notice my upset.

'But! Courtesy of our brilliant Scientists and spy network of archers, this book should answer most of your questions,' he said, tapping the book cover.

I fixed my gaze on the volume in his hands. Would this beautiful book finally be the source of all knowledge, ending my cluelessness?

'Our history is long and convoluted, and I wouldn't be able to do it justice,' added Strat, his tone soft and apologetic. I finally looked up to meet his gaze. I knew my eyes had brimmed with tears, overwhelmed by his thoughtfulness. My mouth went dry as I tried to find a way to express the warmth that flowed through me. Seeming to understand, he tenderly placed his hand over mine as he handed me the book, sending chills coursing through my body in response. It was incredible how safe he could make me feel, even at my most exposed.

Opening up to someone else was still new, but my greatest struggle was acknowledging the sadness I had masked for so long. I had never dared voice any of it, not even to Neer. The sense of belonging I had craved so profoundly. The pit in my stomach would not leave me during those long sleepless nights. The guilt I imposed on myself for feeling like I wasn't grateful enough to the mother that had raised me and for the life she had provided. But now, looking into Strat's trusting eyes, I could feel my conviction deepen – I would get through this, and, like all wounds, I would eventually embrace my pain and allow myself to heal.

Gently cupping my hand, Strat guided me out of my chair and onto my feet.

'Come on, let me show you something.'

Chapter 11

Following the lead of his steady hand, I let Strat guide me through the multiple hallways as I marvelled at the manor's grandeur. Wanting the night to last forever, I interlaced my fingers in his, feeling the calluses on his hand as we made our way to the basement. Dead quiet, I couldn't help but feel like we were doing something prohibited by sneaking around in the lower levels of the mansion. Having walked down to the basement, Strat guided us towards a hidden spiral stone staircase, only to stop halfway between the floors in front of a large metal gate.

I let a small gasp escape, upon discovering a hidden floor, but we weren't in yet. A huge, impenetrable lock hung around the bars of the gate. I looked at Strat questioningly, but his eyes sparkled with anticipation.

'Hey, Gabe! Do you mind letting us in?' he called. The scrapping chair echoing through the tunnel suggested there was a gatekeeper. Patiently waiting, we could hear what sounded like an elderly man struggling to get up as he ambled to the entrance. Smiling broadly, there stood what I can only describe as one of the most striking older men I had ever seen. In his mid-70s, wearing a blue-striped collar shirt under a loose light grey jumper, the tall thin man held an extensive set of keys. His bright wrinkled eyes met mine, and joyful creases folded across his smooth dark face as he took in Strat.

'What are you doing here?' enquired Gabe, his voice echoing with thrilled surprise, although the answer didn't seem to matter as he opened the gate anyways.

Greeting each other in a big embrace, Strat carefully wrapped his hand around the fragility of his slender frame. Three pats on the back later, Gabe released him.

'Here, I brought you something.' chirped Strat as we walked in. He pulled a novel from his jacket, carefully placing it in Gabe's hand.

Grazing his hand over the cover, Gabe smiled. '*The Overstory*. I don't think I've read this one yet.'

'I hope not. I spent hours at the bookstore with your niece going through every book available just to discover you hadn't read one of my favourites,' Strat joked, making my heart warm in response. 'I don't know how you have the time to read so much,' Strat added, looking towards me as I gave him a quizzical look. 'After retiring as one of our most brilliant Scientists, Gabe volunteered to oversee the management of the entire kitchen gardens and guard the Weapon Room,' he explained.

'That's impressive,' I offered honestly. I had seen the grounds – it was no small task.

'It's nothing really, the plants are my friends, and I mainly come here for the peace and quiet – and yet …' He lifted his white eyebrows. 'I can never seem to be able to keep this one away.' Gabe poked Strat in the ribs, making them both laugh harmoniously together.

'I was hoping I would be able to show El the Weapons Room?' enquired Strat as we paused in front of another locked door. I loved the nickname he had given me. My stomach somersaulted every time he said it out loud.

'You know I'm not meant to let anyone but the Committee in,' warned Gabe.

'And it'll be as though we were never here,' persuaded Strat, only making Gabe chuckle as he shook his head in defeat. Raising his hand to the metal door, Gabe wrapped his hand around the biometric sensor and released his Energy through it, causing a series of clicks to unlock the door.

Pulling the heavy metal frame open to a pitch-black room, Gabe stood at the entrance. 'Ten minutes,' Gabe insisted as he pulled up a nearby stool, placing it by its entrance. Leaning with his back to the opened door, he took a seat as he watched us enter.

Strat took my hand and led the way. I stayed silent as we crossed the threshold of the darkroom. 'Stay here a minute,' he instructed, letting go of my hand as he went ahead. Guided only by a faintly lit emergency light, he made his way to the back of the room, causing the automatic lights to turn on as he passed. Every step he took lit up different areas of the room. Each shelf displayed a diverse range of weapons – knives, swords, spears and even axes. I didn't know if it was the darkness of the rectangular room or the mass of deadly weapons lined up across either side of the walls, but the orange fire in me suddenly flared up in response. I stood defensively, trying to tame my fear, holding back the burn of Energy circulating through my arms and hands.

'There's nothing to be concerned about,' soothed Strat, sensing the shift inside me. 'Well, that's not completely true. We'd be in pretty big trouble if we got caught in here. If the Committee didn't punish us, then I'm pretty certain Darren would,' he joked lightly, slightly easing my tension. 'It'll have to be our little secret.'

'I guess it will.' I blushed.

Strat grinned as he walked toward me, but there was no hesitation this time as he retook my hand, leading me deeper into the room.

'This is the Weapons Room –where every Elan gets to pick their weapon and, by default, their crystal. That's if they're ready to finalise their position. Usually, there's a whole ceremony with it, but since you can't officially be here, I figured we'd get you one now. You'll need something to defend yourself against the Defacers.'

'Does that mean I'll no longer need to wear the purple I'm-a-confused-teenager Tetresia crystal?' I beamed, thrilled at the prospect of getting closer to discovering how I might fit in this world.

'I promised you I'd get your position reviewed, didn't I?' Strat confirmed, his emerald eyes glittering.

'You never cease to deliver.' I blushed deeper under his admiring gaze. We'd stopped in front of a large poster titled Mastering Our Weapon hung on the back wall of the room. Showing a series of steps, the sign visually displayed the forging of the weapons.

'All of our weapons are made from a rare alloy made to resist the corrosion of the Defacer poison we lace them with – it's why we can't have any modern weaponry. The serum either dissolves them or causes all sorts of glitches to high-tech devices, making them useless. Plus, we'd rather have the poison's warning signal ward off nearby Defacers than fighting each other constantly.'

'But wouldn't you rather kill them?' I asked, perplexed.

'Oh, we do! But it's not that easy!' he chuckled. 'Similar to Elans, Defacers have the same Energy system as us, only in the opposite direction. Their Lifeline connects them to Pamatan, where they can indefinitely regenerate their Energy. The further they ascend from Pamatan, the more Energy they need to burn to travel to the next Level. By the time they get to Level One, they're usually weak enough that we can stop them from crossing into Earth, but occasionally a few get through. It doesn't help that they have their own version of our crystals.'

I nodded, remembering he had mentioned they had the marron, or Marcax crystal.

'It not only makes the Defacers stronger than us but also fuels them with rage. While we work smarter by focusing on nurturing individual strengths through the various positions, it doesn't make the thought of a bunch of Energy-thirsty Defacers less terrifying.' Strat paused, his expression woeful, before voicing his thoughts.

'Honestly, sometimes I wonder why the Defacers even bother. I understand they have this insatiable thirst, relentlessly driving them to pursue more Energy, but it seems to be never-ending. Having more just never seems to cut it. They seem to live in a constant state of dissatisfaction. If they weren't killing and trying to cross into Earth to quench their thirst, I'd almost feel sorry for them.'

Somehow, despite the threatening environment and being on high alert, his expression kept my panic at bay. I didn't think I could ever get used to his charisma, even if it was reserved. He had humanised the Defacers in a way I didn't think I ever could.

Encouraged by my apparent interest, Strat pushed on. 'Until now, we've always been able to fend off the Defacers, which is why it's so concerning that they've managed to find a way of summoning you. It means they've found another advantage against us. Besides the protective shield around the Academy, we cannot stop them from doing it again.'

His face grew grave, and his voice full of warning. 'Never underestimate a Defacer, no matter how weak it looks.' His gaze fell to the bare floor, lost in thought. A shadow of sadness fell across his face before he redirected a fierce look at me. 'Trust me when I tell you there are no limits to how far they'll go to feed on more Energy.'

Sensing the tension, I watched him as he shook his head slightly as though trying to expel a dark memory. Checking we were out of Gabe's earshot, he turned back towards me and squeezed the sides of my arms. 'Which is why it's so incredible that you've survived,' he said, bravely, although his smile didn't yet reach his disturbed eyes.

'Thanks to you,' I replied quietly.

Following his lead, we returned to the front of the room. Once there, we stopped in front of a collection of large framed headshots, each with their own ornate and descriptive plaque. I looked on with curiosity, only to stop dead at a photo of Darren. A cold thrill ran through my body as I tried to push down the nagging feeling taking me back to the barren black volcanic land of my dreams. It was a young, unscarred version of him with a full set of hair, but there was no mistaking him. His plaque read:

Darren Rose

1968 – Living

Travelled to: Pamatan

Next to him was a photo of a beautiful young woman: projecting a strong sense of authority, she held her head high. Her thick brown hair was perfectly combed back into a stylish high ponytail, revealing an oval face still containing traces of childish rounders. Her pearl skin was radiant, creating a striking contrast with her dark eyebrows, but what drew me the most was the familiarity of her piercing grey eyes: intelligent, daring and determined.

She was a leader, a woman to be followed, a general you would want to fight for no matter the cost. She didn't need anything to distinguish her. She stood out on her own. Dressed in a red uniform, she was wearing a delicate gold chain holding the Elan symbol of the sunset.

'The resemblance is staggering, isn't it? You would think they were twins,' offered Gabe upon entering, confirming that she was Darren's sister. Under her name was written:

Amelia Rose

1972 – 2001

Travelled to: Level Five

'It really is,' I mustered, facing Gabe, hoping he would reveal more.

Strat glanced encouragingly at Gabe, who cleared his throat before proceeding. 'They were inseparable. Despite being the younger sibling, Amelia led, and Darren followed her with blind loyalty, but then again, she seemed to have that effect on everyone. She was compassionate, fearless and relentless in her pursuit of exploring the deeper Levels we knew almost nothing about. Experimenting with consciousness, they were always pushing each other's boundaries to see how far they could go, playing with death until it finally caught up with her.' He trailed off sadly.

'What happened?' I asked.

'One day they went too far…' Gabe continued, his voice mournful. 'They were on yet another scouting trip in Level Five, searching for the last Gate that would lead them to Pamatan, when they got lucky … or so they thought … '

'There it stood, the last Gate that would lead them to Pamatan – a world that no Elan had ever had the strength or genius to find, let alone explore. Completely unguarded, Darren tried to convince his sister that they should return to replenish their Energy and cross tomorrow since they knew the location of the Gates, but the temptation was simply too strong. Amelia had longed to see what was on the other side her whole life and wouldn't wait any longer.

'Dismissive of the risk involved, she convinced her brother that this was their chance to make history. Before he could argue, she had crossed into Pamatan. Unable to abandon his sister, Darren followed her, knowing that he was coming close to total burnout, only to find his sister captured on the other side ...'

Falling silent, Gabe looked down at the floor before lifting his pressed fists to his lip.

Strat picked up where he'd left off. 'Although he was frail, he tried to fight the Defacers that had his sister, but it was no use – he was outnumbered. Not giving up, Darren eventually collapsed into unconsciousness after a Defacer injured him, leaving him with the scar on his face today.'

Like a perfectly rehearsed duet, Gabe, who had recovered himself somewhat, finished the story.

'His Lifeline teleported him back to Earth, but he was so weak that his Energy had burnt out completely – he had hit the bottom of his well of Energy. We didn't know if he would survive. In many ways, he didn't. I don't believe Darren has ever recovered from that day. He would go on to isolate himself and suffer his loss in solitude. We tried to help him, but it was no use: he blamed himself for her death.'

Taking a deep breath, Gabe proceeded. 'After weeks of recovery, Darren eventually quit the Committee. Although he remained a teacher at the Academy, he spent most of his time locked away, working on secret projects until he eventually left.'

I looked sadly up at the photo of Darren, knowing he would never be the same carefree, happy man pictured. He had suffered, and the pain had changed him.

'We hadn't seen or heard from him for a decade, that is, until this week,' finished Gabe. Deep in thought, he said nothing more as he went to sit back in his chair.

Strat jumped in, his voice full of gratitude, naturally lifting the room's mood. 'I was lucky enough to have Darren as my coach at the Academy for a while. I remember the day he told me he was leaving. I felt so mad that he was abandoning me, I burst into tears, begging him not to go.' He let out a harsh chuckle, remembering the day. 'Darren told me he had no other choice, that he didn't belong in the Academy anymore. He said he wouldn't go far and told me I could visit whenever I wanted, and I did. In the beginning, Ms Roberts drove me, and eventually, I was old enough to get a bike and travel myself,' explained Strat.

Strat's green eyes lit up as he lightly stroked the side of my face with the tips of his fingers, letting them rest on my chin. Holding my gaze, he looked down at me as though I was the most special girl in the world. 'Darren helped me through a difficult part of my life, and yet it's nothing compared to what I have to thank him for now ...'

Mesmerised by the glimmer in his eyes, I responded unthinkingly as my mouth parted to let out a curious, 'Oh?'

'Without him, I would have never walked through that forest path … I would have never met you, and for that, I will always be eternally grateful to him,' he affirmed.

Sending my heart into long and deep palpitations, my chest ached. I knew this to be the moment Strat had locked and sealed his grip around my heart.

Interrupted by Gabe's light cough, we could both pick up on the chuckle he was trying so hard to conceal. We tore our gazes away from each other, not realising Gabe would still be able to hear us, smiling shyly as we turned to face the photographs. Strat ran his hand over Amelia's plaque. 'The plaques only record the Levels you've travelled to and returned from, which makes Darren the only Elan to have traversed the entire Helix and lived.'

'Wow,' I responded, amazed, although I wondered how many Elans had died attempting to go to deeper Levels in the quest to keep Earth safe.

'What type of threat do the Defacers create when they cross to Earth?' I finally asked, feeling somewhat silly for not asking such an obvious question earlier.

'Do you remember how I told you Defacers crave more Energy?' he asked and I nodded back.

'They will go after any living thing, anything that has Energy. Unfortunately, humans tend to be their number one target because the dimension of their vibrations and their position within the ecosystem make them excellent Energy vessels.' An involuntarily shiver went down my spine at the thought of Defacers targeting humans like Mum and Neer.

'Exactly,' agreed Strat in response to my shiver, 'which is why we need to get you a weapon!' He threw his arms expressively towards the endless range of weapons displayed in anticipation.

'Finally, I get a crystal, a weapon and a role,' I exclaimed enthusiastically, knowing the weapon and the crystal came as one, and the crystal would determine my position.

'The triple combo,' Strat chuckled.

'How do we do this? Do I just pick a weapon at random?' I was keen to get started as soon as possible. Just the mere presence of Defacer poison made my skin crawl.

'No, no!' objected Strat, who was sharing his mischievous smile with Gabe. 'As I said before, we'd usually have a formal ceremony, but this will have to do for now.' He walked behind me, taking a thick red ribbon out of his pocket.

'Do you just carry that around with you?' I teased, to which he shushed in response.

'Close your eyes and just listen.' He gently placed the ribbon over me and tied the knot in the back of my head. He delicately brushed the loose strands of my ponytail aside, and my pulse quickened in response to his touch. Softly placing his hands on the side of my shoulders, he lowered to brush his soft lips against my ear. 'Let the blade choose you,' he spoke in a seductive voice.

I had just begun to relax into his embrace when he suddenly spun me around like a madman. I could hear Gabe chuckling in the corner as Strat released me to fend for myself in total disorientation. It had served its purpose. I couldn't tell which way was up.

'Strat?' I asked, agitated by the thought of being left on my own in this place, but there was no answer. The room was silent, insulated from all sound. I could crash into a deadly weapon, and no one would hear.

'Just listen,' he had said. Desperate to get out, I tried to embrace the feeling of danger, letting my mind run with it to see where it took me. Shuffling my feet, I extended my arms in front of me as I walked forwards until I felt a wall.

Abruptly stopping, I patted my hand carefully around the wall before pulling my hand quickly back. I was at one of the weapon displays. Reluctantly extending my finger, I touched the hilt of one of the weapons, only to recoil back from the sting.

'Ow! Not that one,' I spoke to myself as I extended my arm again along the wall, tuning into my inner voice. Careful not to touch any more weapons, I tried to listen. I couldn't hear anything at first, but then I heard something. Paying close attention, I could hear a faint vibration from the crystal within every knife, sword, and other killing item displayed.

Taking my time, I placed my hand over the different weapons, listening to their different tunes. For some, it was a tolerable buzzing. For others, a loud siren like those of an ambulance, each equally uncomfortable. Until now, I had felt nothing but tightness in my stomach, my orange fire throbbing, prepared for battle. I continued like that for what felt like an age, going around in circles until I felt something different. Stopping abruptly, I heard the calming sound of wind blowing through trees.

Raising my hand, I hovered it before me, trying to identify the source. Transforming from a gentle breeze into a howling wind, its vibration grew louder the closer I approached it, as though guiding me to it. With my hand still outstretched, I stopped in front of one weapon in particular. The Energy was fiercely strong, yet I didn't feel in physical danger as I had with every other weapon. The weapon once again made a calm, soothing sound, putting me at ease.

This weapon felt right. It was the one I would use. I was sure of it. Asserting my decision, I reached for the item and pulled it out of the display. Expecting the touch of cold metal, I was surprised by the smoothness of the handle. It was short, T-shaped, with a slim neck. Pushing my knuckles forwards, protruding through my fingers, I wrapped my hand around the handle in a clenched fist motion, feeling the inscriptions pressing into my palm.

Impatient to get out of the room, I yanked my weapon out of its socket, almost knocking myself to the ground, as I released the surprisingly light object. Not taking the time to look at it, I rushed to pull off my eye fold as I exited the room, letting the metal door shut behind me. Relief spread through me as soon as I walked out. Letting out a long exhale, I tried to shake off the lingering, venomous threat. I was safe again. Taking another deep breath, I could feel Strat's impatient stare.

'What did you pick!?' he exclaimed eagerly, bobbing up and down as he tried to contain his childish excitement. Quickly matching his enthusiasm, I swung my arm forwards uncontrollably, still not used to the blade's lightness. Giggling, I finally put the short knife in front of us. Untangling my grip, I carefully laid the knife across both of my palms so that we could have a clear view.

It was beautiful, although I felt weird thinking of a lethal weapon's beauty. It was elegant, delicate and cutthroat. The sharp, double-edged blade was made from a single maroon stone. Momentarily responding to the touch of my hand, the 20-inch-long weapon faintly glowed in response. The bone handle featured a skull-themed design, painstakingly etched in fine detail. Strat's eyes ran along the body of the dagger. All his previous childish excitement disappeared behind his increasingly furrowed brow.

'What's wrong?' I asked, my body stiffening to the sudden change in mood. Locking his eyes with mine, I guessed he was making the decision right then whether or not to tell me the truth. Breathing out harshly, he raked his hand through his hair in deliberation. 'It's Marcax,' he stated, agitated.

Looking more critically at my weapon, I saw what Strat was saying. Having seen countless Elan weapons, I knew they had all been forged with the same pattern surrounding a small crystal in the hilt, whilst my dagger was one bold crystal, possessing none of the traditional refinement. Yet, when I looked at my knife, it felt right.

Continuing to watch Strat quizzically, I tried to steady my breath as I ran my hand along the handle when I felt an inscription. Looking more carefully, I noticed something written. 'Ultima mors est,' I read aloud, reluctant.

Freezing in his spot, I heard him murmur under his breath, 'Death is Final,' as though remembering a deeply buried memory.

Snatching the blade from my hand, Strat pulled it closer to his face as he examined it, breathing out, 'Samalas,' before tossing it back into my hands, repulsed by its touch.

'What is it?' I asked, perturbed by his uncharacteristic harshness as I softly placed my hand on his back.

I could see the struggle on his reddening face as he tried to reconcile emotion with logic. Tension hung in the air as I waited. For the first time in a long time, I felt uncertain around Strat. I could feel my heart beating louder than ever before, pressing itself against my chest, preparing to be torn apart.

Chapter 12

'Strat! Strat!' I called out to the boy as I struggled to keep up with him. He'd taken off after examining my new weapon, storming out of the manor's basement without a word of warning or explanation. Unable to get him to stop, I practically had to run beside him, asking my previously ignored question.

'What's wrong?'

'Put that thing away. You can't let anyone see it, especially not the Committee. They'll strip us both of our Energy,' he snapped.

Tucking my dagger away in its sheath and inside my kimono, I had to run to catch up with him again, jogging by his side.

'Speak to me,' I pleaded more forcefully this time.

Ignoring me, he started taking longer strides. Grabbing his arm, pulled him to a halt. 'What's going on?' I demanded.

Staring intensely at my grip around his arm, Strat breathed out heavy and fast. I gently let go of his arm, like you would if you had accidentally touched a wild animal after it had snapped its teeth at you, only to have his piercing green eyes plunge into mine. They held no love or admiration. This was not the Strat I knew.

'I could ask you the same! Who are you? Did He send you?' he lashed out at me, his eyes dark and full of hatred.

Completely taken aback by the venom in his voice, I subconsciously took a small step backwards. 'What are you accusing me of?' I barked back, unable to contain the hurt in my voice.

'Out of all the weapons, you've picked the only one that doesn't belong to us,' he replied with murderous hostility.

Crushing me like a thousand stabbing blades, I quickly understood that the 'us' he mentioned didn't include me. The feeling only worsened with the sensation of acknowledgement sweeping through me, my gut confirming his suspicions. I wasn't like the rest of them. I was once again the odd one out, and I didn't even know why. Doing my best to cast aside the familiar crushing feeling rapidly building inside my chest, I asked the only thing I could think of to help me get some answers.

'Whose is it, then?' I asked reluctantly.

'The Defacers, of course,' he snapped back, pushing his eyebrows further together before marching ahead.

I couldn't believe he was behaving this way. What did he think was going on? Rushing to follow him, I thought of what could have happened. I knew it had to be because of the dagger I had picked, but how was I to know which blade would choose me? Halting to a stop, I looked around to see that we had arrived at the bottom of the stairs, leading to Strat's studio.

'Out of loyalty to Darren, you can continue to stay here until your business is done. You hurt anyone, and I won't hesitate to go straight to the Committee.' A threat.

Before I could begin to process what he'd just said, he turned to leave without a hint of hesitation. As he did, I thought I heard him mutter, 'I'm starting to understand why Darren's been keeping you secret.'

'Wait!' I pleaded, relieved when he stopped. I waited to see if he would turn around to face me, but he remained still with his back.

'I don't know what you think is going on, but I'm completely clueless here. Just a few days ago, I was just a girl whose greatest problem was getting through her A-Levels and in an unbelievably short space of time, I found out about Elans, the Helix, Defacers trying to kill me, and that my whole life has basically been one huge lie. Despite it all, I've been able to deal with it.' I paused, trying to stabilise my trembling voice as I gathered my courage. 'And part of the reason I've been able to stay brave is you.' I could feel my throat tighten as I struggled to keep my emotions under control. 'Whatever you think is going on, let's figure it out together! I promised I wouldn't run, and I meant it.'

I watched with anticipation, completely vulnerable, hoping he would afford me the same trust I had in him. He stood still, his head tilted sideways as if tempted to look at me. I could see his eyes – they looked haunted with some dark, unfathomable emotion. Turning to glance at me, my heart soar before he shook his head and walked away.

I wanted to cry, scream, implode and bury myself. A fiery rage leapt to life within me as my orange Energy exploded through my veins. I wanted to destroy something, anything. Racing up the stairs into the studio attic, I bit my lip. He had hurt me. I hadn't realised the moisture in my eyes had brimmed over. I quickly rubbed my hand across my cheek and grabbed my dagger from its sheath.

I impatiently waited for it to light up to my touch like it was meant to, knowing I needed to channel my growing rage, but nothing. I knew it was possible. All the other Elans' crystals lit up in their weapon when they directed their Energy. It was how they activated its benefits. Squeezing it tighter through my whitening knuckles, I closed my eyes, determined to get the maroon blade to light up. When I opened them, there was still no light, and I could no longer stop the tears rolling down my cheek.

Giving up, I fought to resist the crushing feeling in my chest, managing only short, sharp breaths as I started practising solo Krav-Maga drills. Pushing myself to exhaustion, I tried to clear my mind of the relentless, repetitive flashbacks of my fight with Strat.

I trained hard, trying new combinations, including a straight punch with the knife and an upper-cut targeting under the rib cage and into the gut. Playing with my flow, my Base Energy and body weight, I worked through my pain as I delivered moves with savage power. Slashing the air with my pale knife, I continued experimenting with the angles until I couldn't breathe anymore.

Panting loud and heavy, I fell to the ground in exhaustion, watching my opaque weapon as I released it. My body hurt, feeling broken beneath me. Getting up, I got into the shower, letting the hot water pour over my hair and aching muscles, trying to rid myself of the day's worries.

'It'll be okay,' I muttered repeatedly as I let my tears flow. 'Everything will be better tomorrow,' I tried to convince myself even though I longed to run after Strat. I wanted to clarify things and go back to how things were before I picked the bloody dagger. Impatient and frustrated, I didn't dry my hair and went straight into bed.

I took deep breaths, trying to connect with my Energy, but whenever I tried to focus on the chatter, my mind returned. Forfeiting, I wished I knew why Strat had whispered Samalas' name when he saw the inscription on my dagger. Did it have any reference to my past? Ordering myself to stop thinking, I reminded myself there was nothing more I could do today. Tomorrow I'd speak to Strat and find out about Samalas, but right now, I needed sleep.

Chapter 13

'It's okay, baby. It'll be okay. I promise,' she said with a trembling voice. We were sitting on the ground, and I was lying across her crossed legs with my feet touching the chilled ground. Covering my eyes, I couldn't see her face. Caressing the top of my forehead, she repeated the soothing motion rocking me side to side. We stayed like that for a while. I relaxed my head on her shaking body as she tried to contain her sobs. I wanted to say something but simply squeezed her forearm, only to have her repeat softly, 'It'll be okay,' over and over again. Rubbing the back of her hand across my forehead, she wiped the tears rolling down her cheeks. 'We'll make it out of here,' she promised.

I woke up in a panic.

My heart was pounding, and I could feel a weight crushing my chest as though a tonne of bricks rested on top of me. Unable to catch my breath, re-living the total despair I felt that day, I could only manage short, sharp inhales. I desperately tried to cling to the memory of my dream, but I couldn't seem to remember anything. There was total darkness, leaving me to deal only with the antagonising aftermath as I struggled to pull air into the crushing hollow where my lungs should be. Sweat formed rivulets along my brow, tickling past my ears and down my neck, disappearing into my cleavage.

All I could hear was the pounding in my ears as my vision blurred. I'd seen Neer have a panic attack before. I recognised the signs as I tried to run through his exercise to calm my mind. Holding onto my consciousness, I looked around me, trying to name three colours around me. I could see the camel leather sofa by the fireplace, my blue kimono on top, and the deep chocolate bedsheets covering me. Next, I named two objects: the bedside table beside me and a photo frame hidden behind the lamp. I hadn't noticed the photo before. It showed Strat as a young boy, laughing while holding onto the hip of a shorter boy who looked a couple of years younger. They had the same chestnut hair and nose crinkle when they laughed. There was no doubt they were brothers. Occupying my thoughts, my breath slowed, wondering why Strat had never mentioned his sibling. Closing my eyes, smelling the humidity of the morning dew, I completed the final step of my exercise through scent, already feeling calmer, more connected to my body.

Slowly reopening my eyes, I deepened my breath to oxygenate my brain, helping get rid of the black spots that had crept into my vision. For now, all I had to do was clear my mind and find stillness. After a few minutes of mindful breaths with my eyes closed, I felt slightly recomposed. Trembling from the dampness creeping into my clothes, I got up even though my alarm hadn't rung. I wouldn't be able to sleep anymore anyway.

Rushing to the bathroom, I was almost surprised by my face. Other than the normal redness, I remained utterly unchanged. I stared at myself, looking for a sign in my rose-beige skin, something and anything to reflect the turmoil and growth happening inside, but to no avail.

It's just a dream, I reminded myself again, but I knew that was a lie. I'd been having flashbacks of my childhood since the unsealing of my Energy. Strat had been right, someone had wanted me to forget who I was, and I was going to find out who it was and why. Dressing in my navy kimono, I took out my newly acquired dagger from the inner pocket, watching it glimmer in the bathroom light. Tying my hair in a high ponytail, I looked at myself in the mirror one last time before grabbing the dagger and placing it in my inner pocket; after all, it was now rightfully mine. I threw my phone and the book Strat had gotten me into my backpack and headed down for breakfast.

Walking down towards the dining hall, I straightened myself in preparation. I doubted Strat would be waiting for me after last night. The worst part was that, even though I was sure he wouldn't be there, I still hoped. I couldn't keep my eyes from sweeping the place looking for him, feeling a pang of disappointment as I realised he wasn't there. I moved through the hall alone, feeling small. I couldn't believe he had questioned my integrity. His rejection stung. I had never liked anyone before. I'd had short-lived crushes, but nothing compared to the chemistry I had felt with Strat.

He seemed so at ease, finding the perfect balance between his carefree boyish charm and seductive masculinity. His dazzling smile could lift my spirits, the same way a single look from his piercing emerald eyes could awaken every part of my body. Just thinking of him made my heart ache, and I couldn't help the gloom that engulfed me as I realised I didn't know how long I would have to wait before I saw him again.

Grabbing my breakfast, I sat at one of the corner tables in the dining hall. It was still early, so most seats were still empty. I sat down at a table and opened the book Strat had given me. I flipped straight to the back to look through the index, and bingo, there it was: Samalas. There was a whole chapter dedicated specifically to him. I turned to the indicated page and saw a drawing of a young man. There he stood, Samalas, above a terrified Elan who had fallen to the ground. He wore a seamless black suit with a stiff collar and a deadly grin. Pumping his fist in victory with one hand and holding a sword with the same maroon blade as mine, he looked poised to plunge it through the Elan's heart.

Sending shivers through my spine, I became painfully aware of the Defacer's Marcax dagger pressed against my chest. Frantically scanning through the pages, I tried to understand Strat's accusations. He had implied a connection between Samalas and me. I moved restlessly in my chair, the fire in me roaring in response. Why couldn't I have picked a weapon made for Elans?

Barely able to focus, I skimmed through the pages, picking up critical pieces of information along the way, when a paragraph caught my eye:

'Ridding himself of all contenders to the throne, Samalas has proved himself to be ruthless and tactical in his rise to power. Demonstrating fearless strength coupled with an unprecedented ability to organise the Defacers effectively, Samalas was the first to assemble a united Defacer army. It is believed that his creation of the Marcax crystal blades and the crystal's ability to provide magnified strength first secured his position.

Limiting its production to seven blades, Samalas would offer the blades to a select six, a small but influential group of Defacers, to act as his disciples. He would organise a coup with his disciples, dethroning Chief Tambora. Claiming the position for himself, his reign marked the start of the Elan Defence strategy.

Although it has not been confirmed, it is suspected that Samalas' command over his army has allowed him to retain his position for over two decades. If not the most powerful Defacer, Samalas is arguably the most feared Defacer that has ever existed.'

The words 'most feared' resonated in my head, sending my heart pumping hard enough to punch a hole through my cheat as I laid my hand over my dagger. It suddenly felt like a heavyweight. I looked back at the book, only to jump when I looked at the drawing below the text – Samalas was surrounded by his immediate council, all holding glowing weapons with the same maroon blade and bone-white handle as mine. The front of their faces was stained with black masks, their eyes still bright, reflecting lingering tints of purple. The blood drained from my face in realisation. They had just killed and fed off an Elan's Energy.

I slammed the book shut. My hand wiped over the inscription on the back:

'For the countless Elans killed in pursuit of the knowledge found in this book.'

Feeling a shiver roll down my spine, I rose from my seat. I couldn't deal with anything more. It was all too much.

Dropping off my tray, I kept my head low and headed to the training centre to meet Darren in the Grounding Room. Trying to push aside the relentless thoughts in my head, I checked my phone. There was a text from Neer.

'Morning! How are things going?'

He must have chilled out after receiving my response yesterday, and I was happy he had – I didn't think I could cope with any additional uncertainties or changes right now without breaking down. I felt relieved as I typed my response, giving voice to my fears:

'Hey back! Things have been... intense. I'm pretty sure Darren knew me before I was adopted and has been lying to me this whole time.'

I paused for a moment, wondering whether I should or could tell him about Samalas' weapon picking me and Strat becoming distrustful of me because of it or that I was having visions of my forgotten childhood. I started to write it all, letting myself vent in a long message, before deciding to delete most of it. I didn't want to have to explain myself, especially when I was uncertain about so many things, so I simply sent him the part I had initially written up.

When I arrived at the Grounding Room, Darren was already sitting in the centre of the chilled room. He was in the same position as yesterday: cross-legged with his eyes shut in meditation. I quietly took a seat opposite him. I could feel his Energy flow through me, sensing my nervousness. Opening his eyes softly, he observed me, taking note of the bags under my eyes as he assessed my levels of distress.

'We're going to practice the alternate nostril breathing technique this morning to balance your flow of Energy. It will help relieve your anxiety and get you in a state of focused relaxation, which will prepare you for deeper meditation,' suggested Darren. I was relieved he didn't probe further and asked why I was in such a state.

'I want you to start with your right hand: curl your index and middle finger inwards and extend your thumb, ring finger and pinkie. You're going to use your ring finger and thumb to alternate between closing first your right nostril and then your left nostril, very lightly and without pressure.' Taking my hands, he helped me to place them in the correct position as I pressed my fingers lightly to my nose.

'Now, inhale through both nostrils… Lightly place your thumb to close your right nostril, and exhale lightly and evenly through your left nostril. Inhale slowly through your left nostril.'

Engrossed in the task, I found my worries starting to ebb away as my shoulders began to relax.

'Change your hand positioning, so your ring finger lightly closes the left nostril. Exhale evenly through your right nostril. Then inhale through the right nostril.'

It was surprising how uneven my breathing was as I struggled to exhale with the same intensity through both nostrils. Closing my right nostril once again with my thumb, we started a new round and continued for three more until I had evened out the imbalance of my Energy flow.

'Now allow your breath to return to its natural rhythm,' instructed Darren, satisfied with our progress. I noticed that my heart rate had lowered and how much more open my Energy felt, although thoughts of my fight with Strat lingered in the back of my mind. Not letting me dwell any longer, Darren launched straight into our next exercise.

'Today, we are going to take a more proactive approach towards using your Lifeline to travel back here,' said Darren. 'First we're going to start by focusing on tightening your connection here, and then we're going into the Helix, where you'll practice using your Lifeline to return here. Do you feel ready to do that?'

Travelling into the Helix was a big step, and we both knew it, but I needed answers, and I knew this was part of my journey. Building up my determination to succeed, I nodded with conviction. I was ready.

'Okay then,' replied Darren enthusiastically, letting his disfigured lips curve slightly. He grabbed my hand and pulled me up on my feet before opening the bag beside him. Filled with dark protective armour, Darren helped me strap on two shoulder protectors falling just above my elbows. Surprised by their lightness, they held steadily in place, creating a cross across my torso. Fastening my forearm guards, I kept quiet, feeling more and more like an imposter. I stretched my arm, testing my unaffected mobility, determined to give my best, before tightening my thigh cover, completing the final piece of my armour.

'When we're in the Helix, I need you to be quick with your focus and listen carefully to my instructions so that we spend as little time as possible there. I don't know if they can reach you in the Helix, but let's not risk the Defacers suddenly summoning you. Okay?' confirmed Darren holding my gaze, searching for reassurance that I would obey.

'Got it,' I replied, nodding my head overenthusiastically. After everything that had happened, it was nice to spend time with a familiar face. I had missed our old dynamic.

'I want to hear you say it,' said Darren like an overbearing teacher.

Rolling my eyes, I tried to hide the amusement in my voice as I parroted his instructions back to him in a robotic monotone. 'I promise I'll be focused and listen to your instructions when travelling through to the Helix.'

'Good,' Darren replied, a small smile gracing his face before he grew serious again. 'I want you to lie on the floor, palms facing down towards the ground, and close your eyes. Let the ground fully support you. Take a deep breath. Ground yourself in this room. Listen to the recording playing through this room and embed the sound of the constant crashing of the waves deep in your memories.'

Following his instructions, I took a deep inhale and exhaled. Closing my eyes, I focused my thoughts: first on the weight of my body pressing into the ground, then on the cold air making its way up my sleeves. I followed the chill as it spread through my body.

'Good – now focus on the Base Energy within you.'

It was incredible how much easier this was becoming every time I did it. Finding my orange Energy within me, I could still sense traces of the tension I was still holding onto from the latest events.

'I want you to let go of any preoccupations, past or future,' instructed Darren softly, as though reading my mind. 'Let yourself be free from those thoughts. Take a deep breath and exhale those negative thoughts through your mouth in a heavy sigh …'

I let out a steady breath from the back of my throat. I could feel the air from the depths of my belly make its way through my lungs, up to my oesophagus and finally out of my throat in one big exhale, banishing the knot I had created.

Giving myself a couple of minutes to settle in my newfound freedom, I laid still, letting my Energy flow synchronise with the rhythmic sound of the crashing waves. Warmth spread along my body, counterbalancing the chill in the room and bringing me into a deeper state of relaxation.

Darren lay next to me, clasping his hand tightly around my forearm.

'Engaging your Energy, I want you to find the source of your Base Energy – I want you to just observe the fusion within you,' he warned explicitly.

Taking a deep breath in, I returned my attention to the orange sun that seemed to rest in the centre of my body. Observing it, I looked deeper, feeling the same hypnotic sensation I had felt in the forest when all this had begun. I was utterly mesmerised by the intensity of its burning core. It was a white hot mass of Energy, an explosion the size of a golf ball creating all the Energy within me, and just like the sun's rays, I had only felt snippets of its strength. Despite my closed eyes, I could feel the amazement displayed on my face as I explored the boundaries in which the continuous explosion confined itself.

'The strength of that core is your baseline, your Base Energy Level, that is as strong as your Energy will ever be,' Darren interrupted. 'It will be important for you to familiarise yourself with its base strength to learn how to use it efficiently in battle and as you travel. It's also vital that you recognise when your Energy comes close to depletion so you can avoid burnout.' He paused. 'For us to enter the Helix, I want you to return to that core fusion within you, but this time I want you to let this fusion engulf you. Let yourself be pulled in by the repetitive nature of the pattern.'

Feeling my stomach knot and my heart pumping faster, the all-too-familiar hypnotic feeling pulled me under. It was as though I was reliving the moment before my first summoning, but this time I wouldn't lose my nerve.

Checking on the strength of my connection to the ground, I let myself ponder momentarily on the reassuring presence of my Lifeline to this world. Recognising my apprehension, Darren squeezed my arm in comfort.

'I'm with you,' he reassured.

Clenching my jaw in determination, I searched for the white hot core in the centre of my Base Energy, and before I could think about what I was doing, I let the hypnotic pattern pull me inwards.

Chapter 14

I sprung my eyes open, discovering the most enchanting view I had ever seen. Endless rolling hills lay in front of me, covered in vibrant green grass. They were home to an assortment of tall bushy trees, each providing shade from the bright sunlight shining through the cloudless blue sky. Feeling a light breeze flow through my clothes, I noticed my Base Energy depleting from the slow and steady consumption of Energy demanded to exist in the first Level of the Helix. Conscious of the sparseness of my time here, I absorbed the calm, carefree atmosphere reminiscent of my childhood summers in the English countryside.

'This is incredible,' I exclaimed, turning towards Darren standing next to me as excitement coursed through my already adrenaline-high body. I couldn't help but think of Strat, how his emerald eyes would have matched the natural harmony of the hills ahead.

'Isn't it,' Darren agreed gazing in awe at the view ahead.

'Is it always this sunny?' I asked, briefly closing my eyes, enjoying the heat from the rays. These were precious moments, especially since we weren't getting much light back home. No wonder the Elans all looked so healthy.

'Not always but it is a midnight sun. We get roughly ten consecutive 24-hour periods of sunlight, after which the sun starts to set, taking up to four days, before collapsing the Helix and remerging for another cycle. Its irregularity and the unpredictability remind us of its danger, daring not even the Defacers to wander through its Levels during sunset.'

Looking up ahead, I took a moment to absorb it all, wondering how much longer this world ahead would exist. Further down the hills, a group of Elans ran into a forested area surrounding the gliding stream.

'What are they doing?' I asked, pointing below the hill.

Darren looked in the direction of my hand. 'The descending Gate to the next Level must be down there.' Feeling a stiffness, I knew this meant that the Defacers could be passing through that Gate at any moment. Just as it was our entrance to their world, it was their route to ours.

'Come on,' encouraged Darren, who had already walked away from the view. Turning to follow the sound of his voice just a few yards behind me, he was standing next to the final ascending Gate. Large, iron cast, it stood unsupported, defying the laws of gravity. Guarded by a group of experienced Elans, they stood straight, respecting the grandeur of their post. They were humanity's final line of defence; anything that passed that Gate would be unleashed into Earth.

I nodded with respect, the guards eyeing us as we walked closer to the Gate. My gaze focused on the intertwined pattern that covered its ancient gothic doors. It was the same design I had seen on the Gate in Pamatan. It must be the final descending Gate. Bursting with questions, I turned to look at Darren standing with a guard by the Gate.

I could feel my Energy amplify with my surprise, attracting the attention of one of the young guards. His eyes tore away from the distance before meeting mine. His almond eyes widened like an owl in the night, absorbing every detail before settling into a lined smile.

Trying to rein back my excitement, I closed my lips into a timid smile of acknowledgement as I walked past the boy with the large round glasses. He was dressed in light armour, featuring an amber Oliupite with three large rays. His left hand gripped his bow revealing three silver-stained fingers. I glanced at his right hand – it was unmarked, clean and smooth with clay undertones. The small glimpse into the Level Three Archer's artistic personality made me grin.

'Don't mind them,' stressed Darren, referring to the guards, tearing his dagger eyes away from the friendly boy. 'Let's be safe, come on.'

Abiding by my promise, I turned to face Darren, ready to comply with my instructions. 'Closing your eyes again, I want you to focus on identifying your Lifeline.'

Doing as he asked, I didn't need to close my eyes to find the grounding sensation linking back to the Grounding

Room in the training centre. It was hard to describe, but the connection felt so clear that the prospect of travelling back to the Grounding Room felt effortless.

'I've got it,' I replied cheerfully, surprised by the ease of the task.

'Well, let's go then,' he urged in quiet amazement, and just like that, I grabbed onto my link and pulled myself back.

≈

A smile spread across my face as tears of satisfaction filled my eyes. We were back in the Grounding Room! Sitting up, I looked across at Darren, who was still holding onto my forearm, his eyes full of pride, as we burst into animated laughter. I couldn't believe what had just happened. It was like pulling onto a rope in one sharp motion, and BOOM, we were back!

'Strat was right! Travelling felt as natural as flying is to birds!' I exclaimed in mid-hysteria. Wiping away the tears rolling down my face, I grinned. I felt alive like I never had before. I was getting closer to discovering the truth, and I knew I was on the right path.

'How have we not done this before!?' I burbled mindlessly, still high from all the excitement, and instantly regretted the words. The atmosphere turned a hot 180 degrees as Darren took my statement for criticism. I felt tension sweep through my body as Darren turned, giving me a piercing look. My heart pounded as my brain scrambled to compensate for my misgiving. We didn't talk about the past. We didn't even allude to it. I had crossed the line.

Dropping my eyes, I could still feel his gaze piercing through me. My shoulders dropped back down as soon as he released his gaze. The seconds passed as I waited, only to hear Darren sigh as he recomposed himself.

'How was that?' he asked, his voice controlled. He was giving me a chance to move past my mistake and sweep it under the carpet. It didn't matter that I suddenly felt freer than ever before or that the anchoring weight that had bound me here all these years had suddenly broken. I was, of course, dying to know the answer to my question, but this was how things were between us.

'I'm taking it you found that rather easy?' he asked with apprehension, sensing my newly found hesitation.

'Yes, very easy,' I finally replied in compliance, accepting this was how our dynamic would remain, but I wouldn't completely roll over. Not this time. I was hungry for more. I wanted to go back – I was finally getting to know myself, and I wasn't ready to stop.

So, I tried a different approach.

'I was surprised by how natural it felt,' I commented, hoping it wouldn't blow up the fuse.

'Yes …' Darren agreed pensively. He remained calm. This was okay.

'I'm ready to go again,' I told Darren, my voice resonating with determination. Examining me with contemplative eyes, I could feel him analysing my Energy. It had already regenerated itself back to its previous fiery strength. I had done what he had asked. I had obeyed him in the Helix. He couldn't deny me the chance to return, hopefully further this time. Taking a deep breath in, Darren exhaled, making his decision. 'Okay,' he said calmly, 'but you must follow my instructions.'

I nodded in agreement, eager to go back, as I laid myself back down.

Placing himself parallel to me, Darren clasped his hand on my forearm. I cleared my mind and let myself become engulfed by the hypnotic pattern of Energy in my core.

Startled by the light breeze flowing through my hair, I flinched, but this time I wasn't afraid. Looking around to get my bearings, I spotted the artistic Archer standing near the Gate, looking in my direction. He smiled as he greeted me with a tip of the head. Smiling back at him briefly, I quickly turned to face the comforting view of the open hills ahead where I could be free from observers.

Taking a moment to reconnect with my Base Energy level, I noted that it had slightly weakened just as before, although I knew I still had a lot of Energy left before I started worrying.

'All okay?' checked Darren, walking towards me.

'Yes,' I replied all too eagerly.

‘Well then, I think we can go deeper, don’t you?’ Darren suggested. I gaped up at him. I never imagined he would consider taking me to the next Level on my second attempt!

Smiling broadly, I followed his lead as we walked back towards the artistic Archer, his distant gaze replaced with renewed curiosity. Taking off his worn cap as we approached, he ruffled his short thick pitch-black hair before combing through the side sweep. His eyes were unblinking, steady and intense as he watched us thoughtfully. They widened further, and I could see their almond colour clearly in the sunlight. I gave him a small reassuring smile, recognising my own tension, before shielding my eyes from the sun’s brightness.

‘At least it doesn’t harm us anymore,’ he offered, his eyes lighting up, as I turned towards him, asking for an explanation. ‘Back in the 1990s, the UV radiation used to be so strong that Elans had to fully cover up, to protect their skin, before travelling through Level One.’ I raised my eyebrows, wanting to ask him what had happened to the ozone layer, and how they were monitoring it, but before I could even engage, Darren interrupted.

‘We’re looking for the next Gate,’ enquired Darren in an authoritative voice. Straightening, the young Archer stared at Darren’s fully-fledged badge before giving him a series of ultra-precise directions, finishing off with a casual, ‘It should only be about 10 miles away.’

I felt my previous smugness replaced with inadequacy.

'Thank you.' Darren nodded, unaffected by the Archer's evident admiration. I looked back as we walked away, just in time to see the Archer watching us with the same thoughtful expression before switching shifts with the newly arrived guards.

Glad to be out of earshot, I huffed. Settling my mind for the long journey ahead, I put one foot in front of the other as I let myself enjoy the beautiful scenery surrounding me. I didn't make it far before turning back to look for Darren, who was still standing in the same spot. He stood with his arms crossed across his chest as though patiently waiting for me to pay attention to him. I raised my right eyebrow inquisitively. Suddenly, Darren sprung himself towards me like a gazelle, and in one fluid motion, he was beside me. My face washed blank with confusion. It was like the cogs in my brain couldn't turn fast enough to process the information transmitted by my wide eyes. I worked on trying to collect myself, but every muscle in my body seemed to have frozen.

I eventually choked out, 'How? What? How?'

'That's what we call Augmented Strength,' offered Darren, trying to ease the shock registered on my face. Although his voice remained serious, there was a slight smile on his lips. 'It's the same technique you used when you punched me off my feet at the studio after your Energy first got released,' he reminded me.

I remembered how invigorated the bright orange light within me had felt that first time, and automatically I started searching for the fiery sun within me. Focusing on a nearby tree, I began channelling some of my Base Energy through my legs as I thrust my feet off the ground and through the air. In one long jump, I was next to the tree, putting a hand out on the trunk to steady myself.

Throwing my arms victoriously into the air, I turned to face Darren as I revelled in my achievement. My heart felt like it was about to burst from the radiating Energy that was coursing through me. I had never felt more invigorated.

'Let's get going. Every minute we stay here is another minute the Defacers can summon you,' reminded Darren. 'Try to be efficient with your Base Energy,' he added as he leapt forwards.

Channelling a continuous stream of my Base Energy into my legs, I followed Darren. I tried to mimic his long horizontal leaps as he moved effortlessly across vast swathes of land, zigzagging through the trees. Letting the rhythm flow through me, I quickly picked up my pace to match Darren's, using alternative legs to spring myself from side to side.

I let out a joyful, triumphant, 'Whoop!' It was like discovering how to run for the first time.

Slowing down the pace, Darren returned both of his feet to the ground, indicating for me to copy. Stopping behind him, I wiped away the sweat rolling down my forehead as I tried to catch my breath. Darren waited patiently, having barely gotten his heart rate going.

'How are you not tired!?' I breathed out loud, bewildered by his stamina. I could have sworn our fitness was not that dissimilar, not when we trained anyways.

'Shhh,' he hushed, 'not so loud.'

We must have been close to the Gate. I looked around curiously, still catching my breath. There were green, bushy trees surrounding us in almost every direction. Darren took off, walking slowly and deliberately.

'It's unlikely there are Defacers, but we must always be ready,' he warned, and I hurried to keep up with him. Snapping my senses to high alert, I put my hand inside my kimono and grasped the hilt of my dagger – this time, I would be ready. We were leaving the shelter of the trees and approaching a clearing. I could see the Gate ahead, gleaming in the sun where it stood in the middle of the field. Standing still for a moment, we listened attentively. Every colour seemed brighter, every noise louder, and every bird passing by made my heartbeat more fiercely.

'It's safe,' called a low female voice nearby.

Relaxing his stance, Darren lowered his bow, its amber Oliupite luminous in its hilt. Although it was only slightly exposed, I could sense the Defacer-poison on his blade ringing warning alarms within me. I had been so focused on a potential attack; I hadn't noticed the pitched sound coming from his weapon until now. Somehow, it didn't make me feel any safer. As we walked into the clearing, I dropped my hands by my side. A short, middle-aged woman greeted us. Dressed in her armoured kimono like mine, she carried a spear with an electric green Calmond gleaming – she was a Scientist and yet, to my surprise, she had travelled to Level Four. Four other Elans were strategically positioned to attack anything unexpected coming through the Gate.

The one wearing the Squad surcoat approached us, easing her stance slightly when she saw my Tetresia crystal. 'You're a bit old, aren't you?' she commented pointedly, much to my irritation. Despite her role as a Healer, I definitely wouldn't be going to her for any emotional healing, that was certain.

'Do you have anything to report?' asked Darren, ignoring her statement. Her eyes flowed from his scar to his badge, showing six rays as though confirming his identity. She straightened her body in response.

'Nothing, sir,' she replied more respectfully.

Standing outside the Gate, Darren turned to look at me, his eyes burning with intent. 'If we see anything unexpected, I want you to use your Lifeline to travel back, okay?'

The serious tone of his voice did nothing to lessen the pit forming in my stomach. 'Okay,' I replied firmly, checking on the intensity of my Lifeline, ready to be used at any point. Holding my sullen dagger tightly, I followed Darren as he put his hand on the handle of the Gate and pulled it open. As he took a last look at me, we walked through the Gate.

≈

The cold wind blew strongly through my hair. I could smell salt in the air and hear waves crashing down below. I opened my eyes to the vast ocean horizon. We were atop white cliffs extending along the coast. Breathing heavily, I could feel my Energy burning strongly. I hadn't expected Level Two to be so taxing on my Base Energy as I struggled to breathe evenly.

I didn't have long to adjust to my new settings when screams pierced the salty air. Bellowing ferociously, a group of Elans ran in our direction with raised weapons ready to be used. Shining brightly, I could see the Energy flowing through their weapons as their crystals radiated, mimicking the intensity of the Energy powering through them.

'Behind you!' an Elan yelled from the top of his lungs. Coming from the coast, a small group of Defacers were using their Augmented Strength to propel themselves onto the cliff top, where we stood. That's when I saw a female Defacer sprinting towards me, ten yards away. Her fiery-red hair flowed behind her as she ran, one hand clutching a sharp sword. And I was her target.

All the general fear I'd been feeling condensed into an immediate moment for this woman, this predator who might kill me in seconds. Swinging my dagger out of my kimono, I ducked out of the way, feeling the breeze of her blade. Her sword swung above my head as I pivoted, turning to face my attacker. Her black eyes gleamed purple like the small

Marcax crystal glowing brighter in her sword – she was giving herself more strength.

I jolted my hand repeatedly, desperately wishing my blade would suddenly magically light up. The strong gusts whipped my hair against my face, reminding me of my fragility. The female held my gaze, the depth of her eyes letting me know she would bring me to see their pit. I shook my crystal again, trying to get my Energy to flow through the blade, but all I could sense was the tightness in my orange sun, weakening every moment I continued to exist in this Level. I would have to do this the old-fashioned way.

Sliding my left leg back, I solidified my stance, locking eyes with my attacker. Letting out a piercing screech, her scream rang in the wind. She swung her sword more forcefully towards me this time. Pushing through the exhaustion, I quickly jumped back, avoiding her attack.

Adrenaline shooting through me, I seized my opening. While the Defacer was still hefting the heavy sword up from the ground, I turned to run full speed. I was ready to strike when I was yanked hard to the floor. She had managed to grip onto a piece of my trousers, slamming my body against the ground. Using her Augmented Strength, she dragged me across the floor. I helplessly knotted my fingers into the damp grass, scrabbling for purchase. Grappling with learning how to use my abilities, I scrambled to focus on finding my core. Grabbing whatever Energy I could get hold of, I rushed to channel it through my body. Using my arms to lift my upper body, I used my Augmented Strength to create the momentum I needed. I swung my leg across her face, slamming my heel into her iron grip, freeing myself.

Shock swept across her face before she launched herself at me. And before I could comprehend what was about to happen, I thrust my dagger out in front of me. The blade pierced into the delicate skin of her throat as we fell to the ground. Staring into the Defacer's eyes, black sludge poured out under my knife as her body became limp.

Shaking, I yanked my dagger free. My eyes blinked black as I caught a glimpse of Darren rushing over. Swiftly pulling the body off me, I could feel nausea crawling up my throat as I slid myself out from under. Checking I was unharmed, Darren's eyes dropped to the dagger still in my hand. It was dripping with black-coloured fluid. He turned his glare on me, having seen my weapon.

'Get out of here,' he ordered, but I remained frozen. Sitting on the cold ground, I watched as the fervent ocean wind scattered the remaining dust that was once the Defacer's body. Grabbing me from under my arms, Darren lifted my body to its feet, but my brain remained numb.

'Go!' Darren yelled more forcefully, shaking me awake. My eyes finally responding, I could see more Defacers climbing to the top of the cliffs, rushing towards the Gate crossing into Level One.

Adrenaline pulsing through me, I closed my eyes and tried to focus as my heart beat wildly in my chest. Like before, I found my Lifeline, but another force was pulling me, grounded somewhere else. Confused, with only seconds to decide, I pulled on the Lifeline I recognised back to the Grounding Room.

Feeling the chill of the room, I sprung my eyes open. I was back in the Academy. Standing up too quickly, I stumbled. My head felt dizzy from the blood rush. I took a breath and looked around. I was alone – Darren wasn't back yet. Looking at the dagger in my hand, I threw it to the side with disgust. I had killed a Defacer. In the space of minutes, I had become a murderer.

Nausea rushed up my throat as the enormity of what I had done dawned on me. I tried to force down the bile, but it was too late. Chunks of this morning's breakfast spewed from my coughing, choking mouth. My stomach rolled violently, forcing everything up. I lurched forwards as I sunk to my knees, the pungent stench invading my nostrils as I heaved even though there was nothing left anymore.

A hand on my shoulder startled me. Crouching down beside me was Darren. I let out an exhausted sigh of relief. Handing me a cloth, he watched me trying to regain control of my breathing as I wiped the dripping bile away from my white face.

'Go wash up and take tomorrow off,' said Darren coolly as he stood up. Picking up my dagger from the floor, he stared at it for a long moment before placing it on his belt. He returned to my side, bringing me a glass of water. Taking a few sips to wash down the acid in my throat, I took his offered hand and let him pull me up.

'I'll clean this up,' he offered as I walked out of the room, conscious of his eyes on my back as I left.

Chapter 15

Overstimulated, emotionally drained and physically exhausted from fighting the Defacers that had ambushed us in Level Two, I left feeling like a zombie. I zoned out, letting my body slump where I sat in the empty shuttle heading back to the manor. It must have been mid-afternoon. Classes would be in full swing and running for a few more hours before dinner. I doubted there would be any leftovers from lunch in the canteen and, even if there were, I didn't think I could eat. My Base Energy was close to depletion, but it wasn't the physical recovery from my travels that I was worried about. It was the dark cloud looming over me that was weighing on my mind.

In the space of an afternoon, I had become a killer.

The shuttle pulled up to the manor. I clambered out in a daze. Adjusting my eyes to the dim light shining through the grey clouds, I embraced the fresh air as I stepped out of the stable and into the gardens. With no one in sight, I contemplated running away. I would never do it. Still, I entertained the thought anyways, imagining a world where I could be free from Elans, Defacers, Humans and anything else, just for a moment. Yet here I was. My limbs felt like wet laundry hanging limp on a cold, still day, leaving my every muscle strained. I wished I could go to sleep but my body wouldn't let me. I was still too wired.

Diverting from the path leading to the manor, I let my legs lead me towards the dense woodland ahead. Hitting the impenetrable wall, I knew I needed to temporarily disassociate my spirit from my body if I was to allow my soul to recharge. Stumbling across a small pond, I sat close to the water, watching the subtle ripples from insects and tiny newts in the water. Folding my arms against my chest to keep warm, I laid myself on the soft soil below. Looking up towards the sky, as I had so many times from my bedroom, feeling slightly comforted by its familiar sight. I let my eyes close under their weight, wondering if this was the cost I had to pay to discover my past. Just for a moment, I let my mind drift.

I reluctantly extended my arm as he wrapped an elastic band above my elbow. Making me wince, he squeezed it tightly, the tips of my fingers going numb. Pinning my arm along my body, he held it tightly against my hip as he searched my bare arm. Stopping along the inside of my elbow, he seemed to have found what he was looking for as he squeezed my hand tighter against my body, making sure it wouldn't move. Heart throbbing, I frantically searched for his face, but the tears in my eyes blurred my sight. The glint of metal caught my eye, and I looked to see a giant needle in his hand. Tearing my eyes away as he stabbed me in the arm, I watched the four stone walls I called home fade into the darkness. My eyes falling shut, I fought to stay awake, hoping to see Mama one last time, but the darkness beckoned me deeper as he inserted the liquid into my bloodstream.

I jerked myself awake, the cold air snapping me out of my sleep as my body shivered in the frosty wind. It was pitch dark. I must have fallen asleep. Taking my phone out of my pocket, I turned on the torch and checked my arm. There, where my arm still throbbed from the phantom sensation of the needle puncturing my skin, I found a small scar. It was barely visible, but a scar in the same spot confirmed my fears, causing the muscles in my stomach to tighten. There was no doubt left my dreams had been snippets of my forgotten memory.

Pulling my sleeve back down, I lifted myself off the ground. Wiping the dirt from my clothes, my mind raced to try to make sense of my dream. Using my phone to light my way back to the manor, I could feel the weight of the dark cloud loom over me again. Trying to shake off the sensation, I forced myself to shift my focus.

Checking my Base Energy, I could feel it was now fully restored as it shone brightly within me again. At least my rest had been useful for something. As I walked towards the dining hall, my mind defaulted to Strat. Sending a flutter in my stomach, I hoped I would see him at dinner. If only he would allow me to explain, he'd realise that I was equally clueless in all this and that my link to Samalas was also a mystery to me.

I fed off the memory of his ear-to-ear smile, letting the soothing feeling momentarily wash over me. I knew better than to hope – not because I didn't think there was a chance Strat would be there, but because I didn't think I could deal with the disappointment, especially after everything that had happened today.

Walking into the dining hall, I couldn't stop myself from scanning the room for Strat, but there was no sign of him. Feeling the prick of disappointed tears and exhaustion bubbling up, I cast my head down, hiding my face as I walked through the busy hall. As I reached the buffet counter, my stomach rumbled, and I started piling everything I could find haphazardly onto my plate. I looked for a free space to sit. My body slumped with exhaustion as I caught the eye of the artistic Archer I'd met in the Helix. His eyes widened as our gaze met.

He stood up and walked over. 'Hi,' he said abruptly, flexing his fingers around the untouched apple in his hand.

'Hi,' I replied, pleasantly surprised by his unexpected boldness. A beat passed as he fiddled with the apple in his hands and I tried to think of something to say. 'Is it locally sourced?' I finally asked, my tone gentle, directing my gaze to the apple.

'We pick them from the orchard out back,' explained the boy, 'wrap them in paper and store them in the cellar to consume during the dormant seasons.'

His hand was now soothing the apple's shiny red surface.

'Because of the early blooming, we now need to eat them sooner,' he added.

It didn't surprise me. Neer had written an article on the impact of warmer temperatures and changing rainfall patterns distorting the UK's apple production. He gazed up, glancing around as though checking I wasn't waiting for anyone. Even with no one in sight, his tone was uncertain when he asked, 'Would you like to sit with us?'

His almond eyes met mine as I nodded gratefully. Leading us to his table, he shuffled the chairs to make space next to him. I sat down at the end of the table, relieved he didn't make me introduce myself to the broader group. I could only manage a small smile to the others. Although I knew Darren would disapprove of my mixing with the Elans, it didn't stop the warmth I felt from not having to sit alone again. I justified I wouldn't have many chances to mingle, and it was just one evening.

'Thank you ...' I lingered, recognising I didn't yet know his name.

'Mikhil,' he filled in the silence.

'Mikhil,' I repeated. I could feel him waiting for me to introduce myself, only to be rescued by the commotion at the front of the room. Silencing the entire room, all eyes turned to the short woman striding to the front of the room. I recognised her golden surcoat, along with her bouncy blonde hair from my first evening in the Academy. She stopped at the centre of the room.

'As many of you already know, there has been an attack in Level Two by a group of Defacers, three of which have crossed into Earth.'

The room gasped.

'We have already sent our best Squad members to deal with the leak, but until we can better assess the situation, all travel to the Helix is banned.'

Outrage broke loose.

My thoughts immediately went to Strat – was he one of them? The panic in my eyes seemed to show as the young boy sat in our group whispered, 'Don't worry, they didn't send him.'

I looked at the eight-year-old. 'How …' I started, only to be interrupted.

'What about our brothers and sisters?' someone called over the crowd's chatter.

The Committee member lifted her hand, demanding silence. 'I feel your concern, but there is nothing you can do for them now.'

'Bull,' coughed the young boy at our table, only to be silenced by one of Mikhil's looks.

'We will let you know as soon as we have more information." The Committee member finished, her voice uneasy – she too knew this wasn't going to be enough to appease the crowds.

We all turned back to sit at our tables. 'She means she'll let us know once when Diamor allows it, while children are having their Energy Awaken pre-maturely in response.' snapped the girl with the flaming blue hair, sitting opposite me. 'I'm so fed up with them keeping us in the dark.' Her voice started to rise. 'You know the Defacers kidnapped TWO, TWO of our Troopers – where was that information in her bogus announcement?'

The girl started to rise from her chair, her body visibly trembling, only for the young boy to grab her hand. His tiny fingers tugged her back down. She sighed, looking into his clear blue eyes before ruffling his messy hair.

No one spoke, waiting for the girl's anger to boil down to a simmer.

'Gaten, is this true?' Mikhil whispered, looking at the mischievous boy.

The boy's first glance was towards the blue-haired girl, waiting for her approving nod. 'They went straight for the less experienced Troopers. Dragged them back with them,' Gaten explained. The news sounded even more disturbing in his youthful voice.

I felt a shiver go down my spine. I had seen the red-haired Defacer look at my Tetresia crystal before lunging towards me – it had been a targeted attack. I could feel my stomach turn, realising how close my escape had been.

‘Damn Tetresia crystal,’ I muttered loudly, gripping my fork tightly.

‘Were you there?’ Mikhil asked, surprise and shock clouding his usually soft and calm voice. The small gang stopped and stared.

I stiffened a hard lump building in my throat at the mention of this afternoon. I knew the rules were different here, but I felt so guilty that I lied, shaking my head before registering what I was doing.

They let out a collective sigh of relief.

‘Where are you from anyways?’ asked the young spy, darting his eyes in my direction.

My mouth hung open for longer than was normal, only to mutter, ‘Why would the Defacers do this?’

That seemed to distract the other two, even though I doubted Gaten would ever take his eyes off me. At least I knew Strat was safe.

‘Maybe it’s linked to how strong they’ve become,’ suddenly suggested Gaten, who, unlike the others, didn’t seem to enjoy thinking in silence.

His answer seemed to intrigue Mikhil enough to break the concentration behind his eyes. He lifted his eyebrow in response before letting his gaze once again wander into the distance. We all waited, hoping he would return with the answer, but he shook his head, snapping back to the present. He looked back at me, remembering I was here before returning to the group.

'I don't know how kidnapping Elans would strengthen the Defacers, but maybe Gaten's right. We used to see only a few Defacers get through the mid-Levels, and now groups of them are storming through Level Two. Maybe it's all connected,' he theorised.

'You've got to tell the Committee about your maps. Tell them to let you back into the Helix,' urged the blue-haired girl, looking at Mikhil.

He shifted in his seat, pushing his glasses up the tilt of his nose, 'What good would that do? You heard them, Zirong. They've banned entry to every one of us – no exceptions.'

'How long do you think it'll last?' I enquired, peering at my head, feeling guilty for only contemplating the impact it would have on my training. I didn't think I could convince Mum to let me take an additional week off school. But if I was honest, the coward in me wished this whole thing would disappear. All I wanted to do right now was to go home and have Mum rock me like a babe while telling me everything would be alright.

'Probably a few days until the Gates' sequence changes again, although even that's become hard to predict' replied Mikhil, interrupting my ruminations.

'What do you mean?'

'There used to be warning signs allowing us to accurately calculate when the Helix would collapse, now it's impossible to tell if we have hours or days before the sun sets and the Levels reset.'

I crossed my arms at the news, and Mikhil mimicked the motion, the frown on his face deepening in response.

'Gaten and I could sneak you past the guards,' Zirong insisted looking at Mikhil. 'We might still have enough time,' she pressed, desperation now lacing her fierce words.

He peered at her from under his glasses. The look seemed to mean a non-negotiable 'no' as she huffed, raising from the table, before dragging Gaten away with her.

'Why were you hoping to go through the Helix?' I pried now we were alone. I was curious as to how this news affected him.

He sighed. 'I truly believed this was our chance at cracking the complete sequence to the Gates. We've finally managed to track their location through to Level Four, which is rare, basically impossible, since the Defacers have strengthened their ranks. Who knows how long it'll be before we get another opportunity?'

'That's frustrating,' I offered sympathetically, wondering if the strengthening Defacers also had any connection with my summoning.

'The worst part is that figuring out the sequence is our only hope in stopping these attacks. We've got to start becoming proactive, rather than be constantly reacting to the Defacers' attacks if we want to break any ground.' Mikhil pinched his lips together as though trying to hold himself back. I wondered how long he had been thinking this through. I admired how, even now, he remained calm and collected – only his eyes offered a glimpse into the mind frantically working in the background.

'What will the Committee do?' I wondered out loud, my stomach clenching at the prospect of more Defacers crossing into Earth. If they were anything like the one that had attacked me, humanity wouldn't stand a chance.

'My sister Babi reckons they'll probably get as many Troopers as possible enlisted into the Squad's training and hope they can shape a few elite warriors within the next few years. In the meantime, it leaves us with no choice but to dispatch more unprepared Troopers onto the battlefield, hoping to hold the Defacers off.' Mikhil frowned, his expression dimming. Again, this was something he had already thought about.

'It'll be okay,' I comforted.

Mikhil let his shoulders sag, the tense look leaving his face, giving way to an apologetic smile.

'I just wished they'd let me go ahead and scout for the next Gate. Our only advantage is learning to crack the Gates' sequence. Without it, I don't know how we'll be able to protect ourselves sustainably,' Mikhil explained. 'The Committee can't seem to understand, sometimes we need to make a push, and this is one of those times.'

'Isn't it at least worth asking the Committee for permission to enter the Helix?' I suggested.

'You're starting to sound like Zirong.' Mikhil smiled ruefully. 'Although she never asks for permission. I'm guessing you're new?'

I knew I had to pick my next words carefully in case I gave my true background away. 'Doesn't it work that way?' I asked back, 'Aren't they meant to listen at a minimum?'

'I wish it was that easy. We've got to do this by their rules. There's no way they will let me go against their orders and risk getting caught by the Defacers,' he said but seemed to contemplate the idea before swiftly shaking his head. 'They'd probably rather lock me up and strip me of my Energy,' Mikhil argued to himself, but my mind was racing. Strat's reaction to my dagger was making more sense. I hadn't realised the Committee was so heavy-handed. It also helped explain why Darren had insisted on sneaking around.

'Especially if I tried again,' Mikhil muttered under his breath resolutely before biting his lip. My eyes redirected to him and judging by the pinkness that had crept into his cheeks, it was something he wished he hadn't let slip out. I couldn't help but grin. This innocent-looking boy had an edge to him. I raised my eyebrows, hoping he would elaborate.

'I may have previously used the Level's map for unauthorised research and ended up being interrogated for days,' he said with a tight-lipped smile, his wide eyes fixed on me as I laughed.

With all that had happened today, it felt incredible to laugh. 'I knew you couldn't be all saint-like!' I pointed out, still grinning. He tried to contain his smile, but it broadened as he chuckled. The sound was ever so gentle. 'Now that you mention it, I didn't know we kept records of the Levels?' I asked, pressing the tip of my fingers to my lip. A plan was beginning to form in my head.

'Sure, we draw the landscapes and Gate locations,' replied Mikhil, watching me attentively; now, the cogs of my mind were turning. 'It's the Scientists' main database and pretty much the only thing they can use when trying to hypothesise the location of the new Gates. But, since they aren't the ones usually doing the scouting of the Gates, they tend to rely on us Archers to sketch the maps for them.'

This explains the silver lead stains on his left hand, I thought back to when we first met.

'Can I see them?' I asked tentatively. I had no idea what was allowed.

'Technically, no, the Committee decided to revoke universal access to the maps a couple of years ago.' Mikhil paused, assessing my disappointment, before leaning in to speak in hush tones. 'However, as the artist, I believe in keeping copies of my work.' He smiled shyly, but there was a glint in his eyes.

He grabbed his scuffed shoulder bag, dragged it onto his lap, and pulled out papers from inside. I made to grab his arm, stopping him before he laid the maps on the table in front of us. 'Surely, not here,' I objected, glancing over my shoulder for prying eyes.

'The Committee is so preoccupied with the attack, they won't be paying me any attention. As for the rest of the Elans, most of this group know I circulate the maps on the downlow. Who knows, we might even draw in some new puzzlers.'

I leaned back as though to look at him again. 'Who are you!?' I asked, a grin playing on my lips. This time he let his smile widen freely before sealing his mouth and looking down at the maps.

Returning to this focused demeanour, he walked me through reading the maps, outlining the location of the current Gates across the Levels. I had to say, his passion was infectious, and I found myself looking carefully through his sketches, trying to memorise their locations, uncertain what I was yet to do with them.

'You can have them if you want,' my new friend encouraged. 'I've got plenty more copies.'

'Really?' I was surprised he was trusting me.

'Sure,' he said, and just like that, I understood he'd be there if I ever needed anything. Getting out of my chair, I couldn't ignore the niggly feeling inside.

'Mikhil?' I asked, grabbing his attention as he raised his wide eyes towards me. 'Why do you it?' I asked hesitantly.

'What do you mean?'

'Risking your Energy being stripped to share maps of the Helix's Gates?'

He sighed, and I found myself disappointed to see his smile replaced by a frown. 'I just don't see another way... Someone is due to crack the sequence – I'd just rather it be one of us.'

I smiled, amused by the thought of this angelic-looking boy smuggling drawings around the Academy. 'Quite the rebel artist,' I complimented. Just as I was about to leave, I paused and saw the hesitation in his eyes. I waited, looking at him to give him an opening.

'I can show you our interpretation of the sequence that lies underneath it all if you're interested?' he asked, his voice soft and reserved.

'*Our?*' I questioned, needing to check who else was involved before I got too excited.

'Babi's and mine. Although mainly Babi's, she's the brains of the operation.'

I smiled at the image and nodded eagerly, telling him I would love to see their work.

'It's more of a puzzle,' he warned, glancing away.

'I'd still love to see it if you'll let me,' I reassured him, my head now nodding eagerly. My answer only seemed to cause Mikhil's face to scrunch up further.

'You can't backtrack now,' I tried to convince him, uncertain of what was happening behind the deep frown.

'No, it's not that. You just took me by surprise,' the Archer opened up.

'You did offer,' I reminded him, doubt now clouding my tone. I hoped he wouldn't withdraw his kind proposal.

'I know, it's just… I usually need to convince people to have a look at my research,' he explained, a phantom smile appearing on his lips. 'This is nicer.'

I couldn't contain the grin that spread across my face at his words. 'You had me at "puzzle".'

The pinkness in his cheeks returned, and he shook his head, but I could see the gleam in his eyes.

≈

My phone started ringing in my pocket almost as soon as I had closed the trap to Strat's studio. There was still no sign of him. Feeling the day's weight taking its toll once more, I looked down at my phone. Mum was calling. I felt relief as I picked up.

'Hello, darling! How are you?'

Just hearing Mum's loving voice was enough to bring tears to the brim of my eyes. Coughing to try and mask the dryness in my tone, I did my best to conceal any sign of sadness in my voice.

'Good,' I replied as enthusiastically as I could. 'It's been … challenging … but good.'

'You don't sound *good*,' interrogated Mum. There was no way to fool her 'motherly senses', as she called it.

I took a deep breath, attempting to stabilise my voice. 'It's hard to explain.' I paused, thinking about how I could speak truthfully without revealing too much.

'They just train differently here. I thought I fit in at first, but I don't think I'm like the others. Not anymore, anyway.' I could hear the tightness in my voice as I thought of Strat's hurtful words. *'You've picked the only weapon that doesn't belong to us.'* I didn't even have my dagger anymore, Darren had taken it from me after the attack, and I doubt he'd ever give it back. It felt like it had all been for nothing.

'I'm sorry to hear that, darling, but sometimes all you can do is be the best version of yourself and trust it's enough. Just give them some time, and they will soon come to know and adore you as I do. And if they don't, that's fine as well. You're not going to get along with everyone. If it's any consolation, you know Mummy loves you.'

I couldn't help but smile, 'Thanks, Mum.' Something loosened inside of me listening to her comforting words, and I allowed myself to moan.

'I just need to show them they can open up to me, which is basically impossible since Darren doesn't want me speaking to them. He's treating it like a game where only he's allowed to know the rules, leaving the rest of us no choice but to follow blindly. Ignoring the fact that it's my life we're dealing with. He can keep me in the dark all he wants, it wouldn't change the fact that—' I had to halt myself before saying, '*I know I'm neither Elan nor Human.*'

'Why won't he just trust me, let me in?' I whined.

'Have you asked him?' enquired Mum.

'No,' I admitted, knowing I'd always been too much of a coward to even think about challenging our unspoken rule or ask any real direct questions. We had a deal, Darren would give me certain freedoms, and I wouldn't abuse them. I could miss training sessions to go out as long as I made up for the time, and he would recount small episodes of his childhood as long as I didn't ask follow-up questions – he would bring me to the Elan Academy as long I respected his boundaries. But it wasn't cutting it anymore. He had lied to me, omitted a part of my life I had a right to know about. If he couldn't trust me with the truth, I couldn't trust him either. The conclusion left me feeling betrayed but mostly confused, just like my Tetresia crystal showed.

'Can I give you some advice?' offered Mum.

'Please.'

'Take responsibility. You're the bravest, kindest and smartest person I know. I'm sure Darren has his reasons, but sometimes you need to trust your judgement might be better than his. I would much rather you made mistakes and started backing yourself than be held back by fear. If there are answers you need to uncover, then go get them.'

I found myself nodding vigorously at the empty loft. Mum was right. Looking at the maps in my hand, I had an idea. It might not be the most failproof plan, but it was my story that lay hidden in the depth of Pamatan. If no one would tell me anything, I would either have to accept that I would never get the answers I sought or I would have to go and get them directly myself. I was alone, frustrated and tired of being kept in the dark. The Gates location would change soon, and I would likely never be able to return to the Academy, yet here I held a semi-complete roadmap of the Gates position, unlocking access through the Helix, promising the tiniest chance at getting answers. It was a foolish plan, but this was my last shot. My only shot. I had to try – I knew what I had to do.

'You're right, Mum! I've got to go. I love you.'

'I love you too,' she replied, her voice beaming with pride. I hung up the phone, feeling far more confident.

Grabbing Mikhil's sketches, I threw them across the floor as I poured over them.

Chapter 16

Stretching my limbs across the bed, I let out a loud yawn, feeling truly refreshed. Despite yesterday's events, I'd had a nightmare-free night. Getting dressed, I started making my way to the dining hall for breakfast, only to find everyone rushing outdoors. Following the crowd out of the manor, my ears were filled with the noise of ambulance sirens. My stomach started to knot as my thoughts went automatically to Strat. Losing no time, I pushed through the crowd as I crossed the bridge. I saw the top of the ambulances, their red lights flashing, sending my heart pumping rapidly in my chest. Forcing my way through, I wiggled my way to the front.

Relief flooded me momentarily as I saw Strat standing in the midst of the commotion, healthy and whole. He held onto Ms Roberts' hand as the medics carried her on a stretcher towards the ambulance.

'Is she going to be okay?' I asked the girl standing next to me, perturbed.

‘She should be,’ she said reassuringly. ‘Poor Ms Roberts gets so freaked out by the thought of Defacers crossing into Earth that she won’t even let our Healers attend to her. It’s the same after every major attack. It’s as though she’s reliving her son’s death all over again.’

Staring back at Strat, I watched him delicately place Ms Roberts’ hand over her chest as they lifted her into the ambulance. Pausing momentarily, he looked over the crowd around them, almost like he was looking for something, when his eyes caught mine. Frozen under his gaze, I was struck by the agony in his glorious eyes. His expression was so pure, and the moisture in his eyes revealed an emotion so raw that anyone who looked could have seen the depth of his sorrow. Softening his gaze, I could see his chest fall as though he’d been holding his breath. Recognising the emotion, I, too, could feel the tightness in my chest ease as he let a small, sympathetic smile slip. Wishing I could be there with him, I smiled back, feeling the tears fill my eyes as they closed the ambulance doors.

We might be okay after all.

Placing my hand over my soaring heart, the crowd dissipated around me as I watched them drive off.

‘Ella!’ I heard my name being called out by someone in the crowd, and I turned around towards the source.

‘What are you doing here?’ I exclaimed, shocked as I saw none other than Neer rushing to take me in his arms.

‘I wanted to surprise you. Your Mum told me you sounded upset when she spoke to you yesterday, so I thought I’d come to cheer you up,’ he said, handing me my favourite granola bar.

Hugging Neer tightly, I quickly became aware of everyone around us. Looking up at my best friend, I realised he was scanning their faces, searching for something.

‘He’s not here,’ I said, unable to hide the disappointment in my voice, answering his unspoken question about Strat. Neer frowned at the expression on my face.

‘You shouldn’t be here,’ I whispered, smiling, as I led him away from the crowd. ‘How did you even get here?’

‘I’ve got my tricks, you know,’ he replied smugly, only to crumble under my oozing gaze. ‘If you must know, I can still track the location of your phone from when we gave each other indefinite access.’ He paused as I recalled the memory. He was right.

‘In case of emergencies,’ I reiterated what I had said back then. ‘It’s a gross invasion of my privacy, and you’re definitely not allowed to be here.’

‘And yet…’

‘A little part of me is relieved to have you here.’

‘Well, I hope so. It wasn’t easy getting past the main entrance. Luckily, the ambulances showed up, and I could tail them in.’

‘Very sneaky.’

Neer looked around, taking in the remnants of the crowd. 'Is everything okay here?'

'Hopefully,' I replied optimistically, hoping Ms Roberts would be able to recover swiftly. I looked again at my best friend, still struggling to comprehend that he was actually here. 'I'm so glad you're here!' I exclaimed as I wiped away joyous tears.

'Hey,' he comforted me, squeezing my hand, the same way I did when he had panic attacks or needed comforting. 'What's really been going on with you?' he asked softly, looking at my watery eyes, and that's when it all spilled out.

'Oh, Neer! I know I'm meant to keep this all to myself but I can't keep lying, especially not to you. Nothing's been easy. We got attacked by Defacers yesterday. And I killed one of them,' I admitted in a whisper, my voice filled with guilt, despair and relief as I was finally able to share the burden of my crime. Feeling the ball of tension fill my stomach again, I sat on the grass, comforted by the stability of the floor below.

'Ah, the thing you've come to 'beat'. I presume the Defacers and the creature that infected your bloodstream, making you all vicious on your birthday, are one and the same?' he enquired, sending my back straight as I rushed to whip the tears from my face.

'You knew!' I launched, my voice pitched.

'I saw Darren and Strat inject you with the serum, heard them saying how the Defacer must have left traces in your bloodstream after you were summoned,' Neer revealed.

'Why didn't you say anything?' I asked softly, to which he shrugged.

'I tried probing you to tell me, but you kept clamping up, so I figured you'd tell me when you were ready.'

'So, you faked your amnesia,' I concluded. 'How are you not freaking out?' I asked incredulously.

Neer just shrugged. 'I got over it,' he explained as if that was explanation enough, and in many ways, it was. I squeezed his hand tightly in recognition before he continued. 'So, tell me, why are you upset? Surely, it's a good thing you killed one of them?' reasoned Neer, confused by my guilt. 'They're evil after all, aren't they? One of them tried to kill my best friend, so they must be,' he said, giving me a reassuring smile.

'I guess so… But it still didn't feel right.'

'Is it because your mum's a doctor?'

'Possibly,' I replied. After being always taught to help others, I felt like I was doing the opposite.

'Do you know why they attacked you? What they're after?' pursued Neer, returning to his usual investigative journalistic manner.

'I don't know why they are targeting me specifically, but I do know they're trying to invade Earth to devour all of humanity's life force,' I summarised, remembering my short lesson with Strat.

'Ah,' he sighed, I turned to look at him knowing there were probably thousands of questions flooding his mind, but he pinched his lips together, recomposing his expression before turning back to me. 'Well, you see—case in point. You have nothing to feel guilty about. In your own way, you're also saving lives, just using a more preventative approach.' I shot him a look, surprised by his unexpected restraint. Still, he only held my hand before adding, 'You know I'll have a long list of questions, which I have no doubt will take us many days to go through when you come back, but for the moment, I only care about getting you back on your feet.'

I couldn't help but smile back at him as Neer put his arm around my shoulders. 'I don't think you did anything bad, Ella, more like the opposite,' he said softly.

'Then why does it feel so wrong?' I asked. 'I will never be able to wipe the blood from my hands. I killed another being, and yet this is what I must now do to be part of this other world.'

'You don't need to do anything you don't want to,' reminded Neer. 'But maybe it's not so bad as long as you know your actions serve a greater good?'

I stared at him, thinking. Maybe he was right. Maybe I had to accept I would have to kill and live with the consequences to protect others. When I looked into Neer's kind eyes, perhaps the burden wouldn't be so heavy if I knew I was doing it to protect him, Mum and all the others I loved. Sitting in silence, merely comforted by his presence, I thought back to the last few days as he patiently waited for me to open up, knowing there was more to come.

'I've been having dreams, flashbacks actually of my forgotten childhood. I didn't want to believe it, mainly because I didn't understand what I was seeing at first, but when I recently saw a photo of Darren as a young man, I remembered. He's been lying. He knew me as a child before Mum found me,' I admitted, finally accepting the truth.

Shock crossed Neer's face until it turned into something else, an expression I had never seen on him before. Shooting up, Neer's fists knotted at the sides of his body before he stalked off to the nearest tree. I just watched, intrigued by this unfamiliar side of him, as he stomped around before sitting himself back down. I stayed silent, watching him take a deep breath as he calmed himself, before saying, 'How could he!' louder than I'd ever heard him speak.

'Sorry, I didn't mean to. I'm just so mad! How could Darren not say anything? He knows how difficult it's been for you – why! Why would he hide this?' questioned Neer, the same way I had, and I gave him a look letting him know I still didn't have all the answers.

'I don't know, but I'm pretty sure I'll find the answers I'm looking for in the place where this all started. Where I first got summoned. In Pamatan.'

'Is that safe?' Neer asked.

'It's where the Defacers live, so I'm going to go with no. But before you say anything, that's where I first remember seeing Darren, and it's where this sickly woman has been calling me from,' referring to the woman I first saw when I was summoned to Pamatan.

'You can't seriously be thinking what I think you're thinking?' exclaimed Neer. It came out so comically dramatic that I couldn't help but smile, making me feel normal for the first time in what felt like a long time.

'I don't know, maybe – if it's even possible. But that's not all of it,' I said, making Neer's eyes widen further. 'It's all very hazy… but the weird thing is—'

'How can it get weirder!' interrupted Neer in an exaggerated way. He was just trying to be funny now, to cheer me up, and it was working.

'The weird thing,' I persisted, but smiling this time, 'although I was terrified when I first landed there, I also had a niggly feeling of familiarity." As I said it, I realised the truth in my words. Sensing Neer's astounded eyes, I could feel a blush creep up on my face. I knew how ridiculous I sounded and tried to brush it off. 'But, of course, that's impossible! I'm losing my mind!' I laughed.

'When were you ever sane?' teased Neer, smiling.

I shoved him lightly in protest.

'So, what's the plan?' he asked, raising an eyebrow quizzically. 'Come on, Ella, spit it out. I know you. Of course, you have a plan, and most likely, it will be a crazy one, but you're going to do it anyway, so you might as well let me know what it is.'

'Well… I did have an idea on how to start getting some answers,' I admitted. Neer smiled widely. I felt hopeful excitement flow through me. I went on to tell Neer everything I knew about the Gates and the maps.

'I can't believe you're seriously contemplating going to Pamatan,' he sounded bewildered.

'It's the only way,' is all I could say, and just like me, Neer knew going to Darren demanding answers wouldn't be an option. Neer looked unconvinced, but I was resolved to follow through with my plan – successful or not, I would at least try.

'What if the Defacer summons you again while you're travelling? You won't be protected by the Academy anymore,' challenged Neer.

'Then it saves me having to travel through all the Levels,' I shot back. 'I know you're worried, but I'm better prepared this time. I can defend myself. And honestly, I don't think the woman calling out to me is trying to kill or bait me. I'm not even sure she's a Defacer,' I added.

Neer scoffed incredulously, 'How can you say that? After you were almost killed by it.'

'Not really! I've been thinking about it. It was the freaky Defacer nurse that tried to murder me. Start believes it's a trick, but I know she's real and she needs my help. I know I it sounds impossible, especially because I was in Pamatan, and technically only Defacers can survive there, but something tells me this is different. This woman, whoever she is, has been calling me by my birth name. You've got to admit, it can't be a coincidence.'

'No... I don't believe it is,' admitted my best friend.

'And there's something else,' I admitted, causing Neer to raise his eyebrow.

'I have this feeling that stirs every time I think of my encounters with her.'

'What is it telling you?' probed Neer.

'I'm not sure. It seems to be mixed,' I closed my eyes, thinking back to the first time I saw her. I remember seeing her in the straw bed, looking frail and thin, and how my heart jumped in response, not out of fear but – possibly in recognition. Although it was barely noticeable, I remember the quality of her Energy. 'It's like a sensation of longing laced with warning.'

I could see the frown deepen on Neer's face. 'How curious,' he finally breathed out. 'And you're sure this is the best plan you can come up with? What about Strat?' he asked, some of his previous worry resurfacing.

'What about him?' I shot back defensively.

'Don't pretend with me. I can see it all across your puppy wounded face that something happened. Can't he at least help you?' he pushed, to which I narrowed my eyes, only for him to go on further. 'I know you claim not to need anyone, but it might be nice to have some backup – especially since you're putting your life on the line. Don't you agree?'

'I'll be careful,' I promised. After all, I had no idea where we stood with Strat, and I didn't want to go through it all with Neer now.

'You'll think about it?' he tried again. He wasn't going to let this go.

'I'll think about it,' I resolved. In the meantime, I needed to find out what the woman knew about my past, and soon, judging by how sickly she looked. I doubted she'd live much longer, which meant I had to act soon.

'What can I do to help?' offered Neer, finally supportive of my plan.

Standing up, I offered him my hand as I pulled him up from the ground.

'Nothing at all. Having you on my side is more than enough.'

'But I want to help,' Neer insisted as we made our way to his car. The expression on his face told me he wouldn't let go.

'I'll need to catch up on my missed classes when I'm back, so if you want to help me stay in class and keep an eye out for Mum until I get back.'

Nodding in agreement, I hugged Neer as a send-off, watching as he jogged towards the exit.

≈

I had a plan and plenty to prepare for it. First, I'd have to find my new Elan friend and get more information about those maps. Heading towards the dining hall, I soon spotted Mikhil's large round glasses as I walked in. Before changing my mind, I grabbed breakfast and sat next to him.

'Good morning,' I said pleasantly.

'Morning,' he replied wide-eyed, his tone uneven. He blinked twice, this was different for him, but he didn't seem to mind as he scooched over. I smiled widely, trying to put him at ease. I settled beside him, and to my wonder, his eyes crinkled with joy.

Looking at him closely for the first time, I realised that I had never noticed how handsome he was. His almond eyes contrasted with his brown skin. But what compelled me went beyond anything physical. It was his essence – soft, calm and ever so warm. It was so subtle that I knew many people would miss it and misinterpret him as just being awkward. While there was no missing the intellect behind his sharp eyes, it would take time to uncover the infinite sensitivity that hid behind his restrained emotions. Yet, there was something incredibly endearing in his gentleness.

Shifting in his chair, he took another sip from his empty mug. It was my cue.

'Where are the others?' I asked, referring to his gang.

'Sleeping, forget ever seeing Gaten or Zirong before mid-day unless dragged out by force,' he explained, making me smile.

This was turning out better than expected.

'I'm hoping we can go through your puzzle, and you could get me every map of every Level Five that's ever been recorded,' I asked, coming straight out with it. I would have probably needed to dance around the request for a while with anyone else, but as I predicted, he didn't seem to mind.

'What are you trying to find?' he enquired, his tone inquisitive but trusting. I could see him absorbing the hesitation in my response. I didn't know how much I should tell him without compromising my plans or his safety if things went wrong. I picked up my apple, ready to bolt, Mikhil's eyes now wide as he spoke in his usually calm demeanour.

'Depending on what you need, I can either give you sketches of the landscape that show you how their environment has changed in the last fifty years despite being stable for thousands of years before then; or share with you my findings on the sequence, which includes where I think the Gate to Level Five is located.'

I put my apple down and picked at my porridge again. I had so many questions. I wanted to know both of those things but, for the moment, just needed to focus on the one. I took another spoonful, unsure how to ask him without directly asking him.

'I'd be happy to talk you through both,' he encouraged, most likely recognising my struggle to find the right words, breaking my silence. I took a sip of my tea, trying to calm down the intense beating of my heart.

'Just like that?' I asked suspiciously.

The suggestion of having to trade it for something seemed to amuse him as he restrained a smile

'Sure,' he answered nonchalantly like he wasn't offering me a massive favour.

'I'd feel better if I could at least give you something for it,' I responded, thinking of what I could offer him as my eyes settled on my apple, which I now extended to him in offering. The corner of his lips curved as he let out a little chuckle, a rarity. He must know how desperate I was for those maps.

He raised his hand to turn my apple down. 'Hopefully, I can save you from slowly descending into madness,' he joked softly as his eyes fixed on the table before glancing up to gauge my reaction.

I grinned wide. 'It does seem to be a rite of passage around here, though.'

'If that's what you're looking for, you should meet the rest of my family, they only talk about sustainability.'

'You're the ones who did all of this!' I waved my hands, thinking to the group of engineers pioneering the development of the Academy into becoming carbon negative. 'I wish we could talk about your projects, but not now.' I forced myself to say, regretfully knowing I'd probably never meet them.

‘Can I assume your restraint is linked to why you’ve purposefully avoided telling me anything about yourself?’ he asked candidly.

‘You’ve noticed, eh?’

‘Even I know it’s odd when someone doesn’t give you their name.’ His eyes crinkled again. I wanted to tell him then and there, even though I knew I wasn’t allowed to share my name for my own safety, or so Darren claimed. ‘Either way, the maps and my findings on the sequence are yours’, he clarified. I smiled, grateful that he hadn’t pressured me. ‘I’ll warn you, though, I’m not sure they’ll be of much use to you for much longer. As soon as the sun starts to set, travelling through the Helix becomes a death sentence waiting to be served.’

I stared at him intently, knowing this added danger didn’t change anything. *‘Sometimes we need to make a push,’* I quoted him.

He nodded, repeating in agreement. ‘Sometimes we need to make a push.’

We smiled at each other for a heartbeat before I presented my hand before him, ‘My name is Ella. Ella Barnardo.’

He shook my hand confidently. ‘It’s nice to meet you, Ella Barnardo,’ Mikhil replied, and with that, I lifted myself from the table.

‘I’ll come find you later,’ I planned. I paused for a moment making a judgement call as I asked, ‘Mikhil, out of curiosity, how difficult would it be to get a weapon?’

He frowned but gave it some thought before answering. 'Unless the Committee hands it to you, very hard, practically impossible.'

My shoulders slumped in response, understanding what Strat had done for me had been an enormous risk, yet I had been foolish enough to lose it to Darren.

'Having said that, the benefits of having a weapon are only as good as your ability to channel your Energy through your crystal,' added Mikhil. He was, of course, right. I had gotten 'lucky' earlier against the Defacer's attack. I could have been holding a sharp stick, which would have provided me with the same level of protection. It wouldn't be a fair fight until I managed to connect to the crystals.

'And, theoretically speaking, how would one practice without going into the Helix?' I probed.

'By mastering your Base Energy –' He could see me open my lips to ask, as he continued, 'Hold yourself in limbo, in that sweet spot between this world and Level One, just before you let your Lifeline pull you through.'

I felt the tightness in my stomach relax. Hopefully, I hadn't revealed too much – I was, after all, disguised as an Elan trainee.

'Thanks,' I whispered back, satisfied with my progress.

'Us rebels need to stick together.' Mikhil smiled. He was still smiling as I walked away.

≈

Striding out of the manor, I walked toward the pond I had found last night. Secluded from the crowds, it was perfect. I had the directions to the Gates and the determination to go all the way – now, I just needed to muster enough Energy to get me there. I tried not to linger too much on the task's difficulty and focused on getting to the next step.

Shoving doubt from my mind, I lowered myself to the bank by the pond, laying comfortably on the green grass. Taking a few deep breaths, I took a moment to absorb the sunrays hitting my face. Relaxing, I tried to extend my every inhale and exhale with each breath. Closing my eyes, I attempted to clear my mind and focus on the now. Listening carefully, I heard the distant sound of fallen leaves bustling in the gentle breeze, the slow motion of the still water moved by the newts in the pond, as I let my body sink further into the ground below.

Focusing within, I found the orange sun within me, shining bright as I looked deeper into my hypnotic core. I could feel my Base Energy pulsing readily, ready to pull me into the Helix through its white hot core. Channelling my Energy, I could feel my Base Energy levels spike and fall, mimicking the intensity of my effort. Continuously fighting to subdue and control my Energy, I tried to hold myself in limbo, precariously balancing at the edge of a precipice, trying not to let myself be pulled into Level One nor grounded in this world. Pushing myself further, I knew I had to get better at this, and quickly. Panting loudly in exhaustion, in a draining dance-off between my Base Energy and Lifeline, I knotted my fingers around the slippery grass below me, forcing myself to use the remainder of my depleting Base Energy. I needed to hold on, just a little bit longer.

'El?' called out a voice not far off, pulling me straight back to the ground below me. I immediately recognised that low, alluring voice as tingles exploded along my back.

Chapter 17

He called my name again, breaking my concentration. My heart flipped at the sound of his voice. I grasped hold of my Lifeline, grounding me back to the soil underneath me. Sitting myself up, I could hear the sound of his footsteps close behind me. Panting loudly, I placed my head between my knees, desperately trying to catch my breath from my Energy training. Calming the sound of my breathing, I could feel my Base Energy starting to refuel itself, but my heart was still pumping faster than usual, my body full of apprehension. Lowering himself behind me to the rim of the pond, Strat lightly touched his fingertips to my elbow. Anxiously trembling under his touch, I felt a jolt as a stream of electricity blazed through us, his touch reaching the depths of my heart. But, unlike before, this time, he didn't let go.

Letting the weight of his hand fall on my shoulder, the electric current between us began to intensify as he closed the space between us. Squeezing my shoulder reassuringly, ever so slightly, I could feel myself relax under his touch while the butterflies in my stomach multiplied with every passing second. Sending pulsing vibrations along my body, I could hear his breathing intensify, responding to my reaction as he gently turned me around. Side to side, our faces burning, only inches apart, I could hear his heart beating strongly against his chest as he brushed his fingertips delicately up along my neck, absorbing the texture of my skin. Letting out a quiet gasp, I brushed my cheek against his hand, surrendering any resentment I may have been holding onto, yielding to the comforting touch of his rough hands.

Pulling back to face me, he lowered his eyes before revealing the full devastating impact of his emerald eyes.

'I'm so sorry,' he said, his words burning with sincerity.

Holding myself back, I cast my eyes on the ground, avoiding his gaze. I had to be cautious. I couldn't let myself go through the pain again. Lightly plucking my hands from the side of my body, he placed them in his. 'You have no idea how sorry I am, El. I promised I would be there for you and I let my own issues cloud my judgement, I shouldn't have blamed you for something outside of your control. Worst of all, I let them get in between us.'

My heart flipped in my chest at the mention of us, but I had to resist. Feeling Strat's eyes searching to meet mine, I kept my eyes cast down, although I could feel myself wavering.

'What about the Committee?' I asked, my voice barely louder than a whisper, unable to directly ask the question we both knew I was truly asking. What if there was something darker in me? What if I wasn't like every Elan?

'Well, they're just going to have to cope with it!' he challenged, trying to lighten the mood, but his voice grew solemn as he saw my unwavering concern.

'I broke my promise once and for that I'm truly sorry. You've shown me nothing but honesty, and I let you down when you needed me the most. Nothing will ever keep me away from you again. As long as you'll have me, I will always be here for you, keep you safe. Whatever we discover, whatever we go through, we will deal with it together. You and me, as one, like I promised.'

Pausing to take a deep breath, I could hear the tightness in his voice.

'Please will you forgive a foolish boy who didn't know any better?' he pleaded.

Feeling a blush deepen on my face, I glanced warily from the corner of my eye. He was frowning deeply, and my heart ached to touch him, but I was still hurting, and he could tell.

'Please, El?' he begged softly as he brushed the tip of his fingers against my cheekbone.

'I'd rather face Samalas again than bear being apart from you any longer,' he spoke sincerely, but I could hear the edge in his voice.

'Again?' I asked, unable to restrain my curiosity.

Sitting beside me, Strat kept hold of my hand while running his fingers nervously through his hair.

'Samalas murdered my brother,' he finally let out. 'When I saw the blade, the same one Samalas had that night… It was like I was eleven again. It transported me back to the evening it had happened.' He took a sharp breath in. I could see the effort it took him to recount the events.

'We had sneaked off to the garden shed for another sleepless night of practice travelling through the Helix.' He swallowed. 'We were obsessed with trying to out-compete each other.' He smiled sadly.

'That night, we were going through our usual routine where I'd distract the guards, Angus would cross through the Helix's gates, and I'd follow straight after. We were just two kids messing about when it happened. I'd just …' His voice trailed off, his brow creasing. I could hear the tightness in his throat as he took another deep breath, trying to stabilise himself. I couldn't bear to see him this way: so vulnerable, so hurt. I squeezed his hands.

'Strat,' I interjected. 'You don't need to tell me the rest. I understand.'

Squeezing tightly in return, he looked at me thankfully, but refused to look away. His lips trembled, and his shoulders heaved with emotion. 'I want to tell you,' he insisted, unwilling to back away from his pain.

He sat, watching the calm water ahead. His dark lashes brimmed heavily with tears while his hand rubbed briskly up and down his thigh. I could see the desperate battle he was having trying to contain his grief. Managing to soothe the fears of his child self, Strat spoke in an unnaturally calm voice, recounting the events.

'I'd just followed Angus into Level Three when I saw Samalas. His face had wrinkled and his hair had changed since announcing himself as Pamatan's new Chief, but I immediately recognised his Energy. Violent like a tsunami, I could feel his thirst – raw, savage and destructive as he plunged his blade through Angus' heart.

'I remember time slowing. The numbness in my body, the blood draining from my face, and the sickening feeling booming in my gut. Before I could think, I threw myself onto Samalas, screaming at the top of my lungs. But Angus was too far away from me. I could already see the blood gushing out of his body.'

Strat paused, taking in a shaky breath.

'I'll never forget that white-hot exhaustion inside as I burned through the final remains of my Base Energy, only to be thrust effortlessly aside by Samalas, knocking me straight out.

'I woke up the following morning wishing death had taken me but knew I couldn't give up just yet. The thought of Angus dying alone gave me the strength I needed to drag myself into the house and call out for our parents. I knew I was barely making any sense, I was so drained, but I remember calling Angus' name over and over again, hoping we could still somehow save him. I blacked out shortly after. I only survived because of the Healers, because of Angus.'

Falling to barely a whisper, Strat hung his head. I put my arm around his shaking body and took his spare hand, which had reddened from the aggressive friction against his jeans.

'We never even found his body,' Strat whispered, and with his admission, the floodgates opened. He wept, tears streaming from his emerald eyes, silent, heavy sobs torn from his throat as I pulled him tightly into my embrace. Gently rubbing his back in a circular motion, the same way Mum had done so often to me, I held him, hoping to soothe him. Taking a few hiccupping breaths, I could feel his heartrate slow as he pulled himself back to wipe at his tears.

'I felt so guilty and felt his loss so painfully that I lost myself in my grief. I couldn't remember who I was anymore. No matter how often I told my parents Angus' death was my fault, they refused to blame me, making things worse. I hated myself for being weak and wanted them to punish me for it. Every time I comforted them, they would try to protect me from the punishment I sought so desperately. After a year, I couldn't bear to look at them anymore, and I asked to move to the Academy. I was so depressed that they didn't have much choice but let me try living in a different environment.

'My recovery wasn't immediate, but I did get better. The structure of the classes helped direct some of my anger, and eventually, I met Darren. He was kind and understanding, especially since he had also lost a sibling to the Defacers.

Unlike the others, he didn't try to make me feel better. He understood my pain. Instead of fighting it, he encouraged me to surrender to it. '*You need to get to know your shadow to love your whole self truly*,' he said, and so I did.

'Giving into the devouring black hole of my mind, I surrendered to my grief. My state went from bad to worse. At one point, I needed to close myself off while I faced my inner demons completely. Until eventually, I managed to calm my mind. Only when I addressed the blockages in my Energy, causing me illness and suffering, was I able to find the silence I needed to re-establish a free flow and forgive myself.' He smiled shyly. 'Or at least needed to start forgiving myself. But I understand if this is too much for you. I wouldn't blame you if you wanted to leave. I sure have thought about it.'

'Never,' I said fiercely as I wrapped my arms around him again, seeking and offering solace as I imagined a small, green-eyed boy lost and pained, watching his dying brother.

'You're one of the best people I know, Strat, don't ever believe otherwise,' I whispered as I tightened my arms around him. We sat there for some time, me breathing in his heavenly scent, when my stomach rumbled loudly, breaking the sobriety of the moment.

Strat shook his head. 'Ella Barnardo!' he exclaimed, my favourite ear-to-ear grin bursting across his face.

My face burst into flames, I stared at him with wide eyes, refusing to admit my embarrassment. 'What, I'm hungry!' I defended myself, unable to contain my matching grin.

He was laughing, louder than I had ever heard him before. Unable to resist his enchanting laugh, I joined him, and he helped lift me off the ground.

'I guess we better get you some food,' he said, grinning, slowly returning to his naturally spirited self. He brushed a few stray hairs to the sides of my face. His emerald eyes gazed deeply into mine.

'I was worried I'd lost you,' he admitted. 'I want to be your go-to person, El,' he said, taking me by the hand. His eyes looked guilty. Eying him suspiciously, I wondered what had brought this along when I remembered Neer's earlier visit.

'Did you see me with Neer?' I asked, narrowing my eyes in suspicion.

Strat ignored my question, not wanting to reply.

'Strat? Are you … jealous?' I asked again, smiling widely. I would never have fathomed a boy being jealous over me, least of all Strat.

'Why was he here?' he enquired innocently.

Placing my hand on Strat's shoulder, I looked into his eyes. I wanted to get the message across. 'Neer is just a friend, and he did what friends do when someone is upset – he came to cheer me up.' Pausing momentarily, I could feel my heart racing again as I decided to answer his actual question. 'You know I only have eyes for you,' I murmured, glancing down at my feet, blushing at the boldness of my confession, but it seemed to have caught his attention as his eyes flashed back to mine. Their intensity seemed even fiercer than before.

He grabbed me by the waist, pulling me closer until there was no space left between us. I could feel the vigorous beating of his heart against my chest, the euphoric warmth burning up along my body as my face reddened.

'If you're confident enough to pull "a Darren", then it must be true,' he smiled.

I look at him wide-eyed and then burst out laughing until tears make their way into my eyes.

'How did you know?' I ask, still shaking.

'I overheard your conversation with Neer while packing about how Darren always puts his hand on your shoulder when he's trying to say something important. I now have to stop myself from laughing every time Darren lifts his arm.' He beamed before catching a strand of my hair that had come loose. Placing it carefully behind my ears, the atmosphere shifted, and his eyes caught mine.

His voice was low, and I swallowed nervously as he gave me that look that made my knees go weak. 'Darren never stood a chance,' he mused, to which I looked at him curiously. 'I knew it the moment I saw you in that forest path, I would never again let you out of my sight, that this was it for me. How could he expect me to keep away when everything about you is beautiful – your courage, Energy, resilience and goodness, all of it making it impossible for me to leave you alone.'

'I didn't realise you had noticed,' I said, pleased to hear he too had picked up on Darren's glares every time he saw us together.

'Darren's not the most subtle when it comes to hiding his emotions – it was pretty clear from the moment he turned me away at the Grounding Room he wanted me to take a step back, but I physically couldn't, so I didn't. I knew it would annoy him, but I figured as long as you wanted to see me, I'd be there.' He smiled ruefully. 'I, unfortunately, had a momentary lapse of judgement, but I hope even after my mistake you'll still have me?'

'Always,' I breathed. I could say with certainty I was truly, completely, irrevocably head over heels, and there was no turning back. Wrapping the whole of his hand in my hair, I let my hand glide slowly down his chest and slid it under his shirt, settling back up to feel his heartbeat and the heat of his skin.

'Mmm,' Strat groaned softly as he tilted my head towards his. Very, very slowly, he pressed his lips against mine.

The air around me crackled with intensity as he parted my lips. His mouth was so warm, and the caress of his lips was softer than I could have imagined. It felt like I was walking on air as our lips perfectly intertwined, and then he gently tugged at my bottom lip.

The tiny, primal response sent my heart racing, filling me with insatiable lust and need for his kiss. Head spinning, heart bashing against my chest, I felt like my body might collapse. Nothing could slow down the adrenaline coursing through me as he expertly tilted his head further to deepen the kiss, claiming my mouth as his. Matching his intensity, I kissed him back, my hands knotting in his hair, pulling him closer. He groaned, a low sexy sound, as he broke off the kiss, panting. His eyes were deep with hunger, firing the already heated blood that was pounding through my body.

'I... you… you're driving me crazy,' he said breathlessly, his eyes still wild, as he leaned his forehead against mine. Holding my hand against his heart, I could feel it thumping rapidly. He closed his eyes in concentration, flooding me with his Energy – I could feel it melting over me in waves as I allowed it to flow freely through me. Warm, bold and powerful, his Energy hid nothing. Exposing the rawness of his vulnerability of his whole self, he was putting everything on the line as though screaming, '*This is me'*.

'My heart is yours, El. It's always been yours,' he confessed. My face scrunched up, feeling the knot in my throat grow as I tried to hold back the elevated feeling that was bursting in me.

'I love you,' I confessed burying my face in Strat's shoulder. Feeling him flash my favourite ear-to-ear smile, I could hear the tease in his voice as he held me tightly.

‘I thought couples usually rejoiced when they first declared their love for each other – should I be worried?’ he asked, chuckling lightly.

‘I wish this moment would never end,’ I admitted, wrapping my arms around his neck and hugging him tighter than ever.

‘Me neither, but I’ve got to admit I’m afraid of what might happen if we don’t feed you!’ Strat joked as he led us back to the manor. ‘You’re like a grizzly bear when it comes to eating. I’ve never seen anything like it!’ he barked in laughter as he pulled me closer under his arm.

Smiling infectiously back at him, I settled in his arms. It still felt surreal, like a dream.

‘I’ve never seen you so…’ I paused as I thought of the right word, but I found myself speechless. Looking down at me, the Striker gave me one of his wicked smiles as he swept me off the floor and swung me around in circles, roaring with laughter.

‘Crazy! That was the word I’m looking for,’ I squealed gleefully in his embrace.

‘I did call it, although I didn’t expect it to happen before my death-by-relentless-questioning,’ he teased, making me hit his arm one last time before we had to calm down. We were approaching the manor. After all, we weren’t meant to be drawing any attention. Falling into silence, he kissed the top of my head before we crossed the bridge into the manor and headed towards the dining hall.

Chapter 18

Basking in the joy of our reconciliation, Strat and I made our way back from the pond to the dining hall, hoping to score some very late lunch.

'It seems like we're too late,' I sulked, feeling the pangs of hunger in my stomach.

'Don't worry, I've got you,' he assured me, and with a dazzling smile, he pulled up two chairs and indicated for me to sit. He walked to the kitchen and disappeared for a moment before reappearing, carrying two full plates of food.

'My saviour!' I called out, eyeing the food greedily. Leaning down to place my plate in front of me, he pecked me on the lips before sitting himself down. Rummaging through my food, it was like life itself was making its way back into me. Minutes later, I let out a loud, satisfying sigh, having cleaned my plate. Lifting his eyebrow, Strat looked down from me to his watch.

'Just over three minutes! That must be some sort of record!' he teased, having barely touched his food.

'Hey,' I said, unable to restrain my childish pout.

‘What were you doing by the pond, anyways?’

‘I was practising managing my Base Energy,’ I replied, choosing to be honest.

Strat shifted in his seat and lifted his eyebrow at my response. ‘Can I ask why?’

I was hesitant to respond. I knew Strat would disapprove of my dangerous plan, as any sane person would. ‘I’m taking responsibility for my destiny. I figured if I wanted to discover the truth about my past, I should be willing to uncover it for myself. For the moment, finding the woman summoning me is my best shot at getting some actual answers,’ I revealed.

He frowned but didn’t immediately object. ‘I’m not one to shy away from a challenge – I am First Spear after all- but are you sure we want to be travelling to Pamatan? We did almost die the last time we went there.’

‘This is the plan, you can either come onboard or sit out’ I replied firmly. I was determined, unwilling to waiver under Strat’s concern.

‘And you’re sure she exists and isn’t a Defacer trying to murder you?’

‘I am. It’s hard to explain, but we have a connection that could never be faked. I can feel it. It’s what got me to enter the stone building in Pamatan in the first place. It wasn’t curiosity. It was her. She’s innocent, and she needs my help.’ The more I thought about it, my conviction to find her grew. I just knew I had to find her.

Looking at me intently, Strat grew silent, like a chess master determining his best next move.

'You know it's not safe, right?' he asked rhetorically. 'And the chances of you even getting to Pamatan are minuscule to none,' he tried to reason.

I said nothing, and Strat remained silent as if he thought he might be able to sway me to stay, to wait, but I wouldn't budge and held his gaze firmly.

'You can either help me or stay behind,' I reiterated.

I could see him rub his hand over his thigh before running it through his hair. He exhaled loudly, saying, 'Shit, El,' before shifting his gaze back to mine. 'It's a suicide mission, especially during sunset and with powerful Defacers on the loose. You're not trained enough…' He trailed off as though he'd finally had a realisation, the thought turning his face back into a calm mask. 'Fine, but you'll have to run this by Darren first, and the moment I deem it too dangerous, you'll pull your Lifeline directly back,' he demanded.

'I'll *try* running this by Darren, and I'll pull my Lifeline when *we* deem it too dangerous,' I negotiated, unwilling to yield to his overprotectiveness – I had just started breaking free from one overbearing Elan.

'You're not experienced enough to make that judgement. It's on my terms or nothing,' stated Strat, his face showing nothing but pure resolve.

'Fine,' I snapped back, sealing the deal. It was as good as I was going to get from him. He leaned back into his chair.

He'd gotten what he wanted. It was clear as day that he was betting I'd fail. Even if I somehow overcame a lifelong habit of cowardice by confronting Darren about the lying, he knew the odds were I'd never make it close to Pamatan.

'When you're ready, he's in room seven.' His smile widened further as the heat in my cheeks grew. I could hear the crack in my jaw, but I bit my tongue as I replied as sweetly as I could manage, 'Brilliant. It gives me a chance to recuperate my dagger.'

He chuckled at the challenge – if he wanted to tango, I could tango. Just when it looked like he was going to win this round, I spotted Mikhil's head peering in to the dining hall entrance. As though answering my silent prayer, I waved Mikhil over, his body stiffening as he approached.

Rejoicing the momentary confusion that flashed across Strat's face, I gave Strat a feline smile. 'You didn't think we were going into this blindly, did you?'

He said nothing, despite the disapproving frown that clouded his face.

'I've got the … thing,' Mikhil said elusively. His eyes filled his large circular glasses as he took in Strat before settling back on me. Strat's frown deepened. I could see his eyes dart to the three-rayed Archer badge pinned to Mikhil's chest as he recalculated his odds. A moment passed, and he suddenly relaxed.

'It's nice to meet you,' initiated Strat, a smirk on his lips, as he rose effortlessly from the table to shake Mikhil's hand.

I urged my face into neutrality, despite the glow that now filled my cheeks. The arrogant Striker still believed he had the upper hand. Doing my best to ignore him, I glanced up to see Mikhil mentally assessing the fine man in front of him, uncertain what to make of him or know whether to trust him by exposing his research.

'I'm the boyfriend,' answered Strat, reading Mikhil's mind, revealing a threatening edge. His possessiveness sent a thrill down my spine. He was insufferable, yet I couldn't help that my heart melted with the glint in his eyes.

Picking up my plate along with his, Strat readied himself to leave. 'Where are you going?' I asked, unable to keep the disappointment from my voice.

'I need to check on Ms Roberts, but I'll see you later in the evening.'

My chest tightened as I nodded eagerly. After everything we'd been through, it was silly how that little promise set off flutters in my stomach. Walking around the table, Strat gave me a quick kiss on the head, his eyes fixed on Mikhil.

'Don't let my girl get you into too much trouble,' he joked, but there was no mistaking the edge to his voice. Still chuckling, he walked out, taking my heart with him.

≈

As soon as Strat was gone, I turned my attention to Mikhil. I was eager to get a look at his findings. It was critical if my plan was to work. I reached out to take it from Mikhil but he handed it over to me.

'You didn't need to lie to me, you know,' he said hesitantly, his voice ever so quiet. My lips tightened as I turned to look at him, tilting my head. 'I looked through the Elan birth registry and never found an Ella Bernardo.'

My nose wrinkled at the news, making him frown. It wasn't the answer he was expecting. 'Every Elan ever born has been registered in our records, but you are not,' he further elaborated, his almond eyes watching me intently.

'I was adopted,' I offered up as though in explanation. Mikhil paused for a moment and looked into the distance before blinking twice.

'It shouldn't make a difference. Your Energy would still have been felt and recorded,' he stated, discrediting my theory, but he continued to look outwards as the cogs of his mind turned to solve my mystery.

I bit my lip, watching him intently, my gut already knowing what had happened.

'Unless someone erased the records?' I hypothesised, feeling the fire in me rise.

My coach had already sealed my Energy. Why not make me disappear altogether? It was the easiest way of covering their tracks. Mikhil didn't move. I waited for confirmation before he blinked and turned to me.

'I see no other explanation,' he concluded, watching my reaction intensely.

Burning hot under his intrusive gaze, I could feel the fury glow in my cheeks. Abruptly pushing myself up, I scraped the legs of my chair against the floor.

'Please excuse me. There's someone I need to deal with.' Before Mikhil could reply, I stormed towards Darren's room.

≈

Wild ideas ran through my head as I tried to find explanations for Darren's behaviour. What did he have to hide? What was he so ashamed of that involved me? From the start, he had been so secretive, never explaining why the Committee couldn't find out about me, just expecting me to follow him blindly. He was always watching me as though he was waiting for something unexpected to happen. But what really hurt were his lies. Before my adoption, he had known me as a child and had never shared what he knew about my past.

I marched down the passageways leading towards Darren's room. As I got closer to Darren's bedroom, I heard his voice. He was arguing in whispers with someone. Ducking into one of the nearby passageways, I concealed myself from them as he fumbled with his keys, trying to unlock the door to his room.

'Lily, I need you to make that serum for me again. We have no other choice,' Darren urged Dr Vera.

'Don't drag me back into this. You chose to bring her back here, of all places!' she accused, in a harsh whisper.

'I had no choice,' he barked back, the words seeming to erupt from him before he could control them. 'You said it yourself, the seal around Ella's Energy should have been unbreakable. The Academy was the only place she'd be safe. The Defacer calling her is powerful, stronger than we've ever experienced before, and it's trying to summon her again. If we are to succeed, we need to act quickly before the Committee finds out about her.'

'Even if you manage to kill the Defacer summoning her and conceal her Energy again, there is no guarantee for her safety. The Defacers won't stop until they get what they want,' Dr Vera challenged back, unaffected by Darren's harsh tone.

'Unless it's just the one Defacer that's after her, and I manage to kill it,' he said, hopeful. 'It's a chance we need to take and hope that's the end.'

Peeking ever so slightly, I could see Darren's back as he reached for her slim hand. 'Please, Lily, I wouldn't ask you if I had any other choice,' he pleaded. 'I promised Amelia.'

'And her memories?' she asked, her voice defiant, but I noticed that she left her hand in his.

'Is there any chance we can limit the amnesia to a couple of weeks?' he asked, his voice soft. A cold shiver forced its way down my back. I laid my back against the wall, needing the support. Darren's words were slowly sinking in, but my head was spinning as I tried to make sense of them.

'Best case scenario, I might be able to limit it to a couple of years, but we won't know until after you've injected her.'

I could hear Darren exhale as he deliberated.

'It's a small price to pay,' he replied, sounding almost regretful. 'It's better if she doesn't remember.'

There was a long, silent pause as Dr Vera seemed to consider Darren's words. I held my breath, trying to keep the nausea down my throat. I felt sick to my core.

'I'll have it ready by tomorrow,' Dr Vera eventually whispered, and then all I heard were footsteps fading away.

≈

As soon as I heard Darren firmly close his bedroom door, I ran. Tears were streaming down my face, full of frustration, betrayal and pain. My mind raced. I couldn't believe he'd been so quick in deciding to erase my memories. Had Darren been referring to his sister, Amelia? If so, why would he be doing this for her? I could feel the pressure in my chest build, squeezing the air out of my lungs as I struggled to catch my breath. Wiping the tears from my blurry eyes, I raced towards Strat's studio, running headlong into Mikhil.

'There you are,' said the Archer, recovering swiftly from our collision.

I didn't want Mikhil to see me falling apart.

'Oh,' he said softly, his eyes widening the most I'd ever seen them. 'Are you alright?'

Barely able to contain my sobs, I simply shook my head.

‘Can I get you a glass of water?’ he asked as he urged me to sit at the bottom of the stairs. I would have laughed at his quintessential British reaction if it wasn’t for the fact I was still holding in my breath. Feeling the pressure building in my chest, I did my best to swallow. I would have to deal with Darren’s betrayal, but not now. Not like this.

Taking a sharp breath in, I shoved the feeling deep down until I finally managed to say in a small voice, ‘It’ll be okay.’ Peeking at him through the curtain of my hair, I could see him take in the redness of my eyes and the flush in my cheeks. Giving me space, he sat silently.

Seeing how his hands gripped his knees, I took a final steadying breath. ‘I’ll be okay,’ I reassured him again, wiping away the redness in my eyes as I gathered myself and stood back up. Mikhil stood with me, his weight shifting in his feet as he clung to a folded piece of paper. I eyed it curiously as I shoved the shock of Darren’s betrayal firmly to the back of my mind.

‘Is that your research?’ I asked.

‘You want to go through my research right now?’ asked Mikhil, his tone weary as he took in my glazed eyes.

I nodded in confirmation as I wiped the remaining dampness from my eyes and forced a smile. ‘I’m fine,’ I lied. I had to move forward with my plan to travel to Pamatan, especially after hearing Darren’s intention to reseal my Energy, erasing years of my most recent memories.

I could feel Mikhil's eyes on me. I knew he noticed the shallowness of my breath, the tension in my shoulders and the pinching of my lips as I fought to stop myself from unravelling. But I didn't give him time to contemplate this further, and I took the research from his hands. I needed to find out the truth if I didn't want to be turned into a lab rat, and I didn't know how much time I had.

Mikhil stilled but made no attempt to stop me. Neither of us breathed. I gave him a tentative smile, which he returned. I took a deep breath and opened the findings that would determine my fate.

Doing my best to keep my face neutral, I took in what lay in front of me. It wasn't a traditional map, that was certain. Without taking my eyes off the sequence, we sat on the staircase. Mikhil constantly shifted beside me as though waiting while I assessed his work took all his willpower.

I glanced at him in invitation. It seemed to be enough to open up.

'It's a personal interpretation of the underlying structure of the Helix,' Mikhil rushed to explain. He must have seen the confusion flash in my eyes because he leaned back. 'I know it looks unconventional ...' He trailed off.

I cursed my reaction, recognising the hurt in his eyes.

'Will you explain it to me?' I added as softly as possible, hoping to ease his wide eyes. 'Please?' He must have felt the genuineness of my request because it seemed to soften the itch in his hands.

'Have you heard of the Law of Nature?' he asked.

'The one that states that symmetries underpin the making of the universe, explaining why we see numerical patterns within sunflowers and breeding ratios?'

Mikhil paused, his eyebrows momentarily hitched. I forced my face into neutrality, trying not to let his surprise bother me.

'Yes, exactly. It allows us to look at the pattern on a leaf and predict with certainty the infinite repeatability of its sequence.'

'And you believe that, if these symmetries existed across the universe, they could also be found in the Helix?' I said, my answer once again causing him to pause. He probably wasn't joking when he said not many people engaged with him on this topic because he started to smile. His grin was constrained to the corners of his lips, but there was no mistaking the light that shone through his eyes.

'We know they're there,' he emphasized, edging closer. 'Amelia Rose proved as much. She discovered there was logic to the positioning of the Gates. It's why she had to cross over to Pamatan when she found the last Gate. It was the only way for her to prove her theory. It would have forever tilted the ongoing battle to our advantage.'

'But you never found the framework she had been using?' I guessed, to which Mikhil shook his head in resignation. 'So, you've been working towards discovering the sequence that underpins the Helix ever since because if you can uncover the pattern that makes up the Helix, then you can predict the future locations of the Gates.'

I turned to look at Mikhil, smiling broadly, his eyes gleaming. I mirrored him in mutual understanding. There was no thrill equal to two minds working together to solve the impossible.

Mikhil blinked, once, twice, before turning his gaze away as the rosiness in his cheeks returned.

'After her death, the Scientists spent years trying to uncover her findings and unlock the Helix, but they were eventually told to redirect their efforts towards more tangible outcomes. They've since been focusing on symmetries within the individual Levels. In the same way, there is a sequence to the entire Helix, there are also micro-symmetries within the individual Levels. It's those patterns the Scientists have been uncovering.'

I frowned. I understood why the Scientists had redirected their effort. It's likely what made them so good at setting up their defences in the earlier Levels. But to completely give up on finding the macro sequence that flowed through the Helix, which could forever help protect Earth, made no sense to me.

'So, they just stopped?' I asked, unable to keep the judgement from my voice, to which Mikhil nodded in agreement. And then I remembered Mikhil's puzzle in my hand, a smirk spreading across my face.

'They all stopped trying – all but one, the unsung hero, the rebel artist that would stop at nothing, not even the Committee's interrogation,' I announced, in my most newsworthy voice, as though reading one of Neer's school paper top headlines.

Mikhil's cheeks pinked as he looked away.

'Babi led the effort,' he reflected. 'I'm just her sidekick that happens to know how to draw and has access to the location database,' he tried to clarify, but I could see the crinkle in his glowing eyes.

'Although I did have our eureka moment during my interrogation,' he revealed, looking at me from below as he rested his elbows on his knees. 'I realised we had been making things too complicated with too many variables when the answer had to be simple, elegant. We'd been distracting ourselves with superfluous details like the changing landscapes when we should have been looking deeper, so we stripped the Helix back to its basics.

'Focusing solely on the constants within each Helix, we plotted the location of the Gates in relation to the sun within each Level, and you can see an independent pattern for the ascending and descending Gates starting to emerge.'

It was true: there seemed to be a logic to how the Gates moved along the page. 'It looks like the ascending Gates have a four-step sequence, while the descending Gates have a three-step sequence,' I commented, 'but we'd need to map at least one more Level to know for certain.'

Mikhil nodded in confirmation, our minds flowing in the same direction of thought. 'It's why I'm so desperate to go back into the Helix,' he explained. We both frowned. We were so close to what would be a breakthrough, both for the Elan society and my selfish motives.

Staring intently at the puzzle as though expecting the paper to provide him with the answers, Mikhil finally sighed in forfeit. 'Take it,' he encouraged, his voice hopeful.

Carefully folding the paper, I pressed it against my chest. I had a decision to make. It was riskier than I initially thought, even reckless, but rescuing the woman calling to me was the only chance I had at uncovering my past and, hopefully, persevering my newfound freedom. If I didn't want Darren to continue determining my fate, I needed to decide to what lengths I would go to discover who I was and wanted to be.

'Thank you, Mikhil,' I repeated as I took my leave.

'Ella…'

I turned around as he called out hesitantly.

'I'm here if you ever want to talk,' he vowed. Looking deeply into his eyes, I could see the sincerity of his words, and I smiled before walking away.

Chapter 19

It felt like the middle of the night when I heard Strat's honey voice waking me up.

'El?' he whispered as he caressed my face before tucking my hair behind my ear.

Pushing my eyes open, I tried to clear the sleepy fog clouding my mind as I pulled myself up against the headboard. 'Are you okay?' I enquired, my eyes scanning him for signs of injury.

'Yes, yes,' he reassured me as he handed me a hot mug of breakfast tea.

I looked at the clock: it showed 5 a.m. Rubbing my eyes, I let them adjust to the darkness, reaching for Strat's arm.

'Come,' he whispered with anticipation.

Breathing in the fresh aroma of the tea, I gave myself a moment to wake up as I threw my legs out of bed into the cold air. Looking out through the windows, I saw it was still pitch-black outside, lit only by rare twinkling stars. Pulling on my kimono, I rinsed my face and brushed my teeth before tying my hair in a high ponytail. Glancing in the mirror, I could see the bags under my eyes from the lack of sleep. I had worked late into the night, waiting for Strat, but had fallen asleep before his return. My memory was blurred, but I remembered him tucking the covers over me and wishing me sweet dreams before heading back out.

Hurrying out of the bathroom, Strat was already holding open the latch to the attic trap. Quickening my pace, I walked in front of him, preparing to descend the ladder when he grabbed my wrist and tugged me closer, flashing me a lazy grin.

'Good morning,' he soothed, tracing the tip of his nose against the nape of my neck. I tilted my head backwards, further exposing my neck, unable to resist as I leaned in. He lifted his deep emerald eyes to mine, the tip of his nose soft against mine. He delicately pressed his fingers to my chin, lifted my head, and closed the space between our lips.

The pace of my heart sprint violently in my chest as our lips touched, awakening my whole body. Soft and slow, comforting in a way words would never be, he rested his hand below my ear as his thumb caressed my cheek.

'I'm sorry we didn't get to spend the evening together,' he apologised.

'Is Ms Roberts okay?' I asked, worried that something had happened to her.

'She will be. I wanted to make sure she fell asleep before I left,' Strat explained.

‘I was worried,’ I admitted, only making him pull me closer as he pressed his tender lips once again against mine.

‘I’d never let anything happen to you,’ he reassured me, misinterpreting my concerns about myself even though Darren was planning to re-seal my Energy and erase my memories – including those of us.

‘I was worried about you and Ms Roberts,’ I explained. ‘I was fine,’ I said, refusing to need a hero.

‘Now that I have you, I’ll never let you out of my sight!’ He squeezed me tightly, making his point.

‘Okay, okay!’ I giggled in response, starting my descent down the ladder.

Leading me by the hand, we did our best to be quiet as we sneaked out of the manor and towards the training centre.

‘Are you finally going to tell me what we’re doing sneaking around at this ungodly hour?’ I questioned as we ran across the crisp air towards the shuttle.

‘Be patient,’ teased Strat as we crossed into the training centre and the changing rooms. Strat riffled through his backpack until he pulled out a one-piece black swimming suit and handed it to me. Raising my eyebrow quizzically, I held onto it as he grinned at me, keeping me in suspense.

‘Trust me,’ he simply said. ‘I’ll see you at the pool – and bring your clothes!’ he added as he walked into the men’s changing room.

Wrapping my towel around my waist, I wished I’d let Neer pack the beautiful bikini Mum had given me as I walked down towards the pool, only to see Strat waist-deep in the water. Pulled to a stop, I watched Strat as his muscles tensed up from the temperature drop. Staring, I could distinguish the individual muscles in his broad shoulders pulled towards his ears as though trying to distance himself from the cold water. My jaw almost dropped when he turned to face me as his trunks hung low on his lips, revealing the toned 'v' beneath his abs. Sending my face afire, I realised I was gawking but couldn't seem to pull my eyes away.

My gaze made its way from his ultra-defined abs to his smooth chest, along his strong shoulders, to finally rest on his smug grin. I could tell he knew the effect he was having on me, and I was helpless trying to hide it as everything south of my body clenched in response. Dramatically clearing my throat, I took my time to place my towel and pile of clothes next to Strat's in a desperate attempt to normalise myself.

'How's the water?' I tried to ask casually, but the pitch of my voice was too high.

'Come see for yourself,' invited Strat as he approached the pool's ladder, which I was descending. It was heated but cold enough to keep swimmers fresh when exercising. Standing beside me, I could feel the heat radiating from Strat's body as he took my hands and led me to the shallowest part of the pool.

'It's slightly unorthodox, but this is where I've done my best training. There's something about the stillness of the water that's always helped me easily connect with my Base Energy. Since we're pressed for time, I figured it was worth a shot.'

I raised my eyebrows, thrilled to see he had decided to become cooperative.

'Do I want to ask what's caused this change of heart?' I probed, making my voice as sweet as possible, hoping it wouldn't rock the boat.

Strat shook his head in fake annoyance.

'Just thank Ms Roberts when she's back. For someone who hasn't met you, you seem to have won over quite the ally,' teased Strat.

I smiled, making a note to get her a bouquet of flowers in thanks. I was so very lucky. Anyone who could get through to Strat was a rare breed. Just like the Scottish wildcat, I suspected very few existed.

'And this way, I can oversee your training myself.' I smiled, liking that idea.

'So we agree no more going to the pond alone then?' he asked innocently.

It caused my eyebrows to meet, but I nodded in agreement, biting my tongue. I'd learn to keep my mouth shut if it meant we'd be on the same side.

He smiled ruefully in response. 'Now, come. Float on your back.'

Doing as told, I extended my body along the water. Placing his hands under my tights and another under my shoulders, Strat helped keep me afloat.

'Try to relax,' he instructed, feeling the tension that had crept into my body due to the unfamiliarity of his touch on my bare skin, no matter how amazing it felt.

'I've got you,' he assured me as I eased into the water.

'Close your eyes, and take a few deep breaths,' he instructed, taking a deep breath in and out, leading by example as he extended each breath. Closing my eyes, I let myself melt into the softness of the water around me, feeling myself float a little higher every time I breathed in and sinking a little when I breathed out. Quickly finding the orange sun of my Base Energy within me, I unlocked it, setting it free to flow through my body.

'I want you to activate the core of your Base Energy and Lifeline at the same time. Engage both of them without ever giving into either, holding yourself in limbo between worlds, maintaining yourself in a perfect state of balance.'

I connected with my white-hot core just as I had by the pond. I could feel my Energy levels once again spike and fall, mimicking the intensity of my effort as I fought to impose control over my Energy. Feeling my face wrinkle, my heart raced as I tried to maintain myself in limbo, yet I could never find the stillness I hoped to achieve.

'Stop fighting it,' coached Strat. 'This is not a battle. You need to start acknowledging and accepting these conflicting forces within you. Relax, let's start again. First, connect with your Lifeline: feel and explore the grounding feeling, connecting you to this world.' Doing as he instructed, I reconnected with the secure link that kept me there, floating in Strat's arms as he pressed the palm of his hands against my bare skin.

'Good,' he encouraged as my face softened. 'Now, I want you to look within and find the source of your Base Energy. Its core is where the particles of your Energy collide to create the power needed to transport you into the Helix.'

Once again, looking within, never letting go of my focus on my Lifeline, I drove my mind's eye to my white-hot core, radiating the intensity of my Base Energy. Allowing myself to get closer to the continuous explosion confined within me, I let myself absorb the ripples of Energy while staying connected to my Lifeline.

'You're doing great, El. Now, maintain that balance and familiarise yourself with that sensation – this will help you maintain and control your Base Energy burn rate.'

I felt a thrill go through me: I was doing it, although it wasn't without much effort. Refocusing my attention, I found it much easier to stay in limbo as I let myself feel the hypnotising pull of my Base Energy while holding onto my Lifeline, keeping me in the pool.

'When you are ready, I want you to travel into the Helix. I'll be just behind you.'

As quickly as before, I let the repeatable pattern engulf me into the Helix.

≈

Strat appeared a couple of seconds later. Frozen in the spot I had arrived, I couldn't tear my eyes away from the sun disappearing below the horizon. I guessed hours from now, the sun would disappear in the shadow of the rolling hills ahead, collapsing the Gates and the worlds in each Level with it.

'This isn't good,' said Strat as though reading my mind as he handed me my clothes. 'It won't set as quickly as it does on Earth, but it's become so unreliable it's hard to say if it'll last longer than a day- if that.' Quickly dressing up, I could feel my shoulder tense as Mikhil's words rang in my ears. Who knew when we'd next locate this many Gates? We were so close to unlocking the sequence to Pamatan. We couldn't give up, not when I had so much at stake.

Grabbing my hand, I felt reassured by Strat's warm fingers interlacing with mine. My stomach tensed at the silence around us. The place held still as though it knew death loomed around the corner.

'Let's go,' Strat encouraged as he propelled himself forwards, bringing me with him. Giving me no time to overthink it, I engaged my Base Energy, quickly matching his pace. It was much easier to activate my Augmented Strength with his guidance.

Slowing down to our human walking pace, we quietly approached the Gate to Level Two. There was still no sign of life, yet Strat lifted his hand, indicating I should stay put. He pulled out his two golden semi-circular blades, the Demnite in its hilt glowing brightly, as he checked the surroundings for any unwelcome visitors. I waited in apprehension, trying to ignore the ringing from the Defacer-poison on his blade, wishing I had my weapon to defend myself, making the decision then and there that I would get it back from Darren upon our return, even if I still didn't know how to use it properly.

'It's clear,' Strat called from the Gate entrance. The knot in my chest eased. Again, no signs of the guard or anything, not even the lonely sound of the common grasshopper.

'Is it always this quiet after an attack?' I finally asked.

'It's the sunset. Neither Defacers nor Elans travel through the Helix during this period,' clarified Strat.

'When I said we probably have less than a day, that's just a guess. We don't precisely know when the Helix will collapse, and we definitely don't want to still be here when it does. The Defacers don't risk it, and frankly neither do we,' he admitted. 'We're breaking all the rules,' he concluded, only making me want to hug him tighter.

'Thank you,' I reiterated, taking in the weight of our actions. I knew Strat wasn't exactly an exemplary student, but I could tell even he wasn't comfortable with the risk we were taking.

He shrugged, squeezing my hand as he placed the other on the Gate's handle. 'One sign of danger too many, and…'

'We're out of here,' I finished his sentence, clearly remembering the terms of our deal. I rolled my eyes, desperate to make a snip comment about how he had started sounding like Darren but bit my tongue. It was best to stay on this overbearing Elan's 'nice list'.

Taking a deep breath in, we walked through to Level Two. Hitting me with the same intensity as before, I gasped for the ocean air as my Energy burned with fury. Leaning over, hands on my knees. I tried stabilising my Base Energy, thinking back to the balance I had reached in limbo.

'Close your eyes and think back to how light you felt in the pool,' encouraged Strat, seeing the exhaustion entering my body.

'You should be using about 30–40% of your Base Energy,' he said, although it felt like it was taking me much more effort than expected, probably because I was so new to it all. I did as Strat instructed, remembering the soft, smooth water playing along my skin. The peaceful balance that had entered my body, both taut and embracing, the two forces working together. I could feel my racing heart slow. I took a steadying breath and pulled myself upright.

I grunted, the tearing sensation ripping through my body, urging me to pull onto my Lifeline.

'We can stop. You don't need to do this now,' started Strat, but I shot him a look that made him stop.

'Let's continue,' I urged, knowing this was as good as it would get. I could see Strat bite his lip, his eyes widened at the sight of my body in pain, but he said nothing and led the way to the next Gate.

Propelling ourselves along the tops of the beautiful white cliffs, the cold wind blew through my face, keeping the sweat trickling from my forehead clear of my watery eyes. I'd had brutal workouts with Darren in the past, but nothing compared to the physical strain I now felt. Coming to a halt at the cliff's edge, Strat looked at me, worried.

'Try and breathe through the pain, accept it,' he offered supportively, his tone soft as though wanting to show he could accept my decision. Standing beside him, I looked over the cliff's edge, following his gaze to find the third Gate on the pebbled beach below.

I could feel my jaw clench in response. We would need to speed up if my Energy was ever going to last us to Pamatan. That's when I remembered seeing the Defacers propelling themselves up the cliff during their attack.

'We're going to have to jump, aren't we?'

Strat nodded in response, a smirk playing on his lips at the sight of my displeasure.

'Brilliant,' I added sarcastically, making Strat's eyes glint with amusement.

'If you want to succeed, you're going to have to learn to trust yourself, push past your fears and unlock your full potential. Embrace everything you are,' he added cryptically.

'What do you mean?'

'Sometimes you just need to take a leap,' he grinned. Giving me a quick kiss, Strat looked down below and jumped into the void.

Chapter 20

I screamed, gripping the cliff edge as I watched Strat jump to the ground. Landing on all fours, like a jaguar about to pounce, he swiftly leapt back to his feet. He waved from below, with what I suspected was a smirk plastered to his face, as he urged me to follow him. I let out a loud sigh before unclenching my fists from the grass, reminding myself I'd have to kill him later for not warning me – assuming I survived.

Jumping off the cliff to reach the Gate to Level Three felt reckless, yet I didn't have the time or Energy to find another way. We were only beginning our descent to Pamatan, and I was already struggling much more than I expected. If I were to succeed at rescuing the sickly woman summoning me to Pamatan, I had to take a leap, both metaphorical and figurative. I had already promised myself I would give my everything and this was my first test, fight or flight, stand or run, be brave or be a coward.

Adrenaline surged through my veins as I asked myself, *What would I do if I wasn't afraid?* And with that, I set my mind. Taking one last look at the target, I imagined my runway as my feet dug into the ground below, readying myself. Not giving myself another second to lose my nerve, I jumped.

Everything was a blur. There was the sky, the cliff's edge, the ocean and Strat staring from below. Then it all tilted. The wind hammered my face. My eyes sucked into the back of their sockets, and my breath stuck in my throat. I tried to inhale through my teeth but the air rushed by me as I plummeted towards the pebbled beach. My Lifeline flared up in pure panic, desperate to pull me back to the safety of the Academy. Turning my chest parallel to the floor, I pushed my Lifeline away. I had to fully trust in my abilities if I was going to succeed. I had to trust myself.

With a loud thump, I hit the ground on all fours, my Base Energy absorbing the shock. I lifted my hands off the dead shells, turning them over, as I stood myself up, body intact. Followed by a second of pure silence, Strat broke into a howl of celebration. Pumping his fist in the air, he clapped in congratulations and smiled widely. Inhaling deeply, savouring the realisation that I had lived, I let out a silent laugh of exhilaration as I let myself drop back to the floor. Laying myself down on the floor in pure disbelief, my mind felt high from all the adrenaline coursing through me as my body trembled in shock. Staring at the clear sky above, Strat's grinning face appeared in my vision.

‘You! You are amazing!’ he let out, beaming with pride as he extended his arm. Grabbing his hand, I let him help pull me off the ground.

‘I can’t believe you let me do that!’

‘It’s a necessary rite of passage,’ Strat explained, raising my eyebrows. ‘Without it, there was no chance of letting you cross into the next Level. It’s the easiest way of ensuring training Elans can handle the upcoming strain on their Energy without completely burning out.’

‘High risk!’ I joked while similarly alarmed by the extremity of the trail.

‘A calculated risk,’ Strat corrected me seriously. ‘They don’t call me the First Spear for nothing.’ He smirked. ‘Plus, I’m pretty sure I would have been able to catch you.’ My eyes bulged in response, much to Strat’s satisfaction, as he let out his honey laugh. ‘You are, after all, what I hold most dear,’ he added sweetly, his teasing breath caressing my lips. I couldn’t help but lean in, wanting nothing more than to close the space between us.

‘Don’t let yourself stop now,’ he encouraged, pulling himself back, indicating the next Gate. I turned my eyes to the Gate, suddenly acutely aware of the loud thumping in my head and the strength at which my Lifeline was tugging away. The adrenaline from the jump was wearing off, and the creeping exhaustion told me my Base Energy was starting to run low.

Imagining this to be the moment for which I'd been building my mental and physical endurance, I started dragging my feet towards the Gate to Level Three. Standing on the shoreside, I tried to rebalance my Energy, taking a moment to appreciate the force of nature around us as the waves crashed on the pebbled beach with the strength of the gushing wind. Silently leading the way, Strat didn't interrupt my process as I stood straight, trying to hold onto my fading warrior demeanour.

'Ready?' Strat asked, standing outside the Gate as he reached out his hand in support.

I looked around, taking in every detail, remembering this might very well be the last time.

'Tell me we'll come back, that you'll take me swimming here someday?'

Strat looked at me intently before the green in them slightly softened.

'Let's see,' he replied hesitantly.

I smiled, hopeful. I knew there was something Strat wasn't telling me, but for the moment, this was enough. I turned to face the Gate, bracing myself, and gave Strat a nod.

I could feel his body tense, giving in to a moment's hesitation as he pinched his lips together. He placed his face into a seamless mask and squeezed my hand in his.

'This should start to feel like 50–60 percent of your Base Energy,' he warned. Never easing his grasp on my hand, we walked through the third Gate.

≈

Feeling a tear through my body as we entered Level Three, I bit down on my lip, grasping Strat's arm as my legs gave out under me. Quickly catching me, he placed his strong arm around my waist, carrying the bulk of my weight as he gently sat me on the floor. Strat sat quietly as he watched the unsolicited tears flow along my face. I wanted to bang my fist against the ground, but my body wouldn't respond. This was not normal. This Level was burning through every inch of my Base Energy, requiring much more effort than it should.

I closed my eyes, but all I could focus on was the thick, spike-like pressure driving down in my belly, straight to the core of my Base Energy. My body screamed, filled with a burning sensation, letting me know I shouldn't be here. Hearing Strat breathe beside me, he too was taking long heavy breaths, letting out a raspy hum with each exhale, rubbing his hand comfortingly up and down my arm.

He was watching me to see whether I would be able to cope. I finally forced my eyes open to meet his. There was sweat dripping down his forehead. His body's tension was building and releasing as he tried to find balance in his own Energy. My eyes were burning, getting drier from the desert air. Opening my mouth, no sound came out. The roof of my mouth was dry. I couldn't swallow. My whole body flinched as another stabbing sensation swept through my body, plunging into the void that was becoming my Base Energy.

Wiping the tears flowing down my cheek, my lip quivered more violently. My Lifeline flared up, tugging so fiercely that I didn't think I would be able to resist it.

'Alright,' reassured Strat, seeing that I was at the end of my tether. 'I know it seems like your pain is only getting worse, but it can't. It will hit its threshold, and until then, you need to try and embrace it. This is the only way you will be able to overcome and look beyond the pain.' Moving to my side, he swept his hand in front of us to catch my attention. 'Look at the landscape ahead. Direct your focus to what you see.'

Looking at the deserted canyon ahead, I saw that we were sitting at the bottom of a dried-up river bed, fringed by noble walls carved by nature. My gaze followed the river, winding through the dusty bed. It was bordered by red cliffs and arid grandeur and threaded through a sea of desert. Absorbing its vertical, the canyon was filled with amber-gold rocks gleaming in the sun, dipped below the horizon, taking with it the fleeting colours of dusk as they began to fade away.

'Observe the curves of the walls, the deepest of the soil, and let that calming sensation settle within you. And let your Lifeline take you back when you're ready,' Strat soothed.

Closing my eyes, impatient to return to safety, I rushed to pull the first Lifeline I felt.

≈

An initial rush of Energy enveloped me in its comforting embrace as soon as my Lifeline had transported me back to safety. As though given a single pump of oxygen, the aliveness of the world around washed away the tearing sensation of a hollow tank of Energy and upcoming burnout – however weak the transmission.

Letting my body collapse on the rough floor, I kept my eyes closed. I gave myself a moment to breathe in deeply and enjoy the air once again flowing freely through my lungs. Every unique particle transmitted a bit of its Energy to me, helping regenerate my weakened sun. Its orange flames dimmed to its core.

Touching my palms to the rock below, I let the pulsing Energy in the warmth of the stone below flow through me, bringing my Base Energy to a steady burning flame within minutes. Lifting the cloud that blurred my mind, I jolted myself up, registering I was dry! I hadn't returned to the Academy's swimming pool. Instead, I was surrounded by the familiar pitch-black landscape of Pamatan.

Forcing myself to my feet, I moved as quickly as my exhausted body could, hiding behind what looked like a nearby lava formation. I could see the Gate leading back to Level Five. I was close to where I had last landed during my summoning, but this time, it felt different. Checking my Lifeline, it was firmly grounding me here, but I also felt something else, another link pulling me elsewhere. I frowned at my own realisation. Was it possible that I held two Lifelines? One connecting me to Pamatan and another to Earth? Before I could spiral, I felt the sickly woman's presence tugging me towards her. Peering around, there it was, the stone structure where she was held, and once again, there were no Defacers in sight – I had clear access. This was my chance.

Taking a long, energising inhale, I ran ahead, directing the little Energy I had to regenerate into Augmented speed for my legs. I moved towards the front of the metal door entrance when I remembered the window around the side. As swiftly as possible, I anchored myself below the tiny window and peeked through its square jailed frame. While I couldn't see clearly, I could see the multiple shadows cast around her extended arm without revealing myself. A shiver ran through me as I watched the needle drawn into her paper-thin skin.

Trickling into a small transparent bag was her scarlet-coloured blood, her cheeks hollowed with every drop drained. Yet, she fought against the exhausting weight of her eyelids, fluttering them wide enough to lift her gaze to where I stood. Sending a gasp through me, I covered my mouth, trying to silence my weeping. Unable to tear my gaze away, her mouth dragged open as though to speak, the action being enough to want me to run in there now. The urge itched my legs, ready for action, but I clenched my fists shut, putting the idea at bay. I had to be strategic. There were too many Defacers, and if I were going to succeed, I'd have to plan and return.

I didn't have long. I took one more glance, memorising the room's layout, and assessed the faintest of the woman's Energy. Almost non-existent, I knew she would be too weak to survive the trip back through my Lifeline. It would require too much of the Energy she didn't have. I'd have to get her out through the Gates. It was our only option.

Tearing away, I rushed back towards the Gate leading to Level Five. I needed to find the missing information. I would have to locate the Gate that connected Levels Five to Four if I was to have a chance at cracking the sequence unlocking access through the Helix. The pit in the centre of my body clenched, letting me know my Energy was weak, possibly too drained to make it through the Level before my Lifeline demanded I return to replenish, but I had to push through. Opening the Gate, I walked through.

My rough breath fogged in front of me as I breathed into the cold air. My heart pumped furiously in my chest, my muscles tensing at the intensity of the effort. I tried to steady myself, but my mind wouldn't even allow me to think of unwiring. It just begged me to leave. Panting sharply, I instinctively wrapped my arms across my chest, trying to preserve my body heat from the freezing breeze, holding back from burning my Energy, conserving the little left. I was running out of time and I had to act quickly.

Tucking my stiffening fingers under my armpits, I squinted ahead, trying to make sense of the foggy landscape before me. Unable to distinguish beyond a few yards, I would have to orient myself with the sunset to find the cardinal directions of the Gate. Staring up at the sky, I could only see glimmers of the sun setting above. I remembered our geography teacher's mnemonic reminding us the 'sun rises Early in the East' and thus sets West. It was silly, but it had stuck in my memory. I'd have to climb a tree to see the direction of the sunset. There would be no way of orienting myself from down here. Luckily, the forest was full of pine trees.

I knew I wouldn't have sufficient Energy to scout for the next Gate, but if I just found the directions of this one, then it might be enough. Dragging myself to a nearby tree, I searched for the fiery core of my Base Energy within me – finding a dimmed flame. Focusing my intention, I started channelling some of the little remaining Energy through my legs as I thrust my feet off the ground and landed on the first branch, using the momentum to propel myself up along the branches until I finally made it to the top.

Wheezing, desperate for more Energy, my heart crashed relentlessly against my chest. My eyes were blurry as my body started to shut down. Pushing through the stabbing pain diving down to the core of my Base Energy, my eyes met the glorious face of the sun setting. I turned to reference myself against the Gate, making a mental note. Searching for my Lifelines, this time, I pulled onto the weaker one, hoping it would bring me home.

Chapter 21

Rushing towards me, Strat pulled me out of the swimming pool, where my second Lifeline had returned me to the Elan Academy.

'Oh, thank goodness!' he exclaimed, looking flustered and worried as he engulfed me in his wide embrace. I clung to him wetly.

'Where the heck have you been?' he asked shakily, throwing a towel around me. 'I used my Lifeline to return straight from Level Three after you, yet I landed here alone.' His eyes were wild with concern.

'I'm sorry,' I murmured. Rubbing my eyes, I leaned into Strat's embrace and let the lids of my eyes close for just a minute, inhaling his citrusy smell as I rested my head against his chest.

'I didn't mean to worry you,' I soothed, hearing the frantic beating of his heart. I pulled myself up to face him and gave him a small reassuring smile. Leading me by the hand, Strat brought me to the lounge chair. I sat, letting my legs melt below me. Taking a moment to rest, I could feel my Base Energy greedily absorbing the particles in the room, quickly regenerating itself to a working state within breaths.

Crouching beside me, Strat handed me a granola bar. Looking at him gratefully, I took it from him and took a bite.

'It won't regenerate your Base Energy any faster, but it will hopefully make it a little easier for your body to recover,' he teased, knowing that I would jump gleefully at the sight of a treat.

'I saw her,' I started explaining, keeping my eyes downcast, avoiding Strat's gaze – unwilling to confront the shock that would undoubtedly cross his expression.

'I have another Lifeline that connects me to Pamatan,' I carried on, hardly able to believe it myself. I glanced towards Strat, unable to stop myself, only to see his eyes fixated on my badge – two new rays shone brightly. One positioned in Level Three and the other in Level Six, each a handprint of the dimension of Energy I had survived in the distinct worlds. The further widening of Strat's eyes and the drop in his lower lip confirmed the irrevocable truth: I was different from other Elans.

Before he could say a word, I continued before my courage would waiver.

'I don't know how, but Pamatan is where my other Lifeline is grounded.' I paused for a moment, breathing in deeply.

'I went to look in the stone prison where they've got her. She's there, barely alive. And that's not all.' I swallowed, feeling the tightness that crowded my throat.

'They're taking her blood, Strat.' A shiver ran through my spine as I ushered the words. 'I don't know what for, but we need to stop them.'

Running his hand deeply through his hair, Strat stared intently at the floor, probably distilling the implications of my discovery, calculating the risks. I had been lucky not to get caught by the Defacers. The odds, I was all too aware, might not stack in my favour again, especially after what I was going to suggest.

'I want us to go back. Today. Bring the woman through the Gates.'

Lifting his intense gaze, his hands started to tremble as he locked his dark eyes onto mine.

'No.'

'She won't live a couple more days. We need to do this now, while we still know the location of the Gates,' I urged.

'What are you even talking about?'

'I've got a map.'

'What, from the Level Three Archer?' he snorted.

'Yes,' I snapped stubbornly, standing up.

'I don't want to dampen your enthusiasm, El, but those have never worked,' he said.

Like hell, they didn't. I believed in Mikhil, in his logic. The sequence he'd given me was the first one of its kind, and now that I had the location of two of the remaining Gates, we would be able to unlock the sequence to the Helix – I had no doubt about it.

'Hear me out – based on the last two times we've been to Pamatan, we've never seen a permanent guard. Assuming the Defacers only visit the woman when they need to, I estimate we've got just under 48 hours. That's just enough time for her body to reproduce the equivalent volume of blood before making another visit. If I'm right, this gives us the perfect window of opportunity to travel there through my Lifeline, grab her and bring her through the Gates. If I'm right, we won't even have to see another Defacer.' I planned out loud, feeling more and more convinced with every moment, but the tension in Strat's jaw didn't ease.

'It's still too dangerous.'

'And you don't understand the opportunity,' I snapped back. I forced my hands to unknot.

'You don't understand the risks,' Strat shot back, his voice now booming. I flinched. He shoved his hands in the pockets of his towel dressing gown and took a deep breath.

He took a tentative step toward me. 'You have no idea how deadly it is out there,' he said softly. 'You'll never make it, and even if we miraculously survived the Helix, the Committee would get us. They're watching everyone like a hawk. If they ever learned about your abilities, they wouldn't understand.'

‘Then I’ll go alone,’ I urged, a strain echoing through my voice. This couldn’t be the end, there needed to be something we could do.

‘Like hell you will! I promised to keep you safe, and that’s exactly what I’m going to do. You’re not going anywhere. Not when your Energy is so depleted. And when the Helix is about to reset.’ He set his jaw in resolve.

I could feel the knot tightening in my throat. It would be so easy to give into the fire that was brewing inside me. But I forced myself to take a deep breath, remembering what had happened to Strat’s brother. I didn’t want to fight. I needed to get through to him.

‘What happened to listening to Ms Roberts?’ I soothed, trying a different angle.

Strat’s eyes darted back to mine. I could see the plea behind them. I couldn’t stop myself from going to him, grabbing his hand in mine. He clenched my fingers, intertwined in mine, before placing his hand on either side of my shoulders. ‘We can go another time, in a couple of days, when we’re better prepared,’ he tried.

I rested my forehead against his hard chest. It would be so easy to give in. Do it his way. But I had thought through my options already, and I knew I didn’t have much choice; between Darren’s memory-erasing serum and risking my life to uncover the truth about my past, I would rather choose the latter. The Committee was just another complication I’d have to deal with, assuming I lived.

As though feeling my hesitation, Strat grabbed my face between his hands, forcing me to look up into his eager, determined eyes.

'I love you,' he breathed.

'And I love you,' I replied, finding no better words. And with that, Strat kissed me tenderly, his lips soft and warm against mine. His lips suddenly started to move more urgently against mine. Our teeth pressed against each other, and then his tongue was in my mouth. My whole body was exhausted, and yet I couldn't stop the heady rush as my body responded to him. I started kissing him back, matching his fervour, my hands knotting in his still damp hair, pulling it, trying to close any space between us. He groaned, a low, sexy sound in the back of his throat and suddenly grabbed my legs from under me, pushing me against his hips. He brought us to the corner of the room, hidden from prying eyes. He was kissing my throat, my lips… running his hands into my wet hair. I felt the cool, smooth tiled wall at my back as he pushed himself against me so that I was caught between his heat and the chill of the ceramic.

'I want you,' I breathed, and then his hands were on my thighs, gripping them tightly before easing them back down, letting my feet touch the ground. Using the wall to push himself up, he created a small partition between our bodies.

The gap was too much to bear. I wanted him closer. Needed him closer. I lifted to the tip of my toes, kissed him, and then again – stronger this time. I tangled my hands around his neck, urging him to respond, but he gently unravelled my hands and wrapped them around his waist.

'Not like this,' he soothed, his voice rough and heavy, as he rested his forehead against mine. A blush spread across my face as steam evaporated from my wet skin, but Strat didn't seem to notice. His eyes were set on my face. Tucking away strands of my damp hair behind my ear, he let out a long exhale.

'I can't lose you, El. Not you as well,' he breathed. 'He's already taken too much from me. Please, promise me you won't go,' he pleaded, his voice full of fear.

Looking at him, my heart ached, almost giving in to his request. But I knew I couldn't make that promise to him, not when the stakes were this high. Cupping his face with my hand, I gently stroked his cheek before leaning in to give him a gentle kiss.

'Come, let's get changed,' I replied, avoiding answering his question.

≈

I was quick to open my locker and pull out Mikhil's map. Using the sunset to orientate myself, I plotted the location of my newly discovered Gates. The map had a sequence to it, and I now had enough information that I should be able to decipher the unpinning code.

The sequence wasn't clear, but then nothing had been easy. I needed time to put my head down and figure it out. Mikhil had said he'd stripped everything back to basics, and

I had to do the same. Setting the puzzle aside, I rushed to get changed into my kimono and put my badge into my bag.

Exiting the changing rooms, I found Strat sitting outside the changing room on the nearby stairs. The floor was still empty, but you could feel the upcoming flow of students that would soon appear for their first class. Noticing the tension in his shoulders, I thought about showing him Mikhil's map when I was startled by an abrupt noise. I shoved the map back into my pocket just as Darren walked through the Academy entrance. I felt a cold shiver go down my spine: I'd hoped I wouldn't have to see him so soon.

'You're early,' pointed out Darren, meeting my gaze, his eyes wandering over to Strat before focusing back on me. 'Let's go,' he ordered, walking down the stairs towards the Grounding Room.

'I'll be right there,' I replied, flashing him a fake smile. Realising this was our opportunity to retrieve my weapon, I quickly turned to whisper in Strat's ear. 'He's got my weapon,' was all I said, but Strat nodded, understanding. Giving him a quick kiss on the cheek, I headed downstairs.

≈

All the lights were on when I walked into the Grounding Room. Darren was getting some boxing pads ready. It looked like today we'd be doing a physical workout. My body was so weak that I doubted I'd have the strength to fight Darren, but I had to keep him busy long enough for Strat to sneak into the room and retrieve my dagger.

Handing me the tape for me to wrap my hands, neither of us said anything. I couldn't bring myself to look Darren in the eyes, knowing that I wouldn't be able to hide the anger and hurt I felt. Instead, I focused on wrapping my hands carefully as the tension between us grew.

Darren broke the silence first. 'You know you're going to need to stop seeing him.'

I was unable to stop my eyes flashing irritation at him. I had noticed how dismissive he had been of Strat, but he'd never explained why he had cast Strat aside, treating him like a dispensable ally. Ignoring him still, I returned to wrapping my hands, feeling my anger starting to stir, but my silence didn't discourage Darren.

'If the Committee finds out Strat's involved, he'll lose everything he's ever worked for. They'll strip him of his Energy, kick him out of the Academy forever,' he explained, his tone firm and commanding.

Like a child unable to control my anger, I snapped back, 'It didn't stop you from involving him at the beginning!' It wasn't Darren's fault I had fallen in love with Strat so quickly. But I was enraged just knowing he probably hadn't even considered my relationship with Strat when deciding to erase my memory.

'You're right, Ella, but things have changed. We're now explicitly going against the Committee's orders. We can't have him being a part of this.' he persisted, his voice ringing with authority.

It annoyed me how concerned Darren had suddenly become, but it didn't frustrate me as much as it angered me that he was right. After this morning's adventure, it had become increasingly clear that I had more in common with the Defacers than I had initially thought. I hoped I could put off having to think about the Committee, but I couldn't seem to escape from the pile of problems that found their way to me. If the Committee were as ruthless and rigid as they appeared to be, there was no doubt they would strip me and anyone else involved of our Energy if they got the chance.

'I know,' I finally yielded in agreement. Strat had made the Academy his home, and I couldn't let him jeopardise that because of me. He had already lost too much. Strat had said the Committee were attentively watching the Helix. I couldn't risk him getting caught. Letting a cold, calm flow over me, I embraced an emotionless state as I turned towards the disgusting face of my betrayer.

Staggering to my feet, I placed them slightly wider than my hips, bouncing slightly back and forth as I found my balance. Warming up in silence, I tried to be as efficient with my Base Energy as possible, trying to conserve the little I had left, much to Darren's disappointment as he threw the boxing pads to the side of the room.

'Why are you so tired? We're never going to be ready if you can't focus,' Darren lashed out impatiently. Scrabbling for an excuse, I knew I couldn't let Darren suspect anything if I was going to pull off my plan.

So, I blurred out the closest thing to the truth. 'I've been having nightmares. They've been keeping me awake.' He seemed to buy it as his shoulders relaxed slightly in compassion. I had, after all, just killed my first Defacer.

'I'd like to tell you you'll never have to kill again, but we still have one more job ahead of us. Can you do it?' he asked, to which I nodded in resignation, accepting blood would be the price I would have to pay to be part of this world.

'Good. I want five more minutes of your focus, and then I want you to rest for the remainder of the day. We've got a big day tomorrow.'

'Tomorrow?' I didn't expect Darren to insist on travelling in the Helix during sunset. I had figured he would want to wait at least another day. 'What about the sunset?' I questioned, hearing the panic in my voice grow.

'You said you were summoned directly to Pamatan, so there's no reason we should need to travel through the Levels if we use our Lifelines to return,' Darren explained.

I stared unblinking, not seeing any way to refute his plan. Forcing my eyelashes to work, I nodded in understanding, my mind spinning. Unlike me, Darren intended on fighting the Defacers, summoning me head-on, whereas my success depended on the element of surprise. I knew this confirmed I'd have to rescue the mysterious woman before tomorrow morning. Time was ticking.

'Ready?' asked Darren.

I squared my shoulders as I adopted my stance. 'Yes,' I replied. I was ready in more ways than we would ever know. Dead or alive, this would end. I had decided to act rather than let Darren seal my Energy and erase my memory, the same way he had a decade ago. Just the thought of his lies made my blood boil. It was his fault I was in this predicament, fuelling my body which now thirsted for violence as I threw my boxing gloves off. If we were going to do this, we would do this properly.

I don't know who threw the first punch, but suddenly my fists were moving in a flurry of movement intended to inflict pain. My blood hammered through my veins as determination and anger took over, using my legs to try and trip him. I let a growl escape my throat as I threw myself recklessly at him, but he changed direction at the last minute, pinning me to the ground. With a sharp elbow pressing down on my windpipe, my eyes frantically searched for a solution as air rapidly escaped my lungs.

'Tap out,' encouraged Darren. He knew he had me. There was nothing I could do; my body was too tired to fight, but I couldn't give up. Stars danced across my vision as it blurred, giving way to my other senses as a drop of Darren's sweat fell onto me. A vague sense of familiarity washed over me as I inhaled the mixture of garlic and spicy peppers, making something click. Whether it was the lack of air or the adrenaline coursing through my body, something seemed to unlock a deeply buried memory.

Coming together before me, all my flashback nightmares merged into one: Darren hiding behind a volcanic rock, watching me swirl in the confines of our small gated courtyard outside our home in Pamatan; Darren stabbing the syringe with the memory-erasing serum into my arm; the scent of Darren's musty sweat as he carried me unconscious in his arms before pulling me through his Lifeline; and finally, Darren arriving at the front door of my adoptive home in England, introducing himself to me as though it was the first time we were meeting.

Tapping the floor with my hand, Darren released his grip as I shoved him off.

Tears of betrayal flowed. I grabbed my bag and stormed out of the room.

'Ella,' called Darren.

I stopped in my tracks, keeping my back to him. My knuckles whitened from clenching the strap of my backpack.

I could hear him pause.

I waited. My finger was now tapping the fabric against my T-shirt in anticipation. But he let out a sigh of resignation.

'Straight to the manor, no lingering around the perimeters today.'

'Sounds about right,' I muttered, walking out.

Chapter 22

Bruised and battered from my fight with Darren and the unexpected trip I'd taken to Pamatan, I stumbled back to Strat's studio on autopilot. Turning the shower water to boiling, I stripped off my clothes and embraced the comforting feeling of the water rolling over my every inch. Closing my eyes, I was too tired to feel anything beyond the numbness in my body and just listened to the sound of the water gushing out of the showerhead, hitting different parts of my body, as I turned around. I flinched, hearing the trap door to the studio slam shut, disturbing the momentary peacefulness I had found.

'El?' called Strat. It was so unbelievably good to hear his voice. I felt the hovering cloud of despair vanish as he spoke.

'Give me a minute,' I replied in a pitch higher than usual as I reluctantly stepped out of the shower. I knew this moment would come, but it didn't make it any easier. I was trapped between two choices, neither of which gave me a future with Strat. If I did nothing, Darren would erase my memories, including those of us. Whereas if I survived travelling into the Helix, I'd hopefully uncover the truth needed to stop Darren, but likely reveal my affinity with the Defacers to the Committee, who would potentially imprison and strip me of my Energy, unless … I could think of a way of keeping it secret.

While I understood the risk I was taking to discover my past, I hadn't considered the impact on Strat, and now that I knew his fate would be tied with mine, my heart ached. No matter how I looked at things, I was going to lose him. At least with the second option, Strat would be able to continue his life in the Academy as usual, and I'd hopefully get some of the answers I'd been seeking for so long.

It was decided. I was done second-guessing myself, and this would be our last meeting. If I was going to protect Strat from the Committee, I had to cut my ties with him and make sure nothing would trace him back to me. But I knew Strat wouldn't simply let me walk away: I would have to lie to him. I let the waves of torture at that thought wash over me. Then I pushed them back and readied myself to face him. The only expression I could manage when I stepped out was a dull, dead look. I saw the alarm in his expression, and I didn't wait for him to ask.

'I'm just really exhausted,' I explained, my voice lifeless. At least it wouldn't betray my emotions.

'I assumed you'd go straight to the dining hall. I've brought you a snack and – ' He pulled my dagger out of his bag. 'This bad boy. It wasn't easy to find – Darren had hidden it in a dark corner of his room.' Strat flashed me my favourite ear-to-ear smile, and I locked the image to the depth of my memory, knowing this would be the last time I saw it.

I turned away: I couldn't let him see my face. I needed to get him away from me, preferably even get him an alibi.

'Why don't you spend the day with Ms Roberts?' I suggested, keeping my voice level. 'I'll probably be sleeping most of the day. You should be with her.' I let out an exaggerated yawn.

'Are you sure?' he asked, his voice careful.

He could see me coming apart at the seams. I had to keep it together. I flashed him a small, fake smile, nodding my head in encouragement. 'Definitely. You might as well stay through to dinner, too. We can discuss our plans tomorrow.'

I could see the pull on his lip, probably debating whether he should question my change of heart or simply accept that I had, at the risk of swaying me back to my previous decision.

I needed him gone, far away from the mess I was going to create.

'You were right. I'm too untrained, it's too risky, especially with the Committee watching. We'll find another way,' I lied, unable to look him in the eyes.

Frowning, he seemed to be deliberating but decided to trust me as he pressed his lips together before revealing an approving smile.

'Thank you,' he replied as he stepped to kiss me.

I stopped him in his tracks, knowing I would crumble under his touch. I wouldn't have the strength to say goodbye.

'Off you go now,' I said as I shooed him away, to which he chuckled before heading out.

Still wrapped in the damp towel from my shower, I sat down on the bed, unable to rely on the stability of my legs. Before I could think about it any further, I lifted my phone and sent a text to Neer.

All's well. Please take care of Mum. I love you.

I immediately turned off my phone, unable to bear the possibility of a response. If my plan went wrong, it would devastate them. At least, they would have each other. Burying the worry far, far away, I put my hand over my heart, trying to ease the crushing feeling. I felt sick to my bone. I had lied straight to their faces.

Letting the cloud of depression creep over me again, I leaned back onto the bed and let my eyes close under the crumpling weight of my broken heart.

≈

It was mid-afternoon by the time I woke up. I was starving, and my whole body ached, but at least my Base Energy seemed fully recharged – my Energy was more durable than I had expected. Strat had been right once again. When I thought the pain would only continue getting worse, it hit the ceiling. I would be able to push myself further next time. I just needed to work with the pain rather than against it. I made a mental note to keep on going even when my Base Energy would feel completely depleted and have faith that I'd be able to recover.

Still wrapped in the towel from the shower, I got ready methodically, concentrating on each little task. I put on some dry clothes and took my time to style my hair until it flowed in perfect, black waves around my face.

Putting on my trainee kimono, I took my dagger and placed it carefully on the inside of my kimono, feeling the presence of Samalas pressed against my heart. I packaged the map with Gates' sequence in my bag and walked towards the dining hall, hoping I might be able to score some leftovers from lunchtime.

As expected, the dining hall was empty. The chairs had been placed on the tables while the Elans trained. Making my way to the kitchens, I recognised one of the cooks. He had been a friend of Strat's. Feeling a blush rise to my face, I walked towards him, preparing myself to beg for any leftovers they might have, when he turned around and handed me a plate full of food. Stunned, I could feel my eyes widen, which made his chubby cheeks rise with a smile.

'Courtesy of Strat,' he clarified. 'You're lucky to have caught such a good egg,' he added, which only made my stomach twist further, but I reminded myself I was doing it to protect him. I thanked him and went to grab a seat.

Slowly, slowly my thoughts started to push past the brick wall of pain. I needed to plan. For I had made my choice: I would rescue the woman calling me tomorrow in the early morning and face the consequences of the Committee when I returned. First, I had to ensure I didn't get murdered by the Defacers or engulfed by the collapsing Helix. I had no guarantees, nothing that would ensure that at least one of us would live. I could only hope that I would have enough Energy to carry us through the Gates before the sunset crushed us into oblivion. Despair gripped me, the odds were slim, but without answers, I would be hopeless against Darren and his memory-erasing serum. I had no choice: if I did nothing, I'd have to give up my memories and Energy, give up who I'd become. Pushing the terror back, I knew I would rather risk my life than relinquish the knowledge of who I was.

I strengthened my resolve. It did no good agonising over the outcomes, and at least I took comfort in knowing Strat would be safe. Taking the map out of my bag, I pulled it out in front of me as I munched through my food, trying to figure out the sequence.

≈

I don't know how many hours I spent staring at the puzzle, but my brain was aching from trying to figure out the sequence that would unlock the Levels when it finally dawned on me. The brainteaser Neer had given me earlier this week, the Da-Vinci inspired lock, he'd said it would allow me to create my own sequences.

I quickly opened my bag, now frantically searching for the golden cylinder. Taking it out, I counted a dozen rings hanging around its body. As fate would have it, the ascending and descending Gates would each have a perfect six. My hands were already moving, with excitement as I reassembled the mirrored sequence of the Helix.

I fixed the settings to match the number of steps in each sequence and locked in the known Gates' positioning so it accurately mirrored the assigned rings. I tested the four-step sequence to the ascending Gate, locking only half of the sequence before adding the second half I had discovered during my latest journey to Pamatan. The cylinder clicked, confirming it was correct. I just needed to figure out the sequence to the descending Gates, with only the Gate location in Level Four left to deduce. I held my breath as I worked. My destiny hung by a thread. I needed to get it right if only to confirm the sequences were indeed interdependent, and I wouldn't be left to die, engulfed by the collapse of the Helix.

I twisted the rings in every combination the contraption would allow, my fingers reddening with the roughness of my gestures. I was ready to discard the object when something in me urged me to rotate the cylinder upside down. I carefully watched the sequence in front of me with a new perspective, studying it carefully. I turned the final ring into position, revealing the final click. The lid popped open.

I could feel the blood drain from my face in one fluid motion, my mouth falling open. I pulled out the lock's body, and there lay a tiny note. My hands trembled as I unfolded the message. Written in Neer's messy handwriting was my favourite quote, *'What would you do if you weren't afraid?'*

≈

My heart leapt to my throat as I rushed to my feet. My first instinct was to run to tell Strat when my brain finally caught up. The ache in my heart squeezed. I couldn't let my previously gloomy mood win over me. I needed to focus. Bringing my plate back to the kitchens, I checked the clocks. It was getting close to 6 p.m. I had to start preparing for my early morning rescue mission and still needed time to recover my strength fully.

I checked that the shuttle ran all night, which it did. I grabbed some supplies from the vending machine for some early morning and hopefully post-rescue snacks. Next, I checked the infirmary was open all day and night for the life-threatening support I suspected we might need. I repeatedly ran over how I envisaged the rescue mission would plan out and visualised the location of the Gates until it was deeply ingrained in my memory. I did every task I thought I had to do and went beyond, delaying the inevitable. I was soon left with only one thing to do: write my note to Strat. Luckily, I could set back my task a little longer when I spotted Mikhil's black hair gleaming under the library lights, waving me over. I walked over to him.

‘Hi,’ he called out pleasantly.

‘Hey,’ I replied, smiling back. It was nice to see the Archer, despite the tear in my heart that was consuming me like an open flame. An idea occurred to me: if I could do nothing right, at the very least, I could help Mikhil.

‘I’ve got something for you,’ I offered as I handed him the finished map of the Gates’ sequence. ‘Don’t ask me how I got it. I just wanted to thank you for all your help.’

Taking the paper, he didn’t unfold it. Instead, he pressed his hand against my arm. His almond eyes looked troubled, and his smile had turned into a frown. ‘Why do I get the impression you’re saying goodbye? Is this to do with why you were upset yesterday?’

Avoiding his gaze, I felt both embarrassed and touched. I wasn’t used to strangers caring so much about me. No, not strangers, friends.

‘It’s linked to it,’ I answered honestly.

‘Can’t I help?’ Mikhil offered. I shook my head, his expression becoming more concerned. ‘Not even your friend?’ he asked, referring to Strat.

‘This is something I need to do alone,’ I stopped him, my tone forceful. I didn’t need anyone coming to my rescue.

‘Just keep it to yourself, until tomorrow at least,’ I warned him, glancing towards the map in his hand, thinking especially not Strat. I couldn’t risk Strat attempting a heroic rescue. Not wanting to reveal any more, I gave Mikhil a small farewell smile and headed towards Strat’s studio.

I was ready for my rescue mission with only a few hours to go. I felt wired. I was fully dressed, prepared to leap out of bed into battle, and it felt good wearing my clothes again. Carefully folding the kimono Strat had stolen for me, I smiled at the memory as I set it on the sofa. Remembering his deep emerald eyes, the comfort of his warm, rusty voice and the safety of his strong embrace. I knew there was one outstanding task I couldn't delay any further.

I went towards the bed and knelt beside the little bedside table to write. Looking at the photo of young Strat with his deceased brother, remorse filled me once again. Pushing back my guilt as I had been doing all day, I reminded myself that going about my rescue mission alone was the best thing I could do to protect Strat.

'*Dear Strat,*' I started. My hand was shaking, the letters hardly legible.

You were right. This mission is too dangerous. The odds of living are slim, and even if we do, there is no guarantee the Committee won't strip us of our Energy. You've built a great life here, surrounded by Elans who love you and need you, which is why I've decided to release you from your promise and make you one in return. I promise, if I survive, I won't ever mention you to the Committee. It will be as though we never knew each other. I hope you understand this is the best outcome we can expect.

I love you. Forgive me.

El

Placing the note under the kimono, I slid under the bedsheet covers, hoping to catch a few more hours of sleep before the final rescue.

Chapter 23

My eyes burst open as soon as my alarm vibrated under my pillow. Sliding my hand under my pillow, I checked the time. It was 4 a.m. Based on my calculations, I had two hours to go to Pamatan, rescue the woman and come back. It was the perfect slot between when the Defacers might next visit my rescuee and when the Academy would go from being empty to having its first visitors. I pressed my hand against my cheek, trying to absorb the last of Strat's touch. I vaguely remembered hearing him slide through the trap door of the studio. Sitting on the corner of the bed, he'd adjusted the covers around me before placing a kiss on my forehead, leaving behind traces of his familiar smell.

Before the feeling of nostalgia consumed me, I focused my mind on the mission. Grabbing my backpack from under the bed, I placed it securely on my back and slipped discreetly out of the studio. Relief washed over me as soon as my feet touched the bottom of the ladder. Losing no time, I made my way to the shuttle leading to the Academy.

Breathing in the cold autumn air, I looked up at the glistening stars I had gazed at for so many hours as I prayed their good luck would shine on me tonight.

Deadly quiet, I made my way to the training centre. The knot in my stomach further tightened at the sight of the Grounding Room. I had decided to use it as my base with the logic that it was public enough that Darren would have no choice but to call the medics if he found us in the morning and busy enough that we could slip by if, by some miracle, we still had some Energy left in us.

My hands started sweating in response, trying to cool the furious pumping of my heart.

'You can do hard things, Ella,' I said out loud, trying to convince the coward in me this wasn't a terrible mistake. Giving myself no choice, I pulled open the door and set my plan in motion.

Switching on the focal light cast in the middle of the Grounding Room, as I had during my training, I turned on the cold air and played the sound of the crashing waves. Visualising my plan one last time, I took a deep trembling breath, attempting to swallow the lump in my throat.

'I can do hard things,' I repeated more calmly, laying out my mat in the centre of the room. Laying myself down, I closed my eyes. Taking 25 speedy breaths, I inhaled deeply through my nose for two seconds, letting the air fall out, passively through my mouth for a second before repeating the sequence. My face started turning flush, warm and alert as I shifted the chemistry in my bloodstream, tricking my mind into a temporary state of calm alertness.

Stretching the orange flames of my burning core of Energy, their power flowed through my veins until they reached behind my eyes. Fortifying the nerve ending behind the sockets of my eyes, I could feel my pupils dilating to my predatory state. The tremor in my hand had stopped and any hesitation I had felt transformed into fierce determination.

Without needing to pause, I followed the sequence of my training. First, I took a moment to find and reconnect to my Lifeline, linking me to the earth beneath me and familiarising myself with its pull before moving on to the second link pulling me towards my destination, Pamatan.

Letting the air roll up the back of my throat, I restricted its exit, creating a powerful, raspy noise, commanding my focus. Embracing the fury of my glowing core, I touched the Lifeline connecting me to Pamatan and pulled.

≈

Blinking my eyes, I saw I had landed in the same spot as yesterday, midway between the Gate to Level Five and the stone building. Taking out my dagger, I attempted to activate my crystal blade one last time. I closed my eyes, imagining my Energy flowing through it, the same way I had when using my Augmented Strength, hoping it would suddenly light up, only to open them again to an equally dim blade. Rolling my eyes in frustration, I shook off my failure, wishing I had at least thought of warming up in advance as I circled my stiff muscles. It would just have to do.

Quick to observe my surroundings, I noticed the sun hanging low. The chilled air shivered down my spine, reminding me of my younger self, cold, scared and abandoned in a discarded alleyway. And how I had fended for myself, how I had overcome my fears and how I had survived. I could do hard things. With no time to waste, I hurried towards the stone building, where I could see two Defacers sitting outside the block, guarding the front door. I cursed under my breath. Someone must have seen me yesterday. Why else would they suddenly set up guards? Even then, my body moved before I could reconsider my plan, urged by the sensation pulling me to her.

Remembering my years of Krav-Maga training, I knew the element of surprise would be my best ally, especially against two large, male Defacers. My only hope was to attack them from behind, taking them out before they got a chance to defend themselves. Pressing myself against the side of the rectangular building, I waited for one of the guards to do his loop, allowing me to attack.

Closing my eyes, I took a moment to reconnect with my fiery Base Energy, willing it to my command, feeling it flow through my veins, prepared to augment my strength for combat. As the first Defacer stepped out, I moved quickly, propelling my elbow forwards, pushing his head downwards before slamming the back of my dagger against the base of his neck, sending his body crashing to the ground. But I was too slow to protect my exposed back as blood filled my mouth from the sudden jerk, hauling me backwards. I could hear the slight rasp of the material tearing my collar as the second guard dragged me to my feet. Holding back a scream, I lifted my hands, muffling down the pain as I tried to block his punches. Ducking another punch, I slipped through the small opening between his bear-like arms, mounting his back as I stabbed him in the gut. Unflinching, I pulled my dagger out, dripping black-coloured blood, readily awaiting to go again, only for the Defacer to crumble to the ground.

With no time to lose, I continued until I stood outside the main entrance, pausing just long enough to calm my heavy breathing. Listening to the pounding in my ears, I steadied myself, counting down from three.

'Three…'

'Two…'

'One.'

I gently pushed the handle to peek through the wooden door. Holding my dagger firmly, my senses turned to a killing calm the moment I laid my eyes on the straw bed and who was standing by it. Just as the first time, the pale woman lay directly under a single light in the middle of the room. A wave of deja-vu flowed over me as I entered the room to face the man standing over her, delicately brushing her hair. Recognising the strength in his form body and the seamless inky black suit, I knew this was Samalas.

Reacting to the noise on my left, I angled towards the two perpetrators. A girl was standing guard in the corner, wearing a red leather tunic. She looked similar to me. We were both the same age and height, with similar features except for her pixie black hair. Her lethal gaze never left me as she held the tip of her glowing Marcax knife towards me, awaiting the order to plunge it into my body.

'I've been wondering when you'd next show up,' mused Samalas, not bothering to look in my direction. His voice was carnal and cruel.

'Imagine my surprise when I was informed that you had come by yesterday,' he shared. His voice carried effortlessly across the room, its tenor automatically sending familiar waves of horror through my body. I squeezed the handle of my blade tighter, trying to ease the nausea, turning my stomach at the forgotten memories. His eyes remained steadily cast on the woman in the bed.

'It seems you've found yourself quite the route. I'm sure your mother would be pleased to know it runs in the family,' he purred. His eyes moved to me. Watching. A small satisfactory smile escaped his lips as confusion crossed my eyes. Time stood still as I frantically glanced over the woman's fragile face as my brain tried to assess the truthfulness of his words. My eyes paused on the thin gold necklace, holding the Elan sunset symbol, resting against her exposed collarbone, before widening at the sight of hundreds of scars displayed along her wrists and elbow hidden under dark blue bruises.

'What have you done to her?' I demanded, horrified. My voice turned raspy from the tightness in my throat. I tried to hold onto my anger rather than let the despair I felt take over.

'Taking care of her for you, of course,' he said as though I had forgotten his grand generosity. His dark eyes rested on mine, provoking me, waiting to see what I would do next. I could feel the orange sun in me burn brightly, my body aching to launch itself at him, the clench in my jaw only making him grin further. I forced myself to hold it together. I tried to adjust my weapon to attack discreetly, but his bodyguard was watching me, and she let out a low warning hiss, letting me know of her presence as she loyally waited for her master's command.

'I wouldn't do that if I were you,' Samalas warned, looking towards my dagger, his eyes lingering momentarily on my dim crystal blade before returning to mine. 'Especially one as untrained as you,' he scowled.

I couldn't help but wince, feeling the flush grow in my face, his words slicing as intended. I was the weakest one in the room, I had no idea how to use my dagger's properties, and Samalas was making a point of reminding me. One move and I would die a slow, painful death at his mercy.

He sighed. 'Maybe I should just let Neon have you.' His eyes briefly lit up, their brightness like the moon on a clear, dark night. 'I dread to think what my dear Neon would do to you without her morning beatings.' He grinned, causing my stomach to clench as I imagined him picturing it in his head.

'I will not disappoint you, Master,' replied the girl eagerly, the maroon crystal in the knife glowing brightly at her command.

'Quiet!' he shouted angrily at her, making me flinch, giving her a look of disgust. I couldn't help but glance at the girl with sympathy as she bowed her head apologetically. She had wrongly read his wants and would surely have to pay for it later.

Neither of us dared say anything as he picked up a rubber band from the small medical utility cart beside him before tightening it around his bicep. Letting his vein swell, he plunged in a syringe, slowly extracting his blood until he had filled the vial's content. He turned his head towards me, the palms of my hands sweating intensely.

'You've come here because you want answers, and I am here to help you,' he purred as he snapped the needle from its container, now only holding his blood.

'I'm not looking to make a deal,' I growled.

'It's not a deal. It's an opportunity,' he snapped, correcting me like you would an insolent child. He moved around the bed like a spider trying to lure me into its web as he came closer. My feet instinctively took a step back.

'I'll take what I've come for and be on my way,' I tried to say firmly, but even I could hear the lack of conviction in my voice.

'Oh, you can take her,' he said dismissively, making me feel as though I had completely misunderstood the situation. It was enough to make me start doubting myself.

'But she won't live without my help. You see, to keep her alive for so long, I've had to infuse her with Defacer blood.' He paused. 'My blood.' He held up a black-coloured vial of blood held between his fingers. My heart stopped, remembering the first time I had seen the nurse inject Amelia with the same sludge. He had lured me effortlessly into his web using this woman he claimed was my mother as bait. He had made sure I was trapped without him. I could try to fight but doubted I would win a fight against the two of them, let alone have enough Energy to return through the Gates. And even then, how was I to keep the woman alive without Samalas' blood? If I wanted to have a chance of bringing both of us back alive, I would need to give him something in return. I didn't see what choice I had.

'What do you want?' I started, trying to keep the panic in my voice at bay.

'Simply a chance to show you the vision we can bring to the world by working together. When I call upon you, you will do as I ask,' he explained. I could see the bodyguard's head snap towards him in response. This was news to the girl, and judging by the tightness of her grip, I guessed she didn't like it.

'I won't hurt anyone,' I insisted.

'And I won't ask you to,' he assured me. 'I merely want to show you how we could best utilise your … abilities,' he added in his usual demeaning tone, as though I wouldn't be able to figure it out without his help.

'Tell me, are you simply able to regenerate your Energy in both extremities of the Helix, or is there more?' he enquired, watching my face for any tells.

'I'm not here to talk,' I shot back, knowing I'd never been a good liar. My rudeness caused Neon to launch forward, only to halt at Samalas' command.

'It's a shame.' Samalas shrugged like this didn't seem to bother him. 'I have no doubt you will tell me in due time,' he concluded, speaking with such conviction that I took a step back. He was so certain I would accept his proposal, yet despite every fibre in my body telling me it was a trap, I couldn't see what choice I had.

Samalas was intelligent, manipulative and powerful, all the things the book had described him as. I doubted he would allow another solution for my exit. I fought back the panic, trying to claw its way up my throat. I was a fool to think my plan would work so smoothly. If I was going to give myself up, I would at least try to set the terms.

'You can call upon me once,' I tried to negotiate. The atmosphere in the room darkened along with Samalas' eyes, revealing the threat behind the Defacer.

'This is not how this works,' he hissed, his body tensing, emphasising the enormity of his statute. 'You will come when I ask,' he said cuttingly, holding my gaze.

My whole body raced to the pulse of my heart.

'You will let us go freely,' I tried again, my statement sounding more like a question, barely above a whisper.

Samalas leaned back, relaxing his shoulders as he grinned in satisfaction. I had underestimated him, and he had gotten exactly what he wanted.

'I will see you soon, Eloisa,' he finished, dropping the vial of blood in my hand as they walked out. I shuddered. This was a Defacer used to getting his way, and he had made sure I learnt that.

Putting the vial in my pocket, I rushed to the woman in the straw bed. Could Samalas be telling the truth? I looked over her delicate face, worried that the journey back might break her, but something about her faded features told me she was strong. Her necklace reminded me of Amelia's portrait in the Weapon Room. The design was identical to the one in the portrait. Could this be Amelia? Was it possible that Darren's sister had survived this long?

'It'll be okay, Amelia. I'm here to take you home,' I reassured her, hoping she could still hear me in her weakened state. She was so light that I managed to sling her across my back in a fireman carry, using the strength in my legs to stand myself up. Using my hand wrapped around her leg, I grabbed onto her wrist, allowing me to keep my right hand free as I used my Augmented Strength to rush us to the Gate. Our troubles weren't over yet.

≈

The cool air caught my breath as we crossed into Level Five, the fog as heavy as before. I tightened my grip over Amelia, feeling her skin grow increasingly cold, letting me know we had to rush. I propelled us forwards, taking giant leaps in the direction the sequence revealed we would find the next Gate. Other than the rhythmic sound of my breath, the surroundings were still silent as I hurried across the swamp. I tried to maximise the use of my Base Energy that was burning faster than expected. I wasn't used to the additional weight no matter how light Amelia was, and I was suffering because of it.

Using the sunset to orient us, I threw my free hand to the sky, pushing away the air around us to create a clear path to the fiery sky above. Using vague coordinates, I redirected us a few times before finding traces of a trodden path leading us to the next Gate. Only yards away from the iron frame, I heard a distant sound, stopping me in my tracks. I listened, but it was quiet again. Ignoring the tightening in my insides, I crossed into the unknown.

It was like receiving a punch in the stomach, as the pressure on my Energy pulled out from me, Level Four was demanding more of my Energy than before. Sending my heart pumping vigorously, I gasped for the warmer air, trying to find a rhythm to my heavy breathing. Wiping the sweat trickling down my forehead, I examined my new unfamiliar surroundings.

I was in the middle of a rocky dried-up valley, yet I could see the tip of the mountains filled with melting snow. Fortunately, there were also traces made by the Defacers' footsteps where they, too, had made their way to the next Gate. The path ahead was loose with rock, each washed smooth by the river that had once run freely over them. I braced my feet, attempting to guard them against the inevitable roll in random directions, but my ankles tumbled left and right regardless. Charging ahead, I weaved between the thick dark green boughs arched over the path from the sides, competing for the sun, which had reached the horizon. Lifting my eyes, I heard the distant sound of avalanches crashing down.

Stopping for just a moment, trying to manage the burning sensation in my legs, I shifted Amelia, who seemed to have tripled in weight. Despite the cold mountain air blowing around us, I could feel the stickiness of my clothes drenched in sweat. Desperate for a break, I beckoned my legs to move, refusing to sit down. If I did, there was a good chance I wouldn't be able to get up again. Gritting my teeth, I stood straight and pushed the soil from under my feet as I propelled us forward again.

Spinning towards the bristled sound echoing behind us, I brought my dagger out in front of me in one fluid motion. There was no one there. No one I could see anyways, but my gut told me something was following us. Burning more of my Base Energy, I broke into an Augmented run. I had to get us to Level Three if I wanted to have a shot at levelling out the playing field. I would be weaker, but so would our stalker, and just maybe it would be enough to make the Defacer give up. I reached the next Gate and crossed.

≈

I let out a cry as a piercing tear ripped through my body, slicing into the void that was becoming my Base Energy. Biting down on my lip, my body felt frozen, struck by the sudden sharp stabs diving into my belly. Managing only short, shallow breaths of dusty air, I reminded myself the pain was an illusory sensation, and my mind would work with it if I accepted it. Strat had said it was the only way to live through this constant strain on my Energy.

Recognising the beginning of my burnout, I settled into the burning sensation, letting my gaze wander to the deserted canyon ahead. I focused on the dried-up riverbed winding through the cliff walls, allowing my tears to roll freely along my cheeks as I got my legs moving again. Making our way through the sandy road ahead, I looked for boulders to conceal us from the scorching rays. Even during sunset, the heat was beating down, making me feel like an old piece of leather, drying and cracking in the heat.

Wincing more and more with every step, I tried not to duel on our vulnerability or the imminence of my depleting Energy. What an easy target we were! The Defacer would merely have to shove me over and kill us with my own dagger, and I'd have little strength to resist. My thoughts turned to Amelia, to the tortured scars along her arm. For her sake, I had to keep going. I couldn't let them take her back.

Turning to the crumbling rock off the cliff wall behind me, I spotted the tip of a red leather boot peeking out from behind a boulder. My shoulders tensed, despite the alleviation I felt as I put Amelia down behind a nearby rock. The words were coming out of my mouth before I could stop them.

'Why are you following us?' I demanded, my voice bouncing against the valley walls. For a moment, I got no response. Then Samalas' bodyguard, Neon, ran out from behind the boulder. Knife in hand, her dim crystal blade visibly strapped to her waist. I heard the first knife whizzing on my right side and avoided it. Turning just in time to kick her in the chest, I managed to get the lower part of her leg, but she was quick enough to prevent it from being fatal.

Racing towards the rock, I tried to move Amelia to shelter. Neon threw a second knife towards my forehead. It slid above my right eyebrow, a slice that sent a gush of blood running down my face, blinding my eyes and filling my mouth with the sharp metallic taste of my blood. I staggered backwards, leading her away from Amelia, only for Neon to seize the opportunity to slam into me. She knocked me flat on my back, the action cracking one of my ribs, sending a roaring pain through me, Neon quickly pinned my shoulders to the ground with her knees.

I shrieked as the rocks from the canyon floor stabbed into my back. I could feel my Lifeline blaring, begging me to pull myself to safety, but the defiance flowing through me kept me going in this Level. This was it, I thought. If my Energy burnout didn't claim me first, I would die at her hand. I only hoped that my death would be fast. But she meant to savour the moment.

'What does he even see in you?' she spat out, referring to Samalas.

'I'm not a murdering stalker, for starters,' I snarled back at her.

Using my last shred of strength, I screamed at the top of my lungs. 'I'm here!'

It was a lie. Of course, no one would come to rescue us. We were alone, just the way I had foolishly planned. But I couldn't help trying to scare her off. Maybe if she thought there were more of us, she'd leave, but I doubted she'd turn away from an opportunity to kill.

She jammed her fist into my windpipe, effectively cutting off my voice. But her head whipped from side to side, and for a moment, I knew she was at least considering whether I might be telling the truth. Since no one appeared to save me, she turned back to me.

'Liar,' she hissed, reminding me of Samalas. She opened a zip in her tunic, showing an impressive array of throwing knives. She carefully selected an almost dainty-looking number with a cruel, curved blade.

'That crown is mine,' she snarled, anger dripping from her words. 'I've done everything Master has asked. I've proven my devotion to him over and over again. I am worthy, unlike you,' she accused. 'I. Will. Not. Allow. You, of all people, to take away what's promised to me.'

Fighting the black spots appearing in my vision, I could see the intensity in which her chest moved. She tried to hide it, but I could see the enormous effort it took her to exist in this Level. Grinding her teeth, her Energy was depleting, and it would only be a matter of time before she'd have to return to Pamatan. Even under the crushing feeling of the hot burning flame consuming me, the survivor in me couldn't help believing that I might be able to outlast her.

Feeling a dash of hope flow through me, I tried to unseat her, but struggling against her grip was no use. She now breathed heavily as she fought me back, unwilling to lose to her prey. Basking in the hold she had over me, she panted, enjoying watching my desperation as unconsciousness slowly claimed my dying body. Only for her to violently shake me, jolting my eyes awake.

'I'm not done yet,' she taunted. Having managed to keep me conscious, she carelessly wiped away the blood from my wound with her jacket sleeve and surveyed my face.

'Now, where to start?' she asked herself, tilting my face from side to side. Before giving in to the numbness seeping into my body, I made a last feeble attempt to bite her hand, but she grabbed the hair on the top of my head, slamming me back to the ground. I let out a cry, although it sounded more like a moan.

'I think…' she purred, 'we'll start with that insolent mouth of yours. I'm sure it would please *him.*' I lay there hopelessly as she teasingly traced the outline of my lips with the blade's sharp tip. Recognising the pit of my Energy, I reconsidered letting myself die first. Just as I was about to feel her first cut at my lip, a form yanked her from my body, making her groan loudly.

'El!' called a beautiful voice from above the deep waters. Gripping the tiny shred of Energy I had left, I let a small sound escape my dry throat as I fought to find my sight. Through the long tunnel my eyes had become, I saw something that gave me a flicker of hope. Mikhil's arrow pointed directly towards Neon's chest. Sitting on the dirt of the floor, she flashed me a malicious grin as his fingers released the arrow before disappearing through her Lifeline, and then my eyes slammed shut.

Chapter 24

Travelling through nothingness, I drifted, deathlike stillness echoing throughout my body. My mind floated independently from my broken body, so peaceful yet fearful as the unknown quickly approached. I was standing at the edge of the void, my insides tightening inside me in anticipation of the darkness that would come with the fall.

Brought back with a jolt, I felt a flow of reviving Energy rush into my body as soon as my body hit the cold surface of the Grounding Room. Bringing me back, almost to the surface, I could hear the distant sound of the familiar soundtrack of the crashing waves, yet I couldn't find the surface through the deep water drowning me from above.

'Oh no! El, no!' the smooth voice cried in horror. 'El, please! Ella, stay with me, please, El, please!'

I wanted to say something, anything, but I couldn't find my lips under the dark water.

'Darren!' the voice called, agony ill-fitting the usually cheerful voice. 'El, no, oh please, no, no, no!' I could feel a sudden weight leaning over me, the moisture of his face touching my skin. His touch became hotter and hotter, filling me with a comforting warmth from head to toe, bringing me closer to the surface as my every cell awoke. Strat was giving me his Energy.

Replacing the numbness was the fiery flame of burnout ravaging through my body like wildfire. I wanted to scream and tear it off, but I still couldn't move. I was still too deep. Then, it started to ease. As the vitality of Strat's warm Energy broke through the darkness to me, wretched pain began to replace the numbness in my body. I cried out, gasping, breaking through the dark waters.

'El!' he cried, full of gratitude and elevation.

'She's got a few injuries, but it doesn't seem too bad,' a calm female voice attested. 'We've got to get them to the Healers. They're not out of the woods yet,' the methodical voice continued.

Not letting go of Strat's hand, I felt my consciousness slipping again as the pain subsided. Although it felt different, I was afraid to fall into the black waters again, fearful that I would lose him to the darkness.

'Strat,' I tried to say, but my voice was heavy and slow.

'El, you're going to be okay. Can you hear me, Ella? I love you.'

His energy flow intensified, dulling the burning sensation of my depleted Base Energy.

'Strat,' I tried again, my voice clearer this time.

‘Yes, I’m here.’

‘Give her this,’ I breathed out, taking out the vial of Samalas’ blood from my pocket.

‘We’ll give it to her,’ he promised, letting out a weak, wet laugh as he squeezed my hand.

‘Thank you, Strat.’ I sighed, contented, closing my eyes. The burning flame was gone, and the other pains softened under the sleepiness seeping through my body.

‘I love you,’ he said again.

‘Me too,’ I managed weakly.

‘We need to move them,’ ordered a female voice.

‘What about the Committee?’ asked Mikhil, concerned.

‘One problem at a time. Let’s first keep these two alive,’ instructed Darren.

Placing his arms under my body, Strat swooped me in his arms, cradling me against his chest. I breathed in my favourite citrusy smell.

‘I’ve got you,’ Strat soothed as I let my eyes fall shut under their weight. ‘Rest now,’ were the last words I heard before darkness swept over me.

Chapter 25

I felt horribly raw. I tried to force my eyes open, only to peer at the unfamiliar room before me.

Squeezing my hand, Strat's beautiful face appeared in front of me.

'Sleep,' he soothed encouragingly.

I tried to remind myself that I was safe. I had succeeded in my rescue mission and was alive, and with the comfort of Strat's presence, I let the light take me under its blanket.

I didn't know how many hours or days had passed, but when I next woke, my body was stiff like I had been run over by a bus. My mind was dazed and slow but no longer so foggy. I was in a white clinical room filled with living plants. Watery sunlight slipped through the blinds of the nearby window. I was propped up on a high bed with rails on either side. Oxygen pumped through the tube under my nose. I looked at my hands twisted with clear tubes. I had made it.

Turning my head slightly, Strat sat on a chair with his head resting on the side of my bed. His face turned towards me. I watched him sleep peacefully. I could see the bags under his eyes, reminding me of his Energy flowing through me. I wanted to touch his perfect face but didn't want to wake him up. Behind him was Amelia. She was also in a hospital bed but had more tubes attached to her. Darren was by her bedside, holding her hand. His gaze lifted to meet mine. His eyes started to tear up when he saw me, easing my previous suspicions.

'Thank goodness,' Darren whispered, but it was enough to wake up Strat.

'El?' Strat croaked, his throat thick with sleep, catching my full attention. He flashed me my favourite smile stretching from ear-to-ear, his emerald eyes dancing.

'Oh, Strat! I'm so sorry!' I choked out.

'Everything is alright now,' he consoled me.

'How did you know?' I asked, still unable to believe Strat and Mikhil had come to our rescue in Level Three, saving us from Neon's knife.

'Mikhil came by my room after you had left. He was worried about you. He thought you might attempt travelling through the Helix by yourself. When I found your note, I knew he was right. I called Darren to alert the Healers while Mikhil and I went into the Helix, searching for you.'

He paused. His eyes tormented. 'I was almost too late. I could have been too late,' he whispered.

I huffed out a heavy breath, tears pricking my eyes. 'I was a fool thinking I could go through the Helix alone. I should have accepted your help,' I admitted.

‘And I should have trusted you with the truth,’ interjected Darren. We both turned to look up at him, but he was staring at the ground resolutely.

‘I’ll leave you two to talk,’ offered Strat as he prepared to give us some privacy, and my heart sped up at the dreaded thought of him leaving.

‘No, please, Strat. Stay,’ insisted Darren, much to my relief. ‘This apology is as much for you as it is for Ella,’ he said, looking at Strat before turning to the both of us. ‘When I saw the two of you get closer to one another, I let my distrust of the Committee get the better of me when I should have been protecting you against their inordinate fears. I should have realised my plan for Ella and me to return to our normal human life wouldn’t work.’ He paused, flicking his eyes to me, his tone turning remorseful, ‘Not when you were already too involved. I should have trusted you with the truth.’

I could feel the sides of my lips turn up in response, both shocked and relieved that Darren had provided an explanation. I could see his expression soften as he saw my anger start to fade before directing him to Strat again.

‘Ella is special, but she is also good, and we’ll just have to make the Committee see it.’

I wanted to forgive Darren fully, but I still had a nagging feeling there was still one explanation he had to give.

'Does this mean you won't try to erase my memories?' I asked rhetorically, my tone still sour, disbelief flashing across Strat's face as he turned to glare at Darren.

Never had I seen Darren as embarrassed as he was then. 'I'm sorry you heard that. I can't imagine what you must think, but please believe me when I say everything I did was to protect you,' he justified. I believed he was telling the truth. He may have made some horrible decisions, but the same way I could see it in his eyes when he first knocked on Mum's house door, I knew Darren would always look out for me.

Which is why he was going to scowl at me. 'How mad are you?' I enquired, letting him know I had forgiven him in not so many words.

'Furious,' he said. 'Even with Amelia back, I don't know how we're going to be able to explain what happened here without revealing your "extra" abilities to the Committee.' He frowned. 'They've heard you've brought someone back through the Helix, and they're waiting to interrogate the both of you,' he whispered, looking towards Amelia and me.

'I can't begin to imagine their faces when they find out it's Amelia you've returned,' grinned Strat, making Darren's frown deepen. I imagined he was considering telling off Strat for not taking the situation seriously but chose to ignore his comment, maintaining the seriousness in his expression.

'We've managed to get an alibi for Mikhil and Dr Vera, stating they simply helped carry you both here, but the four of us are under investigation,' Darren agonised, breathing out loudly. 'This is why I didn't want you to be part of this world,' he explained.

'I've hidden from the Committee for too long to hold any authority anymore,' Darren huffed. I could hear the self-blame thick in his voice as he looked at me with glazed eyes. 'I can't protect you against them and worry how they will react when they find out.'

'If they find out,' I interjected, an idea forming in my mind. 'All the Committee know is that I've been able to retrieve someone from Pamatan. They don't need to know the specifics of how I got there. If we show them the solved sequence, they'll have to assume I cracked the sequence and travelled through the Gates.'

Strat's eyebrows raised and a wicked grin spread across his face.

'It's risky,' considered Darren. 'If they have the slightest inkling that we're lying, they won't hesitate to lock us up.'

'It's brilliant,' asserted Strat, his forest eyes gleaming. Calculating risks was what Strat did best, and it appeared the stakes were high enough to make our ruse worthwhile.

'Plus, a bunch of people have already seen me talking to Mikhil in the dining hall,' I added, tidying up loose endings. 'Mikhil's already known for working on the Gates' sequence in secret. It wouldn't be a stretch of the imagination to say he had an accomplice,' I proposed, hearing the excitement grow in my voice as I helped paint the picture of our lie. Strat's smile broadened in response while Darren continued to stare at us, the cogs turning as he tried to find any apparent gaps.

'It's the best we've got,' insisted Strat, sharing a look with Darren as we heard a knock at the door.

≈

Dressed in a Squad surcoat, a young arrogant-looking man with fiery red hair and a slicked back quiff walked into the room, his shoes stomping against the hard floor, signalling his entrance. Behind him walked in thee Committee members dressed in a perfectly tailored kimono and golden surcoats. First came in a thin, lanky Scientist followed by the short blond Healer, I recognised from my first evening in the dining hall. And finally in walked one of the most strikingly fierce woman I've ever seen. Tall, elegant, with a long neck, her short-cropped hair only accentuated her angular jaw, framing her wide catwalk eyes. Stepping aside, she moved towards the front, her glowing, midnight skin contrasting with the young Striker's.

I would have remained transfixed were it not for the Striker barking orders. 'We will be moving you,' he announced loudly.

I could see Darren's posture stiffen as he and Strat moved protectively in front of our beds, standing between the

Committee and us. I could see the tension in Strat's jaw as he prepared to object.

'No, you won't,' spoke a weak voice in the corner of the room. All of our heads turned to look at Amelia. In her fragile state, she was trying to sit herself up. Darren rushed over to help her.

'You won't be taking any of us,' Amelia commanded. Her voice was frail, but there was no mistaking the authority that rang in her voice. Making the short woman gasp, her eyes widening at the sight of Amelia. Pushing her long hair backwards, hope lifted in my belly as I remembered her being one of Amelia's super-fans. I could see the conflict in her eyes as she glanced over to the other two Committee members looking for guidance – this revelation had changed things. I could only hope it would work in our favour.

Dismissing her, the fierce-looking woman took a step forward, the arrogant Striker falling behind her as she took the lead – her expression revealing nothing.

'We are glad to have you back, Amelia. But we have reason to suspect that the girl contains Defacer attributes. You understand we cannot let her be free.'

Amelia's grey eyes stared back at the woman, matching the fervour of her gaze. Her bony stature became more imposing every time I looked at her. This was not a woman to be trifled with. She was the leader Elans had venerated and cherished for so long and still mourned.

'Would you rather turn on one of your own rather than believe someone is better than you, Diamor? Are you so afraid that the Roses will continue to outshine you that would rather lock up my daughter than believe she too managed to crack the sequence of the Gates?' I could feel all of our chests drop as Amelia perfectly delivered our cover story.

The Committee's eyes flew back to me, probably taking in the family resemblance. Darren, Amelia and I all shared the same black hair and unmistakable grey eyes. Diamor's face faltered as I watched. Her confident expression had wavered, at first incredulous and then doubtful, before she calmed it into an icy mask.

'No one has been able to travel through the entire Helix…' she started, but her voice was off. Amelia had thrown her off-guard.

'Other than me,' retorted Darren. 'What else did you think I'd been training my niece for all this time?'

Diamor's lips twitched, her gaze still firm.

'You can check with my associate. He'd be able to tell you all about our work together,' I added, meeting her stare.

'We know all about your meetings with Mikhil,' Diamor replied. 'Daughter or not, she did this without the Committee's permission, making her a loose cannon and a danger to us all,' Diamor concluded.

I could see Darren's face grow redder by the second, his body tensing like a volcano about to erupt, to which Amelia squeezed his arm, telling him to let her handle this.

Amelia swung her legs to the side of the bed, holding onto Darren as she stood herself up and moved slightly towards Diamor. Her expression growing, Amelia looked curiously towards Diamor. 'Have you learnt nothing this last decade?' she asked to which Diamor remained silent, only for Amelia to roll over her.

'Are you still too petty and self-involved to see the bigger picture? Or are you finally able to distinguish your allies from your enemies?' Amelia asked, her tone belittling – she was letting Diamor know who was in charge.

'Do you not find it odd that Elans have been kidnapped rather than killed? Have you not stopped to think of Samalas' plans?' Amelia reproached Diamor, giving her a long, disappointed look when she kept mute.

Shaking her head, Amelia further lifted her chin. 'What you failed to see then and what you fail to see now is that Samalas is building an army of Defacers, infusing them with Elan blood to make them more powerful than before so that he can come storming into Earth.'

She paused, letting her captured audience digest what they had just heard as she sat back on the bed.

'Now, rather than turning on our own, why don't you tell the rest of the Committee that Amelia Rose is back and that we've got a war to win?' ordered Amelia, dismissing the stunned Committee.

No one moved. Diamor seemed frozen. The seconds passed, and I grew increasingly anxious, wondering which way the scale would land. Another agonizing moment passed, and the young man's voice broke the silence.

'This isn't over,' he threatened on Diamor's behalf.

Strat's eyes lit up, gleaming with admiration as they started to leave.

'Does this mean we are free to leave?' Strat called out.

'Until we gain more clarity on the situation,' confirmed the lanky Committee member.

'But don't think for a moment we won't be watching,' lashed out the young Striker as the door closed, leaving us alone to our victory.

≈

'That was incredible!' I complimented Amelia, who was once again lying in her bed.

'It was nothing. I just gave her something to think about,' said Amelia. Her voice was much softer than the menacing tone she had used on Diamor. She began to cough, and Darren rushed to her side, bringing her a glass of water as he tucked her back under the bed covers.

'Please, come closer, Eloisa. I want to have a look at you,' cooed Amelia. I started to lift myself when Strat touched my hand. 'Please let me,' he offered as he rolled my bed next to Amelia's. Extending her hand, she placed my hand into hers.

'I'm sorry you've had to find out this way, but I'm so glad to see you. I never imagined I would get to see you after Darren rescued you.' Her eyes seemed to freeze on the features of my face.

'You don't know how many times I called your name, wishing I could see your face one last time. And then a few days ago, I felt your presence in my room, and I thought my heart might burst.'

'I was there,' I reassured her, squeezing her hand more tightly. 'I could feel it too.'

Our connection had been so strong that it was a relief to hear that she had felt it too.

She smiled weakly. 'I was so weak and delusional that I was convinced the heavens had come for me, but then I felt your presence again a couple of days later. Simply knowing you were alive filled my heart with hope in a way I hadn't felt in years. But I worried – I knew Samalas had been keeping me alive for a reason, and I couldn't let him get to you again.'

'Which is why you told me to run,' I said aloud, putting the pieces together.

'Yes, but I can't tell you how glad I am that you didn't listen,' she said proudly.

‘I’m sorry,’ I said apologetically, feeling ashamed. ‘If I had just opened my heart sooner, I would have heard your call. I would have been able to rescue you sooner.’

‘Don’t be. I know it couldn’t have been easy. What you did took courage and bravery.’

‘She takes after her mother,’ added Darren, making Amelia’s eyes shine.

‘Why didn’t you tell me?’ I asked Darren, still hurt from his secretiveness. I understood why he didn’t want me to know about being an Elan, but he could have told me about Amelia and his relationship to me.

‘To begin with, I had no idea that you had a Lifeline connecting you to Pamatan. If I had known, things would have gone very differently,’ he huffed. ‘It all started when I first took you through my Lifeline from Pamatan, and you unexpectedly dropped back in a different location to me. I had no idea if your Energy would be able to regenerate on Earth. I was horrified at the prospect of the journey killing you. I searched for you for weeks. I looked in every street, hoping I would find you, and when I finally did, you had already been adopted by June. You seemed so happy, and she was so kind that I figured she would do a better job than I ever could. I couldn’t raise you, but I could keep my promise to Amelia and look after you. Which is when I decided I would become your Krav Maga coach.’ Darren now looked away, unable to look me in the eyes.

'It's no excuse, but, in some ways, I always hoped the human life we had built was enough.' He took my hand in his and gave me an apologetic look. 'I now realise it probably wasn't the best approach. I'm sorry it's taken so long for you to find out where you are from.'

Feeling the tears overflow my eyes, I bit down on my trembling lip as I tugged Darren closer to me. Walking around the beds, I pulled him to hug me. It was only then that I realised I was shaking hard, my entire frame vibrating until my teeth chattered, and the room around me seemed to wobble and blur my eyes.

'I'm sorry for the pain I've caused you,' grieved Darren, his voice breaking as he pulled me deeper into his embrace. A few seconds passed as we both took deep, settling breaths.

'Who knew you were capable of so many emotions?' I teased, letting out a snotty laugh as we both let go. Wiping our tears on our sleeves, Strat brought us some water.

'It's been a tiring day for us all,' justified Darren, his face pink.

'We better all get some rest,' suggested Amelia with a weak smile. Nodding in agreement, I pulled Darren close to me one last time.

'I'm glad we can be friends again,' I said.

'Me too,' he agreed, his eyes still watery.

'Get some rest now,' he said, rolling our beds apart to separate sides of the room before closing the curtain partition between us, giving Strat and me some privacy.

'Yes, Uncle,' I called out after him. I could hear him chuckle on the other side of the curtain.

≈

Sinking deeper into my bed, I could feel my eyelids fall under the weight of my exhaustion as I struggled to keep them open.

'You can sleep now, El,' murmured Strat, his expression soft. 'It's over.'

I knew he meant the immediate danger, but the reality wouldn't be true for long. I had made a deal with Samalas, and he would come to claim my side of the agreement.

'I don't want to sleep. Not yet,' I insisted. I wanted to look at Strat's comforting face for a bit longer before giving into unconsciousness. Flashing my favourite ear-to-ear smile, he nudged me to move to the side of the bed to lie next to me. Wrapping his strong arm around me, I rested my head against his shoulder, the tip of my nose touching the bottom of his chin.

'Just tell me, how did you do it? How were you able to make your Energy last the journey?' he asked curiously.

'Honestly, I'm not sure. For some reason, Levels Five and Four weren't as taxing as Level Three – that's where I really struggled,' I explained, not having had time to reflect on this beforehand. 'They were actually similar to how I felt in Levels One and Two,' I pointed out, recognising the similarity.

'Like a bell curve,' observed Strat. 'Fully charged on both ends of the Helix and gradually getting harder as you reach the middle.'

'Yes, exactly,' I agreed, pondering what this would mean for the war ahead, only to have Strat's expression switch to his usual playful self.

'I would have missed you, you know,' he teased.

'Really?' I asked, playing along.

'It appears I've grown rather fond of you.'

'Oh?' I asked as he pulled his arm from under me so that he could lower himself to face me. The tip of his nose touched against mine.

'I know you're all about saving the world by yourself, but how would you feel about having a sturdy sidekick?' He grinned mischievously, making his emerald glitter in amusement.

I pretended to think about his offer. 'It's a full-time job. Are you sure you're up to it?' I challenged, my face matching his enchanting expression.

He placed his hands on either side of my face as he stared into my eyes. 'Always,' he vowed. And he leaned down to press his warm lips to mine.

Chapter 26

Almost everything returned to a version of normal – or so it appeared to my human family. After returning victorious from our 'Krav-Maga Championship', Mum insisted on checking every part of my bruised and battered body daily until she was satisfied that I was in better shape than when I had left her. She was pretty shocked when she first saw the state of me, but she didn't scowl at me for taking such a beating. Quite the contrary, although she would never implicitly encourage me to fight recklessly, I'm pretty sure I saw her smile proudly when I returned, walking ahead of Darren. I had, after all, followed her advice and decided to trust in my judgement. I may have gotten beaten up over it, but if it meant I'd finally started to believe in myself, it was worth it.

Neer had done right by Mum by providing me with detailed notes on all the school content I had missed. Although he wasn't pleased to hear that my recklessness led to Strat having to come to my rescue, his tone quickly changed when I told him we had succeeded in our mission and that I would be returning to class on Monday.

Although Neer was initially protective of Strat joining our two-person band, he relaxed once convinced of Strat's 'worthiness'. I can't even imagine the questions he must have asked during their lengthy interrogations. Luckily Strat survived the tortuous process and claimed to have won over Neer. But I reckoned it was seeing us happily together that ultimately convinced Neer of how much Strat cared for me.

As expected, school became all-consuming as I prepared to sit my A-Levels and led our effort in rewilding the school's playing fields. One might have thought things had returned to normal, but they were better. Much to the satisfaction of Ms Lancy, I had a newfound interest in physics, particularly in the many-worlds theory, courtesy of my time in the Helix. To my great struggle, I had started studying in the mornings to adjust to the increasing workload and make time for my private Krav-Maga training sessions with Darren and his new, ruggedly handsome assistant – Strat.

Strat had moved in with Darren while I finished my studies and had taken on the task of learning everything ever recorded on the Defacers and Samalas. Amelia and Darren had agreed, after my close burnout, I should rest for a month before continuing my training, but with a new focus. This time, Darren would teach me how to use my Base Energy in the Helix and combat. In the meantime, Amelia and Mikhil, now known as MK after his heroic rescue, stayed at the Academy to deal with the backlash from the Committee.

News of Amelia's survival after spending a decade imprisoned in Pamatan spread like wildfire. She was quickly amassing a strong Elan following and was swooping her way back to the top ranks of the Committee. We had shared a few moments to get to know each other better, but she was determined not to interfere too much with my 'normal' life. She often came by my training, giving a few tips of her own. And for the moment, the arrangement worked for both of us.

Everything was going smoothly, and with Strat around, it was hard to worry – even about Samalas and my unclaimed promise to him. When I did think of it, I always felt a mixture of shame and anxiety. I felt guilty for not telling anyone about my deal with Samalas in exchange for Amelia's life and anxious for not knowing when Samalas would turn up and show me his vision for a new world. We had agreed I wouldn't hurt anyone or anything, but his bodyguard's reaction made me believe there was a broader play at hand, and I hadn't figured it out yet.

Weeks passed by with nothing happening. I tried to convince myself that I'd never have to hold my half of the deal, but I knew Samalas would eventually come. It started becoming a constant worry, like a fuse about to burst.

Walking along the rim of the nearby reservoir, I let Strat lead me by the hand as we weaved through the forest.

‘Where are we going?’ I asked curiously for the fifth time that morning.

‘You’ll see,’ teased Strat, flashing me a mischievous grin as we walked into a small clearing. There stood the cutest tiny house I had ever seen. Lit up with warm, inviting light, Strat led me inside. In the middle lay the most romantic picnic, beautifully arranged on a red woolly blanket encircled by fairy lights and flowers. I turned to Strat, willing an explanation, communicating only through my widened eyes as my mouth hung dry.

‘We never got to celebrate your birthday,’ he explained. ‘And I promised you a swim. It’s not the acidified water of the ocean in Level Two, but the reservoir should be much safer and equally as freezing.’

I lifted my hand to my face, an infinite number of questions about the Helix’s growing instability and the delicate balance of each Level’s tipping point rushing through my mind. I thought about the Helix’s healing ozone layer, dried-up valley, sterile swamp, snowy avalanche, absence of animals and Pamatan’s smoked sky and degraded soil – each linked to Earth’s planetary boundary. Before I could feel any excitement attached to the possibility of discovery, I was bulldozed by crippling guilt.

‘I lied!’ I cried out. ‘I’m sorry! I can’t hide it anymore, especially not after all of this,’ I admitted, waving to the display of love. ‘I met Samalas when I rescued Amelia in Pamatan!’ I blurted, feeling a wave of relief as I finally shared the burden of my secret. 'He wants us to work together, bring his vision to the world,' I practically shouted.

'Please don't tell me you agreed?' pleaded Strat, shutting the door securely behind us.

'No! Of course not. But, in exchange for the vial of his blood, I did agree to come to him when he calls upon me,' I confessed, feeling the full impact of my agreement. Looking away from me, Strat raked his hand through his ruffled hair, pacing to stare out the window. He was silent for a long moment.

'I knew you were hiding something from me, but I never thought it would be … this.' He sighed. 'I don't know if anyone has told you, but you're terrible at keeping secrets.'

'I am, and it's been killing me keeping this from you for so long,' I whispered. 'Please understand, I had no choice.'

'Is there anything else?' he asked calmly, still looking out the window.

Hesitant, I spoke up. 'The Defacer, Neon, the one that escaped when you came to rescue me – she mentioned something about a crown.' I sighed and took a deep breath building my courage.

'I believe Samalas wants me to play a part in his conquest over Earth,' I revealed, shaking my head to dispel the words in my head, watching as Strat's body stiffened in response. 'You know I would never help him or hurt anyone, there is no reason to worry about it,' I tried to soothe him. I wrapped my hands around his lean waist, pressing my face to his back, praying he'd hear the truth of my words.

Turning to look down at me, his expression was soft and calm enough to ease some of my panic. Every time I looked into his piercing green eyes, my heart pounded as the feeling of safety rushed over me. I could feel the warmth of his body as he wrapped his strong arms around me, holding me close as he squeezed me gently.

'Of course, you wouldn't,' he agreed. 'I shouldn't be surprised. Samalas has a way of making sure his way becomes your only option. You did what you had to do to save Amelia,' he approved. 'But I can't say I'm thrilled to hear that your dealings with Samalas aren't over yet … You have a way of making sure trouble follows you, El,' he chortled in disbelief, flashing my favourite ear-to-ear smile. Pulling 'a Darren', Strat placed his hand on my shoulder, automatically making me smile, as he tried to employ a serious tone.

'But promise me we do this together – you and me. No more secrets,' Strat insisted, his emerald eyes plunging deep into mine.

'One team,' I promised, drawing him closer. We would do this together, and this time I wouldn't be alone. I had a community of warrior Elans ready to support me, a family that cared about me deeply, and Strat's arms around me. As long as that was true, I could face anything.

I squared my shoulders, our fingers intertwined, forming a bridge as we let our Energy flow freely between us. It radiated off our bodies, fortifying the depth of our bond.

I was ready to meet my fate.

Author's Note

My mission is to fight global warming and accelerate the Sustainability Revolution by empowering readers to take climate action.

We have already breached four of Earth's nine planetary boundaries. If we do not change course and evolve the way we live quickly, we will drive our fragile ecosystems to collapse, forever destabilising the natural world we have grown to love and rely upon.

While I could have given climate change a more immediate role in the trilogy, I first wanted to demonstrate the power of our most effective solution the awakening of our individual and collective consciousness.

By bringing more mindfulness into our lives we can transcend our fear, anger, anguish and despair about the world we find ourselves in order to cultivate our inner ability to choose the future we want and which we know we need to bring about.

Ella's transformation from a scared orphan into a fearless warrior starts when she decides to break away from her victimhood and take charge of her destiny. By facing the shadows of her past, she liberates herself from the weight of secrecy and builds the self-confidence needed to grow her future climate ambitions.

We too must become fearless warriors and confront the reality of the environmental precipice on which we stand. Only by embracing our fear of human extinction will we be able to break free from our paralysis and transform into catalysts for action.

Breathe in.

This is the present moment, and it's gifting you the choice of deciding how you want to spend your Energy.

Breathe out.

Maybe that one breath was enough to redirect you towards your North Star, reshuffle your priorities and remind you of the love you hold for our planet.

But mindfulness alone will not limit global warming to 1.5 degrees. With that, I ask you to re-examine how you spend your time, money and influence those around you to become cognisant of the signals they are sending to policymakers, business leaders and the community.

I hope Ella's climate activism and the use of the technology described in the running of the Elans' Academy has inspired you with ideas on how you can contribute to restoring the polluted lungs of our planet.

Remember, if our collective awakening is strong enough, our pivot to a regenerative economy can be immediate.

It's up to every one of us to continue saving the world.

And I for one cannot wait to live in the success of your mission.

The following content was helpful when writing this novel:

- Netflix, 2021. Breaking Boundaries: The Science Of Our Planet. Directed by Jonathan Clay. https://www.netflix.com/gb/title/81336476 (Accessed September 2022)
- Netflix: 2020. David Attenborough: A Life on Our Planet. Directed by Keith Scholey, Alastair Fothergill, and Jonathan Hughes. https://www.netflix.com/gb/title/80216393 (Accessed September 2022)
- Speed and Scale: A Global Action Plan for Solving our Climate Crisis by John Doerr. https://speedandscale.com/book/ (Accessed September 2022)
- Spotify, 2022. The Way Out Is In, Plum Village. Available from. https://open.spotify.com/show/5KhMVavoTzH3ssVZTVJNwI (Accessed September 2022)
- Spotify, 2022. Outrage + Optimism: Climate Change Podcast. Hosted by Christiana Figueres, Tom Rivett-Carnac and Paul Dickinson. https://www.outrageandoptimism.org/episodes/outrage-and-optimism-the-podcast (Accessed September 2022)

- IPCC, 2022: Climate Change 2022: Impacts, Adaptation, and Vulnerability. Contribution of Working Group II to the Sixth Assessment Report of the Intergovernmental Panel on Climate Change [H.-O. Pörtner, D.C. Roberts, M. Tignor, E.S. Poloczanska, K. Mintenbeck, A. Alegría, M. Craig, S. Langsdorf, S. Löschke, V. Möller, A. Okem, B. Rama (eds.)]. Cambridge University Press. In Press. https://www.ipcc.ch/report/sixth-assessment-report-working-group-ii/ (Accessed September 2022)

Acknowledgements

Dear Reader,

Thank you for reading The Helix! I want to thank you and foremost for supporting the launch of my debut novel and writing career. And thank you in advance for supporting authors and helping other readers by considering leaving an online review on Amazon, Goodreads and Waterstones.

My heart is filled with gratitude for the people who have made writing The Helix possible. First to my family and friends for their unfailing support. Enormous thanks to my Mum for giving me a lifetime of support and to my brother, Alexandre, who jumped into the tangled web of Defacers, multi-verses and sequencing with both sleeves rolled up. Thank you for embracing the world of The Helix, helping construct the logic that would be the foundation of the world and ultimately moulding it into its best shape.

Massive thanks to my editor, Arabella Derhalli, I am so grateful for your hard work, care, vision and advocacy. I couldn't have made it without you, and I am eternally grateful for your ongoing coaching allowing me to improve the story with every revision. If anyone is looking to write a novel, check Arabella's website as a first point of call.

To my alpha and beta readers enthusiasm, spot-on feedback and enduring support during the challenging times while writing. Thank you Adriana, Hannah, Sam, Egg, Juliette, Mary, Cebeli, Lorena and Phil.

Big thank you to my graphic designer, Ced for creating a cover that gives me life every time I see it and to the Nomad crew for their ongoing feedback. Finally, a big thank you to everyone who has supported me to this point! I particularly want to thank to my marketing director, Laura for furiously promoting my novel. As well as, my friend Josh whose TedX talk provoked my own conscious awakening and kick started my climate activism.

Thank you to my yoga teacher, Bex, who unknowingly helped inspire the Energy and breathing techniques found in this novel and helped me keep sane during the process. And, of course, the innovators, academics, and climate activists who continue to shape our future and for making me realise we have everything we need to succeed in our transition to a regenerative economy.

Finally, I want to thank my partner, Edward, for giving me the space I needed to create and for celebrating every milestone of this magical journey.

About the Author

Yasmeen Cohen finds innovative ways of leveraging technology to create a more sustainable future. She studied Journalism and Economics at City University London. Yasmeen loves to explore the outdoors and has lived all over Europe – in Spain, France, Switzerland and Hungary. She currently resides in London. *The Helix* is the first book in her young adult trilogy.

#TheHelixTrilogy